They yanked th ⟨...⟩ k and
snugged them tig ⟨...⟩ d the
same to the man' ⟨...⟩

Franklin looked at the captive. ⟨...⟩ m, all
right." He talked to the man but got only grunts in reply.
Dobler came up.

"He saying anything?"

Franklin shook his head. "Not a word, Senior Chief."

"Let's pretend to toss him overboard."

Three of them picked up the terrorist and headed to the
rail. They swung him once, twice, and were about to swing
a third time when the man began jabbering in Arabic. They
dropped him on the deck.

"What?" Dobler asked.

Franklin said, "Says there's fifty of them on board. They
have captured the ship and we will all die."

Murdock came up and was told the situation.

"Tell him he has one more chance," Murdock said. "We
know he's lying. If he doesn't tell the truth, he's swimming
in the gulf."

Franklin translated the words for the captive. He spit in
Franklin's face.

Murdock and Dobler picked up the small Arab and threw
him over the rail. . . .

SEAL TEAM SEVEN
Frontal Assault

By Keith Douglass

THE CARRIER SERIES:

CARRIER
VIPER STRIKE
ARMAGEDDON MODE
FLAME-OUT
MAELSTROM
COUNTDOWN
AFTERBURN
ALPHA STRIKE
ARCTIC FIRE
ARSENAL
NUKE ZONE
CHAIN OF COMMAND
BRINK OF WAR
TYPHOON SEASON

THE SEAL TEAM SEVEN SERIES:

SEAL TEAM SEVEN
SPECTER
NUCFLASH
DIRECT ACTION
FIRESTORM
BATTLEGROUND
DEATHRACE
PACIFIC SIEGE
WAR CRY
FRONTAL ASSAULT

SEAL TEAM SEVEN
FRONTAL ASSAULT

KEITH DOUGLASS

B

BERKLEY BOOKS, NEW YORK

Special thanks and acknowledgment to Chet Cunningham for his contribution to this book.

SEAL TEAM SEVEN: FRONTAL ASSAULT

A Berkley Book / published by arrangement with the author

PRINTING HISTORY
Berkley edition / February 2000

All rights reserved.
Copyright © 2000 by The Berkley Publishing Group.
SEAL TEAM SEVEN logo illustration by Michael Racz.
This book may not be reproduced in whole or in part,
by mimeograph or any other means, without permission.
For information address:
The Berkley Publishing Group, a division of Penguin Putnam Inc.,
375 Hudson Street, New York, New York 10014.

The Penguin Putnam Inc. World Wide Web site address is
http://www.penguinputnam.com

ISBN: 0-425-17352-6

BERKLEY®
Berkley Books are published by The Berkley Publishing Group,
a division of Penguin Putnam Inc.,
375 Hudson Street, New York, New York 10014.
BERKLEY and the "B" logo
are trademarks belonging to Penguin Putnam Inc.

PRINTED IN THE UNITED STATES OF AMERICA

10 9 8 7 6 5 4 3 2 1

SEAL TEAM SEVEN
FRONTAL ASSAULT

1

Tuesday, July 23
Damascus, Syria

Linda Walsh jolted upward and took a quick look through the shot-out, barred, second-floor window of the United States Embassy in Damascus, then moved to the left against the solid rock wall. The gunfire came again, a deadly drumming of rifles and machine guns. She winced each time one of the bullets slammed into the wall outside. The smell of cordite and smoke drifted through the window, stinging her nose and throat with an acrid bite.

"The idiots," she said out loud. It would take three hundred of them to overrun the embassy compound, and then it could happen only if they would accept enough casualties. No problem there. The Syrian extremists would love to die for Islam. A martyr's death for Allah was the highest honor any Muslim could pray for.

Linda held her Walther PP automatic in her right hand. She had drawn it instinctively when she first heard the attack. There was no immediate need for it, but she kept it at the ready. Ingrained company training.

Linda stood tall and slender against the beige wall of the second-floor hall. Her dark hair, cut short on the sides, framed her face. Her brown eyes flashed in anger. Why were they attacking the embassy?

When the spate of firing stilled for a moment, she edged up and looked outside. One white-clad Syrian pushed to the top of the embassy's ten-foot-high rock wall directly opposite her. Before he could climb over, a red flower of blood blossomed on his forehead, blasting him backward and out of sight.

Time to report in. This wasn't a chance mob assault. It was planned and programmed. The ranks of white-robed Arabs, all with new Russian weapons. Everyone moving on signals from a manipulator. Arlington had to know.

She ran to the communications room and typed out a report to CIA headquarters. It was encrypted immediately and transmitted at once to the satellite. She told them it was a planned attack, more serious than ever before. A few casualties. She'd do a complete report later.

The radio tech handed her some papers. Two more attacks at two more U.S. embassies in the Middle East all at exactly noon. That meant one hand was behind all of these attacks. Was this the start of a general uprising by Arabs against the United States? The great religious war the Muslims had been promising for years?

She ran back to her post in the hallway and looked out the window, then ducked down quickly. A hot Arab slug burrowed its way into the window casing near where her head had been a minisecond before.

Linda ran to the window just down the hall and took a quick look outside. Three white-clad Arabs rolled over the wall and dropped to the ground inside the compound. One took a round to the chest and died. The other two charged for the outside wall of the embassy itself and moved out of sight of the gunners inside.

She heard a muffled explosion and guessed the Syrians who came over the wall had blown open the locked and unused door just below her. No Marines would be inside at that point guarding it.

Linda went low under the windows and ran down the maroon-carpeted hall to the back stairs that led to the first floor. That outside door was just in back of the steps. She held her Walther automatic ready and crept silently halfway down the stairs. She stopped when she heard whispers in Arabic coming from below her.

They must be the Syrians she saw coming over the wall. She held her pistol high and edged lower on the open stairway. The invaders would have to come past the stairs to get to the embassy's main front rooms.

The Syrians both charged from their hiding place past the stairs. They came in view almost at once, and Linda tracked one a moment, then fired twice with her Walther. The *muhajed* was only ten feet away and hadn't seen her. He took one .380 round in the chest and the other in his neck, spraying the wall beside him with a gushing rain of blood. He stumbled and fell as his automatic weapon chattered, sending lead slugs down the empty hall. The second Syrian turned toward Linda and swung up his AK 74 rifle. Linda had changed targets and fired three times as fast as she could pull the trigger.

One of the rounds hit the Syrian's weapon, jolting it off target. The second and third tore into his chest, rocking him sideways. He stared at Linda a moment with black eyes of hatred, then he smiled, mumbled, *"Shukran,"* "thank you," and died before he hit the floor.

Linda dropped to the steps, looking for any more Arabs. Sweat beaded her forehead and her heart raced. She could smell the raw copper scent of the blood on the wall and pooling on the floor. She kept her pistol trained on the closest Syrian, but he didn't move.

Footsteps pounded toward her down the front hall. She relaxed when she saw three Marines in their show-off dress blues rushing toward her. Each had an M-16 up and ready.

The Marine sergeant nodded grimly at her. "Good work in here, Miss Walsh. If they'd got down this corridor, a lot of us would have died out there. I think we've about got them beaten off."

Tuesday, July 23
Cairo, Egypt

It was hot, even for Cairo.

A devil wind whipped down the crooked street, bringing stinging sand on the wings of hot air that scraped the skin off a person's face and arms if left exposed too long. The local weatherman had promised that this was the last day of the heat wave.

Two young women hurried from one shady spot to the next along Scarab Street, their veils protecting their faces from the blowing sandpaper. They turned into a shop.

Two boys about twelve walked along Scarab Street. They wore white head coverings that protected their lower faces as well. Only their black eyes showed to the world. Each carried a red plastic sack that sagged heavily in his arms. They paused, set down the sacks, and rested, flexing their arms, talking quietly. The taller one looked at his wristwatch and nodded.

They picked up the plastic sacks and walked forward. Twice more, the taller boy checked his watch. The last time he slowed, then they walked casually to the front of a building with a sign in English and Arabic. The English part said: U.S. Petroleum Explorer.

The boys evidently tired again and set down their heavy sacks against the front of the American business and huddled against the facade to escape the savage wind.

They looked at each other, nodded, and walked away, quicker this time. They hurried down the block, around the corner, and out of sight.

Thirty seconds after the boys vanished, the two bags left outside the business exploded with a crackling, roaring blast that demolished the front half of the two-story building. The rest of the second story stood, gaping and exposed like a shameless streetwalker. It teetered there for a moment, then the back part tilted forward, and it all fell with a crashing roar onto the ground floor.

After the sounds of the smashing wood and shattering glass faded and the dust began to settle on the wreckage, one plaintive cry could be heard from the ruins. The cry came again, weaker this time. Once more, it issued from under some heavy timbers. Then it ceased and there was no life left in the American business office.

In three other sections of Cairo that afternoon, at precisely two P.M. local time, three more American business firms were shattered by bombs planted at the fronts of the buildings. Fourteen people died in the blasts, and over forty were injured. Two Egyptians, who worked in one of the firms, survived the blasts.

Ambrose Blount, security officer at the United States Embassy in Cairo and resident CIA man, inspected all four sites within an hour of the explosions. He wrote his report and sent it by top security scrambled radio by three-thirty, Cairo time.

"All four blasts went off within seconds of each other. Two had evidently been set up by small boys who left the bombs in plastic sacks against the fronts of the offices. It was a coordinated attack. I have absolutely no suggestion as to the reason for the terrorism or who could be behind it."

Naval Special Warfare Section One
Coronado, California

Lieutenant Commander Blake Murdock sat in his small office in the headquarters of SEAL Team Seven, Third Platoon, near the BUDS/S training facility. He could hear the surf breaking less than fifty yards away on the foaming Pacific Ocean.

He studied his personnel roster spread out on his desk and flipped down his pen and rubbed his face. Had he made the right choices? Coming back from the double whammy of the Kuril Islands and then the blowup in Korea had left him with three wounded men and the need to replace three others. Two had suffered wounds that would knock them right off the SEAL platoon, and the third one was in federal prison.

On top of that, his boss, Commander Masciareli, top gun of SEAL Team Seven, had ordered him to get with the T&O and put a SCPO on his platoon. A damned senior chief petty officer, who in effect would be third in command of the platoon right after Lieutenant (j.g.) DeWitt. A SCPO. The man had to be a top SEAL, somebody who Murdock and the rest of the men could get along with. He had to have the respect of the men, and they had to be willing to take orders from him. A hard combo for a chief in any field.

Master Chief Gordon MacKenzie had come up with four suggestions. The commander said anyone in the Seventh was available to him. That could cover maybe ten men. He had interviewed four different SCPOs. One was only twenty-six and on a fast track to Officer Candidate School. At last he had picked SCPO Aviation's Mate Will Dobler. He was thirty-seven years old, which would give them some maturity at the top.

Murdock picked up the pen and put on the cap. It had been three months since they came home from Korea. Things were shaping up.

J.g. Ed DeWitt was healed up and strong again. Jack Mahanani had agreed to be the platoon's medic, but he stayed in Bravo Squad. Murdock had to promise him he'd get some time on the big .50-caliber sniper rifle.

Miguel Fernandez had come back well from his chest wound. They picked twelve pieces of lead out of him, but none of it had hit anything vital.

Colt Franklin, who had been knocked out of action in the Islands, was whole and doing the O course faster than before.

That left him still short two men. He'd worked with Master Chief MacKenzie and come up with two good replacements. The first was a mechanic, Machinist Mate First Class Tony Ostercamp. He came from Third Team, was an amateur race car driver who had a car at the El Cajon Speedway, and could tear apart any machine ever made and then put it back together.

For the last man he wanted an armorer, or at least somebody who could repair and work with their weapons. He found him in the pool waiting for an assignment. His name was Paul (Jeff) Jefferson, a black man from Oakland and an aviation's mate second class.

Murdock looked over his completed roster sheet again:

SEAL TEAM SEVEN

THIRD PLATOON*

CORONADO, CALIFORNIA

PLATOON LEADER:

Lieutenant Commander Blake Murdock: 32, 6'2", 210 pounds. Annapolis graduate. Six years in SEALs. Father important

---

*Third Platoon assigned exclusively to the Central Intelligence Agency to perform any needed tasks on a covert basis anywhere in the world. All are top-secret assignments. Goes around Navy chain of command. Direct orders from the CIA.

congressman from Virginia. Murdock recently promoted. Apartment in Coronado. Has a car and a motorcycle; loves to fish.

WEAPON: H & K MP-5SD submachine gun.

ALPHA SQUAD

Willard "Will" Dobler: Aviation's Mate Senior Chief Petty Officer. Platoon chief. Third in command. 37, 6'1", 180 pounds. Married. Two kids. Sports nut. Knows dozens of major league records. Competition pistol marksman.

WEAPON: H & K MP-5 submachine gun. Good with the men.

David "Jaybird" Sterling: Machinist Mate Lead Petty Officer. 24, 5'10", 170 pounds. Quick mind, fine tactician. Single. Drinks too much sometimes. Crack shot with all arms. Helps plan attack operations.

WEAPON: H & K MP-5SD submachine gun.

Ron Holt: Radioman First Class. 22, 6'1", 170 pounds. Plays guitar, had a small band. Likes redheaded girls. Rabid baseball fan. Loves deep-sea fishing, is good at it. Platoon radio operator.

WEAPON: H & K MP-5SD submachine gun.

Bill Bradford: Quartermaster First Class. 24, 6'2", 215 pounds. An artist in spare time. Paints oils. He sells his marine paintings. Single. Quiet. Reads a lot. Has two years of college. Squad sniper.

WEAPON: H & K PSG1 7.62 NATO sniper rifle or McMillan M-87R .50-caliber sniper rifle.

Joe "Ricochet" Lampedusa: Operations Specialist Third Class. 21, 5'11", 175 pounds. Good tracker, quick thinker. Had a year of college. Loves motorcycles. Wants a Hog. Pot smoker on the sly. Picks up plain girls. Platoon scout.

WEAPON: Colt M-4A1 with grenade launcher.

Kenneth Ching: Quartermaster's Mate First Class. Full-blooded Chinese. 25, 6'0", 180 pounds. Platoon translator. Speaks Mandarin Chinese, Japanese, Russian, and Spanish. Bicycling nut. Paid $1,200 for off-road bike. Is trying for Officer Candidate School.

WEAPON: Colt M-4A1 rifle with grenade launcher.

Harry "Horse" Ronson: Electrician's Mate Second Class. 24, 6'4", 240 pounds. Played football two years at college. Wants a ranch where he can raise horses. Good man in a brawl. Has broken his nose twice. Squad machine gunner.

WEAPON: H & K 21-E 7.62 NATO round machine gun.

BRAVO SQUAD

Lieutenant (j.g.) Ed DeWitt: Leader, Bravo Squad. Second in command of the platoon. From Seattle. 30, 6'1", 175 pounds. Wiry. Has serious live-in woman. He's an Annapolis grad. A career man. Plays a good game of chess on traveling board.

WEAPON: The new H & K G-11 submachine gun.

Al Adams: Gunner's Mate Third Class. 20, 5'11", 180 pounds. Surfer and triathlete. Finished the Ironman twice. A golfing nut. Binge drinker or teetotaler. Loves the ladies if they play golf. Runs local marathons for training.

WEAPON: Colt M-4A1 with grenade launcher.

Miguel Fernandez: Gunner's Mate First Class. 26, 6'1", 180 pounds. Has wife, Maria, and child, Linda, age 7, in Coronado. Spends his off time with them. Highly family-oriented. He has family in San Diego. Speaks Spanish, Portuguese. Squad sniper.

WEAPON: H & K PSG1 7.62 NATO sniper rifle.

Colt "Guns" Franklin: Yeoman Second Class. 24, 5'10", 175 pounds. A former gymnast. Powerful arms and shoulders. Expert mountain climber. Has a motorcycle and does hang gliding. Speaks Farsi and Arabic.

WEAPON: Colt M-4A1 with grenade launcher.

Les Quinley: Torpedoman Third Class. 22, 5'9", 160 pounds. A computer and Internet fan. Has his own Web page. Always reading computer magazines. Explosive specialist with extra training.

WEAPON: H & K G-11 caseless rounds, 4.7mm submachine gun with 50-round magazine.

Jack Mahanani: Hospital Corpsman First Class. 25, 6'4", 240 pounds. Platoon medic. Tahitian/Hawaiian. Expert swimmer. Bench-presses 400 pounds. Once married, now divorced. Top surfer. Wants the .50 sniper rifle.

WEAPON: Colt M-4Al with grenade launcher.

Anthony "Tony" Ostercamp: Machinist Mate First Class. 23, 5'10", 180 pounds. Races stock cars in nearby El Cajon weekends. Top auto mechanic. Platoon driver.

WEAPON: H & K 21E 7.62 NATO round machine gun. Second radio operator.

Paul "Jeff" Jefferson: Aviation's Mate Second Class. Black man, 23, 6'1", 200 pounds. Expert in small arms. Can tear them apart and reassemble, repair, innovate. Is a chess player to match Ed DeWitt.

PLATOON WEAPON: Colt M-4A1 with grenade launcher.

Murdock stared at the names and weapons. He remembered the two months of training they had taken to fuse the new men into the platoon. He remembered the nights of talking with SCPO Dobler, bringing him up to date on the men, trying to give him a firm foundation in the team. Had he done it with Dobler? Were the men in the platoon ready?

On the schedule for the coming week, he had put intensified live fire drills. Each man in the platoon had to be at home firing every weapon the platoon used. This was essential.

The walking wounded had rounded out in good shape. All were fit for SEAL duty, and that was rougher and tougher than normal Navy duty. Murdock tried to relax. Bowling used to relax him. He thought about it a minute.

No, not bowling. There you were shooting for perfection. The perfect 300 game. His competitive instincts would take over, and he'd be furious if he didn't do well. Even a 200 game would piss him off. He settled for going home, taking a long hot shower, then diving into bed.

As he turned out the light, he wondered what Ardith Manchester was doing in her apartment in Washington, D.C., about then.

2

The Persian Gulf

Eight wet suit–clad divers came up out of the depths of the black waters of the Persian Gulf twenty miles below Kuwait City. They swam strongly against the bow wake of the huge ship until they came against the black side. There they pushed strong magnets against the steel hull of the super crude carrier oil tanker.

All eight men wore black wet suits, face masks, rebreathers, caps, gloves, and boots. Automatic weapons had been tied across their backs. Each man wore a combat vest with pockets and zippers, and all were loaded with arms. The men rested as the big tanker towed them through the water at her normal loaded cruising speed of eighteen knots. The smallest man in the team lifted out of the water and, using magnets on his hands and feet, worked his way slowly up the side of the tanker at the lowest point, about amidships. He trailed a thin, strong nylon rope tied to his waist. He rested halfway up, then paused at the rail. He looked down the long expanse of the deck, saw no sentries, no one on watch. It was nearly three A.M. Most of the crew would be sleeping.

Of the eighteen in the crew, they estimated that only four would be on duty at night.

The dark-clad man tied off his end of the nylon line to a

11

sturdy iron fixture, then gave it two short tugs. Two pulls answered him from the bottom. The man pushed behind a fixture and blended in with the ship. He watched carefully both ways. A door slammed somewhere on the houselike building forward of amidships. It was made up of three or four decks topped by the pilothouse with the navigation and equipment section, the bridge, and the communications room. There also were quarters in this house for the officers and some of the crew. It was the nerve center of the computer-operated ship.

He could see the poop deck on the stern of the long ship. That area covered the loading and unloading machinery and the huge power plant that propelled the ship. There were quarters there for the crew as well.

In the intense briefing yesterday, he was told that the tanker was 2,400 feet long. That was almost the length of eight soccer fields laid end to end! Fantastic. He would believe it when it grew light and he could see for himself.

They told him it was 430 feet across, farther across the big ship than the width of two soccer fields. The deckhouse was supposed to be seven stories tall.

Their leader said he was not sure just how many crewmen were on board. With every advance in computer technology, they trimmed down the crew. They were figuring that there were still eighteen men on this older ship. It still had one hull, not the double hull the newest tankers had.

He couldn't see the bow of the ship, but up there was the forecastle. There would be no crewmen or workmen in the forecastle, so they would ignore it during the first attack.

One of his men came over the rail from the rope. He sank to the black deck at once. The men came regularly after that until all eight were on board. Their leader came last.

Each man knew his assignment. Four would take over the poop deck area, to capture the crew, killing as few as possible. They would need most of the Americans to run the ship. Four men would go to the large boat house.

Kamel Jaber took off his wet suit helmet and discarded it over the side. The other divers did the same. He gathered his men around him as they drained the seawater from the barrels of their weapons and charged rounds into the chambers.

"You know what to do. We will not fail. We keep as many

alive as we can to run the ship. Your reward will be great. May you go with Allah."

They moved cautiously in the darkness of the night along the huge ship toward their targets.

Jaber took three key men with him. One was a ship's engineer, the other had a pilot's license for the coastal regions of the Persian Gulf, and the third man was his best shooter.

They moved like shadows along the side of the ship outside the array of pipes across the wide deck. Jaber knew the giant ship held its crude oil in all of its ninety holds. It was full and heading to America. He smiled. Not for long. They reached the metal door that led into the deck-level floor of the house. It was unlocked. He edged it open and peered inside. It looked like a dressing room for foul weather. Various lockers covered one wall. Another had pegs with wet-weather clothing and hats. A stairway showed to the left.

Jaber knew the floor plan of the tanker's house. He had studied it for a week. The steps led to the second level, where there were living quarters for the captain, first mate, and chief engineer. He needed all three of them alive and uninjured.

They cleared the three rooms on the first level, storage and supplies. Jaber took the lead up the steps. He had a stun gun and a silenced pistol. The steps were metal, and their rubber-soled diving boots made not even a whisper of sound. Jaber came up the steps to where he could see the second level. Just as in the plans he had seen, there was a hallway with four doors off it, and more steps up to the pilothouse.

He tried the first door. His three men moved in close behind him. Unlocked. He turned the doorknob gently, then edged the panel in an inch. Darkness. He took out the penlight and thrust the door open a foot, then shone the light inside. One bed. The man on it slept with only a sheet over him.

Jaber moved quietly to him, pressed the silenced automatic to his throat, and shook him.

"Wake up," he said in English. The man mumbled and tried to turn over.

"Wake up," Jaber said louder. One of his men had closed the door behind them. The man jolted upward, his eyes wild in the beam of the small, powerful light.

"What the hell?"

"True, my friend," Jaber said, pushing the automatic into the man's side. "One outcry, and you will be in hell. Are you the first mate or the engineer?"

"First mate. What is this?"

"Nothing to get alarmed about. Hands behind you, please."

One of Jaber's men came up quickly and taped the man's hands together behind his back, then put another piece of tape across his mouth. More tape fastened his ankles together. Then they put him back on the bunk.

"You will stay there, First Mate, or you'll be shot. Do you understand? We're taking over your ship."

The first mate's eyes focused on the shadow behind the light, but he saw little. He nodded.

The four men left the room silently.

The next room was unlocked and empty.

The third room was the same size as the other two. They caught the chief engineer in the middle of a dream, and he called out loudly before they could awaken him.

He submitted quietly after that and was taped and left in his bunk.

The next room had to be that of the captain. Jaber knew it would be twice the size of the others. They had plenty of room on a ship this large. He tried the door. Open. Again, he edged the panel in an inch. A faint night-light glowed. He eased the door open fully. It was the captain's cabin. Three times as large as the others. A big double bed, a living room effect, and a door that could lead to a bath.

Jaber moved in quietly, put his hand over the captain's mouth, and shook his shoulder. He was older, in his fifties. He came awake slowly. His eyes flashed as he tried to sit up.

"Stay down, old man. Try to cry out, and I'll zap you with this stun gun. You want fifty thousand volts of electricity?"

The captain shook his head.

Jaber removed his hand. "We're taking over your ship. We want you to get up and get dressed. Then we'll go to the bridge and put my men in charge. Oh, yes, we can sail this big island of a boat quite well. We're all experts in many fields. Quickly now, get dressed."

Three minutes later, the captain led the way up the steps to the bridge and pilothouse. Two men were on duty. The ship was on automatic controls, moving down the middle of the wide Persian Gulf. The radar man kept watching three screens that showed the area far ahead, the bottom line of the gulf, and the area immediately forward.

Captain Norman Phillips, master of the *Jasmine Queen,* cleared his throat. "Gentlemen, we have visitors. Please do exactly what they tell you to do. Offer no resistance."

"Captain, who are these men?" The man behind the wheel asked the question. At once a pistol slashed downward across the side of his head, and he crumpled to the floor.

"Keep quiet and stay alive," Jaber said in English. Two of his three men peeled out of their wet suits. They wore swim trunks under them.

"You two men strip off your clothes," Jaber told the two Americans. They looked at their captain. He nodded.

A few minutes later, the Arabs had put on the sailor's clothes and were manning the wheel and the radar. Jaber and Nuri Haddad checked over the instruments and nodded. They were just as the plans said they would be. Nothing that Nuri hadn't handled before.

Jaber prodded the two men in their underwear and the captain back down the steps to the officers' quarters. He pushed the two crewmen and their captain into the vacant room.

"The keys to lock these doors," Jaber said. He had noticed while inside that they had no night locks on them, could only be opened with a key. The captain produced a master key, and Jaber locked the three doors.

"Do not attempt to communicate with anyone, Captain. Do you have any kind of a satellite radio in this cabin?"

Captain Phillips shook his head.

"Good. We will kill anyone we have to, but we do not crave to see your blood flow. Cooperate with us and live to sail another day."

Jaber locked the door from the outside and hurried down the steps with his fourth man to check on the takeover of the poop deck, where most of the crew would be sleeping.

They jogged down the quarter of a mile to the stern of the long ship and found one of their men on guard outside. He slipped out from some shadows.

"All taken care of here, Jaber. Two of them grabbed hidden guns, and we had to kill them. The rest submitted to our demands and we have them all locked up in a storage room, with one door and no portholes."

"Well done, Abid. How many men?"

"We have eighteen, counting the two dead ones. They said they are one man short on the crew. He took sick in Kuwait City."

"So, if your man isn't lying, we have all twenty-two of them. A larger crew than we expected. Good work. Now we settle down to running this tanker to its new destination."

The Arabs cheered.

"Yes, when we sell the oil, each of you will receive a share of our half of the money. The other half goes to the glorious regime."

"Sir, any idea about how much . . ."

Jaber laughed. "Faud, it is far too early to count our money. We have a long journey, and there could be many problems before we get there. We will be selling the crude at half the world market price, but that still should produce twenty-five million dollars. Half of that and divided by ten . . . would be a million and a quarter American dollars for each of you."

Faud Baali shook his head. "I would not know what to do with that much money. I would be lost."

"That's why we don't count it yet," Jaber said. "We have much work. First, we check each section of the ship we can get to. You remember your assignments. Who went to the forecastle at the front of the ship?"

"Fahim," one of them said. "It is clear of any men. He came back and is in the crew's kitchen."

Jaber grinned. That was like Fahim, his brother-in-law. He had never seen a kitchen, a café, or a restaurant that he didn't like.

"Let's move. Check out all of the areas we assigned, and come back here. Nuri will be in charge of this detail. The other four of us will be with the captain and in the boat house amidships."

Locked in his cabin, Captain Phillips wondered what he could do. He had told the ship's owners they should have more security on board. They had only one man designated for that job. Where had he been? One man against these terrorists would not have prevented the takeover. They had done it so easily. He didn't even protest, let alone try for the Smith & Wesson on the back of his bed.

What could he have done differently?

What could he do right now?

At least he wasn't tied up.

The intercom. It was a type of telephone service, with buttons to push for various parts of the ship. He went to the phone and pushed the button for the first mate.

"Yes?" a tentative voice came on the line.

"Tabler, is that you?"

"Captain! Damn, I wondered if these would work. Didn't want to try. Can anyone else hear us?"

"Not on the wires. At least they didn't tie us up. Who are they?"

"Arabs, all I can figure out. They did tie me up at first, but then undid me. I'm locked in here. What about you?"

"Locked in, but I've got a spare key here somewhere."

"Took all my keys and billfold, everything."

"Even if we could get out, what could we do?" the captain asked. "They'll have the radio room under control with somebody to answer any calls in English. The ones I saw all had submachine guns. Terrible weapons."

"What about Casemore, our safety and security man? Was he captured? He said he was going to work tonight, stay up all night and watch the crew quarters and see if he could figure out who was snipping away at the poop deck kitchen supplies. We have enough food for twice this crew. Why would anybody want to steal cookies and ice cream?"

"For the thrill of it, maybe," The captain said. "You think there's a chance that Casemore saw them coming and hid somewhere? He could be free on the ship?"

"A chance," Tabler said. "I'd say a damn good chance, Captain. Maybe he could get to the radio room and send out a distress call."

"Maybe. Don't try to call anyone else on the phone. We don't know who might pick up."

"Captain, we better get some sleep. Tomorrow, I figure they are going to need some of us on the bridge for the radio, if nothing else."

"We'll fight that battle tomorrow, Tabler. Yes. Sleep will be helpful."

Hidden in the poop deck deep in the machinery used to load and unload the big ship through dozens of pipes, lay Safety Officer Ben Casemore. He had seen the black-suited figures slip on the ship. He was too far from a phone to warn anyone. Then, when he had tried to reach the phone in the poop deck just above the machinery, the attackers swarmed in there and took down the crew. He had heard two shots. Somebody had died.

He stared at the machinery around him. He was the fucking safety officer. Just what was he supposed to do now to retake the ship from the swarm of terrorists who had captured her with only two shots fired? He had no idea.

3

Naval Chocolate Mountain Gunnery Range
Nyland, California

Third Platoon of SEAL Team Seven had made a silent move two miles into the desert mountains from the gate at the big gunnery range that the SEALs used for live firing exercises and training. The bleak nightscape of desert spread twenty-five miles to the north and fifty miles all the way to the Colorado River on the east. There was no chance a thunder of live firing could hurt any civilians.

Lieutenant Commander Blake Murdock watched his new SCPO, Will Dobler, working the platoon. He'd given the senior chief petty officer the problem: Move the platoon two miles to the target. Attack the "bungalow" from two sides, make sure of the enemy casualties, re-form, and move out a mile due north to avoid any countermeasures.

So far, Dobler was working well. He had been a SEAL for six years, two as an instructor at BUDS/S and four with the teams. He had proven himself under fire in eight actions all around the world. He was an easygoing German-Irishman who brought a little more maturity to the platoon. So far, he had the respect of the men who were quickly learning to have confidence in him. He would need that in the days to come.

Murdock watched as Dobler spread out the men in silent

formations in front and to the side of the bullet-absorbing
bungalow. Murdock's earpiece spoke.

"Silenced snipers, both squads, take out the guards."

Murdock heard the whispers of the suppressed NATO
round weapons firing. All weapons but the machine guns had
silencers on. The Motorola personalized radio came on again.
Each SEAL had one with a transceiver on his belt, an ear
speaker, and a lip mike for instant communications up to
nearly a mile. For wet work, they zippered into a waterproof
pouch on the men's combat vests.

"Let's take it down," Dobler said on the radio. "All fire,
now."

The desert landscape sparkled with the flashes of fifteen
weapons. The two H & K 21-E machine guns chattered off
five- and seven-round bursts.

Thirty seconds into the firing sequence, the radio came on.

"Ching, Franklin, two WP forty-mike rounds each on the
target, now," Senior Chief Dobler said. When the four WP
rounds bathed the front and side of the bungalow with star-
bursts of burning phosphorus, Dobler called a cease-fire.

"Jefferson, Ostercamp. Get in there and clear it, then make
sure of the KIAs. That means one round in the head of each
of the dummies in there. Move."

Two points for Dobler. Murdock watched the little drama
play out, heard the clear signal on the Motorola, then the
four single shots that sounded from the bungalow. The two
SEALs came out, charging back to the line of their buddies,
who still lay in the darkness forty yards from the target.

"Phase one completed, Commander. Orders?" the senior
chief said in the radio.

Two more points for Dobler. He was going to work out.
"Gather the platoon around me for a talk-down," Murdock
said.

A pair of minutes later, Murdock stood in the center of
the platoon. "Senior Chief, any suggestions or ass chewing
for the troops on this mission?"

"A few, Commander. He stood up and walked around the
men. "Three of you moved like little old ladies on the hike
up here. I can name names, but you know who you are. Sure,
sure, you're swimmers, wet warriors, but at least half, maybe

sixty percent of all the SEAL ops will be on land. Remember that, people.

"I don't give a rat's ass how much you dislike slogging along like the infantry; that's a fucking big part of our job. Accept it and adapt to it or get the hell out of SEALs.

"Not all of you were ready to fire when I gave the order. With silenced weapons, you all can't hear the commander or Mr. DeWitt or me fire the first rounds as a signal to you. That's why now and again, you'll get a verbal order to open fire. Be ready. That's your job, to put concentrated, deadly fire on the enemy, *when you're ordered to do so.*"

Dobler looked at Murdock. "That's about it, sir. Not a bad operation, but we can stand some work to sharpen up."

Murdock nodded in the darkness. Another two points for the senior chief. He had chewed, then put himself in the picture saying, "we can stand some work. . . ." Yes, good. "The JG has the next phase. What time is it?"

"0223, sir," Jeff Jefferson bellowed.

"Glad somebody in this group can tell time. The senior chief is right; we're getting a little sloppy. With nobody shooting back, we're not digging in like we should. Mr. DeWitt, this bunch is your meat."

Lieutenant (j.g.) DeWitt's leg had healed up as good as new. He led the platoon on a forced march at just over ten minutes to the mile up a ridge, down across a valley, and upward again toward the Lion's Head. It was a peak that the SEALs used for a variety of purposes.

Less than a hundred yards from the top, Murdock's vibrator pager went off. Their contact with the CIA, Don Stroh, had furnished Murdock with a pager and insisted that he wear it whenever he was Stateside.

"Hold it, platoon," Murdock said. "Somebody is on the hot line." He looked at his beeper, which had the message: "SATCOM, NOW."

"Holt, get back here to me at the tail end. Warm up that SATCOM of yours on the way. Methinks that duty doth call."

"What the fuck he say?" somebody cracked on the Motorola.

Holt had the SATCOM radio on receive before he found Murdock. It was on voice transmission.

"Skipper, just had a transmission. It's the master chief, and he sounds grumpy as all hell frozen over."

Murdock took the handset of the fifteen-pound radio that could bounce signals off the satellite or work through cell phones' TAC frequencies, and a half dozen other configurations.

"SEAL Seven, this is Murdock."

"Murdock, it's really hit the fan. Just had an urgent from Don Stroh. He wants you and yours ready to fly out of North Island at noon today. Better get your fannies back on the bus and move it toward town. Not much we can do until you get here. Stroh's breathing fire. He'll meet you at Andrews Air Force Base near Washington, D.C."

"We're moving it, Master Chief. An hour back to the bus, then three hours to your place. It's 0230 now. Say we'll see you at 0630, give or take a bit. Let's start with a big breakfast as soon as we hit the base. Then we can shower, get new cammies, and get our gear ready. Yeah. Can make that noontime deadline."

Murdock signed off and called into his Motorola, "Reverse your march, SEALs. Just had a call from our buddy, Don Stroh. He's hot for our asses again. We fly out of North Island at 1200 today. So let's shag our tails for the fucking bus."

They made their connection at North Island, sweeping in with less than a minute to spare. The next stop was Andrews Air Force Base, just outside of Washington, D.C. They picked up double-sized box lunches and walked stiffly to their next transportation.

"I'm in fucking heaven," Jeff Jefferson said when they stopped next to a Gulfstream, U.S. Coast Guard VC11 executive jet. Most of the other SEALs had been in a Gulfstream before.

"It's got real airliner seats that lean back," Jaybird said. "Hey, we're traveling first class on this one. Which means they have some especially dank and shit-kicking job for us once we get wherever we're going."

They filed on the sleek jet, took seats. There was room for nineteen passengers and a crew of two or three. It cruised at 581 miles per hour and could cover 4,275 miles without a drink of fuel. A Coast Guard commander sat in the driver's seat. His copilot was a Coast Guard JG female. She didn't even look at the men; she was too busy doing a final preflight checklist.

Don Stroh came running out. They had held the plane for him for ten minutes. He grabbed one of the box lunches and dropped into a seat beside Murdock.

"Okay, big spender," Murdock said. "Tell us where we're going and what kind of hell we're going to be jumping into."

"We're going there fast. That's why I wangled this VIP jet. She'll fly us over there in a damn rush. We're late now. I haven't even figured out when we'll arrive or where we stop for fuel."

"Hey, Stroh. Just tell me where we're going."

"Last stop is Riyadh, Saudi Arabia. Another sixty-five hundred miles from here. We've got a small problem in the Persian Gulf."

"Again?"

"Yeah, big buddy, again."

"So, is it a secret?"

"It is. We've had a supertanker hijacked in the middle of the Persian Gulf. The captain on board used a common term that is a trigger word. It means the ship is in terrorists' hands, and he has no control of it. If the terrorists know that we know, they could sink the ship or release millions of tons of crude into the Persian Gulf, causing a die-off of billions of fish and birds and turning the gulf shorelines into a wasteland.

"The tanker, the SUCC *Jasmine Queen* carries one and a half million tons of crude."

"When was the takeover?"

"We're not sure. First transmission of the trigger word was about midnight, our time, last night."

"You move fast."

"The President moves fast. There's a lot of other crap going on as well over there." Stroh told Murdock about the four coordinated bombings in Cairo and the attacks on three U.S. embassies in the Middle East.

"Does it all tie together?" Murdock asked.

"The President wishes that he knew. State doesn't have a

clue. Our Middle East desk is totally in the dark. We're swatting flies in an outhouse here."

Murdock thought about that a minute. "We must be one of the swatters. Our job is to retake the tanker?"

"Good guess. I have the specs on the ship, layout, crew, types of radar, and machinery. Everything you'll need to know."

"We better start planning. Will the tanker still be in the gulf by the time we get over there? How fast is she?"

"She does eighteen knots fully loaded; that's two hundred and fifty miles a day. The gulf is four hundred seventy miles long. Let's say they captured the ship in the dark thirty-six hours ago. The tanker had loaded at Kuwait City near the top of the gulf. In forty-eight hours, the ship will be out of the Persian Gulf into the Gulf of Oman."

Murdock stood up in his place. "DeWitt, Dobler, Sterling, up here for a powwow. Now."

Stroh moved across the aisle. DeWitt took his seat, and the other two stood in the aisle. The business jet was quieter than most jet airliners.

"We're going to the Persian Gulf. Here's the problem." Murdock laid it out for them. They all listened and then began talking at once.

"Hey, easy. We've got lots of time. We'll be on this plane for another eleven hours. We'll chew it around, get some sleep, and then talk about it again in the morning. It's now twenty-two hundred. Stroh says the pilot reports that with two stops, we should hit Riyadh about 0900. So talk to me."

They talked.

4

U.S. Air Force Base
Riyadh, Saudi Arabia

By the time the sleek Gulfstream jet had landed at Riyadh, the SEALs were rested, had worked out a basic plan to take over the tanker, and were ready for breakfast. Murdock was taken to a communications room where he was put in contact with the XO of the carrier *Enterprise,* now working the duty in the southern half of the Persian Gulf.

"Yes, Commander. We received orders and have been tracking all U.S. super crude carriers in and just out of the gulf with our Hawkeye. We've pinpointed six of them and have confirmed ID on all but one. The tanker in trouble is the *Jasmine Queen.* We have her now outbound in the Gulf of Oman about fifty miles from the Strait of Hormuz. She's on a southeasterly course at a steady cruising speed of eighteen knots."

"That's our target, Captain. My orders are to proceed to your ship via COD. Is there one at this base waiting for us?"

"That's a roger, Commander. It's ready when you are. Your orders come from the highest source, and we're ready to extend all services we can to you and your men."

"Good, Captain. We'll need two IBS craft and a chopper

to get us in front of the *Jasmine*. What is your range to the target?"

"We're about fifty miles from the strait, which puts us now a little over a hundred to the tanker. That's out of range of the Sea Knight, which would be the best vehicle. We'll go with the Sea Stallion, which has plenty of room for your boats and men. Sixteen SEALs?"

"Yes sir. We'll need an assortment of ammo and weapons we can talk about when we get on board. We won't be leaving you until near dark, so we can do a nighttime attack."

"Then we have lots of time. I'll contact you as soon as you're on board."

"Thank you, Captain. We'll see you soon."

Ed DeWitt and Murdock had breakfast to order with the rest of the SEALs at one of the mess halls on base, then rode in a truck out to the flight line, where the transport waited. Murdock had dropped in on more carriers in the COD C-2A than he cared to remember. It was a two-engine turboprop cargo plane that could land and take off from a carrier. Its only job was to ferry people, supplies, and mail to and from CVN carriers at sea.

The SEALs grumbled when they filed on board the COD. All had ridden on them before, and they found what they expected: uncomfortable bucket seats along the sides of the ship.

"Hell, it's only about four hundred miles," Jaybird cracked.

"Yeah, and I bet they'll have one of the Air Force's best box lunches to go," Ostercamp said. They all laughed. The stock car racer was fitting in well with the platoon.

When they landed on board the *Enterprise* three hours later, a JG met them and escorted them to an assembly room they could use to get ready for the mission.

"Yes, Commander," the JG said. "We have three IBS craft ready for your inspection. We'll have a man from ship's stores on hand to get any supplies, ammunition, or weapons you'll need."

A messenger waited for Murdock, and when he was ready, took him to the XO's office.

"Are you getting everything you need, Commander?" Captain Arthur J. Small asked. He was a large man with a wind-marked face and brooding green eyes. He wore an aviator's wings on his shirt.

"Yes sir. All's in order. All we do now is wait for the sun to get low enough. I understand the target is now about a hundred and thirty miles downstream. That still is in range of the Stallion, I'd guess."

"Right. She'll do over a thousand miles round trip."

"Sunset is about 1830 here?"

"Closer to 1900 this time of year."

"So we have a little over an hour's ride at a hundred and seventy knots to get ahead of the tanker. We want dark down there, so we'll leave here at 1830."

The captain wiped one hand over his face and grinned. "Have to say, Commander Murdock, that I've never had orders direct from the Chief of Naval Operations before. This must be something damned important."

"Yes, Captain, it's up the scale a ways, but nothing to write home about."

"Another day at the office, Commander?"

"Something like that. Only the place where our office is located changes every time, and the job is different every time. Makes it more interesting. Thanks for your help."

Murdock excused himself and went back to the SEALs. He made sure they had a good meal, then they worked over their equipment and double-checked their ammo. LPO Jaybird took orders and went to sign for the ordnance they needed. Nothing fancy this time, just a straight shoot-and-scoot operation.

Over the Gulf of Oman

The dark, choppy waters of the gulf flashed by below the Super Stallion CH-53A/D. They were rocketing along at only two hundred miles an hour, but when you're twenty feet above the water, it seems twice that fast.

"The pilot told me at this low level, the radar on the big tanker might not even see us," Murdock said. "If it does, the blip will be so small and fading in and out that they might think it's a small ship.

"This terrorist radar man might not be much good at that

job," Murdock said. "Like, he was shoveling camel shit a week ago; now he's a radar tech."

Murdock checked his men in the big belly of the chopper. There had been room for the IBSs to stay inflated, so all they had to do was drop into the gulf, grab the black boat, and climb on board.

"We're about four miles ahead of the tanker," Murdock told his platoon. "We'll go one more mile, then turn into its path. Not much reason it should change course. It hasn't since it left the strait. We get in the IBSs and watch for him. Eighteen knots, five miles, it won't be a long wait."

"Fifteen minutes," Quinley said. Nobody challenged him. Quinley was their computer expert, and he was good at doing figures in his head.

"You know your assignments once we spot the tanker. It won't be easy. Who has the big magnets?"

Franklin in Bravo Squad had two, and Bradford in Alpha had two.

"They don't have floatation devices on them, so don't drop the suckers overboard."

They felt the chopper turn.

"Won't be long now. Double-check everything."

They had decided to do the work in their cammies. They wouldn't be in the water that long, and the wet suits would be a handicap once on board.

The crew chief tapped Murdock on the shoulder. "About three minutes to our drop zone."

Murdock nodded his thanks. "All right, you know the drill. Bravo Squad out first, then the SBIs, then Alpha. Grab the boats and hold them. Check the motors first. We ready?"

"Hoooorah!" the men shouted.

They all felt the craft slow. The crew chief slid open the hatch. The black water showed below, less than twenty feet away. The Stallion came almost to a stop, hovering. The crew chief yelled at Murdock.

"Go, Bravo, go," Murdock shouted.

The eight men ran to the door and stepped out, dropping straight down into the rotor-roiled water. When the eighth man was out, Alpha Squad dumped the bulky SBIs out the hatch, then jumped out behind them. Murdock was the last man out.

· The cold water hit Murdock like a thousand icy needles driven into his skin. He surfaced, saw the first boat ten yards away through the gloom of the night, and stroked toward it. Six men were inside: Alpha Squad. Two helped pull him in.

"Who's missing?" he asked.

SCPO Dobler waved. "Holt, sir. He's right behind you. That damn radio dragged him down."

They got Holt in with the waterproofed SATCOM, and Murdock looked for Bravo Squad.

"The other boat is off about thirty yards," Jaybird said. "I heard them talking." Jaybird kicked over the engine. It caught on the second try.

"Let's find them," Murdock said. Murdock blinked his flashlight three times. To the west they saw three blinks in return. Two minutes later, the two SBIs had a buddy cord thirty feet long tying them together.

He used his Motorola, which he pulled out of the water-tight pouch.

"DeWitt, you on the net?"

No answer. Murdock asked the question again. This time DeWitt came back.

"Yes. We've been off the chopper for three minutes. Should leave twelve until our friend comes by."

"Roger that, JG. As soon as we get close to him, we cut the cord and get through the bow wake and alongside the hull."

"How high is that rail?" DeWitt asked.

"No idea, nobody seemed to know. Your man has three shots to make a catch. Horse has three shots. One of them should catch."

Harry "Horse" Ronson had the Mossburg shotgun out and ready. He tied the end of a quarter-inch nylon line to the SBI and inserted a slender metal probe down the barrel. The top end of the line tied to a fitting on the part of the device that stuck out of the barrel. It had a wad of thick cotton on the part down the barrel.

"This thing gonna work?" Ronson asked.

"Worked in training," Murdock said. It'll work now. You're using the special shotgun shells without any lead pellets?"

"Oh, yeah. I don't want it to blow up in my face."

"The idea is to get the grappling hook over the rail so it'll catch on something strong enough to support our rope man," Murdock said. "Don't get fancy. If the first one doesn't work, go to the second. When it catches, pull it tight slowly, then hang all your weight on it. If it'll hold you, it should hold any of us."

"I've got three coils of a hundred feet of line," Ronson said. "That should be enough."

The Motorola came on. "Commander, I've got some dim lights to the north of us, seem to be moving this way. Could be our favorite supertanker."

"Roger. Wait until she's almost on us before we dig out with the motors. If anybody can read the name on the bow, it will be reassuring we've got the right boat."

"No sweat there, Skip," Dobler said. "Radar said there was no other supertanker for twenty miles around this one. Got to be our baby."

They waited. There was no wind; the water had calmed but was as black as ever. Murdock could see the huge tanker's running lights now. They seemed to be half a mile apart.

"That's her," DeWitt said on the radio. "We're on the port side, so we see her lights fore and aft. Now, that's a hell of a big ship."

"We better motor toward her," Murdock said. "Keep the tether and let's move in together. How far is she off?"

"Six hundred yards, at least," DeWitt said. "Yeah, we better kick these things over there."

The SEALs crouched in the SBIs, hanging on wherever they could, as the little boats slapped through the swells at ten knots. They were on a collision course with the side of the half-mile-long tanker. Now they could see more lights on her deck and her deckhouse.

"Three hundred yards," DeWitt said. "Let's up the throttles so we don't miss her. She's doing eighteen knots."

They jolted forward directly at the side of the big ship; then, when they were fifty yards away, they could feel the swell of the bow wave coming off her.

"Cut the line," Murdock said. "Go with her, get through that bow wake and alongside. Now, full throttle."

The small boats leaped ahead, came closer to the mammoth island-sized ship, and then angled the same direction she was heading. Slowly, they edged closer. Then the three were moving at the same eighteen knots, and DeWitt brought his SBI up toward the towering metal hulk. The bow wave pushed him away. He tried again, and on the third time got close enough so two men reached out and slammed foot-square magnets against the hull. Lines tied the magnets to the sides of the SBI. The lines were pulled tight and the SBI's motor cut off.

Murdock had a harder time moving alongside. When he did, the bow wave kept washing him away like a leaf in a torrent. On the fourth time, he angled close enough that the magnets slammed into place, and he was tethered to the tanker.

"Ronson, you ready? Make sure the coil of line is free."

"Ready, Cap."

"DeWitt, your man ready to fire?"

"Ready."

"Fire grappling hooks until we get one or two set. Go."

Horse Ronson fired the cut-down, pistol-grip shotgun with both hands, aiming the six-pointed grappling hook at the rail far above him. He watched the line peel out of the coil. Then the line stopped moving, and he saw it arc out from the tanker and the hook evidently fell into the water. He pitched the rest of the coil of line overboard. He loaded a second special shotgun shell and the grappling hook and tied the inside end of the second coil of line to the grappling hook. Then he aimed outward more this time, so the hook would clear the side of the big tanker, and fired.

"We have a hookup," Murdock's earpiece reported.

This time, Ronson's line kept snaking out of the coil of rope until it fell in on itself, then stopped spooling out. Ronson put down the shotgun and pulled gently on the line. It came down two feet, then three more. Two more feet of line came down, then stopped. It had snagged something above. Ronson pulled it hard, then stood high, grabbed a loop of the line, and pulled himself upward off the small boat. The hook held.

"Got it, Commander," Ronson said. "Looks to be about twenty to twenty-five feet of line left. A seventy-five-foot climb."

Jaybird moved to the line. All the SEALs still had their

weapons tied across their backs. Jaybird flexed the thick aviator's gloves and reached up on the rope. On the O Course, he was the fastest up the rope climb of anyone in the platoon.

"Go," Murdock said. He touched the lip mike. "Ed, send your first man up. One man on the rope at a time. Go, go, go."

The rest of Alpha Squad watched as Jaybird worked his way up the line. He moved smoothly, all with his arms. He might use his feet on the line higher up, but down here it was partly for show. Moments later, he was out of sight. Ronson sat on the bottom of the line to make it as steady as he could for the climber.

They waited.

The big tanker kept plowing through the Gulf of Oman at eighteen knots. Murdock used the radio. "Ed, make sure everyone has his Motorola out and working. Make a net check on your men to me." He looked at his remaining men. They were digging out their radios from waterproof pouches. Soon the whole platoon was wired for sound and ready to rumble—except the two men climbing up the line.

"I have my first man up," DeWitt said. "He's on the deck, has tied off the line more securely."

Jaybird gave two tugs on the line, indicating that he was on the deck. He checked the grappling hook. It was secure. He looked around. He could see no lookouts, guards, or terrs.

Ron Holt went up next. He left the fifteen-pound radio in Murdock's hands, still in its waterproof wrap. It would be tied on the line and pulled up after the last man was on board.

On the deck of the tanker, Jaybird saw Quinley in a crouch and moving toward him.

"See anybody?" Quinley asked as he bellied down beside Jaybird.

"No. You watch forward, I'll check aft. We stay in place until the rest are up."

Far to the stern of the tanker, they both heard a door open and a brilliant splash of yellow light gush out, then grow smaller and vanish when they heard the door close.

Jaybird motioned Quinley to the inside of the tanker where there were masses of large pipes that were used to fill each of the giant holds. They wedged onto the deck with six inches of cover. They could hear the hard soles of someone

walking down their side of the long ship toward them. There
was no way to warn the men below. The man had a hundred
yards to cover before he came to them. He must be heading
for the deckhouse.

The man turned on a flashlight, and the beam bounced
along, covering the deck directly in front of him. The tanker
man was twenty yards away when a SEAL came to the rail
and clung to it. Jaybird had not heard the signal to turn on
his Motorola. He waved at the man directly opposite him,
but couldn't get his attention. The man rolled over on the
deck, panting from the long climb.

By then, the flashlight beam bounced along, ten yards
away. Jaybird was midway between the man with the light
and the SEAL. No way the man could miss the SEAL on
the deck here where the empty space between rail and pipes
was no more than ten feet.

Jaybird waited until the tanker sailor came directly opposite him, then he stood and slammed into the man with the
light. He knew he couldn't kill him, not until he was sure
the man was a terrorist. Jaybird hit the man hard, and they
both jolted to the deck.

5

On Board the *Jasmine Queen*
Gulf of Oman

Jaybird hit the seaman waist high and drove him to the deck. His hand curled around the man's mouth so he couldn't call out. The SEAL spread his legs to keep the man from turning him over. His right hand jerked the KA-BAR from its sheath, and he pressed it hard against the sailor's throat.

"Are you an American?" Jaybird whispered.

The head nodded.

"Yeah? Who is Jay Leno?"

The man tried to throw Jaybird off him, just as Quinley dropped on top of them both, pinning the man securely to the deck. Quinley had the flashlight the man had dropped. He shielded it and shone the light in the man's face.

"Oh, yeah, he's a damned A-rab," Quinley said. "Check for a weapon." In his belt, Jaybird found a pistol. Quinley pulled the man's hands behind his back and snugged them tightly with plastic riot cuffs. He did the same to the Arab's ankles.

Four more SEALs came over the rail.

"Get Franklin up here," Jaybird told Quinley. Quinley was back in two minutes with Franklin still gasping from the long rope climb. He was the only man in the platoon who could speak Arabic.

Franklin looked at him. "Oh, yeah, he's an Arab. One of the terrs. I'll see what I can get out of him."

Franklin talked to the man but got only grunts in reply. Senior Chief Dobler came up and spread out the men, then looked at Quinley.

"We've got an Arab captive. He tell you anything?"

"He won't say a word, Senior Chief."

"Let's pretend to throw him overboard."

Three of them picked up the Arab terrorist and took him to the rail. They swung him once, then twice, and were about to swing him the third time when he began jabbering in Arabic. They dropped him on the deck, and the Senior Chief stood on his back.

"What?" Dobler asked.

"Says he's one of fifty Arabs on board. They have captured the ship and we will all die."

Murdock came up and was told the situation.

"Tell him he has one more chance," Murdock instructed Franklin. "Make him understand that we know he's lying. If he doesn't tell the truth, he's swimming in the gulf."

Franklin translated the words for the captive. He spat in Franklin's face. Murdock and Senior Chief Dobler picked up the small Arab and threw him over the rail. He screamed only once and then was lost in the darkness. They didn't even hear the splash as he went into the cold waters of the Gulf of Oman.

Murdock put his SEALs on the deck and considered the matter. Jaybird told him the terr had come from the poop deck in the stern, evidently heading for the deckhouse. Murdock knew they had to capture the deckhouse, the control center of the ship. There were enough electronics, sensors, and computer-linked instruments in there to fly a space ship. It all was controlled on the bridge.

Other computer-instructed instruments piloted the big ship and could hold her on a precise course for days at a time without the aid of a human hand. This, regardless of the weather, tides, winds, currents, or changes in engine power. She was locked on to the stars for her precise guidance across the vast oceans of the world.

Murdock still wondered how many Arabs were on board. He didn't believe the fifty the terrorist claimed. At least now they were sure they had the right ship. He motioned to DeWitt.

"Take your squad and capture the poop deck and anyone there. If you find captive U.S. sailors, free them, but keep everyone quiet and down there. Don't let anyone use the phones they must have there and warn the bridge. We both have a hike to get to our targets. Alpha will be taking down the deckhouse. We'll both hit them in five minutes. Go."

The SEALs split and moved toward their targets.

Something had roused Ben Casemore where he hid among the various vents, pipes, and machinery used to load and unload the ship. He lay there without moving; then, when he could see no danger to himself, he lifted up and looked over a huge pipe down the deck of the tanker.

At first they were shadows moving from one bit of cover to the next. Six, seven, now eight men came toward him. He had heard nothing. They did not act like they were terrorists. No. They were attacking! Someone had learned of the take-over and had come to recapture the *Jasmine*.

He started to jump up and was about to yell, but he stopped and shook his head. Not the best idea. A good way to get himself shot. Even in the darkness, he knew the men had rifles and probably machine guns. They had to be military of some sort, Rangers, maybe, or Navy SEALs. He'd heard about them. He watched the men moving down toward the poop deck and waited.

Slowly, he began working his way toward the main doorway into the rear deck. Perhaps he could help in some way. He wiggled past some pipes, slid behind a square shaft, and was within six feet of the door.

The first attacker came up to the door and flattened out on one side of it. Another man went on the far side. Soon six more men were in position near the door.

Ben took a chance.

"Americans," he called with enough force for them to hear him. "Americans, I'm one of the crew. Don't shoot." The nearest man lunged toward him, a short weapon up and covering him at once.

"American. I'm one of the crew. Don't shoot."

The man in a camouflaged uniform rushed him and pinned

him against the bulkhead. At once three more of the men were beside him.

"Who is Jay Leno?" an American voice asked him.

"Late-night talk show host from Los Angeles," Ben Casemore said. "Hey, I'm an American, no shit. You Rangers?"

"Hell, no, we're SEALs," a tall, thin man said. "Arabs took over your ship?"

"Oh, yeah, at night. I was out prowling. They missed me. Been hiding ever since."

"How many terrorists are back here?" Ed DeWitt asked.

"Only three now. One went up the deck a while ago."

"He's swimming now," DeWitt said.

"Good. They did some shooting back here. Bet somebody's dead in there."

"Where would the terrs be?" DeWitt asked.

Ben frowned. "I ain't been inside when they been there, but I'd guess they herded the crew into the storeroom. No windows, steel door. Leave the rest of the quarters back here for the Arabs."

"Is this door locked?" Guns Franklin asked.

"Never seen it locked," Casemore said.

"What's your name?" DeWitt asked.

"Ben Casemore, sir."

"Casemore. You stay here and keep out of sight. We don't want you getting hurt." DeWitt turned pointed at Adams. "You and I'll go in. Fernandez, grab the door and jerk it open. Adams, you go right if there's any room. I'll be on the left. Once we're in silently, the rest of you come in. No shooting unless required. Bullets will bounce all over the place on those steel bulkheads. Fernandez, now."

Fernandez turned the knob slowly, then jerked the door open. Adams was in front. He went through the open door into a companionway. Doors showed to the left and right in the dimly lit area. No one was in sight. Ed pointed to the first door. Adams turned the knob slowly and eased the door outward. Ed used his flash and looked inside the room. A sleeping area. Four bunks. Nobody home.

Four more SEALs were in the companionway now. Two worked each of the next two doors. A soft night light glowed in the second room. A man slept on the bottom bunk of another four-man room.

Mahanani dropped on him with his 240 pounds and clamped one hand over the man's mouth. A moment later, Quinley had his hands and feet tied with the plastic strips and a gag tied across his mouth.

They found one more man in the fourth room, which was as large as the others but with only one bed and a soft chair and a TV set. Ostercamp went in the door, heard a hammer cock, and dove for the floor. Right behind him in the light of the door, Jefferson heard the sound, too. He triggered three rounds from his Colt M-4A1. The silenced rounds sounded much louder in the closed room. Ed DeWitt jolted into the room and shone his small flashlight around until he found the bed. One terrorist lay there with his hand still holding a .45 automatic with the hammer on cock. He had taken three rounds in the chest and died before he could pull the trigger.

"He had me, JG, I was dead meat," Jefferson said. "I had to fire at the sound."

"It worked, and you're alive," DeWitt said. "We'll talk it over later. Let's get the rest of this place clear. Should be one more terr here somewhere."

The last room hadn't been looked at. Ed DeWitt turned the knob slowly, then pulled the door open. Al Adams charged quietly into the lighted room. A terr sat on his bunk, an AK-74 in his hands. He looked up, blinded by the JG's flashlight beam, then lifted the weapon and triggered three rounds.

Adams had his Colt up and returned fire, nailing the terr with three rounds into his chest and neck. He spun back on the bunk, dropped the automatic rifle, and gave a long sigh. In death, his bowels emptied, and the odor was immediate and sharp.

"Anybody hit?" DeWitt asked.

"Yeah, just a scratch on my arm," Adams said, then he sagged against the bulkhead.

"Mahanani up here," DeWitt barked.

The corpsman came in the door and looked at Adams. He moved him to another bunk and sat him down. Blood showed on his left sleeve. Mahanani pulled down the shirt and looked at the wound.

"In and out, JG," he reported. He treated the small entry wound and the larger exit wound on the back of Adams's arm and then bound it tightly with a bandage. He slipped the shirt back on and buttoned it.

"Good as new," Mahanani said.

"Hell, I must not have been much good new," Adams said. "Hurts like crazy."

The medic gave Adams a shot of morphine and nodded at the JG.

"Leave the terr there," DeWitt said. "That should be the last of them. Let's clear the rest of this place in a rush. Bring in Casemore."

Somebody brought in the tanker sailor. They quickly cleared the rest of the sleeping areas. Nobody was on guard.

"Show us where the rest of the crew is," DeWitt said.

Casemore took them to the spare storage compartment. It was locked from the outside. Eighteen men lay on mattresses and blankets on the floor. They cheered when they saw Casemore.

"What the hell's going on?" one seaman asked.

"We just got rescued," Casemore said.

"At least half of the ship," DeWitt said. "Would there be any of the terrs up on the front of the ship?"

"Naw, just in the deckhouse," Casemore said. "Our officers are still there. We gonna go up and free them?"

"That's being taken care of," DeWitt said. "We just stand by here and wait. Are there telephones from here to the bridge?"

"Sure, want me to call?" Casemore asked.

"No. We'll wait for our people to call us when they have the situation under control.

Control was a problem in the deckhouse. Murdock and his Alpha Squad had played it by the numbers. He and Jaybird went in the first door on the deck level, found a changing room with nobody in it or in the rest of the first deck's three rooms. They worked silently up the stairs and discovered the officers' quarters.

"Door's locked," Jaybird whispered to Murdock.

"Who do we have who picks locks?" Murdock asked. Jaybird passed the word for Ken Ching to come up front. He looked at the locks, took out a set of lockpicks he had learned to use when he went to locksmith school, and soon had the first lock opened.

"Locked, so they must be good guys," Murdock whispered. He opened the door slowly and shined his light inside.

"What the hell?" an American voice asked.

"We're Navy SEALs," Murdock said from a crouch near the door.

"Chrissakes, you fuckers got here in a rush. I'm Tabler, the first mate. Bunch of raunchy Arabs grabbed us two nights ago. Or was it one night ago? Damn glad to see you. You have control?"

"No, just arrived. Can you show us the best way to get to the bridge without getting our asses shot off?"

"Local native guide," Tabler said. "How many of you?"

"Eight on this end. Eight in the poop deck."

"Good. Only four of them here. Some of them may be sleeping. Should be two on duty topside. Got a spare weapon?"

"No. If we need to shoot, we'll shoot. How do we get to the two sleepers? Where would they be?"

"In the captain's cabin. They threw him out early on. He's pissed."

"Show us where. Would the door be locked?"

"Shouldn't. They control the place. Let me get my pants on, and I'm with you."

A minute later, First Mate Tabler led the way down the short companionway on the second deck to the end door.

"Captain's cabin," Tabler whispered.

Murdock and Jaybird, both with their H & K MP-5 submachine guns, stood by the door. It opened outward. Jaybird turned the knob, then nodded at Murdock. Jaybird jerked the door open; Murdock went in with his flashlight on and held against the barrel of the subgun. He saw two men in the captain's big bed. Jaybird slugged one in the head with the butt of his subgun. Murdock fell on top of the other one, who was sleeping on his stomach, and pulled the pillow hard against his face.

"Strap them," Murdock said. Senior Chief Dobler had followed them in, as did Ron Holt. Each slipped the plastic riot cuffs on hands and feet and then put gags around their heads, covering their mouths.

"Yeah," said Tabler, who had come in with the others. "I'd like to kick that one called Haddad in the balls about four times. He's a bastard. Can I throw him overboard?"

Murdock grinned. "Maybe later. Right now, we need to get the last two of the guys on this end and hope that DeWitt has wrapped up the poop deck. Where do we go?"

Tabler led them to the end of the corridor and pointed up a set of steel steps. Murdock nodded at Joe Lampedusa and motioned for him to go up. Murdock went second, then had Jaybird right behind him. He whispered to Ken Ching to go get the other ship's officers out of the still-locked rooms.

Lam went up the steps on his rubber-soled boots like a ghost. Murdock wondered if he even breathed. He had his Colt M-4 up and ready. It had the suppressor on.

Lam edged up the steps with Murdock right behind him. He expected to get some resistance. The top men would be in the bridge, making sure the computer sent the ship where they wanted it to go. Murdock had no way of knowing if they had changed the original route to take the fortune in oil to a new customer.

They came out of the steps on a small platform and then a door that led into a brightly lit room. The glass in the door showed the ship's nerve center. The whole thing was computerized, with various display screens and high chairs to sit in to watch the screens and the way ahead through the expanse of large windows that slanted outward.

Only one man sat in a chair. He wore clothes too large for him, with shirtsleeves rolled up three times and pants that must be rolled up at the bottom. He was dark and had a full beard and short hair. An Arab.

Lampedusa turned the doorknob and gently pulled the panel toward him. He had it half open, with his weapon pointing inside, when the door squeaked. The Arab darted a look toward the door and at the same time brought up a pistol and fired twice.

Lam caught the slug in his chest and went down. Murdock's line of fire was clear. He point-aimed the subgun and pounded off three rounds of the 9mm messengers of death. The terrorist took the rounds in his stomach, folded over, and sagged to the floor. He held both hands over his belly and screamed.

Murdock saw that the terrorist was out of action. He turned to Lampedusa, who had sagged against an instrument panel.

His shirt showed blood high up. Lam blinked and shook his head. "He hit me?"

"Just a scratch. Right under your clavicle, right side. What we used to call a million-dollar wound, a going home kind. Don't push it, just slide down and sit on the floor. I'll take a look."

Murdock unbuttoned the top Lam's cammie shirt. The slug had gone just above the clavicle bone, cut about an inch of flesh, and come out. Nothing fatal. Murdock told Holt to keep pressure on the wounds until Doc got there.

Then he looked at the terrorist. He knelt beside him. "Where's the other man?" Murdock asked.

"Go to hell, American devil," Kamel Jaber said in English. "You will surely rot in your own hell for all of eternity." He coughed after he said it and spat up blood.

"You're a dead man, terrorist. You know how bad hit you are. You'll never see home gain. Tell us what we want to know. Your other man should be watching the radar screens."

"Go fuck your mother twice," Jaber said in English. Murdock punched him in the face and felt something break inside the man's cheek. Good.

"Tie him up; let the bastard bleed to death. Tabler, where could that last one have gone?"

"Not many places to hide on this tanker."

"No? This thing is a half mile long. There must be dozens of hiding places. What about down in the holds somewhere?"

"We have ninety-three holds, they all are filled with oil right now. No place there."

"The engine room; must be places down there."

"That's in the stern. Yes, he might be down there."

"What about the forecastle?" Murdock asked.

"Yes, a chance. Easy to clear that one." Tabler rubbed his hand over his face, evidently trying to think. "Okay, I'd say the engine room and front holds for general cargo would be best. The forecastle, a maybe. Clear that first, then we can check the hold."

"Not we. My men know how to check a ship. Can we talk to them in the poop deck?"

"Certainly. The phone's right there. I'll ring them." Tabler picked up the phone and hit three buttons and handed the instrument to Murdock.

"Yes?"

"It's all right, DeWitt. This is Murdock. We've got the bridge secured. We're in control. You have that area clear?"

"Yes, one dead and two prisoners."

"We have one terr missing. He might be back down there somewhere. Keep a look out. We'll be down there shortly."

He hung up. "Senior Chief, take two men and clear the forecastle, and use your Motorola when it's done. Tabler, get your officers up here and run the ship. It's yours now. Your captain would probably like to know what's going on. The rest of you, let's get aft."

"What about the body?" Tabler asked. "He died while you were on the phone."

Murdock pointed at Bradford and Ching and told them to take it down to the storage room on the first deck. Then they headed aft to the poop deck. One terrorist with an automatic weapon could cause a lot of problems on this tanker. They had to find him before he turned deadly and started shooting up people or equipment.

6

On Board Tanker *Jasmine Queen*
Gulf of Oman

By the time Murdock and his men reached the poop deck, the crew had shown Ed DeWitt the two hatchways leading into the engine compartment and the forward hold where general cargo was sometimes stowed.

Access to both was by vertical steel ladders, and DeWitt waited for Murdock before he began any movement down. One of the engine maintenance men volunteered to go with them and show them the engine room. He said there were some good hiding spots down there, and he knew them all.

Murdock told him the terr down there would be dangerous and would shoot to kill. The sailor from Michigan, who said he was Curley, shrugged.

"Hey, I'm twenty-six already. I've been married, had a kid, divorced, been around the world ten times, tried every kind of drug you can buy or steal. Shit, I never thought I'd last this long. You guys wanta live forever?"

"Damn right," Horse Ronson said, and the crew and the SEALs all laughed.

"Can he sabotage the engine down there?" Murdock asked.

"Sure, easy, if he knows anything about big diesels."

"Ed, you take your men and work the cargo hold. Be careful. We'll do the engine compartment with Curley here as our local native guide."

Murdock used the Motorola. "Holt, get back down here to the poop deck. Tell Lam to hold the pressure on those wounds himself. He's tough. Mahanani will be up there soon." He waved the big Hawaiian up the deck, then looked at what was left of his squad.

He'd sent three men to the forecastle; Lam was down for now, Holt was coming back. He had Ronson, Sterling, and Holt. That would be enough.

"Go ahead, Ed. Get a guide from the crew to help lead you down to the cargo hold. The Motorolas might not work too well under all this steel."

Murdock looked at Curley. "How far down that ladder to the guts of the place?"

"Three levels. He could be on any of them. He'd have to be down at the last one to do any damage."

"You shoot a weapon?"

"Did a hitch in the Marines."

Murdock tossed him the AK-74 they had taken from the dead man. "That's the new AK-74, upgraded from the old AK-47. This one shoots 5.45mm zingers. Fully auto or single shot. Be careful with it."

Holt came jogging up and grinned. "I got blood on my hands, so be damned careful of me."

Murdock waved them toward the hatch that led into the engine compartment three levels below.

A tall Texan they called Tex said he'd show them the cargo hold, "Jest so no sucker gonna shoot my balls off." He led DeWitt and his men down the ladder. Nothing happened. They went down the iron ladders into a hold with a jumble of boxes and crates. A man could hide a dozen places in that jumble.

DeWitt and his men swept the hold from one side to the other, protecting themselves at all times. They found no one. They went back the other way, checking under boxes and testing crates. Again they found nothing.

Murdock tried the Motorola. "Commander, we have a clear on the cargo hold." He waited a minute, but there was no response. The heavy steel plates had blocked out the signal.

"Let's get back up the ladder," DeWitt said.

Murdock went first down the ladder with his four men into the engine compartment. He was followed by the volunteer, Curley. At once, the sound of the big diesel engines pounded in their ears. He turned and looked at Curley, who pointed to a metal catwalk going off the ladder. The two of them stepped on it, and Curley did a look around. He shook his head and pointed down. This time, he took the lead.

They went down next to a huge drive shaft of some sort and on down into the bottom deck of the compartment. The noise made talking impossible. Curley pointed and indicated all three of Murdock's men should stay there. Then he and Murdock went down a walkway beneath some more equipment and to the far side of the compartment.

A shot slammed into the other noises and sounded only like a buzz as the round whizzed past Murdock's head. He dropped to the grating and looked ahead. He saw nothing.

Curley had gone down, too, and he rolled to the left behind a large tank. Murdock did the same before a second shot could come.

Curley nodded at Murdock and pointed ahead. Then he shook his head. He motioned to the side and they squirmed around the tank and could see down the same direction they had been going. Murdock saw legs working past another large tank. He aimed and fired a three-round burst, but he figured the legs won the race. The legs got behind cover before the slugs got there.

Curley came to his feet and ran ahead to the tank that had shielded the terrorist. Murdock pushed around him and went flat on the deck and leaned around to take a look. A single shot whistled over his head. He jerked back.

Curley cupped his hands to Murdock's ear and spoke loudly. Murdock could understand.

"No exit," Curley said. They moved slower then, darting from side to side where there was steel cover. The terrorist fired twice more and missed. All on single shot. He was conserving his ammo. Down to his last magazine, Murdock figured.

Murdock put his floppy hat on the butt of his subgun and pushed it just around the corner of their safety shield. A three-round burst almost tore the weapon out of Murdock's hands and sent the hat flying back the way they had come. Murdock screamed.

He looked at Curley and grinned.

Seconds later, they heard feet pounding on the steel deck and a man showed out of the dimly lit engine compartment. He charged up the walkway, his AK-74 aimed in front of him. Murdock waited until the last minute behind his concealment, then swung the stock of the H & K submachine gun at the charging runner's ankles.

The sub gun connected and nearly tore out of Murdock's hands. The runner went down, swearing, and his rifle clattered ahead of him five feet.

The AK-74 behind Murdock chattered off three rounds, and Murdock saw them tear up cloth along the terrorist's back. The Arab gave a groan, then tried to lift up, fell flat on his belly, and didn't move.

Murdock surged up and checked the man. Dead.

He waved at Curley, and they went back to where his other men waited in the blocking position. Murdock pointed upward, and the five climbed up the ladder and left the roaring of the big diesel engines behind them.

Once up the ladder and back on the deck, Murdock took the AK-74 from Curley.

Ed DeWitt looked at Murdock, who nodded. "One terr taken care of. You find anything in the cargo hold?"

"Just a lot of cargo. No terrs."

The Motorolas spoke. "Commander. We've been through the forecastle twice. We have a clear here. Orders?"

"Move back to the deckhouse. We'll meet you there. We found the missing terr."

Murdock turned to Curley "Thanks for your help. Now, you should get back with the rest of the crew and see what your captain wants you to do."

By the time Murdock and DeWitt climbed back to the pilothouse, the captain was in command again, and he had two officers working with him.

Murdock introduced himself and asked if the ship had a TAC frequency that could contact U.S. naval units.

"Most certainly, young man," the captain said. "I understand we have you to thank for capturing the terrorists and returning control of the *Jasmine* to us. The owners are grateful, as the crew and I are. We did lose two dead in this takeover." He paused. "I haven't had to send letters like that for a long, long time." He brushed his hand across his eyes.

"Well, come with me to the communications room and we'll see if we can contact that carrier back in the Persian Gulf we passed a day or so ago."

They did.

A chopper would pick them up at 1000. It was then a little after 0246.

Murdock checked on his two wounded. The tanker had better medical supplies than Doc Mahanani carried. He used them and re-treated Adams left forearm bullet wound and the chip through Lam's shoulder.

The captain suggested the SEALs might like some food. The tanker had enough food to feed a regiment for a month. They found the kitchen and mess hall, and the cooks worked up any breakfast to order they wanted. Breakfast steaks, fried potatoes and onions with cheese, and sides of pancakes and bacon was the most popular order.

The SEALs found bunks and sacked out for the rest of the night and by 0900 they were up and grousing around the big ship until Murdock led them on a two-mile jog around the long tanker.

Two hours later, they had landed back on the *Enterprise* in the Persian Gulf and Murdock wrote up his after-action report.

Stroh was not impressed. He told them to stand down for a day and rest up. Sick bay redid treatment on the two wounded and sent them back to duty.

Two hours later, Stroh came in, waving three sheets of paper Murdock knew came off the encryption machine. He groaned.

"Fisherman of the small yellowtail, I have some news here that you are not going to be too thrilled about," the CIA man said. "You want it straight or with a sugar coating?"

7

The Emir's Palace
Doha, Qatar

The emir of the independent state of Qatar, bulging out into the Persian Gulf from the middle of Saudi Arabia, took his usual early-morning stroll around his gardens. He had spent thousands of dollars to make the gardens grow and thrive. He enjoyed plants and exotic animals. He stopped at his prize row of roses and snipped one off to smell.

At that precise moment, a large-caliber rifle round slammed through the morning coolness and smashed into the emir's chest. Emir and Prime Minister Humand bin Kahalifa alt-Thani jolted backward and sprawled on the carefully clipped lawn. A guard behind him ran forward and bent over the emir, but it was too late. The bullet had blasted through the emir's chest, taking half of his heart with it before it tore through ribs and exploded out of his back.

They never did find the bullet.

Sirens went off. A hundred palace guards rushed outward from the garden toward the only place that had a view into the garden. It was a small grove of trees the emir had planted several years ago. When the guards stormed into the grove, they found only trampled grass, a discarded sack with leftovers from a meal, and one fifty-caliber shell casing.

Before the guards could recover, two companies of the Qatar elite infantry rushed into the palace and took over the grounds, the palace, the automobiles, and the helicopter that sat on its pad. Six guards protested and were shot down where they stood.

General El Hadar, former chief of the emir's military, quickly took over the vital controls and services of the small country and declared himself as the new premier. He would rule by proclamation.

General El Hadar watched as his new palace guard assumed all of the functions of the palace, discharged the civilian help, and arrested any of the old guards who did not surrender. He smiled as his infantry shot down four guards who had barricaded themselves in a storeroom. None of them escaped.

His proclamation came only three hours after the emir was assassinated. The words went out over the state-owned radio and television station.

"The people of Qatar must remain calm. This has been a simple transition of power from the emir to General El Hadar. I will lead my people in new directions. I promise enough food, clothing, and education for all of my people. We will grow and prosper and will create new foreign associations to make our small nation even stronger. All normal government services will continue as before. My door is always open for anyone who wishes to talk to me or bring complaints."

General El Hadar drove from the television station back to the palace and rested. Later that day, he put in a telephone call and talked for more than an hour. When it finished, the premier smiled. Yes, it was good to have powerful friends in high places. The cooperation would continue, and the military equipment would be coming within the week. It was good to be strong, even if your nation had less than 700,000 citizens. It was good to be strong.

Basra, Iraq
Petroleum Loading Docks

The medium-sized tanker lay in her berth next to the loading dock and gulped down the crude petroleum that flowed into her thirty-six holds. She could take thirty-five million gallons of crude, and she would be filled and under way within an hour.

The guards on the pipeline had been tired and inattentive. The next moment, they were dead, and another tanker slid in beside the dock and the Iraqi oil gushed out.

The oil had been long embargoed by the United Nations in retaliation for the Iraqi attack on Kuwait. Now was the time to strike. Now was the time to move out as many tankers as the pipelines would fill. Now was the time for the Iraqi oil to flow once again into the world markets.

Four of the medium-sized tankers had already been filled and now sailed silently and secretly down the Persian Gulf headed for oil-hungry markets that would pay more than the market price.

Ar Ramandi watched the hoses being connected and could hear the oil surging through the tubes. Now Iraq would at last have more hard currency to use for its master plan. More cash, more power.

A workman attaching one of the large hoses tripped and fell, dropping sixty feet between the side of the tanker and the dock. For a moment, there was a piercing cry of pain and anguish, then the big boat surged slightly toward the dock, crushing the flailing man against the piling, and the cries stopped suddenly.

Ar Ramandi lifted his brows. The men were cautioned to be careful but quick. They could be discovered at any time and could face severe penalties. It was a risk that all of them were willing to take since the orders came from so high in the Iraqi government.

Ar Ramandi smiled as the tanker signaled it was loaded, the hoses came out, and the big ship at once loosened the huge tie-down ropes and a moment later eased away from the dock and moved toward the outer bay where it would slip into the gulf unnoticed.

Twelve of the medium-sized tankers loaded and left before the sun came up. By then, the locked and guarded pipeline heads were back to normal and the Iraqi guards patrolled the area. With any luck, the tankers would be out of the Persian Gulf and heading for their customers before the U.N. or anyone else realized that they contained the embargoed Iraqi oil.

Ar Ramandi slid into his big, government car and turned up the air-conditioning. He had the driver take him back to Baghdad. It was cool and pleasant in the car. He would sleep most of the way.

Bahrain
In the Persian Gulf

Emir Usa ban Sulman al-Khalifa, the head of state in this traditional monarchy, attended an outdoor soccer game when the national Bahrainian team played against a team from Qatar. The first period was over with the game tied 1 to 1. The emir came out of his traditional white canvas tent to urge on his home team.

Two men with submachine guns ran from the crowd and fired their weapons on full automatic. The emir was hit by more than twenty rounds. When the weapons ran out of rounds, the crowd dove on the assassins, beating them to death before soldiers could get to the killers to try to identify them or find out who they were working for or what political faction they represented.

TV cameras at the game caught the final shots of the assassins and then the crowd venting its anger on the killers.

Two hours later, General Yasim Nassar attacked the emir's national palace with two companies of rangers, routed the few guards there, killed more than a dozen people who protested, and claimed that he was the new premier of Bahrain.

He went on TV, urging the people to be calm. He said the savagery of the assassins today who killed the emir made it even more important for there to be a strong government to control the island. He said all connections the assassins had would be investigated, and the blame for this tragedy put on the proper country or movement. He said his own move to stabilize the government went smoothly. That all regular governmental operations and services would continue. The eleven thousand in the armed forces had pledged their support for his move, and the country would be ruled for the next two weeks under martial law to try to root out the factions that assassinated their beloved emir.

He said the prime minister, who was second in command of the nation, was missing, and he was afraid that the terrorists who killed the emir might have kidnapped him. There was no confirmation of this, and the prime minister was eagerly sought by the new government to help assure that there would be a smooth transfer of power to the new regime.

USS *Enterprise* CVN 65
In the Persian Gulf

Stroh waved the papers again, and the room quieted. The SEALs knew this man's connections and his power, and all of it directly affected them and their lives.

"We've got big trouble sprouting up all over the Middle East. First those embassy attacks, then the bombings in Cairo on U.S. companies. Then the hijacking of a U.S. flag tanker. Now we have military coups in two nations along the Persian Gulf. Nobody knows what the hell is going on. Whatever it is, it's big and getting bigger. We've had requests from six small nations and emirates and sultanates around the gulf to come and give them some protection.

"There have been military takeovers and assassinations in Bahrain and in Qatar. Okay, not exactly huge places, but those two have been nominally our friends for a while and haven't been helping out Iraq or Iran.

"We told most of the others asking for help that we're not the damned police force for the whole fucking world. Most of them don't understand. They think we have unlimited resources and manpower and planes and tanks. Ain't so.

"Right now, we're getting stretched thin in lots of places. We're relying more and more on the Reserves and the National Guard to fill in and shore up weak spots when we do get a crisis.

"What can I say?"

"So, where do we come in?" Murdock asked. "I know you're coming to it, but my retirement is coming up in about eighteen years and I'd like to . . ."

Stroh swung at him and missed. "Okay, you want it flat out, you get it. The sultan of Oman has asked for help, and in their great wisdom, State and the Joint Chiefs have decided that we can give them some help. To get your geography right, Oman is just down from the Strait of Hormuz, and it curves around the peninsula east and south of Saudi Arabia. It's to hell and gone down there.

"It's a good-sized place, a little larger than the state of Colorado, and has about two and a half million people. Army has about 45,000 men. It does oil, gas, fruits, dates, and fish. So you guys are going down there and try to keep their sultan from getting his head shot off."

"Sounds fair," Murdock said. "When?"

"That's the fun part. You're due down there yesterday. The good part is you're going to Muscat City, which is on the Gulf of Oman, so it's not a long flight from here."

Murdock turned to the men. "Hey, you heard the man. Check out your gear, get loaded up with ammo. My guess, we'll be bailing out of here as soon as we can on a COD. Let's hustle."

8

Muscat, Oman
On the Gulf of Oman

Third Platoon, SEAL Team Seven, landed at the military-controlled airport at Muscat, Oman, just before dawn. The sixteen men off-loaded in bright floodlights and were ushered between military guards to two army trucks and transported to the sultan's palace, a short way out of the city.

Each man carried double ammo, half of it in a small bag that would be stashed in the new quarters. The Oman military looked efficient enough to Murdock, but he would wait and see how good their security was around the palace grounds. He didn't expect much.

The trucks drove into a walled compound. It looked to be about a thousand yards square. Lots of places for holes and weak spots. Murdock, Ed Dewitt, Jaybird, and Dobler were all ushered into a plain room at the outer fringe of buildings where an army colonel sat. They all came to attention, and he nodded.

"Gentlemen, I'm Colonel Khalof, director of the sultan's personal safety and security. I requested your aid. We are pleased that you are here. We are a small country with many enemies. Lately, we have had a number of intrusions and some shooting. We hope you will be able to assist us in our security and to train our people in the best methods of defeating any who try to attack this small fortress. We have a two hundred–man guard force. Do you have any questions?"

"Sir. I'm Lieutenant Commander Blake Murdock, in charge of this platoon. Is it my understanding that we will have some authority to move your men, to suggest different operations, and to assist in the tightening of your security?"

"Commander, you have total authority. One of my officers will be with you to insure that my men comply with your orders. He will also give you a tour of our security and our defensive forces. His name is Major Jabrin."

At the mention of the name, a rather stocky man with a full but closely trimmed beard stood and saluted. He had stripes on his shoulder boards and turned to Murdock.

"My English not good, but will make understand."

"Your English is much better than my Arabic. I'm sure you'll do fine."

Twenty minutes later, the four men and Jabrin toured the wall surrounding the compound. It was eight to ten feet high, had intrusion alarms on top along with razor wire. Murdock stopped the car where a ravine ran under the wall. It was dry now, but he knew it would surge with runoff water whenever a downpour occurred. A fence of loosely connected barbed wire screened the four-foot ditch under the wall.

"This one will need fixing," Murdock said. "Some solid wooden gates that can be opened from the inside when a big rain is expected."

The major made a note on a pad he carried.

By the time the inspection tour was over, Murdock and his crew had found ten places where work needed to be done and security increased. It was nearly dark when Murdock and Senior Chief Dobler talked to the platoon. The men had settled down in a dormitory room with twenty beds and a TV set with a VCR and a rack of more than fifty Hollywood-produced movies.

"We get our feet wet tonight on this security situation," Murdock said. "There are three roving patrols in humvees. We'll have two SEALs in each rig. We'll also put two men at each of the five worst security risks we saw today. We'll begin the watches at twenty-two hundred and run until morning. Any questions?"

"We have weapons free in case of trouble?" Jaybird asked.

"We were given carte blanche in this matter. If you think you should fire, then shoot up a storm. Just make sure it's not some frightened kid looking for a handout."

The SEALs ate two meals with the other troops. Jaybird said the food was fair.

"Don't know what the hell it was, but it wasn't camel nuts. It was good. Not that I'd want to live here forever just for the food."

They watched part of the movie *Battle of the Bulge*, and then it was time to go to work. Murdock stationed the men where he wanted them, then he, DeWitt, and Senior Chief Dobler each took one of the roving patrols with an extra SEAL along.

Murdock and Jaybird settled into the humvee. The driver spoke no English. The other Oman soldier knew only a few words of English. Murdock and Jaybird knew no Arabic. It would be an interesting night.

Murdock checked in by Motorola with his men every hour. By midnight there had been no problems. DeWitt's roving patrol had found two small boys trying to slip in the main gate. They had been caught by the gate guards, given a sound lecture, and sent running back the way they had come.

"They try to steal something," one of the guards told DeWitt. "If they can't steal anything, they hope for a gift of food when they are caught."

The gentle motion of the humvee as it rolled slowly around the compound's outer road lulled Murdock to sleep. Jaybird shook his shoulder when time came for the radio check.

"Dozed off there a little, Commander," Jaybird said. "Don't worry, I won't tell anybody you went to sleep on guard duty. As I remember, that used to be a hanging offense."

"Not true," Murdock said. "It was a simple and immediate firing squad. None of this uniform code of military justice jazz." He shook his head. "This is tough duty. I'm not used to it."

The radio net check went without incident.

Just after 0320, Murdock heard gunfire. He got on the net for a report. It came almost at once.

"Skipper. Bradford. We took five rounds of rifle fire here

at the ravine under the wall. We returned fire at their flashes but don't know if we connected. No more firing. The bad guys seem to have vanished."

"Anything on your NVGs?" Murdock asked.

"Not a thing out there on the night visions, Skipper. We'll keep a sharp lookout for the next couple of hours. My best bet is they took off like a herd of turtles."

"Roger, Bradford. Stay tuned."

The rest of the night was quiet. When the SEALs came back at dawn, they found Lam and Adams waiting for them. Murdock frowned.

"You two were supposed to get a good night's sleep and heal up for when we need you," Murdock said.

Adams snorted. "Hail, Skip, I can shoot just as good now as always. Want me to do some push-ups for you? Damn arm hardly hurts at all anymore."

"Let it heal up, Adams. I catch you doing push-ups, I'll ship your skinny ass back to the ship and slap you in a hospital bed."

Adams grinned. "Aye, aye, Commander. Had to give it a try."

Lam just waved. "Checked out you guys on the Motorola," he said. Looks like you didn't need me after all. I was ready to choggie out there to the hot spot."

Holt walked up to Murdock then, holding out the handset to the SATCOM radio.

"The king of the CIA wants a word," Holt said.

Murdock took the handset. "Yeah, Stroh, what's happening?"

"Too much. We just had a report that two more of the small countries around the area are having trouble. There's a serious challenge to the government in Lebanon. Two regiments of the army have attacked the government offices, and there is heavy fighting. A colonel has declared martial law in Beruit and claims victory. He's premature. Most experts there say that the loyal Lebanon army and air force will defeat this upstart colonel, but it will be close."

"You expect there could be trouble here?" Murdock asked.

"Damn right. It looks like every country in and around the Persian Gulf except Iraq and Iran is either being attacked or is having internal problems. It doesn't seem to be a random situation, according to our Middle East experts in Virginia."

"So, I'll warn the authorities here, hope for the best, and be ready for the worst. Any idea how long we are to stay here?"

"Depends on what happens, if and when somebody attacks. Just hang loose."

"Easy for you to say with three squares a day and a good bed to sleep in. We'll try. Out."

Murdock went to find Colonel Khalof. He was in his guarded office. The SEAL commander wondered if the sultan had such good protection. Murdock told the colonel about his talk with Stroh.

"Yes, we have been hearing. It is bad all over. Somebody is rattling everything. At least our army is loyal. There is no chance for a coup here."

Murdock rubbed his jaw. "Colonel, there's an open space to the west of the palace. I wonder if it would be possible to pull in a battalion of infantry for some maneuvers."

"I don't think that our troops need . . ." He stopped. "Ah, yes, I see. Have them on hand in case anything happens. Good idea, Commander. I'll talk with my general. I'm sure that he'll see the value of a small maneuver program at this time."

Murdock left, feeling a little better. Most of the SEALs slept the rest of the day. They would go back on guard duty that night at 2100, shortly after dark. They would be ready.

This time, Murdock left Jaybird in the roving patrol and he took the most vulnerable location around the perimeter, the eight-foot stone wall at the back of the grounds. He had also asked the colonel to double the interior guards, especially those around the walls. It was done.

Murdock sat with Harry "Horse" Ronson and his H & K machine gun at a lookout port in the foot-thick stone wall. The slot was three inches high and a foot wide and would barely accommodate the NVGs. Murdock scanned the two hundred yards of cleared area in front of the wall.

Nothing moved.

He gave the goggles to Ronson, who took his turn at the view port.

Slightly after midnight, they surveyed the area again. Ronson grunted.

"Take a look, Skip. We got company."

Murdock took the NVGs and checked. He saw an infantry squad of uniformed soldiers moving forward slowly, then dropping to the ground. He hit the Motorola.

"Back wall, we have invaders working forward. Anyone else see them? Fire at will."

A trigger pull later, Ronson laid down a stream of five rounds across the first squad he saw. He could fire through the slot. He checked, then fired a nine-round burst. Murdock checked out another port. Half the men in the lead squad were down. Another squad rushed forward. They were still a hundred yards from the wall.

Murdock heard firing from both sides of his position then. The attacking infantry had no protection, only the semi darkness of a moonlit night.

"Let's use some mike forties," Murdock said. He watched through the port, ducked when a scattering of fire slammed into the rock wall, then looked again. Four of the 40mm rounds landed near the moving infantrymen. More men screamed and went down. A dozen kept running forward.

The machine gun chopped into them again, wounding two, then a 40mm WP hit in the middle of the group, spraying its white, superhot burning phosphorus over the troops. Six more went down, screaming at the pain of the instant burns that kept right on burning through cloth, skin, muscle, and bone. The WP was impossible to put out. It had to burn itself up.

Murdock saw the attack slacken, then stop. "More forty mikes," he said. "Let's push them back where they came from."

Six rounds of HE 40mm slammed into the area, knocking down four more of the troops and sending those who could move charging to the rear.

"Let's hold fire," Murdock said on the radio. Only then did he realize that none of the sultan's troops inside the wall had been firing. Unbelievable. Why not? He'd find out as soon as he could locate Major Jabrin. Where was he? Murdock had seen him earlier. He had no communications to use to contact the colonel. He tried the radio, but none of his men had seen Major Jabrin in his own humvee.

Jaybird came on the net. "Skipper. I parked the humvee

at the gully under the wall. We got in a few rounds supporting you up there. But now, it's too fucking quiet. Where did they go? There must be more of them. Why just one try? Got to be coming back again. My guess is they'll pull back, then hit the hole under the wall."

"We'll wait them out and see," Murdock said. "Might put up a white flare out there just to see what's going on. We'll do it from here. Keep watch."

Murdock had Ching fire a flare, and they watched the front. Some of the wounded who had been moving stopped. Other attackers dropped to the ground and played dead.

"Hold fire," Murdock said. "Just checking them out."

Guns Franklin came on the net. "Skipper, these locals didn't fire at the attackers. I tried to get them to, but they said no. After it was over, I asked them why. They said nobody ordered them to fire."

Murdock remembered that Franklin could speak Arabic. "Franklin, I'm going to ask the colonel the same thing. Let's keep watch."

It was more than a half hour later when Murdock heard the engine sounds beyond the wall. They put a white flare out front and saw the vehicle, an older half-track that once was known as a personnel carrier. It had a 50-caliber machine gun mounted on top, round tires in front, and tracks holding up the back half of the rig.

"Let's take him," Murdock said on the net and began firing his subgun with the suppressor off for better range. In the glare of the flare, the rig rolled ahead fifty yards and stopped. As the flare faded, Murdock could see men come out from behind the rig. They held something he couldn't identify.

A second later he knew. Two RPGs blasted into action and slanted toward the wall. One hit the wall near Murdock and didn't dent it. The second exploded on the barbed wire fence under the wall near Jaybird.

"Machine guns, work that rig's front tires," Murdock said on the net. "You guys with forty mikes, let's stop him. We need a damn close near miss or a direct hit."

Murdock tried for the driver. The windshield was not protected, and he soon had it shot into a thousand granules of glass. The rig kept rolling forward at eight or ten miles an hour.

Ronson blasted the front tires, flattening both, but the rig kept coming, now at half the speed. The forty-mike grenades dropped in closer, but none had a killing effect.

Then Murdock saw a fiery trail of an RPG that lanced through the air from this side of the wall. It hit the slow-moving vehicle right through the blown-out windshield. The explosion shattered the night and lit up the landscape for a hundred yards. Murdock's gunners and snipers picked off a dozen men in the light while the half-track burned.

"Who had the RPG?" Murdock asked on the Motorola.

A laugh came first, then Jaybird's voice cut in. "Dang me if I didn't hit a bull's-eye. The bastard locals wouldn't fire, so I ripped this RPG out of the hands one of them and nailed the sucker. You guys owe me free beer for a month."

"You're on," Murdock said. "How is the barbed wire under that wall?"

"Gone, blown to hell. A wide-open invite inside. Be a damn nice spot for a couple of claymores. We bring any?"

"Should have two somewhere," Murdock said. "Who has the claymores?"

Ching had one, Quinley the other. "Get them over to that hole in the fence; you've all seen it," Murdock said. "Move it now."

Every fifteen minutes for the next hour, Murdock had one of his men fire a white flare over the suspected attack area where the troops had come before. He brought the other machine gun over and had Bradford bring around the 50-caliber sniping rifle. Now Murdock felt more ready.

It was nearly 0400 before the attack came. Six RPGs blasted into the wall, and two went over it. Machine guns from the darkness raked the wall and the firing ports. When the MGs stopped, Murdock fired two white flares. The attackers were running toward them. Everyone on the SEALs' side of the wall began to fire. The machine guns cut chunks out of the hundred men coming at them. HE 40mm rounds jolted into the running mass and chopped down another dozen.

But for the eight guns on that side, there were too many of them. Twenty of the uniformed men charged straight at the hole under the fence. The first one dove under where the barbed wire had been and triggered the trip wire. Three hundred .38-caliber-sized ball bearings exploded out of the claymore, all aimed directly away from the wall and into the path of the shouting soldiers. Eighteen of them fell, mortally wounded.

All along that stretch of the wall, enemy soldiers made it to the wall. Some tried to climb over. Murdock and his men used up their hand grenade supply when the enemies were close to the wall.

Murdock picked off one man who tried to lever over the top of the wall through the razor wire. He took two rounds and fell outside.

"We've got two over the wall here," Jaybird called in the net. "Who's got them?"

"One down and out," Quinley said.

"I've got the other one," Ostercamp called. "Hey, he's just a kid, no more than fifteen."

"Save the next one for questioning," Murdock said.

"Mine is still alive but hurting," Ostercamp said. "I'll save him."

Four more RPGs came over the wall and exploded against buildings in back. Murdock sent another flare up and checked out the port. It showed few of the attackers still in sight. "Next to the wall or gone into the hills," Murdock said. "How's our ammo?"

"Half gone," a voice said. "Damn near empty," another voice reported.

"So conserve and share," Ed DeWitt said. "That might have been their final hoorah for tonight."

"Stay alert on the other sides," Murdock said. "They might think they pulled us all over here and hit at another spot. A flare now and again all around the perimeter wouldn't hurt."

The solid, nasty snarl of an AK-47 drilled through the night.

"One of them got inside," Senior Chief Dobler said. "He's down on my end. We're hunting him."

Two more shots blasted into the night, then silence. The war outside was over for the time being. Murdock wanted to rush down to where Dobler was, but he didn't want to run into friendly fire. He hunkered down and waited.

"No, not there," Dobler's voice came.

"Yeah, right. I see him."

Murdock recognized Fernandez's voice.

A few seconds later, the H & G sniper rifle snarled three times, then an MP-5 slashed in with more than a dozen rounds on full auto.

Silence.

"Yeah, clear to the south," Dobler said.

"Back to your positions," Murdock said. "I want a casualty report."

"Yo," Franklin said. "Picked up a scratch from one of them damn RPGs. Nothing serious."

"Doc, find him. Where are you, Franklin?"

"West side, south of the fence gully. No big deal."

Ten minutes later, Doc Mahanani reported to Murdock.

"Skipper, Franklin has a nasty on his left leg. I'm taking him back to the room and get a good look at it."

"Go, Doc," Murdock said.

They waited out the rest of the night. Dawn came rolling across the deserted landscape about six. They could see no wounded or dead in front of the wall. All had been carried away. The dead half-track smoldered.

Murdock asked Ostercamp if he still had the prisoner.

"Yeah, and he's hurting. I wrapped up his shot leg, but he's a nasty little character. He must be near twenty years old."

"Let's take him back to the colonel and see what he makes of him."

Colonel Khalof was not in his office. An aide said he was in the bunker. He led them to an underground safe house protected with reinforced concrete and double steel doors. The aide rang a bell twice, then twice more. Slowly, the first steel door swung out. The aide rang the bell once, then twice, then once. The inside steel door slid back into the side of the wall.

Inside, Colonel Khalof sat at a desk. He appeared to just have awoken. He turned and stared at Murdock.

"I heard the alarms and the shooting. This is my battle command post, but all of my communications went out. How did it go?"

"None of your troops fired a shot, Colonel."

"What? They had specific orders."

"They said they received no orders," Murdock said. "My

men beat back the attackers and captured one. We thought you might want to question him."

The colonel smiled and rose. He adjusted his uniform, put on his garrison-type hat, and strode out of the bunker. They returned to the colonel's office, where he called in two guards.

"Take this man and interrogate him," the colonel said. "I want to know what unit he was with, who their leader is, and what their objective was last night in the attack."

The guards nodded and took the captured man out the door. He screamed something at them in Arabic. Murdock looked at the colonel. He waved it aside.

"He said he would die before he told them a thing. This is not true. My men have many ways to make a prisoner talk."

That morning, three companies of infantry set up a bivouac in the area where the fighting had taken place the night before. There were three more companies on the other open two sides of the palace.

Just after the noon meal, Murdock was called to the colonel's office.

"We have obtained a great deal of information from the prisoner. Unfortunately, his wounds suffered in battle resulted in his death. We learned that the attackers were a renegade company of my army. My elite guard has tracked down the survivors of the attack and captured or killed them all. They will not be a problem anymore.

"I have reworked my communications system and given all units on guard the freedom to return fire anytime they are attacked."

"Who was behind the fracas last night?"

"Our intelligence operation has linked that renegade company and its captain to a group of foreign agents who are trying to kill the sultan and overthrow his rule here. We have known about them for some time, but this is the first time they have made a direct attack on the sultan. We have rooted out the leaders of the group, and they will be executed tomorrow, the old way. We will chop off the heads of seven men in a public execution with ten thousand of our people watching and cheering."

"One way to take care of the opposition."

"We find it most effective. Almost as good as the way your men killed the captain who led the insurgents last night. He died in the half-track when it was hit by the RPG."

Murdock nodded. "Then would you say our mission here is completed?"

"I would think so. I will contact your superiors and talk with them."

"Thank you, Colonel Khalof." Murdock came to attention, nodded curtly, did an about face, and marched out of the office.

Two hours later, the word came from Don Stroh on the SATCOM.

"Get your rear ends in gear, SEALs. A Greyhound has just left the *Enterprise*. It should touch down there in just a little under an hour, so get yourselves out to the airport. This w!ole damn Persian Gulf region is going to hell in a shit can. Trying to figure out which of three places to send you next. Now move."

The SEALs moved.

9

Near the Presidential Palace
Damascus, Syria

Abou Zawr lay in the shrubbery within sight of the gates that led into the highly guarded Presidential Palace. He had been there for ten hours, since just before dawn when he had slipped in through a row of small trees and brush and hid in the dark of the waning moon.

Now he stretched and touched his companion, a shoulder-fired rocket propelled grenade that had the blasting power of a quarter pound of plastique explosive.

Zawr waited. He was an expert at waiting. He had been in that mode for the last four years, expecting some softening of the rule of the president, Meyadin al-Assad. Zawr knew that al-Assad was little more than a figurehead, taking his orders from the actual rulers of his land, the army generals who made the decisions and backed them up with a harsh justice that every Syrian knew and feared.

There was little freedom, little incentive. That all must change. He had been assured that when al-Assad was eliminated, there would be a surge of political power and military help from a neighbor that would sweep the generals and their front men out of the country. Then the people would take

over the government and their country with the help from
their good friends in Iraq.

Syria's sixteen million people would rise up and overthrow
the last of the old regime. Then there would be a new day,
a new government, a democracy, and a freedom the Syrian
people had not known for generations.

He blinked. Even though the day had been long, he had
not slept. He was waiting for the precise moment. The big
car the president rode in was a stretch limousine, but it was
not armored. The president was not considered important
enough by the generals to give him an armored limo of the
kind they used every day.

The RPG would penetrate the shell of the car and explode
inside it and instantly kill everyone in the vehicle. Yes. Now
all he had to do was wait for the exact moment.

He blinked.

Yes. The gates were opening. As was his usual practice,
the president always paused at the gate to speak with the
guards there. He was a good man, but had been twisted and
turned and convoluted by the generals and their payments to
him. He was one of them now.

Zawr shook his head to be certain. Yes, the long, black,
extended Lincoln came around a slight curve to the guard
gate.

Zawr brought up the RPG, made certain it was ready to
fire, and aimed it at the gate. The limo stopped. Zawr refined
his sight and fired.

The round flew through the air, trailing wisps of smoke.
No one at the target saw it coming. It struck the driver's-
side door of the limo, penetrated, and detonated. At once the
gas tank exploded as well, and the resulting fireball envel-
oped the guardhouse, the two armed guards, and the gate,
reducing everything to flaming rubble and incinerating bodies.

Sirens wailed on the palace grounds. Zawr left the firing
section of the RPG on the ground, stood, stretched his aching
muscles, and walked away, hidden from sight by the slight
growth of trees and brush that flanked the highway. He had
only to move a quarter of a kilometer, and he would be well
beyond the sight of the army guards who even now must be
converging on the south gate.

Should he run? No, that would attract attention. He paused and looked behind him. All he could see was the boiling, rising column of black smoke from the burning car. There was no wind, and the column built higher and higher into the sky.

Abou Zawr kept walking. He had done it. He had struck a solid stroke for liberty and freedom. No one would ever know, but he had brought his beloved country a huge step closer to becoming one of the great free republics of the world.

He felt his heart singing as he left the brush and stepped onto a dirt road that led away from the highway and angled into the low hills. He was only twenty meters up the roadway when he looked up and saw a trio of army guards facing him.

"What are you doing here?" one of the men barked. "This is a restricted area. No one is allowed here under penalty of death."

"I . . . I didn't know. I was out for a walk. I walk three kilometers every day to help strengthen my heart."

Two of the soldiers had their weapons pointed at him. The third used a handheld radio. He spoke softly into the radio and then smiled and put the radio on his belt. He lifted his automatic rifle, covering Zawr.

"There has been trouble at the gate. We are to return you to the palace grounds so you can be questioned."

"I am simply on an innocent walk for my health," Zawr said.

"Then a little more walk to the palace gate should be beneficial," the sergeant with the radio said. It seemed to Zawr that the sergeant's smile was a bit too grim and smug at the same time.

They knew he had fired the RPG.

Someone had seen him walking away.

They would find the launcher and get his fingerprints off it.

Why didn't he wear gloves as the others in his group had suggested?

"I would like to go with you, but my wife is waiting for me. She'll worry if I'm late."

"We'll worry if you don't come with us," the sergeant

said. "I'm sure it will only take a few minutes to clear you, and you'll be on your way."

No, no. The man's smile was too smug. They knew. They must know. Zwar nodded and took two steps toward the soldiers. Then he changed directions, sprinted toward the edge of the road and the drop-off to the canyon below.

The soldiers fired.

The three automatic rifles chattered off five-round bursts. Eight of the slugs hit his body. The first ones hurt terribly. The next two hit so quickly he didn't have time to scream. The last three ripped up his spine and into the back of his head.

He dove down the embankment, dead before he hit the dirt. The three Syrian soldiers stood above, looking down. The sergeant took out his radio.

"We had a runner here, Captain. It may have been the man with the RPG. Send out a vehicle, and we'll bring him back to the guard room for fingerprinting."

The King's Palace
Amman, Jordan

Marilyn Kabariti lounged in the second waiting room of the newly crowned young king, Hussein II. The young man was popular, only twenty-eight, had studied in America, and had many Western ways that irritated many of his advisers and top aides. He brushed them all away and did exactly what he wanted to do.

Marilyn wasn't her real name. She was slender, seductively curved, with breasts that enticed and thrilled the young king. She knew he was power driven, knew that he had a tremendous ego, and that was what also triggered his continual need for sexual conquest. The first time he met her, he said she would be his little blond kitten. He had made her bleach her hair and eyebrows.

Marilyn knew she wouldn't be around the king long. He would tire of her as he had every other woman he kept in the palace. The four and half million Jordanians never knew of his women. He was scheduled to be married in another six months to a proper woman who would be queen. Marilyn knew that after his marriage, he would continue to gather in women the way he did now.

Marilyn was a native of Jordan, and she loved it dearly. She would do almost anything to bring about change for the better. People had made lavish promises to her. She knew most of it was just talk, but the chance that some of it could come true made her take the risk. They had learned of her intimacy with the king. They sought her out and provided her secretly with plans and ideas. Then they gave her a great deal of money.

Realistically, she knew that there would be little chance for her to escape alive. She had planned it carefully and would do her best. It didn't matter. She was committed. She had accepted a great deal of money and left it with her mother in Tul Karm in the north part of the country.

It wasn't the money. It was for the good of Jordan. The kingdom was holding the country back. She stood and walked around the room.

Then the door behind her opened and the king came in. He was bare to the waist and had been sweating. He had just come from his heated pool. He loved sex after a swim.

"My little blond bombshell, you're looking good today," the king said. "Only you are wearing too many clothes."

He pulled her to him, kissed her mouth hungrily, then stripped off the flowing white robe of silk he had given her to wear. She let it drop on the floor and stood erect, thrusting out her breasts and pulling in her stomach.

"My god, but you're beautiful. Three times tonight. Yes, that sounds about right. I don't want to wear myself out." He picked her up and carried her to the soft bed.

After they made love, he turned on his back and closed his eyes, resting. She knew his habits.

"I brought my pencil and pad so I can sketch you," she said, her voice soft and gentle.

"Yeah, yeah," he said.

She left the bed, went to the small stand, and took out all the guards would let her bring in: one wooden lead pencil, sharpened to a point, and a small sketch pad. She took both to the bed and stood over him. Quickly, Marilyn took the lead pencil, pushed the eraser against her palm, and let the wooden shaft extend between the second and third closed fingers. It made a deadly weapon.

She hovered over him for a moment. He was sleeping. She gauged the spot carefully; then, keeping the pencil straight out from her hand and in a line with her forearm, she rammed the sharp point of the pencil downward, slanting off a rib and plunging four inches into the king's chest, stabbing directly through his heart.

King Hussein II cried out from the sharp pain, tried to sit up, but already his heart had failed. He looked at her as his brain raced, then he lost his power of speech and slumped back on the bed.

Sweat beaded her forehead. She dropped the paper she had brought. For a moment, she thought she would throw up; then she bit her lip and bent for the paper.

She waited a moment longer to be sure he was dead. Then she gripped the pencil and pulled it out of the wound. The body moved slightly, then lay still.

Marilyn slipped back into the robe, pushed the bloody pencil into her pocket, and walked out the door that led to the room where she had changed. She found her clothes in the second anteroom, dressed quickly, and pushed the bloody pencil deep into a mattress in the room so it vanished completely. Then she walked out of the room as she had done so many times.

The guards turned away as she passed them. They were not supposed to know that she had been there. It was the same at the gate. She walked down a block, found the small car the king had given her, and drove quickly north out of Amman.

It took her four hours to travel the forty miles over back roads, angling to the northwest until she came to her mother's home in Tul Karm. It was all arranged. Her mother had the twenty thousand dollars in American currency. They would take one suitcase each, drive her car, and be across the border before daylight. Then they would be in Israel and free to watch the great changes that would take place in Jordan.

Marilyn would change her name back to the one her mother had given her. They would build a new life in the democratic state of Israel, where Arabs were at least tolerated if they minded their own business and did not make trouble.

She eased to a stop outside her mother's house, turned off the lights, and started up the walk to the door. Yes, the lights were on inside. Her mother was expecting her.

Marilyn opened the door and stopped. Her mother lay on the floor, spread-eagled and held down by three men. Her skirts were around her waist and her breasts were bare. A fourth man with his pants down knelt between her legs.

"Yes, Marilyn," a sergeant said, holding an automatic rifle aimed at her. "We were expecting you. Don't worry, we found the American money. Your mother has been most helpful."

She ran at him, screaming. He fired seven rounds into her chest, and Marilyn cried out in terror, then slammed backward from the force of the heavy rounds and sprawled against the door. She looked up at the soldiers, gave one small cry, and died.

The sergeant's expression didn't change. "Enough," he said. "Let her go." The four soldiers stood away from the woman, who moaned and sat up, her glance riveted on her daughter, who lay against the wall.

"Murderers!" she screamed.

The sergeant angled his weapon down and fired a five-round burst into the woman's chest.

10

USS *Enterprise* CVN 65

Murdock and Don Stroh sat in the dirty shirt mess working over second cups of coffee.

Stroh pointed a twisted finger at Murdock. "I tell you, everyone at State is in a dither. They don't know what to think. Half of them say that Saddam Hussein is staging the biggest coup of the century. They say look at the 'incidents' so far. Fifteen separate actions that they say almost certainly have gone down with the hand of Saddam behind them."

"Fifteen?"

"Some you don't know about yet. Count them this way. Three embassies attacked, four blasts in Cairo make seven, the hijack of the tanker most certainly by Saddam. Then the Qatar takeover, the Bahrain capture, ten tankers loaded with embargoed oil smuggled out of the Iraq port of Basra, the attack on Oman, the Lebanon insurrection by army units, then the assassination of the Syrian president, and the stabbing death of the Jordanian king."

"I didn't even know about the last two. What's he trying to do, take over the whole Saudi peninsula?"

"Maybe, but he can't do it without Saudi Arabia. No action there at all yet, and I think it's because he's afraid of them. He remembers Kuwait and the bloody nose he got there."

"What about Iran? Nothing's happened there yet."

"True, and he might have them on tap as an ally. Who knows? The one big theory shooting around the Agency, State, and half of Washington is that he's looking for leverage to raise oil prices, and get himself free of the embargo."

"How does he do that, short of a break with the U.N. embargo and running armed tankers down the gulf?"

"Might be what he's thinking. Who knows what the hell that madman has up his sleeve."

"You said something about three places to send us next. What are they?"

"At the time, the boss was worried about Lebanon. Now it looks like they have that situation in hand. The rebels have been routed; a bunch of them killed. Three of their leaders executed by lopping off their heads in a public execution. So that one's in hand."

"So?"

"So the CNO and the Joint Chiefs are all over this. They say that Saddam tried outright aggression last time in Kuwait and got slaughtered militarily and economically. So, this time, he tries another way. He's trying to take over these small countries from the inside. Not much we can do about that. We would be interfering with the internal affairs of the nations.

"This will work for him only on a limited scale. The brass says that once he has a toehold, he has to use his military to go in and prop up the puppets he's put in power. Yeah, works in the small places without the army. But take Syria. He'd need to put a couple of hundred thousand men in there to take over the country, even if he did have a favorable political leader."

"He's got almost four hundred thousand men under arms," Murdock said.

"But his equipment is getting old and worn out."

"Tell that to the guys he's killing."

Stroh finished his coffee and waved at a steward for some more.

"Look at it this way. He wants to get control of the Persian Gulf so he can sell his oil at twice the going price and maybe charge everyone else for using the Strait of Hormuz. What does he need? First he needs a friendly Iran, since they control one bank of the strait. Then he needs that tip of Oman beyond the United Arab Emirates that controls the other side of the strait. If he has those two, he can finesse Saudi Arabia and be in business."

"Sure, but Oman still has that separated chunk of land out there on the strait."

"It was a theory."

"Mr. Stroh?" A sailor touched his shoulder. "Sir, there's a phone call for you. Seems to be important."

"They're all important, son. Where can I take it?"

Murdock finished his coffee and watched Stroh talking on the phone. He nodded, then hung up and marched back to the table.

"Just a theory, huh? That tip of the Strait of Hormuz has just been invaded by three hundred paratroopers and ten landing craft. In two hours, they captured the only city of any size in the area, Al Khasab. This carrier is about eighty miles from there. We're speeding there as fast as we can. The President has ordered aircraft to fly over the area and report what's going on. All communication with the city there was cut off an hour ago."

Murdock stared into his coffee. "Now he needs the United Arab Emirates. It has a commanding view of the entrance to the strait. I'd say the UAE would be the next target. It has to be Saddam. How does he think he can get away with it?"

"With Saddam, that doesn't seem to be a big factor."

"How does he think he can control the strait with the *Enterprise* right in his face and all the firepower that the fleet down here has?"

"Logic has never been one of Saddam's strong points. The question is what the hell are we going to do now?"

"Wait for somebody to yell for help. Did Qatar ask for help to recapture the point out there?"

"Not that I've heard."

"Saddam only put three hundred men in there? That's confidence. They could slip a thousand men across the strait from Iran. Even three hundred against sixteen is not good odds for the SEALs' continuing health plan."

Stroh stood. "I better go call my boss. He may have some new information."

Murdock went back to his men. He had his three with

wounds checked over again in sick bay. None of the wounds was serious, but Murdock wanted them to heal properly. All the men were fit for SEAL duty when needed.

The men worked over their equipment, cleaned and oiled weapons, put their gear in top shape, and made themselves ready for the next assignment.

"Got to be something else popping over here for us," Jaybird said. Murdock had told them about the invasion of the enclave of Oman out on the point.

"Hey, we saved that old sultan's ass once before. We gonna have to go back in and do it again?" Quinley asked.

Nobody had an answer for him.

Three hours later, the SEALs had a new assignment. Stroh talked to them all about it in their assembly room on the big carrier.

"Sultan Aziz of Oman has asked for help. The Navy will be putting five hundred men ashore from an amphibious ship tomorrow at sunup. Before then, they want to be sure the landing area is clear of mines and any other antiship construction. It's a good old basic SEAL operation. Soon the carrier and its task force will be off the strait and waiting.

"The sultan didn't want us to bomb the place into rubble just to get the Iraqis. There will be as little damage done to the land and buildings as possible. Our five hundred Marines will move in with complete air cover and do what they have to, to defeat the land force there."

"We clear the beach and get out of the way?" Murdock asked.

"Right. There will be the fast boats for you to use to get in to shore and back to the carrier. You won't be part of the invasion force."

"Hot damn, that's good," Bill Bradford said. "No sense wasting our special talents pretending that we're infantry."

"But damn good infantry when we need to be," Jaybird yelped.

"Will there be any sound-activated mines?" Murdock asked.

"Not that we know of. Saddam probably can't afford those. We expect the usual old fashioned contact mines, maybe some angled steel, the regular antilanding devices."

"When do we leave?" Murdock asked.

"You'll be a mile offshore in two ten-meter RIBs that will then edge you into within a quarter mile of shore once it's fully dark. Then you go over the side and tote your goods along in buoyancy packs and get to work."

"Piece of cake," Ron Holt said.

"You heard the man," Murdock said. "All SEALs will make the trip. If your gear is ready, sack out for four. It's now 1020. Early chow, then we'll be out of here about 1700. Senior Chief and Jaybird, figure out what munitions we'll need and draw them from ordnance. Lots of two-hour detonator-timers. We'll want any explosions we generate to go off just before dawn so we don't give them advance notice of the landing. Let's move, people."

Murdock had a talk with the commander of the landing forces by radiotelephone.

"Yes, sir, Major. I understand. You'll give us the length of the landing zone. We'll clear everything in that zone."

"Could be mines and steel spike structures to ram our landing craft. We want a clear shot at the beach."

"Understood sir. We'll time our detonations for just before you land."

"Good. You want any help? We have some Marine Recon guys who are raring to go."

"How long a landing zone, Major?"

"Two hundred yards. We'll be going in quickly and won't need a half mile."

"Good. Two hundred yards are easy. My men will do that with no problem. No help needed."

"As you say, Commander. Good luck on the beach."

"Same to you, Major."

The SEALs left the carrier at 1750 in two ten-meter RIBs. There was no rush. The *Enterprise* was only five miles offshore, and they had an hour before full darkness. They crept along at five knots, much to the disgust of the coxswain, who liked to kick the craft up to thirty knots and make everyone seasick.

Murdock left a Motorola with the lead RIB driver and told him to keep it dry and be ready to pick them up on call. He would lay about a mile off the beach waiting for the call well before the landing started.

At last the sun set and the sky grew dark. Murdock motioned the coxswain to head for shore, still at five miles per hour so they wouldn't create a wake for some sharp-eyed lookout to see.

At a quarter of a mile from shore, the two RIBs slowed to a stop. The SEALs in full wet suits, helmets, and face masks but no rebreathers, slid over the sides of the rubber boats and tugged their load of ordnance with them in four neutral buoyancy waterproof bags.

Murdock took the lead into shore with Alpha Platoon. They had checked the shore with NVGs while they waited. They saw no sign of a guard force or even any sentries. Murdock hoped that pattern held.

They stroked silently on the surface toward the shoreline. Just at the surfline, Murdock paused and made sure all of his eight men were with him. He counted, then waved them into their search pattern. He and his squad took the north half of the LZ from the small point of land to the shack that looked like it once might have been a lifeguard tower. The SEALs left their two floatation bags with one holder and dove into the restless water no more than eight feet deep here to check for floating mines or steel bars and other obstacles that would rip apart a landing craft.

On the first dive they found nothing. Murdock scowled. This was high tide, so they should be working farther from shore. Anything set in this area could be on a sandy beach when the tide was low. He waved the men out twenty yards, and they worked another dive. The seven men covered a thirty-yard area, then came up for air. Even in the murky nighttime water they could find anything large and threatening. So far they had found nothing.

Murdock came up and looked around. He saw three white markers bobbing on the surface. Some finds. He swam to the first and went down. A floating mine anchored to the bottom on a four-foot chain. Even at low tide, it would be two or three feet underwater. It was two feet long and as large around as a ten-gallon bucket. It was big enough to take out a small tanker. Joe Lampedusa attached a one-eighth-pound chunk of TNAZ to the mine and gave Murdock a thumbs-up sign. The timer/detonator would be put in just before the SEALs were ready to leave. Then they would set them for the right length of time.

Murdock checked the other floats. Soon there were twelve of them in a rough line along the two hundred yards of shore. They had found no spiked fixtures in the sand, no tank-trap devices to sink or upset the landing vehicles. Evidently Saddam's troops had only time enough to lay out the mine defense on the most likely landing beaches.

They worked for three hours and found eighteen mines. Lampedusa had made a solo infiltration of the beach area. He came back and reported to Murdock that he found no troops, no personnel of any kind. There were houses about 300 yards in back of the beach, but they looked lived in by civilians.

The SEALs' job was done, but it was too early to set the timers. Murdock waved the men onshore, and they faded into the sparse growth and hid themselves against the chance a roving patrol might come by.

Just after 0100, a patrol did swing past along the hard sand. Two men in the jeep were chatting and not paying much attention to their task. Murdock snorted. Not the way to run an invasion of a hostile land.

Dawn would come at 0530. Murdock decided to be well out of the way by then. He told the men to set the detonator timers for three hours. Then at 0230, they went back into the water, pushed the timer detonators into the chunks of TNAZ explosive, and started the timers.

Then they surfaced and swam straight out from the shore. Murdock got his Motorola out and activated without getting it wet as he floated on his back. He called the RIBs three times before they came in.

"Ready to motor," Murdock said.

"Roger that, we're on our way. Keep transmitting, and I'll try to home in on your signal. We'll be coming right off the small point of land where we left you."

The SEALs swam a half mile into the gulf and waited. Five minutes later, the black RIBs came out of the night and idled up to them.

Once on board, the SEALs settled down for a wait. The coxswains wanted to get back to the safety of the five-mile zone, but Murdock said no.

"We need to know that our charges went off," Murdock said. "Then we send a message to the carrier, and it will be relayed to the amphibious ship so they'll know the way is clear on the beach."

They waited. Most of the SEALs slept. Murdock watched the shore for any sign of activity. They were only a half mile off and in rifle range if anyone wanted to try to hit them. If anyone knew they were there.

Murdock had Holt crank up the SATCOM at 0500 and reported to the carrier that the charges had been set on eighteen mines in the 200-yard LZ. They would detonate at 0530.

At 0525, the SEALs were all awake and watching shoreward. Just before the appointed time, the first explosion shattered the morning calm. It went off three feet underwater, so the report was not loud, but they could hear it and see the geyser that shot into the air. Then, in quick sequence, the other mines exploded. Some of them came on top of others, so they couldn't be sure of a count. One man said there had been seventeen explosions. Another one said he heard nineteen.

Murdock got back on the SATCOM:

"SEALs to Flatiron."

"Go SEALs."

"We report explosions on the beach. We set eighteen. Some counted seventeen, some two more than that. We assume they all detonated. Please relay."

"That's a roger, SEALs. Come home."

Murdock nodded at the coxswain who gunned the little boat, and it slanted away from the tip of the shore. The other RIB followed them. A moment later, they saw two landing craft utility boats plowing through the gulf waters at eleven knots, heading for shore. The big landing craft could hold 350 combat troops, or 250 troops and an M-48 tank. A half mile behind them came two landing craft air cushion craft sending spray high into the air. They held 24 combat men, but could do 40 knots, and slide right up the beach, into the sand, over solid ground, and discharge 48 men to put down covering fire from shore for the troops in the slower LCUs.

It worked that way. Murdock could see the air cushion craft spray sand as they charged across the beach and spewed Marines out in all directions to lay down protective fire.

The LCUs hit the beach, the front ramp came down, and 250 Marines charged from each boat through a foot of surf, onto the dry sand, and into the brush. Behind them, from each LCU, rolled an M-48 tank, its big gun swiveling as the gunner checked out possible targets. Murdock heard one of the tank's cannon fire before they were out of sight of the beach.

The coxswain grunted as they put more distance between them and the fighting. "Hey, I'm not used to getting shot at. I'm a blue water sailor."

Murdock tried the Motorola. "DeWitt, any casualties over there?"

He made the transmission twice, then checked his own guys. Nobody had any new hurts.

"Lam, how's that shoulder?" Murdock asked.

Lam had to shout over the sound of the RIB's motor. "Yeah, I know it's there. Think it busted open. No sweat."

"Get to the medics as soon as we hit the carrier. I want them to check out Adams and Franklin, too. Not taking any chances you guys won't be around for the big one."

"What's the big one?" Jaybird shouted.

Murdock shrugged. "Damned if I know, but we've had three or four little jobs on this vacation time. There must be a big assignment for us out there somewhere. I want everyone to be ready."

11

USS *Enterprise* CVN 65
Off the Strait of Hormuz
Persian Gulf

Don Stroh threw down the printout and glared at it. Murdock picked it up and started to read it.

"Straight off the Reuters News Service Web page. As of today, all Western nationals will be excluded from Iraq. All United Nations employees, workers, and volunteers will be put on planes and shipped out of the country. The Iraq Department of Commerce has totally and unilaterally canceled all agreements about imports and exports. Iraq will sell oil to anyone she wishes, anywhere in the world.

"In short, Iraq is declaring war on the U.N. and the Western powers and is defying anyone to do anything about it."

"That's a hell of a bold step for a small country like Iraq," Murdock said.

"But she has one strong bargaining point. About ninety-two billion barrels of oil reserves in her country just waiting to be pumped, loaded, and shipped."

"Sure, but one aircraft carrier sitting right here at the strait can stop any Iraqi tanker that comes this way, or any tanker we know is hauling embargoed Iraqi oil."

"If we'd do it," Stroh said. He flopped into a chair in the

SEALs' assembly room. "Hell, we knew Iraq could do this at any time. So far, we've been able to keep her in chains. Now Saddam is smashing those chains."

A sailor came into the room, looked around, and spotted Stroh. He hurried over.

"Mr. Stroh, a call for you. I'll have it transferred to the phone in here."

"Oh, damn, what the fuck has gone wrong this time?"

He went to the phone and soon was talking a little and listening a lot. After more than two minutes on the phone, he nodded, said something more, and hung up. His hand held the phone on the hook for several seconds, then slipped off as he turned and walked back to Murdock.

"Saddam took the next step. We've just had word that he now rejects all U.N. agreements and operations on the no-fly zone. He says he will defend the territorial integrity of all of Iraq. Any foreign military aircraft flying over any part of Iraq will be shot down without warning."

"I bet that damn Saddam is a poker player," Murdock said. "He sure knows how to up the ante. Any reports from the no-fly zone yet?"

Stroh shook his head. "No, but we have planes in the air patrolling that large no-fly zone. It won't be long."

Iraqi No-Fly Zone

Two F-16s with U.S. Air Force markings slanted along the top border of the Iraqi no-fly zone. Captain Archer Smarthing kicked the Fighting Falcon over into a roll and checked his radar. Nothing ahead. He'd been on thirty-two of these flights and had to chase only one Iraqi MiG back over the line to the north. Sometimes he wondered how valuable this service was.

He knew the Kurds appreciated it, but it took a lot of manpower and aircraft to do the job. He looked over at his wingman, Jeffrey Smith, and waved. They rode in tandem part of the time, then split off for checking the rest of the envelope they had as their responsibility.

Still nothing showing on radar to the front.

If the Iraqi planes intruded, it usually was from due north. The plane-to-plane radio jolted him back to reality.

"Arch, I've got three blips coming hard from the north," his wingman, First Lieutenant Broderson, said. "Looks like we're going to have company today."

Captain Smarthing swung his craft more to the north. There they were on his screen, coming fast. They were already over the line into the no-fly zone. "I see them. You go left, I'll go right," Smarthing said. "Let's give them a reception." He moved the controls only a little and the Mach 2 craft slammed to the right, raced around in a wide arc, and slanted at the invaders from the side. He saw the missile shoot almost when it left the Iraqi MiG. He hit the chaff button to disperse a false target for the missile and did a second sudden turn, then came in behind one of the MiGs. He maneuvered carefully and had the plane in his crosshairs and a lock.

He hit the firing button and felt the AIM-9 Sidewinder drop off the wing and slam forward, trailing a white plume of condensation. The nine-and-a-half-foot-long rocket leaped ahead of the plane at 2.5 Mach, slanting in on the tail end MiG in the group. The target must have shown a missile warning and began to maneuver, but before it completed the first turn, the Sidewinder hit it just in back of the wing. The annular blast fragmentation warhead wrapped in a sheath of preformed rods, exploded with a shattering roar, and triggered the detonation of three Iraqi missiles under the wing. The combination of explosions blasted the MiG into wheelbarrow-sized chunks of scrap metal and bloody body parts that began their long fall to the desert below.

"I've got trouble!" Lieutenant Broderson shouted on the radio. "Two of the bastards. I'm going low and fast. You see them?"

Smarthing scanned the sky but couldn't find his wing mate. He checked the radar screen and moved around, hunting them. Then he saw a flash of sunlight off metal to the west, and he angled that way. Soon he had the three blips on his screen. He targeted the front plane in the trio but received back a friendly signal. The last two were his targets.

He judged the distance and hit the afterburner to catch up, but before he could get into a good firing position, he saw a flash of light in the sky.

"Broderson, come in. Broderson, where are you?"

There was no response. The two MiGs put on their own afterburners and jolted away to the north. He was in no position to follow them. He kept searching the sky and at last found a black cloud slowly rising. Far, far below he saw what was left of an aircraft impacted into a dry gulch in the desert floor. There was no parachute. He slanted down and overflew the wreck. He found one part with the white star on a blue circle, the insignia of the U.S. Air Force. Smarthing swore for two minutes, then climbed back to his assigned altitude.

He switched frequencies on his radio and contacted his home field. "Mother Lode, this is Sweet Sixteen One."

"Go, Sixteen."

"Just tangled with three Iraqi fighters. I shot down one of them, the other two jumped Broderson and they splashed him. No chute. I just flew over the crash. Not much left of the plane."

"Bring it home, Sixteen. Watch yourself. We just had word that Saddam has called off his observance of the no-fly zone. It's open season out there. We're sending up three replacements to work the edges. Get it on home."

"That's a roger, Mother Lode."

Captain Smarthing turned his plane and headed back toward the field near Riyadh, Saudi Arabia. He had a letter to write to a widow. Later, Smarthing heard that his was the first aerial combat of the day that would see four United Nations planes shot down and eight Iraqi fighters blasted from the air.

One of Saddam's Palaces
Near Baghdad, Iraq

Colonel Jarash Hamdoon sat watching his idol and longtime friend pacing beside his big desk in the fifth sublevel of one of his bombproof war rooms. In it were complete communications with his armed forces, with the government, even with his favorite baker. The complex had been stocked with enough food, water, and batteries to last a month. Even the emergency electrical power generator was in place with a separate smokestack and air inlet from the surface to function in another part of the fifth underground level.

Saddam Hussein turned and stared at the colonel. "My

friend, it was not supposed to go like this. We had seven of the eight nations practically in our pocket. We had set up takeovers from inside the countries by trusted and loyal friends. We paid dearly for that friendship. Now we have only one of those nations under our control. We need the larger ones, Syria especially."

"But you have made a statement, Mr. President. You have declared Iraq's freedom from the devil Western powers. You have cut down four of their fighters over Iraqi airspace; you have sent tankers with Iraqi oil into the marketplace. You have declared our freedom."

Saddam slumped into the executive leather chair behind the desk and frowned at his top adviser.

"My good friend Jarash. It has been twenty years, you and I at the helm of this great nation. We are not in the position today that I hoped we would be in back in 1979. What has happened?"

"Iraq has many enemies, Mr. President. They coil and strike like serpents. They are everywhere we look. We must be careful how we walk through the desert in our bare feet."

Saddam smiled, then rubbed his face and his mustache. "It was not supposed to go this way. We must do something quickly, and it must be dramatic. They will not attempt to bomb us into surrendering. They tried that for two months in the Desert War, and it didn't work. It won't work now. So what will they do?

"They will try to isolate us, to cut us off from all the rest of the world. We must do something to shut out the rest of the world from us."

"The Strait of Hormuz?" Hamdoon asked softly.

"Exactly. We have planned for two years. Everything is ready. Iran has given me its word for cooperation whenever we ask. The time is now. Let me make one call to Tehran, then you make the necessary calls to get the program into motion. I want it done tonight. It all must be in place by morning. No ships will go through the strait until Iraq says that they can. That will gain us a lot of respect. Do it now."

Hamdoon went to his separate office next door. Two minutes later, his phone buzzed and he picked it up.

"Yes, Mr. President."

"My call is completed. The door is open. The rest is up to you."

"Thank you. It will be done." He hit the disconnect button, waited a moment, then made three phone calls. For each of them he gave the one code word, *Armageddon*. One navy lieutenant challenged it.

"Sir, for that word, you must have a secondary countersign word. Do you know what it is?"

"No, Lieutenant Aziz. The question is, do you know what the countersign is?"

"Yes sir, 'In Allah's hands'."

"Very well, Lieutenant Aziz. See that it is done, tonight."

In the port city of Qeshm, Iran, on the coast of the Strait of Hormuz, Lieutenant Aziz rousted out his crew of seventeen and fifteen special technicians. They had been in place here in Iran for six months. Every day they practiced. Lately, they had been practicing at night.

Now they would do it at night.

Lieutenant Aziz felt a wave of emotion fill his mind and body. For the greater glory of Allah.

The Iraqi PB-90 coastal patrol boat moved out of the Iranian port at dusk. All was ready on board the ninety-foot Iraqi naval boat. It was the lone survivor of a fleet of fifteen of the speedy coastal craft purchased years ago. Six had been sunk in the war with Iran, three more sunk in the Desert Storm war against Kuwait, three were scrapped, and three left at the naval port of Basra. Only one had been refitted and made seaworthy. Now it would have the honor of bringing the Western powers to their knees.

Lieutenant Aziz felt his heart racing as he went over the plans again as he had daily for the past six months. They would proceed to the narrowest part of the strait, a thirty-five-mile-wide section. However, the ship channel through that area was no more than three miles across. It was a well-known and much-used passage.

His divers knew their job. He went to the hold and to the special containers on the deck and checked to be sure all was ready. The large boxes held relics of World War II that Iraq had purchased seven years ago when the old Soviet Union was breaking up. Many arms and munitions, even atomic weapons, had been for sale back then if you knew the right people to contact.

Lieutenant Aziz heard that their leader, Saddam Hussein, had wanted to buy two nuclear bombs, but he didn't have enough ready cash. Instead, he bought the munitions resting on the deck of the PB-90. Lieutenant Aziz had the commander's trust that he could do the job that must be done to insure Iraq's surge to becoming a world power. Soon they would have all of the clout they needed to do it.

He knew the history of the items in his care. They had been devised, researched, and developed by Germany near the end of World War II. The Nazis never had a chance to use them. By then, they were in a land war on their home country and had no need for naval arms.

He touched the case gently. Soon they would be uncrated and inserted into the Strait of Hormuz at precise locations.

The Germans had been brilliant on this project. They developed a passive mine that could be planted on the sea floor, activated on command, and then would lay in wait with its sensors tuned for the right moment to fire.

Aziz went over in his mind again how the mines worked. They lay on the gulf bottom. The sensitive mine felt the magnetic pull of a large mass of metal, the steel hull of a large ship such as a tanker. The magnetic force moved a pressure piston in the mine in response to each change in the electromagnetic flux. This generated a small trickle of electricity as its armature cut through the magnetic lines of force. With this feature, the mine would gather electricity from the ships moving near it but well overhead.

As with many early naval mines, these were shaped like torpedoes. A titanium casing, developed by the Germans late in the war, protected the mine's interior from any corrosive element in the sea or in the dank caves where they were stored for years.

Inside the mine, a small magnetic generator and a primitive signal transducer still worked. Each of the mines had been taken apart and checked to be sure they functioned.

Once the mines were placed on the strait bottom, they would be activated with a specific signal from a transmitter on board the patrol boat. The mine would hear the signal. Inside the titanium shell, a relay in a spectrum analyzer would click on. Electrons would trickle out of a capacitor and into the firing circuit. At that moment, the mine would be armed and ready to fire.

Then the mines would lay in wait, checking each ship that went over it, until the right signals came. The mine's acoustic sensors would determine the size of the ship and if it fit the right conditions that had been programmed into it. When the right conditions were met, the analog circuits would tell it to fire. When the mine was triggered, it would break apart and fire a torpedo that would slam upward, seeking the steel target. The torpedoes were designed with delay fuses, so they would penetrate well into the tanker before exploding with tremendous force.

Lieutenant Aziz checked with his navigator. They were near the first marker on his map. The patrol boat slowed. Crewmen had the first mine ready. It was lowered gently into the water. It had been designed to settle slowly to the bottom and to remain upright. Divers went along with lights for the first fifty feet to be sure it settled properly. The average depth of the strait here was 300 feet. When the men were sure the mine was moving properly, they returned to the boat and boarded.

Ten times they dropped the mines in a straight line across the three-mile channel through the strait.

It was almost dawn when they finished. Currents had thrown them off line three times, and they had to reestablish their position. Now Lieutenant Aziz held the portable transmitter and eyed it. It was time. He pushed on a switch, then lowered the device into the water. He pressed the sending button on a long cord twice to be sure that the mines would receive the signal to activate them. Even after this long a time, he was sure that all ten of the mines would activate and establish an absolutely impenetrable wall, not allowing any ship to pass. In practice runs, the test mine had activated on each try.

Back in the small bridge, he put the activator transmitter away. He looked at it critically. While deadly for all ships, there was one way to let friendly ships sail through the screen. All he had to do was to send a deactivating signal to the mines, and they would be turned off.

After Iraq's own oil tankers passed through the strait, the

mines could be turned on again, trapping any ships inside the Persian Gulf that were already there and denying entry by any from the Gulf of Oman. It was a brilliant strategy and one that could win the whole Middle East for Iraq.

Back onshore, he left his crew on board and made a telephone call. It was his signal to Colonel Hamdoon that the mines were in place and activated.

Iran knew of the plan and would not send any of its tankers through after midnight. Iraq would not send any of her oil-for-food ships through, either. There had been some discussion between Colonel Hamdoon, Lieutenant Aziz, and Saddam Hussein about giving a warning to the shippers. It had been decided that the first tanker to be blown up would be the first warning to the world.

Then the official Iraqi news agency would tell everyone that the Strait of Hormuz was mined and that no ship of any nation would be permitted to enter or leave the Persian Gulf.

Lieutenant Aziz smiled as he thought about it. Now Iraq had a powerful handle on the oil trade. He laughed softly. Now Iraq could increase the price of oil as much as she wanted to. She could double the price of oil to forty dollars per barrel. As he remembered, crude oil from the Persian Gulf nations accounted for more than 70 percent of the oil consumed by the world market.

With absolute control of the strait, they could force other nations in the gulf to raise their prices, or they wouldn't get their tankers through the minefield. Raise their price to the Iraqi price, and they would be safely passed through.

It was a masterful plan, one that was unbeatable. He would not sleep tonight. He would be on watch to see which oil tanker would be the first to feel the sting of the fifty-five-year-old German torpedo mines.

12

USS *Enterprise* CVN 65
In the Persian Gulf

Murdock watched Stroh with a slight frown where they sat in the SEALs' assembly room on the big carrier.

"Let me understand this, Mr. Stroh. The two-carrier, 350-plane armada of the U.S. military machine is scared shitless of the minuscule Iraq navy. So Third Platoon is nominated to go in and scuttle the whole four to six vessels in their safe harbor?"

"About the size of it Kimo Sabe. Hey, we're not at war with Iraq, so we can't bomb the ships into kindling. But there could be some kind of accident in the naval port and all of their ships suffer such damage that they might never again sail the mighty waters of the Persian Gulf."

"That's CIA talk to hit them before they hit us. Yeah, sure, we can do it. When?"

"Tonight. We'll fly you to Kuwait City, and from there you'll take an army chopper up to the border with Iraq. There you'll meet with a ground party of four Kuwaiti drivers and their civilian vehicles, which will transport you to as close to Basra as they can. Our guess is it's about forty miles."

"We'll need our wet suits and explosives and our weapons. How do we do that?"

"The civilian cars will have Iraqi identification and will be spaced out so it won't look like a convoy. Our sources say you should have no trouble getting to the Euphrates River, which runs through Basra and where their naval base is situated."

"So we could hit the water and work upstream to the base, blow it, and then try to get out?"

"That's what your rebreathers are for. We'll have a fast boat at the mouth of the Euphrates in international waters to pick you out of the wet."

"Might work, if we can get into that river close enough to the base."

"How close is that?"

"Within a quarter of a mile. We'll travel light. Just TNAZ and our weapons. What kind of ships are we talking about?"

"Our latest intel shows that they have one frigate, the *Ibn Khaldoum,* but it is not in operation. It should be taken out. There are two Corvettes shown on their books, but only one we know of was delivered from China and it is not fully operational, and does not have any weapons systems. It went to the dock in 1995 for minor repairs and has not been out of the yard since.

"We understand there are three patrol craft left from the fifteen purchased from Yugoslavia. Most were sunk in wars with Iran and Desert Storm. One of the three left may be operational. These are hundred-foot-long ships. There may be as many as eighty twelve- to twenty-meter inshore patrol boats of the Sawari class. There is also one replenishment tanker of four hundred and twenty-three feet, but it is not ported in Basra."

Murdock looked at his watch. "It's oh-eight-fifteen. When do we leave here?"

"On a COD in two hours. Get twisting some tails."

The phone in the assembly room rang, and Murdock took it. He listened and then looked at Stroh.

"Now there is some real trouble. A Kuwaiti tanker just took a torpedo from a mine of some sort in the Strait of Hormuz. It's on fire and sinking. Saddam Hussein has just broadcast a warning to all tankers in the Persian Gulf. The Strait of Hormuz is closed. It is mined, and any ship trying to enter or leave the gulf will be sunk."

Strait of Hormuz

Lieutenant Aziz had taken his patrol boat out of the small harbor and anchored just offshore. He had his search radar, an older Decca 1226 I-band, watching the approaches to the strait. They had been watching most of the night. Now, slightly before dawn, his radar showed a tanker moving down the channel at eighteen knots. He didn't know what registry it was, but it was steaming into certain disaster.

If his mines worked the way they should, the huge tanker would send a signal more than strong enough to trigger the firing of the closest mine. He wondered if two of the mines might fire almost at the same time, if the ship came between two of them. He didn't know.

He watched for two minutes as the ship sailed closer and closer to his line of mines. Then it was light enough that he could see the ship with his binoculars.

It sailed majestically through the calm waters one moment, then the next, the huge tanker seemed to lift a dozen feet out of the water. An explosion somewhere in the guts of the tanker burst through the deck and spouted fire and smoke into the morning sky. He could see oil pouring out of the ruptured tanks, and then it began burning, lighting the early dawn. He heard secondary explosions and then the craft broke in half. The bow sank almost at once, but the stern half of the quarter-mile-long ship shuddered several times, and another explosion racked the ship. Aziz guessed that might have been when the cold seawater reached the boilers.

Then the rest of the ship sank quickly, leaving only a trail of smoke in the sky and a flaming sea of oil.

He did not move his ship out to look for survivors. He had been ordered not to. He raised his anchor and motored quietly back inside the harbor on the Iranian side of the strait.

It was done. The warning had been given in a way that no one could doubt. Now the world would know what it felt like to be chained and curtailed and badgered and hemmed in on all sides by angry enemies.

Yes, now the whole world would know how Iraq had felt for ten years.

USS *Enterprise* CVN 65

Stroh paced the assembly room. "No, I'm not sure if this changes your assignment or not," he said. "That bastard finally did it. He's trying to close the strait and give himself and his minuscule navy the key to the cookie jar. This way he can let in and out only those he wants to get in and out. Hell, he could double or triple the price of oil, and nobody could challenge him."

"We have mine hunter ships in the gulf," Murdock said. "They've been here since the war. What are they called . . . mine countermeasure vessels. Probably two or three of them are steaming at flank speed down to the strait this second."

"Yeah, but can they figure out the mine pattern or the system quickly enough to keep the strait open? That's the hundred trillion million gazillion dollar question."

"Can you check about our mission? If we go, we need a couple of hours to get ready."

Stroh nodded. "Yeah, I'm still a little shell-shocked over this damn Saddam move. I didn't think he had the guts to do this. Shows what a man will do when he's desperate. None of his other ploys have worked."

Stroh took the phone and called the admiral. Then he called CIA headquarters on the encrypted SATCOM. He came back in ten minutes.

"You're still on. Gonna take the Navy minesweepers a day or so to evaluate the situation and figure out what to do. Those minesweeper-type ships, they really made mostly of wood?"

"What I hear. Oak, fir, and Alaskan cedar with a thin coating of fiberglass on the outside to cut down on the magnetic signature. They even have low-magnetic engines made in Italy."

"I wish them good luck. Mines give me nightmares, especially naval mines." He shivered. "So, the COD will be ready to lift off here at ten-thirty."

"We'll be on it."

Murdock discussed the mission with his men as they readied their gear.

"Yeah, lots of TNAZ and timers and our weapons should

be enough," Senior Chief Dobler said. "We go in light, we hit them hard, and get downstream before they can find their pants."

"You've got a way with words, Senior Chief," Jaybird said. "We going with the rebreathers?"

"Damn fucking right," Harry Ronson said. "Don't want to have to swim down forty miles on the surface."

"Yeah, it might be forty miles," DeWitt said. "That's too damn far. I hear they have a Pegasus with the fleet. This is what they built these little runners for. They do forty-five knots and have weapons. Why doesn't the damn Pegasus motor up the Euphrates quietly during the night and meet us just below Basra? We jump on board and cut out of there at forty-five knots. We're out into the gulf before Saddam knows we've been there."

Murdock agreed. He dialed the phone and found the admiral.

"Yes, Commander, we do have a Pegasus. We weren't sure that it could get up the river quietly enough."

"They will have at least six hours of darkness to move up the river," Murdock said. We'll need that much time to get to the target, hit it, and get into the river heading downstream. All they need is a Motorola on our frequency, and we can pick them up for about three miles."

"Sounds possible. As you said, forty miles is a long swim, especially if you have any wounded. I'll get back to you."

Murdock waved at his men. "Looks like the old man bought the idea. Now he's talking to the Pegasus drivers. The rig has a crew of five and is designed to hold sixteen combat troops. Sounds a hell of a lot better than swimming back."

Twenty minutes before they left for the flight deck, the phone rang, and the admiral's aide was on.

"Commander Murdock. We've talked with the Pegasus crew. They say they can get forty miles up the Euphrates in the dark without attracting undue attention. So it will be a meet in the water somewhere three or four miles below the naval base. If you get there first, hit the beach and talk our boys in with green glow lights."

"Yes sir. Sounds better than a forty-mile swim. We'll be

in place. Can the Pegasus crew get a Motorola like the SEALs use? It will carry about three miles."

"We can do that. Good luck, Commander.

Murdock turned back to the men. "We get the Pegasus up the river for a ride home. Which means we leave our wet suits and that gear here. No rebreathers, either. Five minutes to restow your gear.

Ten minutes later, Murdock checked. "Now, who isn't ready to take a small airplane ride?"

They took off on time.

Just under two hours later, they had covered the 530 miles between the carrier and Kuwait City. The pilot reported that he had counted more than twenty tankers steaming toward the now-closed Strait of Hormuz.

Murdock and his men landed at Kuwait City Airport and had lunch at the nearby air base. They were met by Major Charles Rausch, who would be their contact all the way to the border.

"Commander, we're ready. We'll get you and your men fed and then into a chopper for the jump to the border. We've inserted men into Iraq this way before, but none on such short missions. Usually it's a HALO operation."

"Some food would be good, Major. We have the equipment we need, and we hope it can be hidden in the civilian cars. Somebody said we would be trading our cammies for civilian clothing in case we are stopped."

"The standard procedure. Our drivers know the local customs and the language, of course. Should be able to get you past any road checks. Not a lot of Iraqi military down in this area once you're past the border. I'm sure you and your men won't have any trouble with that. I've seen some of your people operate."

The food was excellent, reminding Murdock a little of a condemned man's last meal.

They boarded a Marine Sea Knight at 1600 and took the sixty-mile flight to a spot along the border with Iraq. They set down at a small village that had an unusually large number of civilian cars, small trucks, and vans. All were nondescript; many with banged-in fenders and some with cracks in the windshield.

Major Rausch led them to a modest building that needed

paint and had one pane of a window broken out. Inside, it was modern and filled with army men and women and Marines all busy at work. The major took Murdock and DeWitt through three doors into an attached building where six civilians worked. Two looked up and nodded at the major. They were all Kuwaiti or Iraqi; Murdock wouldn't know the difference.

"Yes, yes, we have our people here," a small, dark man said. He had a thick mustache and piercing black eyes. "Do you wish to wear the civilian clothing over your cammics?"

"Yes, over them," Murdock said.

Murdock and DeWitt picked up garments and put them on, then watched as the rest of the SEALs came in a side door and put on the latest in Iraqi workingman attire. They all wore some kind of hat to help disguise them. When the small civilian looked at Jefferson, he sighed.

"Sir, you'll have to keep your face and hands hidden if you're stopped by border guards or at a roadblock. We have very few Negroes in Iraq."

Jefferson grinned. "Hey, I been hiding most of my life."

Outside, the SEALs walked with the major to a small building where they would wait until dark. They had their equipment there, and each man inspected his weapon and his combat vest with its variety of deadly goodies and the float bag with the TNAZ. All of this would have to be out of sight during the drive toward Basra.

The major had brought along fresh box lunches for the SEALs. They ate them and waited. It wasn't quite dark by 1800, when the SEALs were split up into the four cars. Four SEALs and a driver. They left the border just at dusk and spaced out a half mile apart. They all drove without lights. They went across the unmarked border at about the same time and saw no one. The driver, who spoke both English and Arabic, assured Murdock that there were Kuwaiti soldiers on guard along the border, but he wasn't sure if Iraq had any or not.

"Never see none," the driver said. He motioned with one hand. He drove an ancient Citroën. Murdock had his combat vest and his MP-5 submachine gun at his feet. The weapon was locked and loaded, ready to fire.

They drove for a half hour, then in the faint light, Murdock

saw a car driving without headlamps come into the same
track of a road that they followed.

"One of ours," the driver said. He stayed behind so far
that Murdock could hardly make out the other car. That must
be the way they always did this, he decided.

"We ten miles across border," the driver said. "Okay so
far, okay?"

Murdock nodded.

A few minutes later, the car slowed from its whirlwind
twenty miles an hour. The driver stopped the rig.

"Trouble ahead," he said. "See lights? Roadblock. Never
seen one out this far."

"How many of our cars up ahead of us?" Murdock answered.

"One, just one. We number two."

"Stay here," Murdock said. "Jaybird, on me." The two
SEALs took their submachine guns and ran along the road
for a quarter of a mile. They split then, one going on each
side of the track for the last one hundred yards to the blaze
of headlights that appeared twice as bright since they were
the only illumination for ten miles around. They eased forward until they were twenty yards from the roadblock.

Everyone was out of the car. One Iraqi soldier held up a
weapon and a combat vest. He shrilled in delight and jabbered something in Arabic.

Murdock looked around the lighted area. Two vehicles.
Three men with weapons holding Ed DeWitt, three other
SEALs, and the driver. Murdock didn't have the Motorola
on. He relied on Jaybird to know what he was doing. He
sighted in on the first guard holding the SEAL equipment
and squeezed the trigger. The silenced round took the road
guard in the upper chest, punched him back a step, then he
let out a small cry and crumpled forward.

Just after he fell, the second guard caught two of a three-
round burst from Jaybird's weapon. Murdock targeted the
third guard and used three rounds to put him into the dirt of
the roadway.

Ed Dewitt leaped forward, his K-bar out, and provided the
proof that the three men were dead. He and the SEALs
dragged the bodies off the road and into the desert fifty yards.
They returned and drove the two patrol rigs forward the way

their car was headed. When the car's lights turned, Murdock heard their car approaching.

He and Jaybird jumped in the Citroën, and they drove forward.

"A small problem that has been solved," he told the driver and the others.

"Yeah, damn small," Jaybird said and took the magazine from his subgun and refilled it with fresh rounds.

Five miles down the track, the SEALs drove the Iraqi cars into the desert, then ran back and got on board their transport, and the convoy moved on.

An hour later, Murdock asked the driver how much farther.

"Depends how close we can get to Basra," the driver said. "They have more guards out now. I don't know why. Two, maybe three miles from the naval base."

"That will be fine," Murdock said. "Can you take back roads so we don't hit any more roadblocks?"

"Not here. One road. Must take. Road goes along river. It's a half mile to the right. We drive up the road as far as we can. Easier than swim upstream."

Murdock nodded. They were passing houses now, strange brick and stone structures, then more of them. The road angled toward the river, and ahead they could see a blaze of lights again. The four cars still were not using headlights. Two hundred yards up the road, they came on the lead car stopped. The second one stopped as well. The driver of the first rig came back.

"Big roadblock ahead. Many men and guns. Best to go by foot now. Maybe along river in trees, most of the way to the naval base on this side of the town."

The eight SEALs crawled out of the two cars. The last two sedans rolled up, and the rest of the men slid out.

"Let's saddle up," Murdock said. "Get on the vests and bring your bags of goodies. We're infantry for a while. Beats swimming upstream. Lam, get out front twenty-five. River is to the right. Let's stay in any concealment we can find. Let's choggie."

Alpha Squad fell in behind Lam and Murdock, and they headed for the brush along the river. Murdock had never seen the Euphrates, one of the fabled and historic rivers of the earliest of civilizations. Some say the Euphrates provided life-giving irrigation to the early city of Ur as far back as the twenty-ninth century B.C. That period of the Mesopotamians fascinated Murdock. The river itself began 1,700 miles upstream in Turkey, came across Syria, and then through Iraq, before it joined the equally historic Tigris River to form the Shatt al-Arab.

Murdock pulled his thoughts back to the present. He was going to be up close and intensely personal with the river before long. They had decided to leave their rebreathers at the base. They wouldn't need them for long, and they would be a hold-back if things got sticky on the way in or the way out. The closer they could hike to the ships, the less surface swimming they would have to do.

Lam dropped to one knee. The men behind him stopped, watching in all directions. Lam pointed toward the river, which was less than twenty yards away. Then the rest heard it: the single chugging of a small boat's motor as it worked its way swiftly down the current of the river. None of them saw the boat.

After a brief pause, Lam moved ahead again. Ten minutes later, they could see lights ahead. Lam came back.

"Looks like security lights," he told Murdock. "This must be the lower end of the naval base."

"Check to see what kind of fences and guards they have."

Lam faded into the night.

Murdock waved the men down.

Ten minutes later, Lam came back.

"Three sets of fences, lights, and walking patrols on the land. I saw no security of any kind in the water."

"Let's get as close as we can, then get wet," Murdock told Lam. They moved ahead another fifty yards, then Lam angled toward the water. The river was wide and deep here. The Tigris came into it a short way above Basra.

The SEALs knew the routine. They would swim just under the surface, break water to breathe, then swim underwater again. When they passed the edge of the naval base, they would keep under the surface for as long as possible. Some of the lights splashed over into the water. Any guard worth his rifle would be checking the lighted water as well as the land.

They strapped their weapons over their backs, adjusted the tied-on waterproof sacks of explosives and timer/detonators, and moved into the water without a splash.

Murdock led the SEALs now. Lam was right behind him. They swam to the light, went underwater and swam as far as they could, surfaced for a quick breath, and went back down. They had only forty yards to go this way before the lights faded and the river opened up into a body of water to the left that had to be the Iraqi naval base.

They swam inside, found a deserted pier, which they swam under, and rested on the muddy bank. Murdock, Lam, and Mahanani made the scouting trip. They were back in a half hour.

Murdock gave them the intel. "The frigate is three-quarters submerged and rotting. Not worth wasting a charge on. There are two Corvettes. One has lights on and a crew. It looks operational. The second Corvette is listing. We'll blow both of them. We didn't see any operational patrol boats a hundred feet long. There are two that are hulks, look like they have been used for spare parts. We'll blow all three of them.

"The replenishment tanker at four hundred feet is not in the basin. We saw about twenty ten- to twenty-meter patrol craft. We'll try to blow them so fuel tanks will explode and we'll have a wonderful pier-side fire." He looked at the men clustered around him.

"Lam, Adams, Franklin. Are your wounds holding you up any? Are you ready for this duty?"

All responded that they were fit for duty.

"Okay. Bravo Squad, take the two Corvettes. Both are bow into the dock. Try to blow the whole ass end off both of them so they'll settle into the muck.

"Alpha Squad will do the patrol boats and figure out something for the twenty-meter jobs. We'll set the timers for thirty minutes. After setting the timers, we all should be back here in fifteen minutes. Then we'll kick out for our meet-up with that Pegasus taxi. Now, gentlemen, let's go blow up the last dregs of Saddam Hussein's navy."

13

Basra Naval Base
Basra, Iraq

Lieutenant (j.g.) Ed DeWitt led out his Bravo Squad, moving silently through the dark waters of the bay, angling for the pair of Corvettes berthed end to end along the pier. They had decided to use four charges of TNAZ on each side of the sterns of each ship. They would do the dark and unmanned ship first.

Jack Mahanani led the way to the silent vessel with Quinley, Ostercamp, and Jefferson. They all had rigged the charges with magnets so they would clamp solidly on the steel hull wherever they wanted them. Ostercamp and Quinley planted their two charges each at the ship's waterline thirty feet in back of the stern on the port side next to the dock. They dropped below the surface just as two sentries walked by on the pier.

Mahanani and Jefferson put all four of their charges at the waterline and about twenty feet back from the stern. They would plant the charges, gather at the stern of the dark ship, and when all were ready, would go back, insert the timer detonators, and start the timers.

DeWitt, Adams, Fernandez, and Franklin moved quietly toward the lighted Corvette. Three sailors moved on the deck.

The SEALs went underwater and came up against her hull. They surfaced without a sound. Two went on each side of the stern of the ship and planted their TNAZ bombs at the waterline. Just as DeWitt checked the ship, he found a sailor looking down at him.

In the stern of the Corvette under the chopper landing pad, there was no more than five feet of freeboard. The sailor leaned down. DeWitt surged upward out of the water, reached up, grabbed the Iraqi sailor's arm, and jerked him over the side before he could cry out. When the two splashed back into the water, it made more noise than DeWitt wished for. Then he was underwater with the wiry Arab, trying for a choke hold, then simply holding the man under the water until he began gulping in mouthfuls of water, probably hoping that it was air.

DeWitt's experience holding his breath underwater made the difference. He came up with his nose and mouth barely out of water and gulped in glorious air, then went back down and dove with the body of the dead seaman deep under the hull, where he snagged his clothing on the propeller.

He surfaced, gasping, directly beside the stern. The other SEALs watched him. He gave them a thumbs up and they swam quietly back to the stern of the dark Corvette.

"Everyone here?" DeWitt whispered. He counted seven heads. "Okay, let's go and set the timers for thirty-five minutes and then get back to that unused pier. Murdock may need a little more time with his targets."

Murdock had split his squad into three teams. Dobler and Holt would do one of the old patrol boats, Sterling and Bradford would take out the second patrol boat hulk. Murdock, Lam, Ching, and Ronson would work on the thirty small patrol boats.

They had a longer swim to the old patrol craft. The teams set the charges on the hulks and waited for Murdock to come back to them.

Murdock and his three men swam another hundred yards to the small docks that moored the patrol boats. There were fifteen in a row on one side of a wooden dock and fifteen on the other. He could see no sentries or guards.

Then a soldier on a bicycle rode down the dock, looked out over the water for a moment, then rode back and disappeared. They had decided to put half of the quarter-pound chunks of TNAZ on the fuel tanks of twelve of the small boats. They picked ones spread out through the group. Once pasted to the fuel tanks, Murdock told them to set the timers to thirty minutes and activate them. They did and swam back to the patrol boat hulks. Their men came out of the shadows of the ships.

"Timers set when we saw you coming," Dobler whispered to Murdock. The eight men swam silently back to the deserted pier. As they passed the manned Corvette, they heard sounds on board. They couldn't understand the words, but it was evident that a search was under way. By the time they were past the ship, it blossomed with all lights available and a dozen men scurried around the ship, seemingly searching for something.

Murdock and his men made it back to the pier, met with Ed and his squad, and talked it over.

"Lots of activity on that Corvette," Murdock said.

"I got spotted by a sailor, but I pulled him overboard," DeWitt said. "They probably missed him and are searching. Maybe it's time we get out of here."

Murdock nodded, and the platoon took to the water. When they hit the current of the river, they grinned in the darkness.

"That's a five-knot current," Murdock said as they floated down the river.

DeWitt swam alongside him. "You still have your watertight Motorola?"

"Safe and sound. We get down a couple of miles, we'll hit the shore and give them a try. Can't hurt."

Just then, a machine gun from the near shore slammed bursts of five rounds of hot lead into the river. The bullets zapped into the water just behind the swimmers, and they dove underwater and swam forward faster.

When they surfaced, they heard the machine gun firing, but now well behind them.

"Somebody getting nervous, or did they see us?" Senior Chief Dobler asked Murdock.

"My guess is the nervous gidgets, a bunch of rookies who have never been in a fight before. Now they get nervous and think they see something."

They heard the first blast behind them, a resounding explosion that reverberated through the night air. Murdock could imagine the Corvette losing its stern and sinking into the bay. Then, in rapid succession, they heard eight or ten more blasts through the silent Iraqi night. The men gave a soft cheer. If everything went right, Iraq had no more navy.

Just another day at the office. They moved on down the river. Murdock swam hard until he figured he was ahead of the rest of the men; then, as they came up to him, he waved them ashore on a sand bar that had some trees just behind it.

When the last man hit the beach, Murdock counted. Yeah, all there. He unzipped the waterproof pouch and pulled out his Motorola radio.

"Swimmers calling Pegasus. Swimmers in the wet looking for Pegasus."

He repeated the call two minutes later but had no response.

The SEALs went back in the water. Murdock stayed at the front, and what he guessed were two miles on downstream, he went ashore with the men and tried the radio again. This time he had a response.

"Yes, swimmers, glad you're coming. Pegasus here. We've run into a bit of a problem. Some assholes onshore with a machine gun and a searchlight have got us at a standstill on the far bank. They can't get their light over this far. If you read this, you're no more than three miles upstream."

"Pegasus, our meat. We'll move down and check out your buddies with the searchlight. Makes them easy to find. Hang tough."

Murdock put the radio away. "You guys heard him. We've got some work to do downstream. Let's move."

Back in the water, they swam with a faster stroke now to help the current.

Sometime later, they rounded a curve in the river and could see a searchlight ahead, probing the water and then moving toward the far shore. The river here was too wide to let the searchlight beam hit the far shore. The far side of the river had trees growing down right to the water. Murdock wondered if the Pegasus was under the screen of branches.

Murdock waved the SEALs onshore. They cleared the water out of their weapons, charged them, and made ready to fight. Lam led out the Third Platoon. Murdock figured they were about 500 yards from the light. He wasn't sure if it was on a boat or on the shore. If it was mounted on a boat, surely they would be on the water moving their light so they could pick up the enemy boat.

The SEALs moved for five minutes along the shore, then Lam went down, and the SEALs followed. Murdock slid into the grass beside his scout.

"Not more than fifty yards, Skip. Looks like a shore setup. A searchlight, small generator, a vehicle, and a fifty-caliber MG. How do we play it?"

Murdock waved the rest of the platoon up. He told them what they had ahead. "Alpha Squad will move up and take them down. Bravo, cover our rear. Let's go."

Murdock and his seven men worked forward, cautiously watching for security. He guessed there would be none. They had their weapons fitted with the suppressors and ready to fire.

Lam edged around a tree. Two men on the searchlight sat waiting in the glow of two bare bulbs. One man on the machine gun and a loader leaned against the small truck the MG was mounted on. Two more men sat against the rig, evidently eating.

Murdock brought the men up in a rough line of skirmishers. They were forty yards from the truck. Silently, Murdock assigned the targets to the men. As usual, they would open fire when his own MG pounded out three rounds.

One of the Iraqi men moved.

Murdock waited. The Arab soldier relieved himself in the darkness, then went back to the searchlight. Murdock sighted in on him, pushed off the safety on the subgun, and spat out three rounds.

At once the other silenced weapons spoke. The searchlight went out first as three rounds hit it and the glass shattered. The two men on the machine gun went down next, with rounds in their chests and head. One man, who had been eating, came up on his knees and reached for his weapon before two 7.62 NATO rounds slammed into his chest, mashing his heart into a froth of bubbles and spurting blood.

The other man who was eating lifted his spoon and turned toward his buddy before he slammed sideways with four rounds in his chest and side that punctured his heart and both lungs. The other man on the searchlight never got off his chair. He took three rounds and slumped over, one hand clawing at the light before he died.

The firing stopped. Then the door of the truck opened and a man came out, diving and rolling. He got almost to the cover of a huge tree before two rounds caught up with him and rolled him into instant communication with Allah.

They waited two minutes. Murdock waved the squad forward. "Make sure," he said. He heard seven silenced rounds as the Iraqis received the classic coup de grace in the back of the head.

Murdock had out his Motorola. "Pegasus, come on to where the searchlight is and pick us up. We need a ride home. This bit of Iraqi soil is solidly in our hands. The bad guys are no longer with us."

"Hey, SEALs, thanks. That's a roger. We've moving."

They could hear the soft growl of the big engines as the Pegasus came out from a screen of trees. In its black coat of paint, the low, sleek boat slid upstream against the current until it was halfway across the river. It turned with the current and slanted in to the shore where the searchlight still stood, now blank-eyed and dark.

The craft eased up within a dozen feet of the shore, and two SEALs grabbed the stern and pulled it in closer and held it. The other men stepped into the craft and moved into the covered cabin on the eighty-two-foot-long speedster.

Murdock was the last man on board. He looked at the ensign and smiled. "Nice to have you come fetch us," Murdock said. "Let's get the hell out of Dodge."

The ensign frowned in the half-light from the ship. "I beg your pardon, Commander?"

"Let's go home, sailor. I'm hungry and could use a huge steak dinner with all the trimmings."

The ensign nodded, and the boat moved down the river at fifteen knots. Murdock found the ensign. "I thought this tub would do forty-five knots."

The ensign grinned. "Sure as hell will, Commander, but not in the dark on a damned river I've never seen before. Then there are floating logs and trees in here and who the hell knows what else. We'll make fifteen, maybe twenty knots and be glad of it."

Murdock nodded. "Right. You're the skipper. Even fifteen knots is a shitpot better than swimming forty miles. You hit any other problems coming up?"

"Just that one searchlight and the fifty caliber. We even took one hit but above the waterline. They didn't know where we were, so they covered the whole tree-lined shore. We were lucky."

Suddenly Murdock was tired. He looked around. Half of the SEALs were asleep already. He waved at the ensign, settled down, and closed his eyes. For a moment he thought of Ardith Manchester, his beautiful lady back in Washington, D.C. He wondered what she was doing today, or tonight, whichever it was back there. Probably at work. He smiled. She would know about this run into Iraq before twenty-four hours were up. She and her dad should be working for the CIA.

He smiled just remembering that wonderful smile she had, the way she walked, how great she was at making small talk and figuring out his exact mood. She should have been a shrink. No, a lawyer was good or bad enough. He hadn't decided yet. The last thing he remembered was her glorious smile when she met him at the door of his Coronado condo. Yes, some things were worth fighting for.

Murdock came awake from a nudge on his shoulder.

"Sir, we've got some trouble. Looks like a river patrol boat coming upstream with a searchlight."

Murdock came awake at once. "How far away?"

"Half mile."

"You have machine guns on here?"

"Yes, a 12.7mm and a grenade launcher."

"Can you fire forward?"

"Yes. Get it ready. Bradford," Murdock shouted. The big guy came awake at once and lifted the McMillan .50-caliber sniping rifle.

"Yes, sir. Where do you want it?"

"Forward, patrol boat coming. Give it ten rounds."

Bradford found a place to shoot over the top of the low cabin and zeroed in on the oncoming boat. His first round was short, his second close. His third ripped into the patrol boat. The next three put it dead in the water.

The Pegasus's machine gunner jolted the craft with the 12.7mm rounds as they stormed past it fifty yards away and at thirty knots. There was no return fire. The searchlight angled upward and still blazed with a shaft of brilliance through the dark night.

Once they made it past the river patrol boat, Ensign Turley looked at Murdock with new interest.

"Never seen you SEALs in action before," he said. "You do good work. So far, we've only run the admiral around. Glad to get in some real action. This boat was made specifically to take you SEALs in and out of places on your missions."

"We've heard," Murdock said. "This is our first ride in one." Murdock went into the small cabin and looked out front. The captain had been right; it was hard to see out there at night.

"That inland patrol boat must have had a radio. If they did, they probably got the word out that we were here. That land machine gun might have had contact, too. My bet that we have some more company downstream. How far do we have to go yet?"

"Thirty miles."

"Plenty of time and distance for them to radio ahead and put out some heavy-duty welcome for us. Can we juice it up to thirty-five knots?"

"Might be safer than running though some concentrated fire from the riverbank." He nodded to the helmsman who revved the throttle. Then he switched off the interior lights. "If they can't see us, we'll be harder to hit."

"How's your supply of forty-mike grenades?"

"Plenty, two cases of HE and a case of WP."

"Good. Our guys might need to borrow some if they run out."

They raced along hard and fast for a while. The river here was fairly straight and getting wider.

Ten minutes later, they saw a light downstream. Turley put his twenty-power scope on it. "Can't tell. Could be a searchlight or maybe a bonfire onshore."

He cut the power and the sound of the two big V-12 diesels that kicked out 4,500 horsepower.

"Whoever it is can hear us but can't see us," Murdock said. "How about hugging the opposite shoreline."

"Dangerous over there, but we'll try it and cut power again. Let's hope we can creep by them."

"SEALs up and at 'em," Murdock bellowed. "Weapons on ready, especially you long guns. Some more company up front. If there's a spotlight, I want it to go first. Snipers decide who gets it."

The SEALs moved from the small, covered cabin to anywhere on the Pegasus that they would have a good firing position. The boat angled for the far shore. The light was on the right-hand shore. They chugged along at about five knots, and the engines sounded like they were idling.

Without warning, they saw a flash from the shore and a trail of sparks and fire coming toward them. It fell halfway to them.

"RPG," Ed DeWitt said. "Damn poor calculation on range. They can get this far."

As he said it, three more flashes showed onshore, and the rockets flew farther this time, but all fell short and slightly upstream from where they were.

The river here was three hundred yards wide. They were still fish in a barrel.

With dazzling suddenness, the light they had seen before turned in their direction, slashing a brilliant shaft of white searchlight across the water. It highlighted the far shore, swung back and forth in a good search pattern, but never got upstream far enough to find them.

"Do it," Murdock said.

Two shots without suppressors blasted from the sniper rifles. Within half a second, the searchlight died.

Ensign Turley gave an order. The SEALs heard the motor revving up and slid back into safety or hung on with both hands. The slender boat leaped ahead, thrust by the four thousand horses. It went from five knots to forty knots faster than Murdock had ever gone before.

A machine gun chattered from shore. The rounds hit well behind them now. Turley aimed the dartlike boat at the middle of the river and pushed the throttle forward again until they were racing along at forty-five knots. Everyone hung on to anything solid he could find.

The machine gun fire faded.

Turley pulled the throttles back to fifteen knots and sailed down the center of the river.

"We didn't hurt them much back there," Murdock shouted over the engine noise to Turley. "They might have some more friends downstream waiting for us."

"Might," the Pegasus captain said. "I'm not counting on it. We didn't see any activity at all on the way in here. I figured we might have to fight our way in and then get clobbered on the downstream run. But now I doubt if it is going to happen. They would have most of their defenses nearer to the navy base. We're a long way from there now. Fifteen, maybe twenty miles to the gulf."

"Hope to hell you're right," Murdock said. "That last bunch really messed up my nap. Gonna try it again."

Murdock found a vacant spot in the cabin and sat down, crossed his ankles, and went to sleep.

14

USS *Enterprise* CVN 65
South Persian Gulf

The SEALs made it down the river to the Persian Gulf with
no more problems, and then on to Kuwait City. The next
morning, they had a big breakfast at the air base near Kuwait
City before they flew on a COD back to the carrier. There
Murdock pigged out on a big steak dinner for lunch, with all
the trimmings he could find. At 1300, he and the SEALs
were working over their gear in the assembly room, when
Stroh boiled in the door, waved at the two officers, and put
them down in chairs at the far end of the big room. He told
them the problem quickly.

Murdock and Ed DeWitt looked at Stroh with surprise.

"What do you mean, the Navy minesweeper guys don't
know what kind of mines those are across the Strait of Hormuz? They must know, that's their rice bowl."

"They've been probing the area for the past day and a half
while you were playing float down the river. They report that
none of their usual testing and search-and-find operations are
working.

"They have located a rough line of chunks of serious metal
on the strait floor in a rough line spanning the three-mile
channel. The metal chunks haven't been there before, and

the specialists say that they must be some kind of mines. They don't know for sure. There are nine of them. Presumably, there were ten before the tanker went down.

"Incidentally, about half of the oil slick is washing into the Gulf of Oman, and the Southern Iranian coastline will also take a hard hit from the oil pollution. Not much of it burned off."

"So how did the Navy find the chunks of metal that may be mines?" DeWitt asked.

"The usual metal detection equipment and a batch of other mine identification and neutralization systems on board the mine sweepers."

"So why don't they neutralize them?"

"They didn't say, exactly. I understand that many marine mines are suspended on cables from anchors on the bottom. They hang in the way of ships passing by, and when one is hit, boom, there goes another rubber tree plant. The mine experts on the *Ardent* and the *Dextrous* say that these mines are not the hanging variety. Instead, they are down there on the bottom of the strait. That's from three hundred to three hundred and fifty feet below the surface.

"So they can't send divers down unless they get a submersible, and that much metal might set off the thing," Murdock said.

"Now you're starting to see the problem. Too deep for free diving, no way to shoot a torpedo at the things to detonate them, kind of hog-tied until they figure out exactly how to set the things off without sending another tanker to its grave."

"These mine countermeasure craft are the ones made out of a lot of wood, right? And they had no trouble moving over and around the nine mines. But one tanker rocked one of them, and it hit and sank the ship. So, how does the bomb get from the bottom, three hundred feet below, and into a tanker?"

"Some kind of cutting-edge electronics and radar and target ID and tracking system?" Ed DeWitt asked.

"Not a chance," Stroh said. "Our people have ruled out any late-tech stuff. They say the things have to be some sort of torpedo to get from down there up here."

"So, what kind of a torpedo?"

"Who the hell knows?" Stroh said. "Oh, the Iraqi know, but they don't return any of my phone calls."

"Ed, remember those torpedo classes we had to take at the academy? They had some on World War II torpedoes. Not nearly as sophisticated as what we have today. But wasn't there something about one the Germans developed late in the war but didn't get to use?"

Ed scowled for a minute. "Yes, some kind of a mine that activated, fired a torpedo that then charged into the ship. Yes, the devices were set on the sea floor. Designed for the North Sea and shelves around British ports. They never got to use them. Two to four hundred feet depth. It fits, but where would Iraq get German torpedoes from World War II?"

Stroh kept nodding. "Yes, yes, yes. It fits. Why don't we get the *Ardent* on the phone and talk to them."

"Stroh, these are the torpedo specialists. They must know all about those German mines and how they work."

"Know, but maybe they forgot. I'm calling. Don't go away."

They got through on the radiophone, and a few minutes later, Murdock was talking with Commander Johnson on the mine sweeper.

"Commander, I know you've thought of this, but what you have there sounds a lot like the German torpedo mines they developed near the end of World War II."

There was a moment of silence. "Keeeeereist. You're right. The same type of setup. They had them programmed in some hand-wired way with electronics and a kind of target-seeking device we didn't understand. That fits the parameters. But where the hell would Saddam get German torpedo mines from WW Deuce?"

"That and the fact that they would be nearly fifty-five years old," Murdock said. "Would they even work?"

Commander Johnson's hand shook so much he almost dropped the phone. "Now, why didn't we come up with something like this?"

"You're too advanced in your field," Murdock said, laughing. "Hey, I'm just a SEAL hoping I don't have to dive to three hundred and fifty feet and deactivate nine mines."

"So how . . . how did you come up with this?"

"We were just kicking around the problem. All that mine

would need is a magnetometer. They've been around for a hundred and fifty years. So the Germans would have them. Then the electrical circuits, and a primitive circuit board, some propellant, and you've got it."

"But how would the torpedo track the ship once it gets a big dose of magnetic signature that its system required?"

"Not the slightest, Commander. Unless maybe it has some way to home in on the magnetic source. Some of your people might know. But it isn't important. All you need to do is ram a high frequency of magnetic force into the strait toward those mines, and they should fire and come to the surface."

"Sure, and blow up any boat they can find."

"True. You have something that could send a magnetic signal into the water?"

"Well, we usually don't do that, but I guess we could. Yeah, possible."

"Only don't do it from a ship. Drop a lead into the water from a chopper and send it that way. The little brain inside that mine gets the magnetic signal, it's large enough to be the right magnetic signature for the firing device to work, and it blasts off and looks for the source of the signal. The thing must have a contact fuse so it couldn't be set off by a foot-square box."

Commander Johnson's voice rose with his excitement. "Yes, yes, it could work. We have a few choppers in the area to launch a missile at the torpedo once it surfaces and starts hunting."

"Good idea, Commander. I just hope I haven't upset your whole schedule."

"Hey, with this we will *have a schedule.*" The officer paused. "If this works, I want you to be on board when we activate it. This is a rush project. We've got over seventy-five tankers lined up on both sides of the strait. Washington says do it today. You're on the *Enterprise?*"

"Right, Commander."

"Who's your boss?"

"Gent named Stroh. He's right here."

"Let me talk to him."

Two hours later, Murdock and Ed DeWitt stepped off a chopper to the deck of a frigate that roamed an area a mile off the line of mines the minesweepers had located. The frig-

ate's choppers were refueled and had full loads of missiles
ready to go.

Murdock was called to the phone. It was Commander
Johnson.

"Sorry, Commander, as close as I can get you. We don't
have landing pads on these mine ships. We've been busy.
We have our target picked out. In an hour, one of the choppers from your frigate will come over for a wild pickup on
a hook and take up a device we're sure will activate the
mines. I've talked to the brass and the chopper pilot. He'll
have a fifty-foot lead, drop the device into the water directly
over the mine, and broadcast those intense magnetic signals
down to the mine. If it doesn't work, it's all your fault."
Commander Johnson gave a short, nervous laugh. "Just kidding. You can imagine the intensity of the tension around
here."

"One suggestion, Commander. The mines must have a
good pickup range. Why not aim your signals directly between two of them. That way you might get two to take the
bait at the same time."

The line was silent for a moment. "Gawddamned if you
ain't right, Commander. We'll give it a try. We just had the
pickup of the device and we'll position the chopper.

"We're about ready to get this moving. We're about a
quarter of a mile off the line of mines, but I don't think one
could sniff us out with a bird dog. The chopper is in position,
and we have two other choppers from the frigates working
their torpedo-finding gear. Here we go."

Murdock could see the choppers in the distance. The frigate captain had been ordered to stay at least a mile away.

Murdock put the radio signal on a speaker, and half the
ship's crew listened.

"Okay, we have contact with the water; the device is sending a huge magnetic signal down to that magnetometer that
must be in the shell of the mine somewhere. We'll keep
sending for three minutes."

The energy level of the magnetic signal decayed the
deeper it went, but by the time it reached the mine, it was
still strong enough to pulse the acoustic diaphragm on top of
the mine. The sensitive diaphragm made a small compression
in the heavy oil reservoir just beneath it, which moved a

piston through a magnetic coil and generated an electrical current in direct proportion to the strength of the sound.

Electrical circuits in the mine studied the frequencies of the energy, judged the fundamental frequencies of the complex waveform to the discrimination standards hardwired into it. The mechanical device determined there was a match. It was a large ship. The device moved on to the next step by determining the strength of the signal to see if the target was close enough. It was.

A relay tripped as all parameters were met for a firing. Power surged into the mine's firing circuit, first arming the torpedo-shaped charge, then activating a small electric motor, which provided the propulsion. The torpedo shot away from the metal casing that had housed the detection devices for so long, determined the direction of the massive electromagnetic signal, and automatically homed in on it.

Another voice came on the frigate's speaker.

"*Ardent,* This is Cover Two. I have a torpedo moving toward my position, still moving. Slow rate of speed. Torpedo approaching the surface, yes, surfacing. I have a visual. I have a missile lock on and firing at the torpedo. It's on a straight course on the surface. Estimated speed twenty knots."

Murdock heard the explosion from a mile away and a great geyser of water spouted into the air.

"We have a hit, mine people. Splash one torpedo."

A great cheer went up on the frigate.

The voice of Commander Johnson came on again. "Now repositioning the chopper between the next two mines. We're ecstatic here, hope for good results eight more times."

The next report from the radio came four minutes later. The chopper was in position and had begun sending the magnetic force into the water aimed at the second two mines.

The voice of the chopper pilot came on again. "Yes, frigate and mine ship, we have one, now two torpedoes coming to the surface. They seem to be converging at the point where the chopper is with the array in the water. Still converging. Chopper with the array, get out of there, move it fast, these two torpedoes could converge all the way and seek out each other."

"Yes, we're out of there, moving away quickly," the chopper pilot said.

The next thing they heard was a pair of dramatic explosions that came so quickly they sounded like one. The helo watching the scene was shaken in its flight but did not go down.

"That's three torpedoes destroyed, *Ardent*. Are we going for more?"

Before the afternoon was over, the sub-hunting helicopters had destroyed seven of the mine torpedoes with their missiles and two more had triggered at the same time and come to the surface and sought out each other and detonated.

The *Ardent* and the *Dextrous* plowed through the Strait of Hormus for an hour, but their sensitive metal detectors could find no more metal on the bottom except the sunken tanker, which was about half a mile toward the Gulf of Oman and in three hundred feet of water, so it posed no transit problem. Neither did they attract any more mines.

Word was passed to all tankers backed up on both sides of the strait that the mines had all been removed. To prove the point, the United States sent through an empty, midsized tanker after giving the captain and owner an ironclad guarantee that if it hit a mine and sank, the U.S. government would replace it. The crew and the watching naval vessels' personnel held their collective breaths as the big tanker plowed through the strait at twenty knots. When it was well clear, the radio crackled with ships getting permission from home ports to let them transit the strait.

On the helo ride back to the carrier, Murdock asked the pilot what would keep Iraq from planting more mines in the strait.

"Hey, we know what they did, there will be a round-the-clock watch on that strip of the gulf. If we see any size ship messing around in there night or day, it will come under considerable attack."

Murdock grinned. "Just wondered. Once burned, twice you not gonna get me again, you turkey." They both laughed.

15

USS *Enterprise* CVN 65
Southern Persian Gulf

"Bahrain is the name of the place," Don Stroh said to the assembled SEALs in their room on the big carrier. "Bahrain was a traditional monarchy, with an emir at the head. It's an island nation of two thousand two hundred square miles. That's the same size as an island forty-six miles one way by forty-six miles the other way. About the same size as the land mass of the city of San Diego.

"Not a big place. But it has a half million people. Three or four days ago, there was a coup there. The emir was gunned down at a soccer match, and a general of the Bahrainian army took over to 'stabilize the government.' He's still there. There has been a request through the United Nations by the former premier of Bahrain who escaped to Saudi Arabia, that they send a force into his country to free it from the conspirator/murderers who control it.

"The U.N. has agreed and assigned the U.S. to make the amphibious landing on the island kingdom. That's where you guys come in. You just did a beach clearing. This is another one. There are only two places where amphibious landings are practical on the island, and both will probably be stoutly defended. Your team and a platoon from Marine Recon will go in there.

"After the beach is secure, you will move with the Marines inland to suppress any enemy fire and to secure the beachhead for the landing."

"All thirty of us?" DeWitt asked.

"Not sure how big a Recon platoon is, JG," Stroh said. "I'll find out. We're not sure, either, how many of the former ten thousand Bahrainian military are loyal to the new commander in chief. I've heard we're sending in seven hundred Marines."

"We'll go in with the rest of the troops?" Murdock asked.

"Not the plan now. After the Marines are ashore, the colonel in command said he would keep the SEALs and Recon in reserve for special assignments."

"Anything the Marines can't handle, they give to us," Jaybird cracked. The men laughed.

"So that's it. You'll be choppered over to the amphibious ship *Boxer.* It will move into position tonight and be ready for a dawn landing. There will be no shelling of the area, no bombardment. The idea is to do as little damage to the real estate as possible yet still kick butt."

"Any contact mines in the surf?" Dobler asked.

"We don't know," Stroh said. "There could be anything there. However, the new regime hasn't had much time to install defensive measures, and the former emir did not think he needed any. So it could be just a walk in the park."

"That'll be the day," Tony Ostercamp said.

"We'll go in cammies and face masks," Murdock said. "Sounds like most of it will be in the surf. We'll know more after our briefing on the other ship. Regular loads of ammo, usual weapons. Bradford, bring the big fifty, leave the PSG1. Bring a hideout if anyone wants to; ankle holsters are best. Any questions?"

"How much TNAZ per man?" Jaybird asked. "We might have some blowing up to do."

"Two pounds per man," Murdock said. With eight timer/detonators."

"I'll draw some more," Jaybird said.

"How we going to work with the Jyreans?" Franklin asked.

"We don't know. They get UDT training, too. We might each take a section, be near but separate."

"Yeah, separate but they're unequal," Jefferson said. The men cheered again.

"Let's get with it," DeWitt said. "We have an hour to chow, then another hour to get on the flight deck, ready to rumble."

Three hours later, the SEALs landed on board the USS *Boxer* LHD 4. Officially, she was a Wasp Class Amphibious Assault Ship. In actuality, she was an 884-foot-long mini-carrier that specialized in helicopters and vertical-takeoff Harriers. She normally carried eight Harriers and 42 CH-46D Sea Knight helos. She had the capability of carrying almost any helicopter the Navy used including the Super Cobra, Super Stallion, Twin Huey, and Seahawk helicopters.

In her holds she could also pack 1,850 combat-ready Marines. Each chopper could move eighteen Marines on vertical assault missions. In the hold were also landing craft and air cushion landing craft.

The SEALs found their quarters and sacked out. They would be going in shortly after dark to start their beach-clearing work. Any demolition they needed to do wouldn't start until daylight, with the Marines hard on their way to the beach.

The briefing for the officer was about what Murdock expected. He did learn that half the Marines would be coming in on one beach and half on the other side of the island at another good landing area. The Recon Marines would clear one beach, and the SEALs the other. Separate and equal.

The *Boxer* had been steaming north all day at twenty-two knots. It would need fourteen hours to get into position. She would lay five miles off Bahrain until an hour before the landing was set. Then she would steam within a mile of the beach and discharge the Marines in a pair of borrowed LCU 1600 Class Utility Landing Craft. They would each hold 350 Marines, and one would attack each coast.

The SEALs and Recon men ate late chow at 1900 and then went to their disembarking point in the stern of the big ship on the third level down. The huge ramp at the stern of the ship opened to let the LCUs move through the water into the open sea.

When they were ten miles off Bahrain, the SEALs would launch in the Pegasus that had sailed to the *Boxer* as soon as the mission was set. By that time it was nearly 0200 and pitch black. They would have the south shore of the island and the Marines the north.

The SEALs boarded the Pegasus and checked their gear again.

"The captain tells me we're about ten miles off the coast. We'll be going in fast for the first eight, then simmer down and move in as close as he can go, maybe a hundred yards, just outside the surf line. From there we take a swim. You know the score on clearing a beach. Anything that will mess up a landing craft, we take care of. We have a little less than an hour's ride. The time now is 0220, meaning we'll have five or six hours to find any obstacles, mines, concertina on the beach, anything at or near the beach that would cause problems. Questions?"

"Yeah. What was all that?" Joe Lampedusa asked. They all laughed.

"Take a nap, you guys. You may need the sleep before this one is over."

Half of them slept. The other half were the least experienced at the real thing: shooting at people and having them shoot back at you. Murdock watched them and looked at the sky. A partial moon, no clouds. At least no rain. He'd been on a dozen of these beach-cleaning missions. The only thing he worried about were pressure-activated mines just under the surface of the wet or dry sand. Maybe they would be lucky.

The constant roar of the two big diesel engines drove them across the open gulf toward the island nation. When the sound toned down and then nearly stopped, Murdock came awake at once and talked to the ensign.

"Two miles out, we're moving in at five knots so nobody will hear us," the officer said. "At least we hope nobody expects us, so they won't be watching for us."

"My hopes exactly," Murdock said.

Another mile closer to the beach, and Murdock could see lights on the island. What did Stroh say, it was a forty-six-mile square? Plenty of room to hide. He wondered how many of the 10,000 troops had followed their murderous leader. They would soon find out.

"Okay, you guys, up and at 'em. Wake up time. Final check on weapons and waterproof pouches. We'll want the Motorolas later. We have another quarter of a mile to go. Bravo Squad off first and work to the shallows where you can stand. We'll join up there and check the situation, then make assignments."

Five minutes later, the ensign running the boat nodded.

"Bravo, over the side. Good luck."

They tipped into the swells and could hear the breakers less than fifty yards ahead of them. They surfaced and stroked easily shoreward with their weapons strapped on their backs.

Murdock's Alpha Squad followed them. They met in three feet of water with breakers pushing them forward with each wave.

Murdock and the SEALs scanned the area. It was a mile-long, sandy beach, evidently a gradual slope that could give the bigger LCUs beaching trouble. So the Marines get wet coming in. He didn't see any mechanical metal tank traps or angled steel to rupture the landing craft. The SEALs spread out in the center of the area. They would clear a section and put up a waterproof rolled-up sign they had brought to indicate the center of the cleared landing area. Hopefully, the coxswain on the landing craft could see it.

For two hours they walked the waves and shallows but found nothing to deal with. It was 0300 when they hit the first problem. Horse Ronson had moved out of the surf to the edge of the wet sand and walked along, gently probing the sand ahead of him with his K-bar. Suddenly, he stopped and didn't move. He had his Motorola out and working and whispered into the lip mike.

"Murdock, we have a problem."

Murdock came out of the foot-high gulf and saw Ronson squatting in the wet sand.

"Hit metal, Skipper. Not the hell sure what it is. Should I take a look?"

"Wait. Get Jaybird up here. Your ears on, Jaybird?"

"Yeah, coming," Sterling responded.

He came up on the wet side of Murdock and Ronson.

"Back the way you came," Jaybird said. "Both use your footprints in the sand as stepping stones. Let me take a look."

Jaybird had become the platoon's mine man when he de-activated six mines left over from World War II that the SEALs discovered deep in the sand at their desert training grounds.

He probed gently with the KA-BAR already in the sand. He withdrew it gently and probed in the wet sand around the point where he knew there was metal. The rest of the platoon moved down the beach in the foot-deep water and out to three feet deep, examining the black water and the sand when they could see it. Their job was to clear a 300-yard stretch of beach for the Marines to land on.

Jaybird looked at Murdock, who knelt in the wet sand right behind him.

"Wish to hell I could use a light," Jaybird said.

They both knew that he couldn't. He twisted one way to let what little moonlight there was shine on the spot. By this time, he had an outline. It was no more than three inches across.

"How in hell did he ever find this needle?" Jaybird said. Slowly, he began to scrape the wet sand off the top of the area. He went down an inch, then two inches. He scraped metal. After that, he moved more cautiously as he removed the sand from the circle around the object.

"Could be an old tin can," Jaybird said. Sweat formed on his forehead and ran into his eyes. He slashed it away.

"Yeah, but more likely a bouncing Betty. Remember them from that training film?"

"Yeah, about three inches across. You step on one, even the side, and a small charge goes off, bouncing the real whammer four or five feet in the air, where it goes off like a grim reaper, wiping out a squad at a time."

"Could do it right here."

"Don't they wish." Jaybird had a hole excavated around the three-inch cylinder. Now he could see the metal sides of the bomb. It was no tin can.

"Yes, a bouncing Betty type at least. Sometimes they put this one together with a pressure-release type mine. Say the Betty is on top of it, like holding down an arming spoon. As soon as a jerk like me lifts the Betty off, thinking he's solved the problem, the arming device clicks in, and whammmo, there goes another rubber tree plant."

As he talked, Jaybird probed down each side of the mine, then deeply under it until he was satisfied.

"Okay, sports fans, no double trouble here. We've got one Betty, but are there any more? If I was gonna spread them out down here, I'd put them in a rough line across the beach, parallel to the fucking shore."

"I'll start looking," Murdock said. He took out his KA-BAR with its eight-inch blade and began probing the wet sand two feet over from where Jaybird worked, doing the final removal of the mine. He took out an orange plastic sack from his combat vest and delicately wrapped the bomb in the sack. Every man in the platoon knew what the orange sack meant. Jaybird began probing the sand, moving the other way from Murdock.

It was a monotonous task. They probed with the knife every three inches in a line three feet wide, then moved up three inches and probed back the way they had come. After clearing a three-by-three-foot section, they moved to the side and did another section. It was slow, agonizing work, and any second one bad probe or one with too much force could set off a mine.

Master Chief Dobler came to where Murdock worked his KA-BAR in and out of the sand.

"We have the surf and the outside wet sand cleared," Dobler said. "Not as certain as you're doing it here, but there are no obvious problems to a smooth landing."

"We still need to check the dry sand. How much here, about thirty yards?"

"Somewhere near. A lot of space to cover."

"Tell Lam to use his KA-BAR and clear a path through the sand up to that fringe of woods. Then have him check it out and in to the point where he finds any humans, civilians or otherwise."

"Aye, sir." Dobler moved away through the water to find Lam, their platoon scout.

"How much we going to do on this, Skipper?" Jaybird asked.

"You know how far three hundred yards are, sailor?"

"Too fucking far. What if this is the only one? What if it

was dropped by mistake on some kind of an exercise by the original home boys here?"

"What if we miss one and it blows up six Marines coming across this wet sand?" Murdock stood, waved up the rest of the platoon, and told them the routine. "Every three inches in a three-foot square. Line up and let's get at it. We ain't got all night."

Lam edged his way up the soft and dry sand, probing two feet wide and moving faster than he should. He made it across the twenty yards to the dry grass and some salt brush. Lam stopped and listened. He couldn't hear the SEALs behind him because of the pounding breakers. He watched ahead. No lights. Small brush, and some trees, but he didn't know what kind. The whole island looked low and flat. He moved into the brush carefully, watching, taking in everything he could see in the half-light.

Nothing.

Nobody.

He went another fifty yards. Still nothing. If they wanted to defend this place, they were going about it in a crazy way. Maybe they had no idea they would be invaded. He hoped so. An all-out war with ten thousand troops was not his idea of fun. Especially since they only had seven hundred Marines backing them up.

A half mile inland, he found the first habitation. It looked like some kind of vegetable farm. A small house, a hint of a valley, with a tiny stream and row upon row of some kind of green crop. Enough. He turned and headed for the beach.

On the way, he neither saw nor heard anyone.

A walk in the park.

He was almost to the beach when a jolting explosion drilled the sky with an arc of light, then the rolling thunder of the mine washed over him along with a wave of hot air. He ran to the edge of the dry sand.

The SEALs had scattered, most of them back into the foaming foot-deep seawater. Lam had no idea where the safe trail was that he had carved coming into the woods. He sat down and waited.

Murdock heard the blast and swore as he left his section. It was to his right. He ran through the foot-deep water to where he saw the small cloud of smoke slowly rising. Two

men lay on the wet sand. Mahanani crawled up to the first
man. Murdock went to his knees beside him. It was Ron
Holt.

"I'm not hit bad, Skip, just knocked me out. Got some
nicks and scrapes, damn shrapnel. It's Al Adams over there
who caught most of it."

They moved cautiously in the water to where Adams lay.
His right arm was torn off. Blood gouted. Mahanani pulled
off his shirt and held it tightly around the bloody arm stump
halfway to the shoulder.

"He's bleeding, so he isn't dead," the medic said.

Murdock checked his face and chest. Blood soaked his
cammie shirt. His face was not marked.

"Lam," Murdock said in his Motorola. "You back?"

"Back, Skipper. Nobody up here for almost a klick."

"Work a safe path for us through the dry sand. Be damn
careful. Adams got it bad, we need a place to keep him off
the beach."

"Doing it. Work better if Dobler could work from the wet
to meet me."

"I'm on it, Skipper," Dobler said on the radio.

"Can we save him?" Murdock asked the Hawaiian.

"I don't know. Shock, blood loss. Haven't even looked at
his chest yet. Be good to get a chopper in here for him. Can
we contact the big boat?"

"Didn't bring the SATCOM. Pegasus can call them. They
must have heard the blast if they hung around. He touched
the mike. "Beach calling Pegasus. Do you copy?"

There was no response. He made the call three times. Then
he heard a faint reply.

"Beach, on our way home. Need help?"

"Triggered a mine. Got two of our men, one critical. I
know we can't get a chopper in here until the attack. That's
still two hours off. Can you pick up our wounded?"

"Check with mother hen. Give me a minute."

Everyone heard the conversation. Adams tried to say
something, then drifted off into unconsciousness again.

"Get his feet up. He's in shock. More blood to his brain
the better."

"Beach, we have a go for ambulance run. Mother is within

five miles. They hit here first, then go to Beach B. Coming in. Any enemy fire?"

"None we've found so far. Just the damn mine. We found one more but have it out. Gentle slope of the beach here, not sure how close you can come. What do you draw?"

"Not sure. We can nose in to ground, then get off easy."

"You have a medic on board?"

"Negative. We're about two miles out and moving in fast. You may be able to hear us. Give me a glow stick to find you. You're where we left you before?"

"That's a roger to both."

"Jaybird, take a green stick, wade out, shield it with your body from the island, and give Pegasus a target."

"On my way, Skip."

Murdock checked out Ron Holt. He had two deep gashes in one leg, an arm wound, and, after repeated probing, admitted that he couldn't see very well.

"The damn flash," Holt said. "Twice as bad as a flash-bang."

"Can you walk, Holt?"

"Yeah, but I won't know where I'm going."

"You're with me. He hit the radio again, Ronson, Bradford, get over here and help us get Adams down to the boat. It should be here in a few minutes."

Murdock led Holt into the water and out beside Jaybird. They heard the Pegasus coming, then it toned down as it slowed. It had no lights, only a murmur now as it idled in the last quarter mile.

Two minutes later, the long craft nosed in three feet from Jaybird until its bow scraped sand. It stopped. The water was chest deep when they walked out to the boat. They lifted Holt on board, and Murdock told them he couldn't see.

Adams was tougher. Ronson and Bradford carried him like a silk pillow, but the men on board the Pegasus had trouble getting him into the ship.

"Mahanani, get in there and help. You're going back with them. Check over Holt for blood loss. Have one of the crew try to stop the bleeding with pressure on that stump. A wet towel might help. Go."

The Pegasus eased backward, away from the beach,

turned, and crawled away on low throttle. They heard it rev up farther out to sea.

Murdock looked at his watch. Nearly 0400.

"Jaybird, get that mine. We'll take it with us. Lam, you know where that safe route is?"

The earpiece came on. "I've got one end, Senior Chief Dobler has your end. Bring the troops into the cover. Nobody up here yet, but I'd guess we'll have some company before the Marines land."

Murdock's radio talked again. "On our way, Skip. Holt is doing well, chest wounds superficial. Lots of blood, not much hurt. He still can't see. Adams is looking bad. We brought the rest of his arm along and the crew has it in a bucket of ice. You know what they can do with severed limbs these days. Almost out of range. Good luck."

The SEALs moved across the safe strip of sand and into the woods. No one else had been touched by the mine. Jaybird said it wasn't a bouncing Betty or five or six of the men would be hurting.

They spread out in the brush facing inland while Lam took another scouting run. He came back thirty minutes later.

"Skip, I'd suggest we move inland about half a klick. There's some good defensive areas there. My guess, there will be someone from the interior over here soon to investigate that mine going off.

Murdock sent them along. Ed Dewitt had the con and Dobler to help him set up an ambush.

Murdock and Jaybird stayed behind. They went back to the wet sand through the safe trail. They marked the trail with an orange flag, then went down to where the mine exploded and put another orange flag. The third one they put on the spot Jaybird had removed the first mine. The flags were three feet square on four-foot poles jammed into the wet sand.

At 0530, Murdock had heard nothing from Ed DeWitt. He said he'd call if they ran into trouble.

Murdock tried a call to the LCUs. They were supposed to have one radioman on board with a Motorola set to the SEAL's frequency. He tried the call again. Nothing. That meant the Marines were still farther out than the three-mile radius of the small radios.

He had to wait. Just as Murdock sat down on the dry sand, his radio spoke.

"Murdock, we have contact. Looks like two jeeps and maybe a dozen men. Is it too early to take them out? If we let them come through, they will see the landing and cause all sorts of hell. The rigs have mounted fifty-caliber MGs."

Infantry tactics. It all depended on the situation and the terrain, they used to say. Only this time, there was another factor: time. If they blasted the rebels now, that might bring a much larger force to defend the beach before the Marines got there. If they didn't take the rebels down now, they would come through to the beach and cause a passel of trouble.

Murdock spoke into the lip mike. "Light them up, Ed. Use all silenced weapons if you can and don't let them fire a shot."

"That's a roger."

Before Murdock could do more than offer a silent good luck to his men, his radio sputtered and a garbled voice came over.

"Bea . . . Beach. On t . . . way. Give us some. . . . Make them t . . . green on . . ."

"Marines. Broken reception. You want green stick lights?"

"Roger th . . ."

Murdock turned to Jaybird. "Let's get in the middle of our little cleared path. I'll tell him by radio about the mines. They have three cleared paths for single file.

That was when he heard some repeated rifle and machine gun fire from well into the trees.

16

**The A Beach
Bahrain**

Murdock stared into the trees where he heard the firefight. Too damn early. The Marines wouldn't be there for another ten, fifteen minutes.

"DeWitt, talk to me," he said on the Motorola.

"Busy, Skip. We nailed half of them, the rest came up shooting. These are well-trained troops. A little firefight right now. The Marines coming?"

"Talked to them, haven't seen them. Ten minutes minimum."

"No problem here other than time. Going to take ten to get rid of these guys. Don't want any running back to the mother lode."

"Roger that."

Murdock tried to listen seaward. At last he heard the faint growl of the LCUs. How long would it take them? He touched the radio mike again.

"Marines, do you copy?"

"Roger, beach. Better reception. Arrive in six minutes."

"Gently sloping beach here. Not sure how far you'll get in. We have green light sticks. Found land mines here. Have three single-file paths cleared. No opposition for landing.

Small firefight about half a mile inland. We have friendlies there."

"Single file, beach? We can do that. Soon."

Murdock and Jaybird could hear the motors now. It was growing lighter. Dawn was coming fast. The Marines should hit the beach just about at daylight. Both SEALs held green light sticks. They would bend them and break the seal and activate them the moment they could see the LCUs.

"Gunfire has tapered off inland," Jaybird said. "Maybe the JG has it under control."

Murdock nodded. He watched the water. At sea level you were supposed to be able to see seven miles before the curvature of the earth bent the land or water out of sight. The Marines had to be closer than seven miles.

Then he saw them, twin dark dots on the brightening waters.

"Got them," Jaybird said. "Light sticks ain't gonna be much good now that it's light."

"They can see them, and it'll confirm they're at the right spot. Let's break the seals."

Each of them held two of the green light sticks and started them glowing.

"Hey, we see your lights, beach. We're on course. You have those cleared lanes marked for our boys?"

"Ready to go with three-by flags."

Murdock waved Jaybird to one of the clear lanes, and he went to the other with its big marker flag. Single file meant it would take the Marines some time to get off the beach and into the woods. If they would run, that would be a help.

"Skip, looks like we're about finished up here," DeWitt said on the radio. "We stopped their vehicle and took down six or eight. But about that many vanished into the brush and must be making their way back to their people. Want us to track them?"

"No, JG. Hold there as a forward outpost. We'll make damn sure the lead elements of the Marines know you're there. They are just about ready to land."

Murdock's radio came on once more.

"Beach, ETA two minutes."

They could see the l35-foot-long LSUs coming, their big defensive landing ramp straight up and charging for shore at

ten knots. They were side by side. They corrected their angle
a little, then charged head-on for shore.

The big landing craft nosed up on the beach, hit the sand
with the bow in about two feet of water, and the big ramp
splashed down. A wave of combat-clad Marines boiled out
of the craft, splashed through the water, and thinned out into
a single file, running smartly toward Murdock. He pointed
to the flag and waved them forward.

"Straight up to the brush," he bellowed. "Stay in line.
Mines around here."

He ran to the middle sign, and a line of Marines peeled
off one of the LSUs and moved toward him. Then they had
three files of combat Marines running across the beach and
up to the brush. Murdock found a Marine captain and hailed
him.

"Captain, Commander Murdock. I've got people up in
front of you. Eleven SEALs who just put down an enemy
patrol. Be sure your lead elements know they are there. I
don't want to lose any of my men to friendly fire."

"They've been told, Commander. I'm Captain Browser.
I'll be with them. Heard you lost a man here to a mine."

"Lost an arm, don't know if he'll make it or not. If you're
ready to go forward, my man and I will go with you. I want
to be sure my lead men are safe up there."

"Let's go."

They came to the lead elements of the Marines five
minutes later. They had formed up and moved through the
woods in squad formations with two scouts out front.

"DeWitt," Murdock said on the Motorola. "The Marines
have landed and are moving up to your rear. We're friendly
back here. Let's hook up carefully."

"That's a roger. We can hear you coming. We'll stay out
of sight until you're close enough to talk to. Any word on
Adams?"

"No contact. Maybe the Marines have a SATCOM."

The lead Marines worked ahead slowly, made contact with
DeWitt, and then the rest of the SEALs were together. They
formed one squad and worked ahead with the leathernecks.

They soon passed the shot-up jeep and six bodies. The
scouts went slower then, moving from cover to cover. By
the time they were inland a half mile, they found the house

and small farm. Just over the low hill, the scouts reported that there was enemy activity.

"Looks like a company digging in, about six hundred yards ahead, Captain. Maybe eighty men."

"Any vehicles?"

"None. Two bicycles for messengers."

Murdock stood near Captain Browser and heard the radio report. The Marine looked at Murdock. "You have a .50-caliber sniper with you?"

"Affirmative."

"Here's what we're going to do."

Fifteen minutes later, the Marines were in position. Bradford lay in a brushy spot where he could see the Bahrainian rebels. He had been checking out the company for five minutes through his scope and at last had found the only officer with the group. He stayed in back of a large tree most of the time but came out now and then, evidently to issue orders.

Captain Browser bellied down beside Bradford. "Any time you're ready, Bradford. You get in your shots and then it's our turn."

Bradford sighted in on the tree the Bahrainian officer used and waited. A full minute later, the officer stepped out from the tree and Bradford fired. He rammed the bolt back and forward and fired again.

The enemy officer was down. At once the Marines opened fire on the company from two sides, putting them in a cross-fire. The rebels weathered the attack for three minutes, then began pulling back, running from the sparse cover into the deeper woods. The Marines ceased fire, formed up, and moved forward again.

The Marine scouts reported that the enemy had not regrouped. They were running and disorganized, charging back through a small village and onto a paved road. The scouts saw no other military units.

Murdock walked beside Captain Browser.

"Our mission is to move up this road and capture the airport at Manama. That's the capital city. The airport is on this side. The other unit will come in from the other direction and take down the government buildings, including the army headquarters. We expected more opposition than this. I wonder where in hell are those ten thousand troops?"

"Let's hope we don't find them," Murdock said.

Captain Browser grinned. "For SEALs, you guys make damn good infantry."

"More than half of our work is done on land," Murdock said. "We get frequent chances to develop our ground combat skills."

"We'll have to talk about that sometime."

The captain's radio spoke.

"Cap'n Browser, we've got a pocket up here with three machine guns and about twenty troops."

"Hold it there. We'll come up and take a look," Browser said. The captain motioned to Murdock to follow him, and they hurried past the stopped troops to the front elements and then on fifty yards to the scout. They peered past some brush and saw the sun glint off metal two-thirds of the way up a small hill.

The scout motioned. "High ground and the MGs. We call in an air strike?"

"Can't. The least damage to the place the better. Range?"

"A hundred and fifty."

"Good range for some forty mikes," Murdock said.

Captain Browser groaned. "Yeah, but our guys haven't fired their forty mikes for six months."

"We've got some guys who can lay an egg in a basket," Murdock said. Shall I call them up?"

The captain hesitated. "Aw, hell. My job is to get past them fast and into that airport. Yeah, bring up your shooters."

Murdock made a Motorola check and Jaybird, Lampedusa, and Franklin soon appeared right behind them. Murdock moved them ten yards apart and explained the mission.

"Alternate HE and WP. Free beer for a week for whoever drops the first egg in that machine gun hole."

The SEALs judged the distance and began dropping in the 40mm grenades. The second WP hit near enough to spray the machine guns with flaming phosphorus. Three rounds later, Jaybird dropped an HE into the bunker.

Captain Browser grinned and motioned his men forward. There was no fire from the bunker.

Jaybird laughed as he walked along beside Murdock.

"Damn but I'm getting thirsty already. I'd guess we have to wait for Coronado before I get my beer."

"Good guess, Jaybird."

Captain Browser came up beside Murdock. "Tell your men nice shooting back there. Glad you're along. My best map shows a hike of about fifteen miles to our target, the airport. Not sure if that's right. It also shows two small towns between the beach and our taxi strip. My orders were a little vague on the subject, but as I understand them, you and your men were to go with us."

"Those were my orders, Captain," Murdock said.

"Good. We might have some more special need for your men's talents. We've been sitting on that ship too long. Our skills get a little rusty."

They kept moving. They met little resistance. One quick firefight in front of them produced six bodies and one prisoner. It was over before the SEALs got there.

The country became more built up. Now there was a paved road and an occasional small car or truck. The civilians seemed to melt out of the way as they passed.

"Captain, we may have another problem. Could you take a look?" It was the Marine's radio. The captain motioned to Murdock, and the two hurried three hundred yards to where the Marine scout lay in a small ditch. Down a slight rise, the buildings were closer together and houses extended back a hundred yards each way from the road.

In the middle of the road, five hundred yards out, sat an armored half-track. It showed a mounted weapon that the captain said was a .50-caliber MG, after checking it with his binoculars.

The scout pointed to the sides and down one connecting street. It looked like more than a hundred riflemen behind good cover.

"Yes, a small problem."

"The fifty could take down that rig," Murdock said. "We use it mostly for destroying hardware, vehicles, radar installations, and a chopper now and then. Want some help on it?"

"Take out the truck, we still have those eighty men down there."

"Do the truck, then more of the forty-mikes. Your men must have thirty or forty under-barrel launchers. We have five. Throw in a couple of hundred rounds before they can scatter, and all you have to do is clean up."

Captain Browser stared at the scene ahead as he thought about it. At last he nodded. "Okay, we move all the launchers up to within two hundred yards. We launch, and at the same time, your man blows that fifty and the truck into scrap metal. Let's do it."

When the riflemen and Murdock's five SEALs were on line and ready to fire, Captain Browser gave Bradford a nod. The first fifty round caught the truck's windshield and blew it out. Before any reaction came, Bradford's second round drilled through the engine. The third hit the fuel tank, and the truck blew up in a huge gasoline fireball, spraying flaming gasoline and truck parts for fifty yards.

With the first .50-caliber round, the forty-mike rounds sailed into the air. About half were short, but enough hit inside the range of the infantry to kill and wound many. The rounds continued to rain down now with more on target. Some shooters lifted their range to catch those who ran to the rear to avoid the death from the sky.

The Marines had been using their M-16s as rifles, too, and blasted anything that moved below. Four minutes after the first round, Captain Browser called for cease-fire.

Ten or fifteen Bahrainian soldiers came out from solid cover and ran to the rear. *Let them go,* Murdock decided.

The 350 men moved out again with the SEALs. So far, Adams and Holt had been the only casualties.

Captain Browser came up with a man packing a SAT-COM. "The force on Beach B ran into a whole shitpot full of trouble. Underwater obstacles ruptured the first LCU. Only half the men made it to shore. They hit ten or twelve mines before they detoured around the open sand and ran into a force of two hundred men who had them pinned down for three hours. Only now are they starting to move toward the capital."

"We picked the right beach, Captain."

"Yeah, but that puts them way behind schedule. We were supposed to have this wrapped up before nightfall."

"Not now," Murdock said. "Not if the B team was supposed to capture the army headquarters."

"So, we take over the airport, leave a force there, and

charge on into town eight miles away and do a frontal assault on the army's GHQ?"

"I hope no frontal assault," Murdock said. "It all depends on the situation . . ."

Captain Browser stopped him. "And the terrain. I took that same course at the academy. Hell, let's take down the airport, then we worry about what to do next. Maybe the other battalion can move fast enough to get it done without help."

"Wouldn't count on it," Murdock said.

They ran into no more trouble or even enemy snipers and came to the boundary fence to the airport just before 0900. Captain Browser and Murdock surveyed the airport from the roof of a small building near the fence. Lam and the Marine scout also studied the layout.

"Kid gloves in here," Browser said. "We're supposed to do as little damage as we can while we take over the airport, without getting ourselves killed."

"No fifties into the control tower or into the military transports on the macadam," Murdock said.

"Yeah. The tower and the administration offices are the primary targets. Also, we've learned there is a hangar being used for troop housing. Three targets. A hundred men for each one. I'll split up the force and make assignments. Murdock, you come with my group. We'll do the admin building."

"Right. Captain, can your SATCOM contact your ship? I need to know how my wounded man is doing."

The captain nodded and pointed Murdock at his radio operator.

The corporal made two calls on the box and gave the phone-type handset to Murdock.

"I've got sick bay for you, sir. They say your man is there. The doctor who treated him will be on in a minute."

17

**Airport
Bahrain**

"Commander? This is Dr. Alspaugh on board the *Boxer*. You're inquiring about Petty Officer Adams?"

"Yes sir. How is he?"

"He's alive. It was questionable when we received him here. We stabilized him and treated his other wounds. He's out of danger now. The arm is the problem. We have the body part on ice and will try to reattach it when he's ready."

"Do your best, Doctor. He's a good man. What about Holt?"

"Superficial wounds, but we're worried about his eyes. It may be a temporary blindness. The intensity of the light from the blast could have damaged the retina. We're watching him closely."

"Thanks, Doc. Do your best."

Murdock and the radioman ran to catch up with Captain Browser and his men. They were on an end run around the airport to come in through the main entrance. They moved down a side road around this back part of the airport and saw no military units.

Their lead men came around a corner, and they could see the main entrance. Two military trucks sat there across the lanes of traffic. A dozen soldiers stood around with their weapons slung, muzzles pointing down.

The Marines went to the ground along the side of the road and began firing at the trucks. The Bahrainian troops scattered, then the trucks started, backed around, and raced down the highway away, from the airport.

The Marines moved up cautiously. Murdock had his SEALs in the second unit. When they arrived at the entrance to the airport off the highway, there was only some broken glass on the pavement to show the encounter. The Marines rushed through the driveway and turned left down a circular road toward a five-story building away from the passenger terminal.

"Administration building?" Jaybird asked Murdock.

"Must be. Where are all the troops? Is this colonel a military man or a ringer?"

Just after Murdock said it, six RPGs slammed into the Marine force. A dozen men went down, injured or dying. None of the rounds hit near the SEALs. Captain Browser dispersed his men and moved them forward slowly, clearing cars and vehicles parked along the road. He made sure the medics took care of the wounded. Then he called for choppers from the *Boxer* to do a medical evacuation.

"Yes, Lieutenant. I said we have wounded. Nine men who need immediate medical care and two KIA. We want them out of here at once. Get those choppers moving."

Captain Browser left six Marines behind to protect the wounded and the medics, then they moved toward the big building.

The Marines were running, charging across the parking lot at the front door of the five-story building. Murdock and his SEALs went with them.

"A fucking frontal assault," Murdock shouted at Jaybird. "I told the captain not to do this."

They were thirty yards from the front door when Murdock realized they weren't taking any enemy fire. Browser split his force, sent half of them to the back and the rest of them charged directly into the building.

Murdock and the SEALs went in the front and stayed on the first floor as some of the Marines moved up the stairs and others froze the elevators and generally cleared the building. Murdock heard no firing.

Five minutes later, Captain Browser came back to the lobby.

"Not a single military man in the place," he said. I talked to one of the people who spoke English. He said the military had been here, but they pulled out this morning. They said something about going to the beach to fight an invasion."

Browser used his radio and contacted his other units attacking the other two targets. The Marines had taken their objectives. They, too, had found no military. The captain told the units to hold fast, let the normal business go on uninterrupted. Flight schedules would be maintained.

He called up his radioman and talked on the SATCOM to a colonel on the B force that had landed on the other beach.

"Yes sir. Understood. Two miles from the edge of the airport. Yes sir. Right away."

He hung up the handset and shook his head. "We leave twenty men at each of the three facilities here and push on to the army GHQ two miles toward town. You want to stay here or come with us?"

"Captain, I've been wondering who fired those six RPGs. Had to be somebody in this facility. Why don't we do security here and try to find those shooters. Should be at least three men, from the way the rounds came in."

"Yes, hadn't thought about that. We'll leave this place in your hands. There should be some choppers from the *Boxer* here soon to evacuate those wounded. When they do, keep the security Marines with you. We'll link up later."

"Make some noise leaving, Captain. We'll lay low here and try and find the shooters."

The Marines left the building, formed up outside, and marched away through the airport parking lot, back out the entrance, and toward town.

Murdock told his men the problem. He put two SEALs in the stairways on each floor with instructions to crack the door an inch and watch for any uniformed men or men with weapons. He and Dobler went behind the reception desk and crouched down, waiting.

Ten minutes after the Marines had left, Murdock heard his earpiece come on.

"Skip, third floor. Just saw three men in brown uniforms get on the elevator. Didn't see any weapons, but they wouldn't be showing them off, would they. Should be in the lobby shortly."

Murdock waited.

"Skip, second floor. Those three men got out here and went down some service stairs. I'd guess heading out the back door."

Murdock and Dobler left the reception desk, ran for the only back door they saw, and waited outside against the building. A service door opened fifty feet down the side of the structure. One man came out and looked around, then the other two left, and they walked toward where Murdock and Dobler hid behind some exterior machinery.

Murdock stepped out when the men were thirty yards away.

"Hold it," Murdock barked. The three men stopped, then drew pistols and fired. Murdock and Dobler dove to the ground and kicked out two three-round bursts each from their MP-5s. The bullets caught all three men and put them on the ground. They dropped their handguns. By the time Murdock and Dobler moved up, two of them were dead. The third one rolled over and tried to fire his hideout gun. Murdock jolted three rounds into his chest, and he died with a scream.

USS *Boxer* LHD 4

Commander Alspaugh shook his head. "We can't do it here. There's a chance we can save his arm on the *Enterprise*. They have the experts who can do it. I'll make the arrangements. Get him ready to travel on a litter. Now."

The medic looked at Al Adams again. He was under heavy sedation. They had another three hours to get that arm attached, or it wouldn't be possible.

The commander used the radio and told the hospital on the carrier that they were coming and to get ready to attach an arm. He wanted everything ready when the chopper landed on the deck.

Dr. Alspaugh took one more look at the other SEAL, Holt. He was awake, alert, and worried.

"I still can't see, Doc. When do I get my eyesight back?"

"Holt, we can't be sure. We've inspected the back of your eye, the retina. It doesn't look damaged, but this is a touchy situation. You could blink once or twice a minute from now and your eyes be entirely back to normal."

"Yeah, Doc, what's the other side of it?"

"You already know that. You could be blind for life, but I really don't expect that. I checked with our experts, and they say a mine doesn't have that much of a flash effect. Its main thrust is with shrapnel. Which leads me to think that your eyes will be okay. I want you to get some more sleep. I'm going to order a mild sedative for you, then you have a good eight-hour nap."

"Sure, Doc. Whatever you say. How is Adams? I heard he lost an arm."

"We're going to put it back on, if it all goes right. You just worry about resting those eyeballs of yours. I'll check with you when I get back."

"Yeah, Doc."

Dr. Alspaugh watched the young man a moment. Amazing that he wasn't dead. Taking the flash from that mine meant he had to be almost on top of it. Most of the shrapnel simply went around him rather than through him. He was hoping for the best.

Three hours later, on board the *Enterprise,* the medical team tried to relax. The attaching operation was over. Now they had to wait and see if everything worked right. Veins, arteries, nerves, tendons, all had to be reattached, sewn together. The two arm bones had shattered and had to be rebuilt and pinned with lengths of rods.

Two of the doctors on the team had done this type of attachment before. Dr. Alspaugh had assisted.

"Will it take?" he asked. "Will he be able to use the arm again?"

"There's a good chance," the senior surgeon said. "Everything went well. But we can't tell for at least a week if the basic veins and arteries are working, then the muscles and the nerves. Somebody say he's a SEAL?"

"Yes, he was on that Bahrainian landing," Dr. Alspaugh said.

"The arm will never be as strong or as good as it was

before, even with optimal recovery. Don't tell him, but he'll never be a SEAL again."

Manama City Airport, Bahrain

Murdock called his men together in the parking lot at the airport and made a casualty check. His medic wasn't there. There were no reports of any wounds or problems.

"Did Al Adams make it?" Fernandez asked.

"They kept him alive. Now they're trying to attach his arm," Murdock said.

"Either way, he'll never be a SEAL again, will he?" Fernandez asked.

Murdock shook his head. "Not a chance. I just hope they get his arm put back and it'll work."

They saw a civilian van driving fast up the highway. It screeched around the corner, slowed as it came into the airport, then speeded up, heading directly at the SEALs. They scattered. The rig stopped and a Marine jumped out.

"Commander Murdock. Captain wants you guys up front, pronto. He says you all can fit in this van we liberated. Climb on board. He has some special work he needs done up front near the army GHQ. Some nasties in there don't want to give up."

"What about the casualties?"

"He said the Marines here could take care of them until the evac helos get here."

"Load up, SEALs," Murdock shouted. "The Marines need us up at the front."

"What they need us for now?" Ching asked.

"Who knows. Something we can do, they can't. Let's go see."

The thirteen SEALs crammed into the van with all their gear. It jolted out of the parking lot and drove three miles down the road through increasing numbers of buildings and houses. They came out on a city street with a large four-story building across from it. Murdock, riding in the front seat, saw Marines in cover all along the block. The van pulled in back of a small building halfway down an alley, and the SEALs piled out, ready to rumble.

Captain Browser came out of the building.

"Commander. We're in a standoff here. We have the general penned in from this side. The B troops have him cut off to the rear. They finally got here about six hours late. I've talked with the general inside by phone. His English is better than mine. Oxford, I think. Anyway, he wants to negotiate."

"Better than a frontal assault on the place."

"Then there's our directive not to harm any real estate if we can help it. Here we can help it and save the lives of a lot of Marines."

"So, negotiate," Murdock said.

"That's the problem. He said he would negotiate only with an admiral or a general. I told him I was the highest-ranking Marine here. He kept off the phone for an hour. When he came back, he said he would negotiate with a U.S. Navy SEAL officer. Were there any with my forces? I told him."

"So, I'm it?"

"Afraid so. No weapons. No hideout if you have one. You'll strip to the waist, and they'll check you out at the door."

"What does he want?"

"He didn't say."

"When?"

"Right now. I'll let you talk to him on the phone. Inside." The two officers went into the small building and the captain handed Murdock a phone.

"General Nassar, this is U.S. Navy SEAL Commander Blake Murdock."

There were some sounds over the line then a strong voice came on.

"Navy SEAL? Where did you train?"

"BUDS/S at Coronado, California, General."

"Yes, yes, I had a tour of your facility there. I love the O Course. I want you to come now and talk. You have safe passage to the front door of the main entrance. Wear only your cammies, no hat, no weapons. Clear?"

"Yes sir, General Nassar. I'll be there shortly."

Murdock stripped out of his combat vest, took a hideout .25-caliber revolver and holster from his right ankle, and emptied his pockets of everything. He was clean.

He left his cammie shirt on and hiked down the alley to the street with the captain.

"Right across there, down the sidewalk, and right up to the front door. We'll cover you in case of any firing. We haven't fired a shot down here and don't think we'll have to. You ready? Tell him anything you negotiate has to be approved by our colonel, who's running this operation."

"Not my kind of assignment, Captain. This is strange, but I'll do my damnedest."

Murdock walked across the street. He had no idea what to say to the general under attack from both sides and evidently deserted by his army. He'd play it by ear.

Two uniformed men without arms met him just outside the big doors. He was expertly frisked and then led inside. Two armed men stared hard at him, motioned him forward. One walked in front of him and one in back. They went into the basement instead of upstairs, where Murdock guessed they would go. They went down two floors into a safe room through a heavy steel door. It clanged shut once he was inside, sounding like a bank vault closing. The large office looked like a living room with upholstered chairs, a coffee table, a sofa, a large-screen TV, bookcases, and several oil paintings.

"Well, Commander Murdock. A SEAL. I have great respect for you men and what you do. I took part of the training, but it was too rugged for me. What class were you in?"

"It was one-eighty-two, General Nassar. You seem to know a lot about the SEALs."

"I was in the States on a training/exchange program. At one time we thought here we might have such a unit. But it wasn't practical, so I recommended that we not form one."

"Yes sir, General, I understand. Now, how can we end this stalemate?"

"I would prefer to leave the country under your safeguard."

"How would we do that, General?"

"A car to the airport. My family is already there. I will use the royal jet, a Gulfstream. We would be granted safe passage to the airport and then on to Libya, which has granted me sanctuary."

"In exchange for this safe passage?"

"I will surrender the remainder of my forces. Most of the troops deserted when they heard about the invasion."

"Do you have any other conditions, General Nassar?"

"Only that I be allowed to take personal luggage and certain assets with me."

"What assets?"

"That would not be revealed."

"Not acceptable, General. Those assets would be gold or funds or diamonds that must rightfully belong to the Bahrainian people. We could not agree to that. Your luggage will be searched at the airport."

The general sank lower in his leather executive chair.

"Very well. Get confirmation from your forces."

"I'll need the phone you used to talk to Captain Browser."

The general pointed to the phone on his desk.

A moment later, Murdock spoke to Captain Browser. He told him the conditions the general had set down.

"Sounds like a winner. Let me check by radio with Colonel Albers with the B troops. It's his baby, and I've been keeping him up to date as we go along. He has to agree to the final conditions the general makes."

Murdock held on the phone. Two minutes later, the captain came back on the line.

"It's a go, Commander. The sooner the better. Tell the general that he should proceed now to the front of the building, where we will have a car to take him to the airport. He should first order all of his troops out of the building without any arms and put them in military formation in front of the flagpole. Then he comes out.

The general waved at Murdock. "One more condition. I must talk to the captain."

Murdock gave the general the phone, wondering what else the crafty Arab had in mind.

"Captain, you must have a superior here. Tell him there is one more condition. To insure that my plane is not shot out of the sky once we take off, I insist that Commander Murdock be my guest on the flight to Libya. That's not a condition I will negotiate. It's the SEAL with me in the airplane with my family and me, or it's no deal, and we go back to square one."

18

Manama City Airport
Bahrain

Murdock and two others inspected the luggage of the twelve family members. They found only reasonable family jewelry, three cameras, a video camera, and assorted goods. No stolen millions from the monarchy. Murdock figured that had already been wired to a Swiss bank.

It had taken an hour to get Colonel Albert's approval for Murdock to go along as the "guest" of the general. With a U.S. Navy SEAL on board the business jet, it was certain it wouldn't be shot down. The colonel had asked Murdock if he would go. He said to end the standoff and the bloodshed, he would.

"Hey, I've never been in Libya," he told DeWitt.

The twelve family members boarded the plane, then Murdock went up the fold-in steps, and the plane rolled to the takeoff point.

The general came around and offered Murdock a drink. He settled for a beer. It was warm and tasted awful.

"What will you do now, General?" Murdock asked.

"Now, my young friend, I am retired. I do not need to work to make a living. Eventually, I hope to come to the

United States. Life is so much more civilized there. That may take some doing, but it is my hope."

"One more question, General Nassar. Americans are not welcome in Libya. How will I get back to the Middle East?"

"I have arranged that. You will be traveling as my aide without a passport, and you will be given diplomatic immunity to return to Cairo and from there back to Saudi Arabia and on to your huge aircraft carrier."

"How can I be sure of that?"

"I made two phone calls before we left. I talked to a high government official, and he guaranteed to me that it will be so. He knows that you are an American. He knows that you will be coming as my diplomatic guest. We will put you in some better clothes so you don't look like a terrorist. I think some of my brother-in-law's clothes will fit you."

They flew over the water to Iraq, then across it to Amman, Jordan, where they refueled and then angled across the Mediterranean Sea to Libya and soon into Bengasi, the capital. Murdock wore the civilian clothes and felt like a geek.

"The pants are too big and the jacket is too tight," Murdock said to the general.

He shrugged. "It's a costume for you. You need it. These people are not as polite as they could be. They may give me a hard time and most certainly will challenge you. It might take me two or three hours to get to the man in the government I called. He probably has forgotten to talk to his police here at the International Airport. Trust me. It won't take long."

Two police cars waited when the steps came down on the Gulfstream. It wasn't an honor guard.

An officer met General Nassar, who had also changed into civilian clothes. They talked for five minutes. All the time, Nassar was getting more and more agitated. At last he shouted something and started back up the steps.

Two policemen pulled him back down and walked him to a car. Then the officer came into the plane and shouted at the others and motioned them outside.

Murdock didn't have the slightest idea what the man said. He went out with the others but was at once picked out as not being a member of the family and taken to one side.

"You are American," the officer said in accented English.

"Guest of Mr. Nassar," Murdock said.

"Your passport and papers."

"I have none, they were lost in Bahrain. I'm the guest of General Nassar."

"You are CIA spy. We have watched for you. Clever. You will come with me."

"I'm not a spy. The general made me a hostage so his plane would not be shot down by the Americans who liberated Bahrain from the general."

The captain of the guards laughed. "Amusing fellow. We'll see how amusing you will find your new accommodations."

"Ask the general. He'll vouch for me. He must be Libya's friend. You let him land here."

"Of course. We wanted the plane. It is confiscated. Now belongs to Libya's Socialist People's Army."

Murdock tried to relax. He should have expected this. He went with the captain to the same car where they had taken Nassar. He was propelled into the backseat, where Nassar sat scowling.

"It's all a mistake. As soon as I can get to talk to General Buruk, we will straighten it out. This officer thinks he's a big man. He will take credit for capturing my plane. It's his now, he says. He said no one told him we were coming."

"But they let you land."

"The tower must have known. In Libya, the chain of command is not as good as it could be."

The captain of guards leaped in the front seat of the car, and it drove rapidly off the tarmac and out of the airport.

Ten minutes later, Murdock was pulled away from Nassar and pushed into a cell in the basement of what Nassar had called a branch police station.

Murdock looked around. No way out. The cell was six by eight and had no bunk, no blankets, not even a chair. In one corner of the room sat a five-gallon bucket that had recently been used as a urinal.

He found a dry spot along the far wall and sat down against it. Two or three hours to straighten it out. Murdock wondered.

Two days later, he still sat in the cell. Night and morning he did exercises. He had been fed twice. The food was strange but adequate. At least he was alone in the cell. He heard other inmates jabbering away in Arabic. He swore again that he would learn something of the language of the land he had to work in. Next time.

Near the end of the second day, a jailer came and unlocked his cell, said something to him, and pushed him along a corridor. They went up the steps to the first floor, and he was pushed into a room that had two chairs and a table.

A well-dressed man sat in one of the chairs. He said something in Arabic, then changed to English.

"Ah, yes, Mr. Murdock, our guest from Bahrain. At first we thought you were a CIA spy. Now we know that you are not. You are simply a common criminal. You will be deported today as an undesirable alien. A friend has purchased a ticket for you to Cairo. You will be on the ten-oh-five flight. Is that satisfactory to you?"

"Yes."

"You are one of the fortunate ones. I have never known the military police to release anyone put in this jail in less than three months. Indeed, a fortunate one. I will be your guard until you are on the plane. You'll wear wrist and ankle shackles. No option."

A man came in the room and fastened the iron and chain shackles on his ankles and wrists. Then the man in the neat suit led him out the front door to a police car that took them both to the airport.

"A common criminal?" Murdock said. "What have been my crimes?"

"The report I saw shows you as a thief, a robber, a molester of children, and a radical against the state. It is enough. No more talk, or I might change my mind, shoot you, dump you out of the car, and cash in your airplane ticket. Quiet."

Murdock never said another word until they were at the airport gate. The policeman talked in Arabic to the check-in clerk, pushed a ticket in his hands, and marched him to a loading door that had not opened yet. The man shouted, and someone quickly swung out the door.

Down a long corridor, then into an airplane. He was relieved to see that it was a large jet with seats six across. The attendant looked at his ticket, said something to the policeman, who shook his head vigorously.

"Egypt has agreed that you may stop over there in the plane, but you must not leave, and you must keep your irons on. Understood?"

Murdock nodded.

His seat was the last one in the cabin. He figured there would be no one around him.

When the regular passengers boarded a half hour later, the plane was only half full, and no one sat within five rows of him.

Murdock slept. No one brought him any food. When he awoke from time to time, he realized no one was served anything. Economy flight, Libya style.

When they landed at the Cairo Airport, an Egyptian policeman came on the plane before anyone left, was pointed to Murdock, and sat in the seat across the aisle from him.

Murdock didn't try to talk with him. Was it still Arabic? He didn't remember. The passengers deplaned, some new ones came on, and just before the plane took off, another man came in, talked to the attendant a moment, then hurried back to where Murdock sat.

"Commander Blake Murdock, U.S. Navy," the man said, grinning so wide Murdock was afraid his eyes would close.

The sudden English surprised him. "Yeah. Yes sir. Something went wrong in Libya."

The man laughed and strapped himself into the seat. The policeman hurried up the aisle and evidently went off the plane.

"We've been hunting you for three days over four continents. Where the hell you been?"

Murdock told him. He motioned to his chains. "Can I get these off?"

"Commander, you outrank me. I'm only a lowly captain in the army. Military liaison at the embassy in Cairo. I just happen to have a key. The Libyan police do this quite often."

"Where are we going?"

"Next stop, Riyadh, Saudi Arabia. No more police. I'd say you'll have a debriefing by our embassy people there. They like to keep up to date on Colonel Mu'ammar al-Qaddafi's jail cells. I bet you can tell them something along those lines."

The shackles came off, and the captain pushed them under the seat. "Oh, I'm Captain Thomas Utts, sir."

Murdock held out his hand. "You know what happened in Bahrain?"

"Yes. Once you got General Nassar out of the picture, the prime minister, who had been in Qatar, returned to the country and was named the new head of the government until a successor to the king can be determined. Our Marines and your SEALs went back to the amphibious ship in the gulf, and the prime minister thanked the U.S. for liberating his country and with such a small loss of life and almost no property destroyed. That could be a record for a U.S. Marine invasion."

"What about the SEALs?"

"My guess is that they are back on the *Enterprise* by now. Oh, one more message. The doctor on the carrier reports that the reattaching operation on your man Adams went well, and they are waiting to see if all of their handiwork is a success."

"Anything on Holt?"

"Your radioman. Yes, the same doctor told me by phone early this morning that Holt's blindness was temporary. He has back almost fifty percent of his sight, and the percentage of recovery is increasing every day. He said something I didn't understand about shock more than damage, and some of it may have been psychological. Holt told the doctor he saw Adams's severed arm lying on his stomach. That was the last thing he remembered seeing."

Murdock felt his stomach rumble. "Hey, they serve dinner on this flight? They have any food on board at all?"

"This is a Libyan airliner, remember that." He chuckled. "I'll go see what kind of clout I have with the attendants."

Ten minutes later he came back with a covered tray. On it were two hot meals, a lunch sandwich, and two cups of coffee.

"For you," Captain Utts said. He sat down and watched Murdock eat.

"I've heard the chow isn't exactly officer's mess quality in Qaddafi's jails."

Murdock mumbled and took another bite of the pepper steak. He was sure that he had never before eaten such marvelous-tasting food.

As soon as they landed at Riyadh, Captain Utts hurried Murdock out of the airport to a waiting embassy limo that drove quickly to the Air Force base nearby. There Murdock was provided with a set of cammies and boots that almost fit him. Then the car drove him to the embassy.

On the second floor, three men sat waiting for him. None wore a uniform. Their questions were simple and followed a pattern that Murdock quickly sensed. Had he been mistreated? Was he given adequate food? Was he in an unheated small cell with no furniture or sanitary facilities? Had his release come about due to help from General Nassar? Had he been forced to wear wrist and leg irons during his time at the airport in Bengasi and on the plane?

His answers were quick, pointed, and soon they both realized that he had nothing of value for them. They thanked him and called in captain Utts, who took him back to the Air Force base where a COD waited for him with its engines warmed up.

Four hundred eighty miles later, the COD landed on the deck of the *Enterprise,* and Murdock let out a long-pent-up breath. Home again . . . well, for a time.

Ed Dewitt and Senior Chief Dobler were on the flight deck to welcome him.

They shook hands, and Ed grinned. "Damn, good to get you back here, Skipper. This bunch of wild men have been driving me crazy."

"Ed, Ed, Ed. I've told you before about this. It's a matter of command presence. You must make the men understand that you're in command at all times, and they must want to follow you. Of course, the easy way is to dump all the tough stuff off on the senior chief."

He shook hands with the man. "Dobler, good to see you again. Thanks for keeping the JG in line."

They grabbed a white shirt and were led off the flight deck without getting anyone killed.

"Is the dirty mess still open? I'm starved. I could go for about three sliders right now with all the trimmings."

"Sliders?" Ed asked. "Skip, you have been away too long. How about a nice, thick T-bone steak?"

"Nope, sliders. That was all I could think of in the damn Libyan jail. Sliders it's gonna be."

Three sliders it was.

19

Hussein's Palace #23
Near Baghdad, Iraq
Saddam Hussein paced the twelve-by-fourteen-foot room. This one was on the sixth subbasement floor of the concrete-and-steel bunker built far belowground to prevent entry by any of the American smart penetrator bombs. He had seen the result of them daggering through three floors of concrete and steel before they exploded, but never six.

He no longer worried about his personal safety. He was angry, nearly furious with the state of his campaign to take over the Persian Gulf. He stared hard at his top adviser and friend of twenty years.

"Jarash, my right hand. Where have we gone wrong? What is there left for us to do to throw off this yoke of the U.N. restraints once and for all and be a free nation again?"

Colonel Jarash Hamdoon rubbed his face and took a long breath. "I don't know what to say. Your plans were good. Our best military and governmental minds put together the master plan that would bring all of the gulf states under our control.

"Perhaps we overestimated the dedication of our people and confederates in these small nations. We still maintain control of only one of them, Bahrain. I don't like to say it,

Mr. President, but we are quickly approaching our final option."

The phrase made Hussein look up sharply at his top aide. He stopped pacing and sat in the leather swivel rocker behind the large desk. "Yes, the final option. It would have been so much better to persuade one or two of the smaller emirates and kingdoms to move into line on our side of the marker. Now we will have to strike quickly and decisively before the big powers can react.

"We have had success in the hated no-fly zone. After three days, we have shot down six enemy planes. They will pay dearly for coming over our territory. As we predicted, they have not launched any kind of a missile or bombing attack on our cities in retaliation. Yes, they are weak, divided, indecisive. Now may be the time for our strike."

"At that time, will we use the red-tipped artillery shells and red-nosed missiles?" asked Colonel Hamdoon.

"Absolutely. We built them. We will use them."

"That will bring a great outcry."

"What will be, will be."

The telephone on his desk chimed softly. Hussein picked it up. He said "Yes," and listened. Slowly he put down the phone, anger building in his face, his forehead flushed, his eyes wide, and fury rumbled in his throat.

"We will do it now! We have just lost Bahrain. The United States sent in Marines and collapsed our control there in less than eighteen hours. Our man there bargained his way to safe passage to fly the royal jet to Libya. I'm sure his Swiss bank account is fat."

Saddam paced again. "Yes, it has to be soon. Tomorrow morning at dawn. No, not enough time to get ready. Begin massing the troops and tanks and motorized men for the attack. Knock heads out there, Colonel, and have the men and the support units ready as quickly as possible. No more than forty-eight hours."

Colonel Hamdoon came to attention, saluted smartly. "It will be done, my President." He did an about-face and hurried to the only door in the room that led to the series of stairs that went up through a separate shaft in various stages and emerged at ground level fifty yards away. There was no way a bomb could penetrate the bunker by working down the stairs. There was no elevator.

Saddam weighed the odds. He had 390,000 men under arms in his active-duty roster. He had 650,000 lightly trained men in his army reserve. He had the use of 2,700 tanks that could slice through poorly defended territory at thirty miles an hour. There were 4,000 other armored vehicles to carry troops, help protect the tanks, and hold territory already captured.

Artillery would surprise the Great Devil America. He had over 2,500 artillery pieces that he would use to reduce any hard site of opposition. They would be the first to be heard from, softening up any defenses that might be in the way.

His ace in the hole that the West was not sure about were his 350 combat aircraft. Many were older fighters, some Fishbed MiG-21bis, but he also had two wings of the newer MiG-23UB Flogger-C jets. They had Mach 1 plus speed and air-to-air missiles as well as air-to-ground, a 23mm cannon with 200 rounds, rocket launchers, and bombs carried on six external hardpoints.

He was pleased with his aircraft. His pilots had not had enough training, but that was always so. They would do well when called upon. His close-support aircraft included 300 helicopters, many fitted with machine guns and cannon. It would be an interesting time.

Now he looked forward to getting the attack under way.

There had long been a master plan for the first strike. The target had been and always would be Syria.

It would be a good fight. Syria claimed to have over 400,000 men under arms, but Hussein had always doubted that. They had over fifteen million people as against Iraq's twenty-two million. The element of surprise would be on his side. He expected great things quickly and perhaps could strike all the way into Damascus, only 120 miles from the Iraqi border.

With his thirty-miles-an-hour attack, he might even get there the first day. His hopes soared. He had a long drink of ice water from a small refrigerator in the corner of the room, and he smiled.

He had asked for reports. He would get them as men and machines began moving toward the border with Syria when it was dark. Syrian lookouts might even notice the movement of troops with daylight tomorrow, but by morning of the next day, everything would be in place.

Praise be to Allah.

Praise be to Saddam Hussein.

The tall, dark man smiled at his own audacity.

In one of the small buildings on the forty-acre site above the underground bunker, Colonel Jarash Hamdoon put his carefully honed plans into action. He called three men on an action tree; these three men called six more, then those called six, and soon the selected men in the armed forces were alerted to the plans for the next forty-eight hours. It was a double-redundant system, so each man was notified twice, eliminating any chance for one branch of the tree not to receive the message.

Activity began at once. Men in barracks and camps were alerted for a three-hour move out. Army trucks and civilian buses were readied for the troops. Just after the three-hour deadline, troops began moving to the west toward Syria. By nightfall, there were more than a hundred thousand infantry soldiers and their support units on their way to spots near the Syrian border.

Everything it takes to support a modern army was soon on the move westward. Trucks, kitchens, hospitals, mail rooms, fuel, food by the trainloads, ammunition, telephones, radios, personnel records, tanks, fuel tankers, weapons carriers, small mobile homes to be used by top-ranking officers, artillery pieces, their caissons, ammunition trucks, a million and one things a strike force of over 120,000 fighting men would need when they drove hard and fast into Syria.

Colonel Jarash Hamdoon called for his car and drove quickly into Baghdad, where he cleared out his office, loaded everything into a small mobile home he had confiscated only last month, and made sure he was ready to move. He kept the telephone and three soldiers to handle the rest of the calls he needed to make. The airfields were alerted, with orders to be prepared to give close ground support and to hunt down Syrian tanks and artillery when the attack came.

This was an attack plan they had practiced for over a year in the desert between them and Syria. Each time they had announced it a day in advance, naming it Desert Preparedness Maneuvers. Syria had brought up some troops each time, and this time might again, but they would not react in force, all of the planners had assured him of that. It cost too much money to throw a hundred thousand men into a defensive line just to find out it was a training maneuver.

The same ruse would work this time.

Colonel Hamdoon had not used the motor home before. It had been taken from some tourists who were in trouble for bringing marijuana into Iraq. He sat on the bed and smiled. Yes, he would have an ideal headquarters. He ran an extension phone out the window and into the motor home and installed it on the small eating table. It would be his desk.

He checked the propane refrigerator. Yes. Four kinds of fruit juices, ice cream, and even ice cubes. Nothing was too good for Allah's fighting warriors at the front.

The colonel sat down suddenly. Soon his men would be fighting and many of them dying on the field of battle. War. It had been described as man's greatest adventure. Where else could a man find such challenges, so much emotion and purpose and the thrill of a good fight? Nothing could match the rush of battle, of pitting your men and machines against those of the enemy, no matter who he was. To fight, to live or die by your wits, by your own skill, by pure chance, or even perhaps by design.

Colonel Hamdoon had no death wish. He would be well in back of any battle. Enemy airpower and land mines would present his biggest danger.

He went over his master checklist. Each of his men right down to a company commander had a schedule tailored to his unit and his duties. The colonel would get no sleep tonight, a little tomorrow afternoon as his motor home moved toward the front. The army had 280 miles to cover to get into position. Some would be ten miles closer than that. Some right near the border. No unit would be closer than twenty miles when darkness closed in on the desert the next afternoon. After dark, the units would move in military precision, each to its own assigned location, ready to do its singular duty come the dawn.

He breathed deeply for a moment as a wave of emotion broke over him. *"To let slip the dogs of war."* He thought of another quote: *"Battle's magnificently stern array."*

His phone rang.

Now it would start. The decisions, the problems, the worry. Now he would start earning his colonel's pay. He picked up the phone and began solving problems.

Even as he did, thousands of men were reporting back to their units from leaves and passes, and preparing to go to war. Not even the midlevel officers knew that this was the real thing and not just an exercise. They would be told later that this was no drill.

The phone rang again, and he picked it up.

USS *Enterprise* CVN 65

Murdock and DeWitt found Al Adams sitting up in his bed in sick bay. The doctor told them that he was still medicated and might not make a lot of sense yet when he talked. He would recognize them, though.

"Hey there, Adams, looks like you got it made down here with nothing to do but look at the nurses."

Adams turned and looked at Murdock, but it took a time for his eyes to focus. At last he nodded. "Hi, Skipper. I fucked up."

"Not so, Adams," DeWitt said. "Hell, could have happened to any of us. We didn't know what kind of mines they had planted along there."

"I fucked up, JG. I'll never be a damn SEAL again. Fucked myself right out of the Navy, too, I bet."

"Hey, we don't even know how well that wing is going to work," DeWitt said. "Might be better than new, with chips and microcircuits. Hell, Adams, you could be the first bionic SEAL."

A touch of a grin flickered across his face; then he shook his head. "No way, JG. Both know it. Won't go to air ops or engineering. I'm a SEAL or I'm a damned civilian. No other way."

"Just hold it there, Adams," Murdock said. "You're a SEAL as long as I say you are. Right now, your SEAL job is to do exactly what these medics tell you to do and get yourself fit for duty. I won't tolerate any other attitude. You read me, sailor?"

Adams blinked, his eyes went wide, and he almost

grinned. "Yes, sir, Commander, sir. Hoooorah."

Murdock smiled. "Yes, SEAL, that's more like it. Anything you want they won't give you?"

"Yeah, Skip. I'd like some M&M's peanut candy. One of them big bags."

"You got it, SEAL," DeWitt said. "You rest easy, and some of the guys will be down to see you."

"Aye, aye, JG. Thanks for coming by."

Murdock looked at Adams's left arm. It was in a complicated brace made of aluminum rods and held rigidly in place. The sewn-together tubes and nerves and muscles and tendons had to have time to heal back together. It would be a long process.

The two officers left the room and found the doctor who attached the arm.

"Can't tell yet how it will do. Most of the patch jobs should take and work fine. It's the number of those that don't that concern us. First, the arm has to have a good blood supply and return. That's the biggest. Without that, there's no way the arm attachment will work. Then comes the nerves and the ligaments and muscles. It's always a chancy thing. Once we know the blood flow works, and the arm will stay alive, then we have a chance to work on the other problems as they arise."

"When will you know about the blood, Doctor?" Murdock asked.

"If it doesn't work right in three days, the arm will start to die from lack of blood. In three days we should know that score."

They thanked the doctor and found out where Holt was. He was ready to be kicked out of his bed. He chuckled when he saw the two coming.

"Hey, no damn funeral arrangements yet for me, Skipper. I'm getting my walking papers out of here. I can see better than when I signed on in this man's Navy."

"For sure?" DeWitt asked.

"Fucking A right, JG. I'm fit for damned duty. What we got on the fire?"

"Glad to have you back, Holt. Now I won't have to break in another radioman." Murdock left DeWitt talking with Holt and located the eye man who had worked on Holt.

"What can I say, Commander," the Doctor said. He was a full commander and the top ophthalmologist on the carrier. "There is no lasting damage to the eyes. If I had to guess, I'd say the blindness was about half shock from the sudden light and the rest from psychological damage of seeing his buddy's blown-off arm almost in his lap. The physical damage is slight, if any, and he's fit for duty. Just keep him away from land mines for a while."

Murdock thanked the doctor, picked up DeWitt, and they walked the deck.

"Not a chance Adams can stay in SEALs," DeWitt said. "That arm will never be strong enough again to do the rope climb or go up a rope ladder into a chopper. He'll be lucky if he can tie his shoelaces."

"Probably, but let's keep his hopes up until he's farther along in his recovery. Can't hurt a thing. You'll be one man short in your squad again."

"Getting to be a habit, Skip."

"True, been wanting to talk to you about taking better care of your men."

They both laughed and kept walking. It was good to be out in the fresh air again and to watch the training exercises as the F-18s and the Tomcats surged off the deck from the catapults. It was the fastest drag race in the books. They went from a dead stop to 150 miles an hour or so in five seconds.

"How is Senior Chief Dobler working out?" DeWitt asked.

"So far, he's been a help. Another couple of missions, and he's going to be wound in tightly with the men. That's the important element. If they won't work for him, then we would have to get a new man. I think he's melding into the platoon well. Any problems with him from your end?"

"No. I'd say he's working well and has been a help in handling the men. He should be taking some of the administration load off your shoulders. That's good. Then we can have more barbecues and have more chess games."

When they returned to the SEALs assembly room. Dobler had the men cleaning and oiling their assigned weapons.

Don Stroh was there, pacing up and down. When he saw the two officers come in, he headed for them.

"Need to talk," he said. They went to their usual conference area at the far end of the compartment where three chairs had been left.

"What'n hell now?" Murdock asked.

"Nothing, that's the problem," Stroh said. "Here the whole place is going to hell in a shitbasket, and the boss hasn't a thing for you guys to do."

"We can't help out on the no-fly zone," DeWitt said.

"No way we can do anything about Saddam's rejection of the U.N. embargoes," Murdock said. "What do you suggest that we should be doing? Want us to declare war on the old boy ourselves and do a suicide run against him?"

"You're a pair of jokers. I could get more sympathy from the back blast of a jet up on deck. We're a whore's breath from an open war with Saddam, and we just sit here doing nothing? Like he says no more no-fly zone. So what do we do, send three hundred planes in there and swamp anybody he puts up? No, we actually cut *back* on our overfly. Now, why the hell did we do that?"

"You're a lot closer to them than anybody on board," Murdock said. "Call them up and ask them."

Stroh shook his head and managed a small chuckle. "You really want to get rid of me, don't you? I do that, and I'd be pushing paper at some weird desk in Langley like the Antarctica Overview desk."

"So relax, Stroh," Murdock said. "Work out in the gym; must be a pool table on board somewhere. Have a game of nine ball."

"Hey, Stroh is getting up there, you know the older man's disease," DeWitt said. "He should be on Proscar, I'm sure. Maybe some BPH pills like Hytrin would bring down his nocturia a little."

"Huh, JG? What the hell you talking about?"

"Your prostate and your urinary life. Older guys like you get the runs at night."

"Ridiculous. I just wish the office would tell me something. We just sit and wait."

"Oh, hell yes," DeWitt said. "We haven't fired a shot in over thirty-six hours. Must be something wrong somewhere. Got to keep them SEALs swimming, or they forget how."

Murdock laughed. "Yeah, Stroh. What you need is something to relax you. Take your mind off the bad stuff. You said you play chess. Ever taken on the JG here? He's the platoon champ. He swears he can beat anybody in the platoon in under ten minutes."

"Ten minutes? Hell, I can stall that long. Where's your set, JG? You're on."

The two played twelve games of chess in a row. Lieutenant (j.g.) DeWitt won the first four in under ten minutes. The next two took him almost fifteen minutes, and the man from the CIA at last won the tenth game. Then the JG got serious and beat Stroh the last two games in under eight minutes.

"Give," Stroh said. He stood up and stretched. "Murdock's right; I'm not mad at Langley anymore. Now I'm pissed at DeWitt."

20

Iraqi Army GHQ
Near Baghdad

Colonel Jarash Hamdoon worked the rest of the afternoon and until nearly midnight in his motor home office just outside of his regular office. He had his lieutenant and sergeant working telephones as well, and at midnight called in the lieutenant to take over while he had three hours of sleep.

Lieutenant Salman was just over twenty-five, eager, a hard worker, and he knew precisely how the colonel would handle things.

"Answer any questions they ask except the one about this being a drill. Tell them as on any such maneuver, they will have to wait until the final time in the field to find out. It is the same as with any mobilization like this."

The colonel was pleased with his work so far. The army was rolling. Already he had more than two divisions on the road. They were self-contained fighting units with their own tanks and artillery and some of his best fighting men. They would give an excellent account of themselves under fire.

Other units were gathering and would be moving soon. All must be on the way before noon tomorrow. His spotter aircraft had reported that the Syrian border where they would attack was nearly free of any units in strength. A company of infantry and two tanks were in one location, and ten miles away, another company of infantry and one tank had been spotted.

The plan called for a five-mile-wide offensive, driving the attack forward with tanks and airpower. They would send 200 planes on a preemptive strike against the three major Syrian airfields, with the hope of knocking down more than half of the Syrian airpower on the first day. That attack also would come at dawn on A day, or Attack day.

Colonel Hamdoon couldn't sleep. After a half hour of trying in the soft bed of the motor home, he got up, put on his boots, and had his driver take him home. He lived on the outskirts of the town in a reserved section for military officers only. The sergeant driver parked in front of the house and Hamdoon went in, woke up his wife, and told her just enough to make her anxious.

He had often compared Arab women with those from the West. Some aspects of Western women he liked, but they were too loud, too demanding, and too disrespectful of their husbands. Not so an Arab woman. She knew her place and was content to live under those ancient traditions.

"You will be gone many weeks?" his wife asked.

"We do not know. It is a secret, and you must not tell anyone. It is a big maneuver on the desert to the west."

"Then I must please you." She took off her nightdress the way he liked, which drove him wild with desire. Four times they made love, and he went into the small kitchen naked and cooked a big breakfast, then returned to her once more and left her panting on the bed, naked, and beckoning to him for one more lovemaking.

"You think I am a horse, woman, and out to stud? You have exhausted me. Not even a naked belly dancer could excite me. Now I must go and make war."

He kissed the foreheads of his two sons, six and eight, patted his one girl, who was ten, where she slept, and went out to the car. The sergeant driver must have seen the lights in the house. He was ready with the back door of the sedan open.

Back at the motor home, Lieutenant Salman was in the middle of an exchange on the phone.

"Just a moment. Colonel Hamdoon is here. He will tell

you." The lieutenant held his hand over the phone. "This idiot wants to know when his army unit will be returning because he has a horse show he must attend."

Colonel Hamdoon took the phone. "What is your name, rank, and unit?" He waited for the reply. "Captain, your job is to work with your infantrymen, not worry about your stupid horses. This is a joint military exercise with the armor and air force. We are not sure when it will end, but your horse show will not be a factor. When is your unit set to leave?"

He listened. "In four hours. So, don't you have many other tasks to perform rather than worrying about your horses? I'd advise you to do your job, Captain. I have your name and unit. I'll check on you later."

Lieutenant Salman grinned as the colonel hung up the phone. "I tried to tell him that, but he kept reminding me he was a captain and I only a lowly lieutenant."

"You did well. Any problems in my absence?"

"One convoy of trucks with food and ammunition is stalled forty miles outside of town. One truck is holding up the convoy."

"Contact the radio and tell them to instruct the convoy commander to push the stalled truck off the roadway, leave it, and continue his trip and to make up the time he has lost. He must reach his designated area on time."

"Yes sir."

"Anything else?"

"Two company commanders can't be located. They were on leave in the mountains."

"Promote the next officer in line as company commander and get them moving on time, or tail feathers will burn."

An hour before dawn, Saddam Hussein walked into the motor home, and the sergeant shrilled for attention. Lieutenant Salman and Colonel Hamdoon came to attention.

"Gentlemen, at ease. I won't distract you long from your work. My reports show many units racing toward the border. We have released an announcement about the maneuvers being held and that no one needs to worry."

He stepped in front of Lieutenant Salman. "Lieutenant, you are hereby promoted to captain. Here are your bars. Wear them proudly." He moved to the colonel. "Old friend

Jarash, comrade of many struggles, you are now to be known as Brigadier General Hamdoon." He pinned gold stars on the new general's collars and saluted him smartly. He turned to go, and the sergeant called for attention again. Then the tall man with the heavy black mustache and black hair walked out of the trailer and stepped back inside his armored limousine.

The sudden promotions took a moment to register, then the sergeant led a great cheer and the captain joined in. After a few cheers, General Hamdoon shook hands with both men.

"Now, I believe it's time to get back to work."

Just at dawn, the sergeant returned with food and cooked breakfast for the three of them.

The phone rang less often now. General Hamdoon decided that he and the driver would leave the GHQ at noon and drive to the assembly point some twenty miles from the border. He would keep in contact with Captain Salman by radio on the hour. Otherwise, the captain would solve the problems getting the last units out of their barracks and on the road from several different towns.

He sent the sergeant out after more food from the supply rooms at the army base. They wanted field food that would last: canned food and loaves of bread, other canned and dried meat and fish. They stored it in the motor home. They refilled the water tank with potable water, and then they were ready.

The roads west were packed with army units. Usually, both sides of the road were taken over by trucks and tanks moving west. Roads were good and handled the traffic well as far as Ar-Ramadi on the Euphrates River. From there the track led almost due west and almost at once into the areas of wadi and desert. For a time, the trucks followed one of the oil pipelines that in better times had transported oil through Syria to ports on the Mediterranean.

This same route had been used several times for maneuvers. In places, road building crews had filled in wadis for easier crossings. Trucks began to fail and pull out of the way. Men and matériel were overloaded into other trucks and the movement continued.

After six hours, they crossed the Wadi Hawran. The direction turned slightly to the southwest now as they were still well north of the desert community of Ar-Rutbah.

Soon units pulled to the side and found their location. Many of the support elements were farther from the border. Some of the infantry and tanker units moved closer, but none within twenty miles of the border with Syria.

When General Hamdoon reached his assigned location a little under twenty miles from the Syrian border, he had the driver bring his motor home next to a pair of tanks and what looked like two companies of infantry. His rig came to a stop, and he got out and stretched his legs in the desert heat. The air-conditioning in the motor home had made the drive less taxing than on the other men.

He soon made radio contact with one of the military aircraft flying over the area and asked the pilot about any buildup on the Syrian side. The aircraft, while staying on the Iraqi side of the border, could see thirty miles into Syria, and the copilot reported that they could make out no buildup or any movement of large numbers of troops or mechanized units toward the border.

The general nodded and went back to his small desk. He sipped at a cold orange juice from the refrigerator and invited the captain and sergeant to participate.

They would sleep now and be up as soon as it was midnight. From then on, there would be much to do.

Captain Hadr saw the motor home pull in beside his tank and frowned. It must be some high-ranking officer to rate such glorious transportation. He had sweat 250 miles in his tank since yesterday early in the afternoon. He was exhausted, dirty, and hungry.

Captain Hadr was not at all amused by this call to arms for a mere exercise, a maneuver. He was one of the tanker reservists called up to take a tank into the battle line. Twice before, he had done the same thing, killing a week of time on each occasion. During both exercises, his small business had lost money. He figured that his partner had profited during his absence by pocketing what otherwise would have been company money.

Now another of these sudden calls to arms. When he saw someone come out of the motor home, he snorted. A damn general, no less. He would expect to be protected. Once they started their fake charge toward the Syrian border, he would be rid of the general. Since everyone knew that generals never came within twenty miles of any fighting.

Captain Hadr had left his wife and three small boys back in Ba'qubah, north of Baghdad, with the promise that he would be back within a week. He had pleaded with his brother-in-law to take care of their small accounting business while he was gone. The man was ten years older than Captain Hadr, which meant he had ten years' more experience in cheating his partner. Sometimes Captain Hadr hated the army. He knew it was necessary, but why such a large one?

Some said there were 440,000 Syrians under arms. Active military, not counting reserves. That was well over 2 percent of the entire population. He had heard that many of the Western nations had less than one-half of 1 percent of their population in the military.

He shrugged at last and ate his evening meal of dried fruit and water. He soon would run out of both. He had learned not to rely on the food supply from the Iraqi Tank Corps. He went back inside his tank and looked at the maps.

Orders were to move forward toward the border three hours before daylight. He was the third man in line in his sixteen-tank company. They would go single file for the first eighteen miles, then spread out in the spearhead tank attack that they had practiced so often but never actually used in battle. Captain Hadr was just as happy he had never had to fire a shot in anger. He wasn't sure that he would be able to shoot and kill another human being, another Arab, another Moslem.

His tank was one of the older Soviet models they had bought early on and now were having trouble finding parts for. It was the T-55. Only the active-duty tankers had the Soviet-built T-62 models that were larger and heavier, with better armor and more firepower. But he'd take what he had. He had mastered the smaller tank and would put it through its paces for the inspectors and judges on tomorrow's dry run at the Syrian border. He wondered how many Syrian tanks would be on the line just across the border tomorrow at daylight to play the little game with them.

It was all a game, and he would glad when it was over and he was back in his own little home and working in his business.

Captain Hadr read his orders again. They said he would wait with his company here twenty miles from the border until three hours before dawn, then move forward to a point a half mile from the border, as determined by his company commander. Then, with first light, he and his company would get in an arrowhead attack formation and would lead the charge through the border and into Syria for twenty miles, where they would pause to let their ammunition and food supplies catch up with them. Then they would charge ahead another twenty miles.

There was no sign that the orders would be countermanded when they were within a hundred yards of the boundary. He doubted if anyone could tell exactly where the border was here in the desert, anyway. It was one scrub bush after another, and no line in the sand to show the border.

On a hunch, he left his tank and walked fifty meters over to his company commander's tank. It was one of the bigger Soviet T-62s. He was Captain Kayf, and in the regular army. He greeted Hadr and offered him a piece of bread and cheese.

They ate in silence a time, then Hadr shook his head. "Our orders, Captain, they don't give the break-off point. Isn't there a chance that we will make a mistake and slide over the border into Syria?"

"No mistake," Captain Kayf said. "I received the word about an hour ago. Tomorrow morning, we go into Syria with our guns blazing. We are invading Syria and hoping we can punch a corridor all the way to Damascus and capture it. It's war, Hadr. Tomorrow morning, we fire the opening shots in war with Syria."

"Captain, it can't be. Surely it's only a trick to make us think this exercise is really important when in reality it's only maneuvers for training."

Captain Kayf shook his head. "No, Hadr. I have had word from The general of the division. We are going in. Did you notice the unusual number of support trucks loaded to their axles with ammunition and supplies? They are here and will be right behind us as we crash over the border tomorrow at dawn. We expect no opposition for the first twenty miles or more. We might not fire a shot for those first twenty miles. We are at war, Hadr. I wasn't supposed to tell the tank commanders until morning, but I couldn't hold it back. This could be my one chance to make major. I must do my best for President Hussein."

"How can this be? I'm only a reservist. I train on weekends and in the summer. My commission is only temporary. How can this be a shooting war? I have my business to go back to, and my wife and three sons."

"With all of that at stake, my friend Captain Hadr, I suggest you follow orders carefully and shoot your cannon with great accuracy. Then you'll have the best chance to live through this six- or seven-day war before we capture Syria and make it one of our provinces."

"I can't believe it."

"You better believe it, Captain. Right now you have less than three hours to sleep before we fire up our engines and move out toward Syria."

"Who can sleep? There are a dozen things to check on the tank. What about the fuel? What about that tread that was slightly loose? How can I get everything done in time?"

"All the tanks have been fueled to capacity, remember? Just after we arrived. Your load of ammunition was checked and double-checked. Your men are sleeping and will be ready. Go back to your machine and take a nap. It will serve you well when we break across the Syrian line."

Captain Hadr stood there, looking at his immediate superior. He started to salute, then shook his head. "Captain, just suppose that one of your tank commanders decided that he didn't want to get into a real war and said he wouldn't take his tank across the line into Syria. What would happen then?"

Captain Kayf smiled in the darkness. In a moment, he had drawn the .45-caliber pistol from his holster and leveled it at Hadr. "Then Captain, I would simply shoot that commander dead, promote one of my other men to take over his tank, and our attack would continue. Does that answer your hypothetical question?"

Hadr shrugged. "Yes sir. It does." He paused, thinking about his wife and boys back home. "I guess I should get an hour or so of sleep. I'll probably need it in the next two or three days."

He turned and walked into the night.

Captain Kayf kept his pistol trained on the man's back until he could no longer see him. Then he returned the .45

to his holster. When the attack began tomorrow morning and all of his men were told that it was not a drill but that they were going to war with Syria, he was sure that he would have one man quit and try to back out. He would be shot, of course.

Yes, there would be one reservist officer turn coward. It would not be Captain Hadr, the company commander was positive of that. He turned back to his own tank and looked over his list of items to have done before dawn. He was almost finished.

With a vague, hostile feeling, he thought of the moment when they would break across the Syrian border. It would be a thrill, the high of his lifetime. Even now he wondered just what it would feel like. How thrilling and wonderful would it be? He could only imagine it now. In four or five hours, he would feel it with heat-pounding reality.

21

Three Miles from the Border
In Western Iraq

Sergeant Hillah made sure his squad of infantrymen was down and sleeping. They had been ferried by truck, then walked, then taken by truck again, as transportation became available. The whole battalion had walked the last four miles forward. Now they lay less than three hundred yards from what their captain said was Syria's eastern border.

Sergeant Hillah didn't understand. None of their war games in the past had brought them this close to the border with Syria. Once they had stopped two miles out and saw that there were more than a thousand men facing them just across the border with tanks and armored personnel carriers and heavy machine guns set up every fifty yards. They had turned and marched away.

Now they were lying in wait, within a fast sprint of the border, and they all had live ammunition. It was dark tonight, so dark he could barely see the end man of his squad. The company captain told them there would be a meeting of all NCOs at midnight. It was ten minutes until that time.

He left his squad and walked quickly to the spot designated as the company HQ. It was a slight depression in the ground at the edge of a wadi. The other noncommissioned officers were gathering. They whispered, but no one knew any more than Sergeant Hillah did. Their captain came right on time and motioned the eighteen men around him. He spoke low, but it was so quiet that they all could hear him.

"Men, this is not a drill. When daylight comes, we will attack across the Syrian border with the objective of taking Damascus before sunset tomorrow."

"We're at war with Syria?" someone asked.

"As of this morning, we will be. We will be following sixteen tanks that come through this sector. They will arrive here at three A.M., be briefed, and strung out in their battle formation. When the time comes to advance, we'll be going behind the tanks as far as we can keep up with them.

"After that, we'll mop up any of the enemy left over. We expect little resistance for the first fifty miles. Other troops will be in vehicles and will follow the tanks closely, dropping off strike teams to take care of civilians or dig out scattered groups of Syrian border guard troops that may be in the area. We expect few.

"The only way we'll get to Damascus is to walk. We may be moved along faster by special trucks if the situation warrants it. Since we'll be in the rear areas most of the time, we should have few if any casualties. That's a lot better than a direct attack with a frontal assault along the way on some hard point. Questions?"

"What about our kitchen?"

"It will be on its usual truck, along with supply, your second packs, and two officer jeeps. We'll get hot meals when we can and sack lunches when we can't. We may not eat much the first day. It all depends on how fast the tanks and their mobile troops can slash forward.

"We'll have all troops awake and ready to march at 0430. It should be light somewhere around a half hour later. We'll follow the tanks. If they move out early, we go right behind them. Don't spread out too far, and keep contact. We don't want any sprinters a mile ahead of the rest of the company. Is that clear?"

"Sir, won't we lose the tanks in the first ten minutes? They can do thirty miles an hour."

"True, but with them out front, leading the way, we should find little resistance as we move ahead. If they get too far ahead, they'll be ordered to stop, or the regiment will move us up with trucks. That's all. Get some sleep if you can. Hard telling when we'll be able to sleep again."

Another sergeant walking back to his squad with Hillah shook his head at the idea. "If they want a mechanized attack, they should give us trucks, all of us infantry, so we could keep up. After the first hour, we won't even hear those tanks they'll be so far ahead. Nothing out here to stop them. I heard the air force talking on a radio. They said there aren't any troops of more than squad size anywhere along this area until you get twenty miles into Syria."

When he arrived at the spot where his squad was, Sergeant Hillah sat down near them, but he couldn't sleep. War! He had known it was possible, but things seemed so settled down. Now he was looking at shooting and killing and getting wounded or killed. All he could think about then was his bride back in Al-Amirah in southern Iraq. He might never see his new baby be born. He refused to think about that. He had a war to fight, so he would fight.

When 0430 came, Sergeant Hillah had his eight men ready. All had their equipment checked, their rifles readied. Each weapon was locked and loaded, and they were in their combat order with Sergeant Hillah out in front.

An hour before, Hillah had watched the tanks come through the infantry. A tanker had walked in front of each of the lumbering, metal monsters, moving infantrymen out of the way so nobody got crushed under the treads.

Now, the tanks sat less than fifty yards from the border and the troops gathered behind each one and spread to both sides. The sixteen tanks were fifty yards apart, covering eight hundred yards along the border. That was about the distance the First Battalion spread out.

Sergeant Hillah looked at the lighted face of his wristwatch. It had been a present from his wife. At 0445 he already he could see streaks of light in the east. Would they wait until 0500 or go when it was light enough? He'd soon know.

Ten minutes later he heard the big diesel engines in the tanks turn over and then growl and purr as they warmed up.

Precisely at 0500, the tankers moved out in a line at a walking pace. The infantry came up and ran after them. Hillah's squad was to the right side of the fourth tank in the line. It had a large 34 painted on the back. He would remember it.

The tanks picked up speed, and by the time they reached what Hillah figured must be the border, they were moving at least twenty miles an hour. Then they went faster. The troops fell behind and settled down to a slogging march forward. Each squad had a section of the desert to cover. Now their line became straighter as they connected with the next squad and moved out with five yards between men.

So far, they had not heard nor seen a shot fired. The tanks rolled forward, kicking up a dust trail across the windless desert. Soon a freshening morning breeze sent the dust cloud chasing the tanks and leaving the men cleaner air to breathe.

Sergeant Hillah bellowed at his men to keep the line straight, to watch ahead. They were not in the tank's tracks, and there could be mines laid along here anywhere. That made the men slow just a little and watch where they walked.

A half hour after the thrust began, the infantry, slogging along behind the tanks, heard the first shots of the war. Two tanks blasted with their cannon, and the sound came rushing back toward the infantry.

"Now the war has really started," Sergeant Hillah shouted. "Look alive now, there could be some Syrians lurking around here soon."

Near Duma, Syria

The flight of twelve Iraqi MiG Flogger-Ds had come out of the Syrian desert just before dawn barely a hundred feet off the sand. They slanted up enough to miss the built-up area as they thundered over the forty miles of heavily populated territory between the desert and the capital. Then they curved slightly north of Damascus and zeroed in on one of the three main Syrian military airfields.

It was just getting light when Captain Muhammad Dasht angled his Flogger-D at the parking area where he saw the lineup of twenty of Syria's best jet fighters. He smiled as he readied his napalm bombs and his total of eight thousand pounds of more napalm and cluster bombs. He dropped four napalm bombs on the first run. On both sides of him, his wingmen did the same, saturating the whole parking strip with the blistering hot flames of the jellied gasoline.

After the first pass, he looked back and could see half the jets burning. Explosions rocked the field as one fuel tank after another on the Syrian jets blew up, scattering more flaming fuel into other jets.

Antlike creatures on the ground scurried from one to another of the jets not yet burning, trying desperately to get them into the air.

They didn't have time.

The second pass of the twelve jets lathered the remaining fighters with more napalm and cluster bombs; then they turned to the hangars and support shops, tearing them apart with their bombs and napalm.

All too quickly, Captain Dasht realized that his plate was empty; he had nothing left but his 23mm two-barrel cannon. He made two strafing runs on more buildings and vehicles, expending his 200 rounds quickly. Then he kicked the big fighter into a climb and searched with his radar for enemy aircraft. He did slow circles but found nothing on his radar.

"Let's go home," he radioed the rest of his flight. They emptied their guns and lifted upward, where they would have better fuel economy and speed, and raced across Syria into the desert and then on home to their base near Baghdad. They did not lose a single plane. None of the twelve had even been fired at by enemy aircraft or from the ground. The Syrian ground defense did not seem to be working, or the strike was such a surprise that no one was on duty to man the antiair defense.

Captain Dasht smiled as he angled his Flogger-D in for a landing. So far, this war was going very well for Iraq. He couldn't wait for the debriefing and to tell how they had wiped out at least twenty jet fighter aircraft on the ground. It would be an attack that would long be remembered in Iraqi military history.

Twelve Miles into Syria

Captain Hadr stood in his tank, watching out from the hatch. So far, he had not used the cannon. There had been no targets. His machine gun had been fired three times at infantry.

The Syrian soldiers had scattered, and at least half had been killed or wounded. Each time, there had been no more than a dozen Syrian infantrymen. They would be no trouble.

His radio came on, and he listened carefully.

"Company, we may have some trouble just ahead. The lead tank reports a pair of Syrian tanks, the T-55 type. They evidently have dug in with just their cannons and turrets showing. It looks like they have been ordered to stand and fight."

"Range?" someone asked.

"Twenty-five hundred yards. They haven't fired yet."

"Flank them," Captain Kayf said.

"Go, Hadr. Take a forty-five to the right. I'll take a forty-five to the left. Fire as soon as you see the side of the tank. Race you."

Both tanks slanted out on an angle and raced through the desert. Captain Hadr kept looking through his sights and range finder to his left. At last he saw a mound that looked out of place. Yes, the tank had prepared a nest. The side bank of dirt wasn't high enough to hide the tank. He swung his machine around; the gunner sighted in on the tank and fired.

Just after the first round, Captain Kayf's tank fired. Both rounds hit the Syrian tank and jolted large pieces of it into the air. Evidently, some rounds inside went off. The second tank in the blocking position turned and charged to the west and was soon lost in the dirt cloud it produced.

The Iraqi tanks re-formed, then charged ahead again.

"Well past the ten-mile mark," Captain Hadr told his crew. "Wonder when we stop and regroup and let the infantry catch up?"

A moment later, a furious geyser of dirt, dust, and shrapnel exploded twenty yards in front of them.

"Hard left turn," Captain Hadr yelled at his driver. He swiveled around to the right to try to find the tank that had fired at him. He couldn't find it. A thousand yards away, a pale haze of smoke hung over some brush near a small spring. Then another puff of smoke appeared in the same spot. Hadr yelled at his gunner and spun the gun around. The tank's old computer figured the range and settings, and before the other tank could fire again, Captain Hadr sent a round in counterbattery. It exploded in the brush, then nothing. No fire from a tank burning, no men running from the brush, no return fire, either.

"We either scared him away or hurt him," Captain Hadr said and reported the shot to his commander.

Captain Kayf took his report. "Good shooting. In another two miles, we'll have come fifteen. There we stop and let the rest of them catch up with us and give us some lateral support. Our flanks right now are wide open."

They had no more action in the next two miles. They went down the gentle side of a wadi and up the other side and set up their line of tanks on a small ridge that gave them a view for eight miles to the west across the desert floor. They could see no sign of life.

"Tank commanders, pop the lid and take a look around. There must be some Syrian air out there somewhere," the tank's radio said. "Let's see that they don't catch us by surprise. Just how effective their air is depends on what kind of air-to-ground missiles they have. Let's hope they don't have the guided kind. Look sharp."

It was almost an hour before any of the other elements caught up. Then it was half a dozen armored personnel carriers. They parked on the near side of the wadi and waved at the tankers. A Russian jeep pulled up next. It hesitated on the top of the wadi, then drove down and up the other side and stopped at the first tank. A bird colonel came out of the jeep and called to the tanker on top.

He was directed down three rigs to the tank company commander.

The Syrian MiG-29 Fulcrum-A came out of the desert without a hint of any forward sound. Someone shouted, then the big fighter dropped a missile. It ignited at once at two hundred feet and jetted at Mach 2 on line at the tank commander's machine. Before the men could more than look up in wonder, the four-hundred-pound missile exploded on the front of the tank. It erupted in a shattering roar as thirty of the high-explosive cannon rounds inside the tank went off in a sympathetic detonation.

The jet screamed overhead and made a sweeping turn and headed back.

The tank was a shattered hulk of twisted metal and smoking shards. The jeep had been caught in the explosion as well, and its fuel tank went up to finish the jeep and kill the colonel and the driver.

By the time the jet came back, the .50-caliber machine guns on the armored personnel carriers were activated and met the jet head-on with a chattering fire of hot lead. It wavered early on, and the second missile missed its target, but the shrapnel killed a tank commander who stood in his machine.

The Syrian MiG-29 Fulcrum made one more run but high up, evidently surveying the mass of men and machines so far inside Syria. Then it streaked away to the west.

Captain Hadr grabbed an AK-47 and jumped to the ground. The commander's tank was gone, disintegrated. The commander and his crew were dead, too. He had slammed three rounds at the Syrian jet when it made its second pass.

He shook his head. In an instant, the commander and his crew were dead. It could happen to him. He watched another Russian jeep drive down the wadi and up the near side. It stopped next to his tank, and a colonel looked at him.

"Captain, one of these tanks yours?"

Captain Hadr saluted smartly. "Yes, Colonel. This one, number 34."

"You are now promoted to major and are in command of this tank group. You still have fifteen tanks. I'll bring you a new radio so I can contact you. When we're ready, you'll move out in the spearhead again and work the way your company did today.

"Too bad about Captain Kayf. Things like this happen in a war. I'm Colonel Irbil. We'll be in this position for the rest of the afternoon and evening. I'll have a platoon of infantry out in front of you as a security patrol. Talk to your men." The colonel shook his head. "No, let me use your radio, and I'll talk to them." The colonel climbed into the tank and used the tank-to-tank radio and told the men about their new commander, Major Hadr. He came out quickly and headed back across the wadi, where more and more troops and equipment were gathering.

Hadr went to the first tank and talked to the men, his men. Damn, he was a major now.

22

USS _Enterprise_ CVN 65
Lieutenant Commander Blake Murdock and Ed DeWitt looked at Don Stroh where the SEALs had assembled in their room on the carrier.

"So that's it?" Murdock asked.

"That's it," Stroh said. "Simple little job. Those two Iranian submarines have been prowling around the _Enterprise_ again, and we've had permission to go in and take them out. Yes, we have some submarines in the gulf, but it's only three hundred feet deep except in two spots. No sub driver likes those kinds of conditions. No place to dive to in case of trouble. One sub commander told me he felt like he was a sitting duck in a bathtub here in the gulf."

"Why doesn't our sub sink their sub?" Murdock asked.

"That would be an official act, an act of war. We're not at war with Iran. But when we send you men in sub rosa, it could be just a whopping big accident, or maybe Syria sabotaged them."

"Syria," DeWitt said. "We're going to get dragged into that one, aren't we?"

"I have no way of knowing," Stroh said. "But if there were an official request from the Syrian government . . . I'll let you decide that one for yourself. In the meantime, we have our small mission. Two medium-sized subs in the Iranian port of Bandar Abbas, which is on the Iranian side of the Strait of Hormuz."

"Night mission," Murdock said. "I'd guess you'll want us to leave at first dark."

"Thereabouts. It's not an easy target. This sub pen is at the port, but there are a scattering of little islands and one big one just offshore. After dark, our guys say they can get you past the islands and hope not to get shot out of the sky. They can move you within two miles of the port."

"A two-mile swim, no problem. A chopper?"

"Your old friend the Sea Knight. Plenty of room for your goodies. Take IBSs if you want. The Knight can get in there at a hundred and fifty miles an hour. It's about a hundred and twenty miles from the carrier over there. We're still watching the strait and flying some guard duty on it, so the Iranians might not get too upset if we stray a little. Well inside the radius range of the Knight. What's your best choice?"

Murdock called up Dobler and Jaybird. "Let's do some talking about it. Then we'll let you know. It's about 1300. Get back to you in a half hour. Oh, how big are these subs?"

"Russian built, two hundred thirty-eight feet long. Diesel power. Been in the Iranian navy since 1992. Carry eighteen torpedoes and can cause a lot of hurt. So the boss wants them out of action. Blow off their propellers, blast a hole in the bow, or drop them in the mud of the harbor. Up to you."

Stroh left the room without a good-bye. He'd be back. Jaybird and Dobler caught the last bit from Stroh.

"A sub?" Jaybird asked. "We're going after an Iranian submarine?"

"Unless it comes after us first," DeWitt said. "Sit down, and let's talk. How can we best take out two Iranian submarines about a hundred and twenty miles away from here?"

"On the Iranian coast?" Dobler asked.

Murdock told them the where, about the islands, and the thought of going in by Sea Knight.

"Yeah, the range is okay," Dobler said. "We can sneak in under any radar they might have. But what about patrol boats? The Iranians have a whole scumbag full of patrol boats of all sizes."

"They also have three frigates and two corvettes with a lot of missile firepower that would make our IBSs mincemeat," Murdock said. "You jokers want to live forever?"

"Yes," the other three said in unison.

"Then what and how?"

"How close can a Sea Knight get us to the harbor?" Dobler asked.

"Stroh said two miles, but we'll have to talk to the chopper pilot. He's gonna be slicin' and dicin' to get in that close."

"Even at that, we'd have to swim in with the rebreathers," Jaybird said. "The IBSs might work, but they would be a much easier target for some patrol boat to see."

"I'd say if they can get us within five miles of the target, we go with our wet suits and rebreathers," DeWitt said. "Might depend on how much ordnance we're gonna be packing."

"First getting there," Murdock said. They booted it around for another ten minutes. Quickly they ruled out a chopper drop on land, negated the idea of a parachute drop HALO, and came back to the Sea King and the rebreathers.

"Sounds best, gents," Dobler said. "If we used the IBSs and got cut up by a patrol boat, we could lose half our ordnance. We go in slower but with ninety-nine percent chance of a surprise mission."

Murdock called to Ching and had him go find Stroh. The CIA man came in. Evidently, he'd been standing in the companionway, waiting for them.

"We need to talk to the chopper pilot who would take us in on his Sea Knight," Murdock said. Stroh went to the phone and made three calls. Then he motioned to Murdock, who took the handset.

"Lieutenant West Jones, Commander," the voice on the wire said. "What can I do for you?"

"You know where Bandar Abbas is opposite the Straight of Hormuz?"

"Right, Commander. Some of us have been talking about a run in there. Shitpot full of islands in front of the navy base there. Don't know if they are fortified or not. They should have some antiair missiles out there."

"Say you're going in there after dark. How close could you get fifteen SEALs to that navy base?"

There was a silence, then the flyer let out a long breath. "Yeah, thought you might be asking that. I talked with my CO, and he says I have the assignment. I'll have to look at the detailed charts we have on that area. Might come down the channel between the coast and that long island. Could surprise them. Have to do some homework. Hell, Commander, I've been shot at before. Just want to have a halfway even chance of coming home."

"Read you, Lieutenant. You have an hour to figure it out. We've got to make some decisions here."

"Will this be a round trip for you on the Knight?"

"Probably not. Since noise won't be a problem coming out, we'll try for the Pegasus. It'll do forty knots."

"Yeah, okay. I'll get back to you on this line within sixty, Commander."

Murdock told the others what the flyer had told him.

"Let's assume that we'll go in by chopper and come out by Pegasus. We're what they built that critter for. So, how do we take down two submarines?"

They worked over that for a half hour. They at last decided how to do the job. Mostly it was a discussion between using TNAZ and the larger limpet mines with shaped charges.

Stroh sat and listened to them. When the talk slowed down, he lifted his brows. "So when do you guys want to go to the dance? Right after dark or about midnight?"

Murdock looked around.

"Midnight," Jaybird said.

"Yeah, midnight to 0100," Dobler said.

DeWitt nodded.

Murdock looked at Stroh. We'll check out of here at 2300, get to our drop point a little after midnight, and swim in. We'll be on site and ready to go by 0030."

"I'll clear it with the captain and talk to the COD for the chopper clearance. You guys better go draw some ordnance."

"You should come with us this time, Stroh," Jaybird jawed.

"Maybe next time," Stroh said and hurried out the door.

At 2310, the big Sea Knight helo slid down until it was ten feet off the Strait of Hormuz water. Fifteen black wet suited SEALs dropped out the rear ramp into the water, each one holding a neutral buoyancy bag filled with the tools of his trade. Standard weapons for each man lay across his back, held on with black rubber tubing.

The SEALs hit the water, teamed with another man, took a sighting on the lights of the naval base onshore, and dove down fifteen feet into the black water.

Up front Murdock checked his attack board, a plastic device with two handgrips and a compass in the middle faintly lighted by a light tube. He adjusted his angle slightly, fastened the eight-foot buddy cord to Holt, and they stroked toward the Iranian coast two miles away.

They surfaced after half a mile. The SEALs had swum underwater with their Drager LAR V rebreathers so much in practice that they could tell within ten yards how many strokes it took them to cover a half mile. The rebreathers recycled the air so there were no bubbles to trail to the surface to give away the swimmers below. Here there was little current, so that helped. They popped up all within twenty yards of each other. Murdock counted heads, waved them forward, and they went down to the fifteen-foot depth and swam again.

The floatation bags they dragged behind them on a line contained all the explosives that they would need. They were waterproof and stabilized with enough air to make them near neutral in buoancy, but the SEALs still had to drag them through the water.

They swam for a mile this time, surfaced to bunch together closer. By now they were little more than a quarter of a mile offshore. They saw two patrol boats with lights flashing working back and forth in front of what must be the channel into a bay, which was blazing with lights. That had to be the Iranian naval base.

The SEALs redirected their approach to the base and swam again. They were near the channel when they saw lights overhead and heard the screws of a powerful boat slamming through the water over them. They were plenty deep to clear these patrol boats, but it kept everyone on his toes.

After the boat raced past them, Murdock and Holt surfaced with just their masks and noses out of the water and checked the channel. Yes, dead ahead, and Murdock saw no searchlights on the water or sentries on the points of land on each side. Good. They went under and swam near the surface until they were inside the channel itself; then they waited for the others to catch up with them.

There was no convenient pier for them to cluster under. Each team surfaced for a peek, then submerged and kept close to the top of the water.

Murdock checked the inside of the base. He saw patrol ships tied up at piers fifty yards from the entrance on both sides. Then the bay swept back into the gloom until it came to a brightly lit area where a frigate had been moored. Where were the subs?

Murdock signaled for the SEALs to dive again. He used sign language to indicate they would go to the far end of the small bay and check around. The submarines shouldn't be that hard to locate.

They swam three hundred yards and surfaced. Murdock checked again. Yes. To the left, under minimum lights, he saw the two sleek black ships resting in the water and tied to a dock end to end.

Everyone came up, saw the ships, and angled away on preassigned tasks.

Four SEAL pairs swam to the farthest sub, found it underwater and surfaced just enough to be sure it was the right one. They scanned it, estimated the distance, then went underwater and opened the floatation bags. They had to support the heavy limpet mines until they could get them positioned at the right place on the sub. The four were in a row about three feet under the water at nearly the midpoint on the oval, undersea ship. They were roughly fifteen feet apart and near the center of the 238-foot-long craft.

The mines were heavy, with a specially shaped charge construction so 90 percent of the blast would be angled inward against the side of the submarine. They were guaranteed to punch a large hole through the outer shell of the sub and do a great deal of damage inside.

The spread-out mines were designed to flood at least three of the watertight compartments if the doors could be closed. They would be enough to drop the warship into the mud of the harbor.

One man went back to the surface and watched. When he

saw through the dim light a SEAL working on the first sub come to the surface and wave one arm, they both dived. The men moved to the mines and set the timers on them, then swam away from the ships at their own flank speed.

Murdock saw that the two submarines were planted with mines, and he and Holt led the charge away from the area. Just the way a stick of dynamite in a pond will kill half the fish, a limpet mine going off underwater sends out a tremendous concussion that will kill any diver caught within a quarter of a mile of it.

The timers were set for an hour. In that time they could be out of the channel and into the strait.

They were about a third of a mile from the subs when Murdock felt the concussion. He stroked to the surface and found the other SEALs there, treading water. He spat out his mouthpiece and checked his lighted-dial wristwatch. The timers had been running for only fifteen minutes.

"Malfunction on one mine," Jaybird said, coming up beside him. "One mine won't sink the subs, but will get somebody out there to check on their hulls. They might be able to deactivate the Limpets."

"No way," Ching said. "These are new ones. They try to pry them off the hull, they detonate automatically."

They heard another ragged roar as another mine went off.

By that time, all the SEALs were treading water and looking behind them. The underwater explosions didn't create any fire or blast into the air. It sent another shock wave through the water that the men could feel.

"Two down," Murdock said. "Nothing we can do to change it. We better get the hell out of here. Surface. Let's make some time."

The SEALs did the crawl stroke and plowed through the channel toward the open water of the strait.

A patrol boat came out of the darkness, snapped lights on, and pinpointed the splashing seals. A machine gun chattered. The SEALs dove to avoid the hail of lead. Rebreather mouthpieces were pushed back in place and they went to twenty feet down. Then Murdock tried to find his men. They had scattered.

He saw the lights above. Heard the big engines on the sixty-foot ship growling as the craft worked a search back and forth where the crew had seen the swimmers.

Murdock swam out of the area the ship searched, and he and Holt came to the surface for a peek.

Nothing.

The ship was off a hundred yards, stopped in the water. Another pair of SEALs surfaced, and then more, and Murdock whistled them over. They treaded water, waiting.

"Anybody get hit?" Murdock whispered. The sound carried. There were several no's.

"I got a nick in the arm. Barely cut through the wet suit."

"Bradford, is that you?" Murdock asked.

"Yeah, Skip, but no strain. Not even any blood. Hell, I can swim twenty miles."

"How many men we have?" Murdock asked.

"I count ten," Jaybird said from close by.

"Ten? Where the fuck are the other five?" Murdock felt like screaming. First the damn mines don't work right . . .

They all felt it then, four more blasts almost at the same time.

"That should be the second sub," Murdock said. "Let's spread out a little and see if we can find the missing men."

They spread out and swam slowly back the way they had come. The patrol boat came alive again, gunned its motors, and moved down channel into the naval base.

They were fifty yards from where they started when Dobler called out softly. "Pink light stick, Skipper. Toward the base."

They swam faster that way, and soon found three men. Lampedusa was holding up someone in the water.

"Skip, got some trouble here. It's the JG. He caught one of them slugs. We kept his rebreather mouthpiece in and waited until the ship left, but he won't be swimming much. We get to that point of land over there?"

"Yes, move that way. We're still missing two men. You hear them?"

"Might have," Lam said. He gave up his burden to Horse Ronson who towed the JG along with a powerful sidestroke.

"We heard somebody swimming toward the point just after the boat left. Could be ours."

Murdock kicked out in a powerful crawl stroke and felt

Holt beside him. They moved to the landmass that was still only a dark blob. Almost there, they heard swimmers ahead of them.

"SEALs," Murdock called softly.

"Fuck yes. Got a man hurt. Making for the shore."

"Ostercamp?" Murdock called softly again.

"Yeah. It's Ching. Took a slug somewhere. Haven't found it yet, but he's not in good shape."

"Get him to the land, and we'll have Doc look at him. The JG caught one, too. Where did those fuckers come from?"

Ten minutes later, the fifteen SEALs waded to shore and stretched out their two wounded men. Doc Mahanani did the best he could in the faint moonlight. He did some bandaging, then talked to Murdock.

"Skip, we got troubles. The JG took one in the chest area. The slug must have gone into the water first, because it didn't go all the way through him. He's losing some blood. But evidently it didn't hit his heart or any vitals, otherwise he'd be KIA.

"Ching isn't so bad. Looks like a graze on his scalp that might have knocked him out, and one round through his right arm, up in the biceps. Neither one is going to swim one hell of a lot."

Murdock checked with the two wounded men. Ching was mad.

"Hell, why they pick on me? Just a scratch, Skip. Shit, I can swim as good as any of you fuckers. Give me the chance."

Murdock grinned at him in the darkness. That attitude was part of what made him a SEAL. "Sure you can swim, Ching, and you'd leave a blood trail a yard wide that would bring about twenty hungry sharks homing in on us from five miles away. Just take it easy and stay down."

The SEALs had automatically cleared their weapons of water, made sure they were locked and loaded, and they spread out in a perimeter defense around the two wounded men.

The JG was hurting.

"Damnit, Skip, I caught one. Not my turn. Your turn.

Don't think I can swim much. I'm a good floater. We should have saved one of those flotation bags."

"No sweat, DeWitt. We'll tell the Pegasus to come in here and get us. Not that many patrol boats running around."

"There will be, Skip, once they realize those subs didn't blow up by themselves. We get both of them?"

"Not sure, the photos tomorrow will show us. Now all we have to do is get home."

"Lampedusa materialized without a sound beside Murdock.

"Commander, we've got some trouble. About ten or twelve bad guys coming toward us from down the bay shore. Could be navy security."

"Get on your ears," Murdock whispered to the closest SEAL. He passed the word. Soon all the Platoon men had their Motorolas on.

"Company from the north. Lam says about a dozen. We take them out silently if we can. Only silenced weapons until we need you big guys."

In the stillness he could hear weapons clicking off safety to single shot or three-shot mode.

They waited.

DeWitt gritted his teeth but a low moan came from his lips.

The SEALs waited.

Two dark shadows appeared twenty yards from Quinley, silhouetted against the light from the navy base. Quinley slammed out five silent rounds from his H & K G-11 with its caseless bullets. One of the men went down, the other lifted his rifle. Two more shots jolted him to the ground before he could shoot or cry out.

They heard some low voices ahead. The next figure that came toward them was low on the ground, crawling. Lampedusa heard him before he saw him. When the scout had a target, he drilled the man with six rounds from his Colt carbine M-4A1. The man bellowed in pain, then died.

All was quiet for a moment. Then, on a slight rise a hundred yards away, what Murdock figured was a tripod-mounted heavy machine gun blasted at them with five- and seven-round bursts.

The SEALs hugged the ground. They had no cover to hide

behind. The machine gun cut off, and a dozen black shapes showed against the lights of the base, charging forward with their guns blasting.

"All weapons," Murdock said into his Motorola. The sniper rifles cracked and the others chattered on full auto or three-round bursts. Quinley finished off one fifty-round magazine and pushed another into place.

Half of the attackers went down; the rest dropped to the ground and kept firing. Slowly, the SEALs' superior firepower drove back the Arabs, punishing them.

"Casualties?" Murdock snapped into the Motorola.

Two more men checked in with minor wounds.

"We've got to get wet," Murdock said. They have the advantage here. That MG is going to open up again when they're sure all their live ones are out of its line of fire. Go now, pull back to the water. Mahanani and Ostercamp, take care of the JG. Ching, you okay to get wet?"

"Damn right, Commander."

"Let's move."

Before the machine gunner had time to check with his men in the immediate area, the SEALs stowed their radios in waterproof pouches and slid into the black waters of the Strait of Hormuz. Murdock squatted in the water and counted the SEALs as they went into the wet.

"Fourteen," he whispered to Holt. "Who in hell is missing? We need fifteen bodies."

"One man must not have not been able to report in on the casualty call," Holt whispered. "I'll go check the beach."

Before Murdock could tell him not to, Holt lifted out of the water and charged the beach. He was on it and checking around when the machine gun on the high ground cut loose again. It worked the other side of the thirty-yard-wide area. Holt quartered the beach, saw nothing. When the gunfire worked over toward him, he dove into a low spot where a small stream came into the bay. The rounds went over his head.

He heard a low moan.

Holt lifted up and looked. No NVGs. Damn. He looked again. "Hey SEAL. It's Holt. Where are you?"

The moan came again from his right. The machine gun worked to the left. Holt lifted up and charged along the sand.

He saw the man then, down and not moving. Holt dove over beside him. Checked his face. Bradford.

"Bradford, can you hear me? We've got to get the hell off the beach. Can you move? Bradford." There was no response.

The machine gun worked back toward them. Holt grabbed the big man and dragged him. He had to stand up to do it. He was giving away forty-five pounds. He couldn't find Bradford's weapon. He tugged and pulled, slipped and fell down, dragged the 215-pound man another three feet.

The machine gun swept the area again. Six more feet. He lunged and tugged and rolled Bradford and at last nudged him into the small depression and slid in beside him.

The machine gun bullets tore up the sand where they had just been. Holt panted from the burst of energy he had used up pulling Bradford into the depression.

As soon as the MG stopped, he'd try to carry the big man to the water. How in hell could he do that? The bullets stopped whining into the sand and he was just about to grab Bradford and move him, when a white flashlight beam nailed him where he sat and someone shouted in Arabic at him. A rifle slammed three rounds into the sand and dirt beside him. Slowly, he lifted his hands.

Shit, he'd be the first SEAL in the platoon captured by the enemy. The Navy didn't even furnish them with cyanide pills.

In the gentle surf forty yards away, Murdock stood and watched the shore. There was no sign of Holt. He had checked Alpha Squad and quickly discovered the missing man was Bradford. If he was badly hurt, there was little chance that Holt, at 170 pounds, could drag him off the beach and into the water. Then that damn MG had started.

Senior Chief Dobler squatted in the water near Murdock.

"They got pinned down by that MG, or blown away," Dobler said. "Look, a light. The damn infantry must have found them. What the fuck we do now, Skipper?"

"We're not losing two good men. Get everyone to move up the channel toward the base. First we nail that bastard on the machine gun, then we get our troops back. Let's go."

The SEALs hit the water and swam silently up the channel

to where they figured the machine gun was. Murdock and Jaybird took the assignment and worked out of the water silently and up the slight incline.

"There he is," Murdock whispered. The gun was set up with sandbags holding down the legs for better accuracy. Two men hovered over it but weren't firing. One man used a handheld radio.

Murdock nodded at Jaybird. "I've got the one on the right," he said. The two SEALs lifted their silenced MP-5s and sighted in. The range was only thirty yards.

23

Naval Base
Bandar Abbas, Iran

Murdock and Jaybird fired their silent weapons on three-round bursts at almost the same time. They watched both Iranian soldiers in the faint moonlight take the rounds. One slumped over the machine gun; the second one slammed away from the weapon and sprawled in the dirt. The SEALs worked up to the gun position carefully. When they were sure the two were dead, they took the weapon apart and threw the pieces in different directions.

Then they moved silently down the slope. All the SEALs had put their radios back on.

"Machine gun clear," Murdock whispered into his lip mike.

Ahead they could see little. They knew the rest of the platoon was working up from the side. All the SEALs were between the Iranian patrol and the naval base.

Murdock froze against the ground as he heard someone in front of him. A lead scout walked forward, watching half the time back the way he had come. When he was six feet away, Murdock put three rounds into his chest, and he jolted sideways and died in the dirt.

"White flare," Murdock whispered.

"Yo," Lampedusa said on his radio. Twenty seconds later the flare went off overhead, turning the point of land into midday brightness. Six of the Iranians went down to the silent shots of the SEALs. Murdock saw Holt grab a dead Iranian's rifle and kill the three Iranians nearest him. There were no more Iranian soldiers alive.

"Cease fire," Murdock said. SEALs from the side charged forward, checked the Iranians to make sure they were dead, then looked at Bradford.

Mahanani sprinted ahead of the others and knelt beside Bradford. He used a small pencil flash and found the wound. It had hit Bradford in the belly and knocked him out. He was barely conscious now. Mahanani bandaged the wound the best he could and found Murdock.

The medic told the platoon leader about the wound. "Quicker we can take him back to the carrier, the better. He's in a bad way. Should have a chopper come and get him."

Murdock used his Motorola. "Pegasus, this is Sailor One. Can you read me?"

He waited. There was no reply. He tried three times. Each time, the speaker in his ear remained silent.

"Move everyone down to the farthest point of land we can," Murdock said into the mike. "We'll try again on the Pegasus. No way we can swim out two miles."

Bradford couldn't walk. Jefferson and Ronson carried him. He passed out from the pain after three steps. They had left the JG and Ching on the point before the rest moved up the channel. Now they came to them, and Murdock made a check.

He had fifteen bodies, but two of them were not able to swim. On the point, he tried the Motorola again. He heard some static, but he wasn't sure if it was the Pegasus.

The SEALs had automatically spread out in a perimeter defense with all of them facing toward the naval base. The two wounded men were in the center of the arc.

Lam stayed out a hundred yards, hunkered down behind a stump, watching toward the naval base. He wondered how long it would be before the patrol was missed and the Iranians sent another one, larger and with more heavy weapons.

Murdock called over Senior Chief Dobler.

"Hang tough here. If we have company, do the best you

can. I'd expect a patrol boat with a light would be checking out this area before long. If it comes, kill the light first, then give them a reception. Move away from our wounded before you fire. Then shoot and scoot to a new location."

"You going for a swim?"

"Only thing I can do. We've got to bring the Pegasus into this point or say good-bye to two good men." He handed his submachine gun to Dobler and started to take off his re-breather. He stopped.

"Yeah, keep it on. You might find a patrol boat out there. How far out you going?"

"Until I can contact the damn Pegasus that's supposed to be out there. No way Stroh would let them hang us out to die."

Murdock walked into the small wave action on the point, then bent and thrust out into the water. A moment later, he was working a fast racing crawl stroke directly away from shore. He knew there were two small islands nearby, but they had missed them coming in, should miss them going out.

He worked three hundred crawl strokes, treaded water hard, and lifted up enough to take out his Motorola from the waterproof pouch.

"Pegasus, this is Sailor One, can you read me?"

He pushed the earpiece in and listened. Only the same static he'd heard before.

Murdock tried the call twice more, then pushed the little set back in his waterproof pouch and swam again. He picked out a star for his aiming point and kept swimming.

This time, he went five hundred strokes, then went through the same routine with the radio.

"Pegasus, this is Sailor One, can you read?"

This time some words came over, but they were too garbled for him to understand.

"Pegasus, if you read, come in closer. We need you on the dirt on the point of land at the mouth of the naval base channel. We have two badly wounded men who can't swim. Come in the hell and pick us up."

Again, the only sound in Murdock's ear was garbled; he made out no single words.

He swam again. He knew his crawl was slowing. He figured he was out almost two miles when he used the radio

again. The garbled words came through again. Then he heard
two words he knew.

"Light stick."

They must be receiving him. Maybe his earpiece got wet
or some other malfunction on the receiver. He used the lip
mike. "Yes, light stick. I'm about two miles off the point.
Light stick coming on." He pushed the set back in his pouch
and rested on the water a moment. Then he pulled the light
stick off his wet suit and broke it. The pink glow seemed
brilliant. He shielded it from the land and waited, treading
water just enough to stay on top.

The light stick said it was good for six hours. He wondered
if that was right. He'd never used one that long. Where the
hell was that boat?

His kicking slowed and he drifted down until the light
went underwater. He shook his head, kicked harder, and held
the stick up with his arm fully extended.

Somewhere far away, he heard the throb of an engine. Yes.
He waited. No. The engine was too heavy, too large. Then
he saw the searchlight cutting through the chop that had developed on the strait. The boat came closer. A damn Iranian
patrol craft. He wasn't sure how big it was, but it was doing
a search pattern. Working closer and closer to him.

He pushed the light stick underwater. It gave off an eerie
glow, but it couldn't be seen ten feet away. He kicked over
and tried to float. The rubber suit was too heavy and dragged
him down. When he looked up, the boat came closer, then
it changed course and angled straight at him.

How could it? The sailors on board couldn't see him. They
hadn't seen the light. He was too small to show up on surface
radar. He waited. It would change course in a new search
grid.

It didn't change course but bore down on him. He pushed
the Drager mouthpiece in place and duck dived down twenty
feet. He saw the craft's searchlight probing, then swing
around. The boat passed fifty feet to one side and was gone.

When the rumble of the motors faded, he went back to the
surface. He kicked out high again and tried the Motorola.

"Pegasus, Sailor one. That patrol boat damn near ran me
down. You see it? Where the hell are you?"

This time he shook the earpiece and pushed it in place. The words came loud and clear.

"Yeah, we're tailing him. Hear you five by five. Show me your light stick. Can't be more than a few hundred yards from you."

"Hear you fine now. Yeah. Light stick up."

"We have it, we have you, coming up slow. There's a landing platform on the back. Just installed. We'll coast in. Grab that platform, and we'll talk."

Murdock looked up and saw a black chunk of the night moving toward him. The purr of the engines sounded. He waved the light stick. Then the black-painted Pegasus slid in beside him, and he touched the hull as it slipped past, almost dead in the water. Yes, the platform. He pulled up on it and hands grabbed him and hoisted him on board.

"Commander, good to see you. Where are the rest of you?"

"I told you, Ensign, they're on the beach. I have two seriously wounded who can't swim. We don't leave our men behind. I want you to run into that beach. It's just west of the channel in to the naval base, about two miles from here."

"Can't do that, Commander. That would seriously jeopardize the safety of my men and my ship."

Murdock grabbed him by the shirtfront and pushed him against the bulkhead. "Listen up, shithead. I have fourteen men in there, and you are endangering their lives. I outrank you, mister. Now get this tub turned around and headed for shore. I'll guide you when you get close enough."

"No, Commander. On my boat I'm the captain, and I outrank you."

"You're putting your own safety ahead of fourteen men? Those are my SEALs in there, mister. You better reconsider your position. The admiral on the carrier personally sent us on this mission. He wouldn't be at all happy with your orders."

"Sorry, I won't jeopardize my boat or my men. That's final. Coxswain, let's head back for the carrier."

Murdock hit him flush on the jaw with his best right cross, and the ensign went down like a sack of wet concrete. The sailor grinned and tossed Murdock a .45 automatic. Murdock pulled back the slide and heard a round slip into the chamber.

"Coxswain, let's head for shore. Low throttle. We don't

want to attract any attention. You have radio contact with the *Enterprise*?"

"Yes sir."

"Get them. Tell them the situation and that we'll want a search and rescue chopper to meet us once we get our men on board and we head for the ship. Have them get in the air now and be here soonest. We're about two miles off Iran and picking up fourteen SEALs. One has a bad chest wound, the other a stomach wound. Both bullet wounds. Go."

The sailor nodded and hurried into the small cockpit.

Murdock hung with the coxswain.

"Sir, the ensign is usually a good man, but tonight he was nervous as hell about this mission. He's gun shy. Never been shot at."

"Too bad he fell down that way and hit his jaw on the rail."

The coxswain grinned. "Yeah, too damn bad, sir. That's exactly what happened. I saw it."

They lifted the throttle to ten knots and drove forward, not making much noise, but Murdock knew it was too much. He didn't care. He wanted his men back.

Three minutes later, he could see the glow of the lights at the naval base.

"Yeah, now ten degrees left. The men are on the west bank of the channel. Ease off the throttle."

Murdock took out his Motorola. "Hey, SEALs, you hear us coming?"

"That we do, Skipper," Senior Chief Dobler said. "Probably half of Iran does, too. No action here. Must be afraid to find out what happened to that patrol."

"Get the swimmers in the water. We'll come in stern first. Use everyone to lift the injured into the boat. How close are we?"

"No way to tell," Dobler said. "Hey, yeah, I can see a small wake, two hundred yards, maybe less. Keep it coming."

Murdock went into the stern. The coxswain would turn the boat around and back in the last few yards until the stern grounded.

They turned, and Murdock could see his men moving into the water, getting ready with the two wounded. The Pegasus hit the sand of the point in two feet of water. Murdock stepped down to the platform and jumped into the water. Jaybird and Dobler had Bradford halfway to the boat. Four men helped lift him in and jumped in to put Bradford down on a stretcher the boat crewmen had brought out.

Then the JG came. He walked partway, then his knees caved in, and Lampedusa and Ronson caught him and carried him to the boat.

In a minute and a half, the wounded and the rest of the SEALs were on board. Lights of a vehicle cut through the night behind them and curved around the rise above them.

"All aboard," Murdock bellowed.

"Hang on," the coxswain shouted, and the Pegasus's engines roared and the sleek boat ground off the shore sand and shot forward into the strait. Behind them, a machine gun chattered, but it was aimed at the wrong side of the beach.

They were almost a mile offshore when the coxswain called to Murdock.

"We've got a patrol boat showing on our radar. He's three miles off to the east and making eighteen knots. He can't catch us. We'll kick it up to thirty knots if your wounded can take the shake."

"Give it a try. How are we with that chopper?"

The crewman who manned the radio came up.

"Made contact, sir. They launched about twenty minutes ago. They want our speed and course so they can intercept."

Murdock looked at the coxswain. "Tell him. I want these men to have medical attention as soon as possible."

"Once we're ten miles out from shore, we'll turn on all our lights," the Coxswain said.

"What happened to the ensign?" Murdock asked.

"He has a bad headache. He gave me the con until we get back to the carrier."

Murdock chuckled. "Yeah, good move."

He went inside the cabin where Bradford lay on a bunk. Mahanani bent over him, changing the bandage. He gave him another shot of morphine.

"In and out of consciousness, Skipper. "What I'm worried about is peritonitis. Round might have ruptured an intestine. All that shit mixed up in the cavity down there works the same way when an appendix bursts. It can kill a man damn fast. I'm watching him. The JG is not in any danger, just a hell of a lot of pain. Damn, Skipper, you know that makes seven of our sixteen men who have been wounded so far on this fucked-up mission?"

They saw no more Iranian patrol boats. Ten miles out, the Pegasus showed every light that it had and stood out in the dark gulf like a firefly looking for a mate.

Murdock heard the radioman talking with the search and rescue chopper.

Ten minutes later, the bird turned on its lights and came over the Pegasus, which had throttled down and stopped.

The radioman came out. "When the basket comes down, be sure not to touch it until it hits the deck. It will have a tremendous charge of static electricity from the rotor wash.

"When it hits, we hold it, get Bradford in first and strap him down, then they lift him away."

Bradford was unconscious again when they carried him out on the boat's stretcher. They eased him out of it, into the basket, and fastened the straps.

The loudspeaker came on when DeWitt was safely in the chopper.

"You men do good work. We have your SEALs safely stowed. We also have a doctor on board who will do what he can on our return trip. We're about forty-five minutes from the carrier. See you there."

The lights snapped off, the chopper slanted away, and then raced at full speed to the southwest.

The Pegasus got under way, then speeded up and hit forty knots, and Murdock used the radio. The radio operator on board the carrier said he'd find Don Stroh and have him call the Pegasus.

Twenty minutes later, Stroh called.

"Stroh, your little boats should be at the bottom of the naval base. We've had some casualties."

"I heard your call for an S&R bird."

"True, the JG and Bradford. Bradford is serious, maybe critical. I want you to get down to sick bay and ride herd on those medics. Let me know what happens. It'll be at least three hours before we get on board. Get me a report on both of them."

"Yes, will do. Congratulations on the prank. Mother is happy."

"Enough of the wild talk, Stroh. Get down to sick bay. They should be landing any minute."

The Pegasus crashing along at forty knots presented the SEALs with a slam-bang ride. There wasn't that much rush. Murdock asked the Coxswain if he could cut the speed to thirty knots. It would take an hour longer, but at thirty, they could get some sleep.

Murdock didn't sleep. He kept going over in his mind what had happened and how he could have done it differently. Getting two men wounded so badly on a mission meant something went sour. He didn't know if it was his fault, the luck of the draw, or the original planning. He'd have a long talk with DeWitt, Dobler, and Jaybird tomorrow and see what they could decide.

It took the Pegasus almost four hours to reach the big carrier. They tied up at the lower hatch, and the SEALs climbed the ladder into the bowels of the ship.

Murdock took Ching to sick bay to have his gunshot and his head graze looked at. They treated them both, then said they would keep him for twenty-four hours for observation, watching for any infection. Murdock asked about Bradford. The doctor who treated him was still on duty.

"Bradford, yes, the SEAL. He's out of danger. Halfway into a bad case of peritonitis, but we nipped it. We stitched up his large intestine and did some repair work in that area. He'll need at least two weeks in the hospital here or Stateside. You're homeported in San Diego. So it would be Balboa Naval Hospital. He's coming along fine. Still in recovery and sedated."

"What about DeWitt?"

"A nasty one. Much worse than it looked. Glad you didn't let him swim out those two miles he kept mumbling about. That really ticked him off. Said if everyone died that it was his fault. Near as we can figure, the round that hit him shattered on the clavicle. Tore up lots of tissue up in there, put one small hole in the top of his lung. Lucky it didn't collapse on him. Some internal bleeding. He's going to be black and blue up in there for a week or two. One shard we found by X-ray an inch from his heart. That would have been bad."

"How long is he grounded?"

"Two weeks at least. Then light duty for another month.

You better take his trident away from him for a while. In two months he should be as good as new."

Murdock found his way back to his quarters and rolled into his bunk. When he looked at his watch, he was surprised that it was 0530. Yeah, when you're having fun.

He turned over and slept.

The damned Iranians had captured him and were banging a bucket they had clamped over his head. The banging was done with an old saber, and he couldn't stand it. Then a door opened and a new voice sounded in the racket.

"What the hell, Murdock, you gonna sleep to noon?"

Murdock made the Iranians go away, but when he buried his head under the pillow, the other voice came through loud and agitated.

"Murdock, you gonna sleep all fucking morning?

Oh, god, he wasn't dreaming. He'd just gone to sleep. He moved the pillow and stared out of bleary eyes at Don Stroh, who stood just inside the compartment door.

"Murdock, get your ass in gear. Something big just came down. The U.S. is officially in the fracas with Iraq. Not officially, by Congress, but we are "aiding and helping defend an ally in any way that we can." In short, Syria begged us to help slow down Saddam the fuck Hussein before he overruns Damascus. We might just as well be at war. And the CIA, the War Department, and State all have a fantastic new assignment for you and your boys."

"We're shot to hell; we can't do it."

"Sure you can. Simple, really. You get awake, have a shower and then about a gallon of coffee, and I'll let you in on your next job. It's a pisser, I mean something the U.S. has wanted to do for years, but had no guts. Now you and your guys are gonna do it."

Murdock stood and headed for the male officer's showers just down the companionway.

"No way, Stroh, I'm serious. Look at my medical report. Half of my outfit is shot up, four in the hospital right now. No damn way are we going to take on another assignment."

24

USS *Enterprise* CNV 65
In the Southern Persian Gulf

Don Stroh followed Murdock down the companionway toward the showers.

"How many men do you have who can walk and talk?"

"Twelve, but four of them have been put on light duty by the medics, which brings us down to eight. Not a good number. Regs require us to have at least a dozen men for any mission."

"Regs my ass. You make up your own regs. Listen to this assignment after breakfast, then see what you decide."

"This would be a volunteer mission, right, Stroh? A highly dangerous, combat-filled operation that could very well get every man in the platoon killed."

"Hell, Murdock most of the missions you go on fit that description. What the hell you so pissed about?"

Murdock stopped at the shower room door. He turned, and his face was flushed and angry. He touched Stroh's chest with his index finger.

"What? You have to ask? I just got half of my squad shot up on this deployment. One is busted up so badly that he can't stay in the SEALs. Another one was on the brink of dying before the medics worked him over. My best friend,

Ed DeWitt, almost bought the farm out there on that rotten chunk of Iranian soil. If that isn't enough, I have four more men with bullet holes or shrapnel in them, and they are hurting by the bucketful. What I have to figure out is why this all happened and what I should have done that I didn't do. Or maybe what I did that I should not have. When it comes down to the final analysis, it's my fault that those men were wounded. My fault, no one else's. Now, do you have any other dumb questions, Stroh?"

Murdock waited a beat, then pushed into the shower room and let a small cloud of steam come out. Stroh took a breath and went to the wardroom for another cup of coffee.

Almost an hour later, Murdock walked into the wardroom and sat down across from Stroh.

"Yeah, yeah, I know. I shot off my mouth at you. I shouldn't have, and I apologize. But who else can I yell at, the admiral?"

Stroh nodded until he looked like one of those little dolls some people have on their dashboards.

"Please don't yell at the admiral. I'm your guy to bellow at. Sorry I came up with the next assignment before you had settled the last one in your mind. My fault."

They both worked on coffee. Neither one said a word for five minutes. At last, Stroh chuckled.

"Okay, inscrutable one. I give. I'll talk first. There really is another situation that we should go over."

"The proposed mission?"

"Right." Stroh looked at Murdock critically, as if trying to figure out what his reaction was going to be. When Murdock looked at him to see if he was going to continue, Stroh said two words:

"Nerve gas."

"Nerve . . ." Murdock scowled. "You've got to be joking. My men have no training in handling nerve gas."

"You did rather well with it in China as I remember."

"That was on a limited scale, and it all was underground."

"You think Saddam is going to have his ace-in-the-hole weapon sitting in a tent out in the desert someplace?"

"From what I hear about him, he might put it in his sons-in-laws' graves."

"We know where it is, what it is, and how to destroy it

without killing off half the population of the Middle East."

"Good, so you do it."

Stroh went on as if he didn't hear Murdock's comment. "We know where it is, and the word from inside the high command at Iraq's GHQ is that Saddam will use it if the war goes badly for him. Our job: Get to the goods and destroy them and the delivery vehicles before the war goes so badly that he lashes out with the missiles aimed at six national capitals, as well as Tel Aviv and Haifa, Israel."

"We still saving this lousy world?"

"Last thing I heard, we are."

Murdock sipped at his coffee. It had turned cold. He drank some anyway so he wouldn't have to answer. At last, he gave a sigh.

"Let's go over the whole damn problem in my compartment. I'd guess this isn't for the ship's loudspeakers."

Stroh stood.

"Sit down, I'm not going anywhere until I have breakfast or lunch or whatever the hell time it is. I'm a bear before breakfast."

Northern Desert
Saudi Arabia

U.S. Air Force Captain Smarthing led a flight of six F-16 Fighting Falcons across the northern reaches of Saudi Arabia, heading for the fighting in Syria twenty miles inside Syria from the Iraqi border. The United States had answered the call from Syria for assistance, and the quickest and most effective way was to provide air cover and attacks on the Iraqi tanks that boiled across the border.

The lines between nations were ill defined in this desert area, but far ahead, Captain Smarthing could see signs of smoke.

"Falcon Flight, this is Falcon One, approaching target area. Keep a check on any Iraqi air, then pick out your tank target and do what you can. We'll split up about now. Two, three, and four take the northern sector. The rest of us the south. Break."

The three other Falcons broke off to the left and raced toward the ground. They needed at least three thousand feet altitude to fire their Maverick missiles. Each of the Falcons carried four of the tank busters. The 637-pound missiles housed a 300-pound warhead and could destroy any tank in this small war.

The big tank killers had IIR, imaging infrared guidance systems, that usually produced an 80 percent to 90 percent hit rate.

"Three tanks to the left," Smarthing's radio reported.

"Roger that, I'll take the first one," Smarthing said. He cranked in the scope and turned to get the tank squarely in a lock in his sights. He had it. He punched the firing button and felt one of the heavy missiles drop off the plane and jet forward at Mach 1 and gaining speed. Below, the tank maneuvered, but the missile's guidance system kept locked on the target.

In the tank below, Major Hadr watched with satisfaction as his company of tanks rolled through light infantry resistance toward the small hill a mile away that was the goal for today. It had been an exciting two days of battle. Thrills of the chase and the battle with two smaller Syrian tanks, which he had won. Now there seemed little to stop his company from taking the small hill.

He had no warning as the heavy Maverick missile bore straight into its target and the 300-pound warhead penetrated the tank's armor before exploding, disintegrating the tank and killing Hadr and its crew at once.

In the air, Captain Smarthing held up one finger and nodded. He had three missiles left. By that time, two of the tanks below had ceased to exist. The hatch popped open on the third, and a man stood up just as another Maverick blasted his armored tin can into scrap metal and a disemboweled and widely scattered crew.

Captain Smarthing and his flight accounted for fourteen tanks that afternoon and finished the day with strafing runs on rear areas behind the lines, looking for fuel dumps and vehicles. They hit one gasoline storage area that erupted in a tremendous gush of flames that spread to tents and a few small buildings.

"Damn, you see that?" his wingman shouted in the radio. "Bet we discouraged a lot of trucks from running any farther."

"Fuel check," Captain Smarthing called. The five others reported in that they had 55 percent of their fuel supply left.

"Better head back, unless some of you want to walk the last fifty miles through the desert," Captain Smarthing said.

They turned, formed up, and headed back to their field in Saudi Arabia.

"Why didn't we get more tanks?" Captain Smarthing asked.

"Damn, that was all there were there, Captain. We clobbered the whole damn tank company. Near as I can figure, we had only two misses with the Mavericks. What a sweetheart."

Smarthing felt better. But on the way back to their base, he still remembered the last words of his friend and former wingman when they patrolled the no-fly zone in Iraq. Nothing would erase those words from his mind. The ache and the empty place would always be there. Today helped make up a little for losing his friend over the skies of Iraq.

Southeast Syria

Sergeant an-Numan had watched the jet fighters come out of the sky and kill the tanks that were about to overwhelm his platoon. His lieutenant had been killed the first day of the war. He had been leading the platoon since. They should have forty-two men, but two days of furious combat had cut his troops down to twenty-two. At this location, the men had dug in, throwing up quickly whatever protection they could. Now the men looked at him.

They had been told to hold this area at all costs.

"Hold your positions," an-Numan shouted. He had no radio. He received instructions by runners, when they could get through. He peered over the dirt parapet toward the still-burning tanks. Where was the Iraqi infantry? The foot soldiers always followed the tanks. Perhaps they had fallen behind the growling monsters.

Sergeant an-Numan had hated it when the tanks came over the small rise ahead of them. They had retreated here early this morning and been told to dig in. There were only a few men behind them. They had to hold. Now they had, thanks to the pilots who killed all but one of the tanks, which turned and sped back the way it had come.

He thought of sending two men up to the dead tanks to see what they could salvage. There might be some useable weapons. He dismissed the idea.

A moment later, he saw the first Iraqi soldier come over the hill. He dropped to the ground at once. He had seen the burning tanks. The figure slithered backward and vanished over the rise. How many men were behind him?

Sergeant an-Numan waved at his machine gunner. The weapon was the best they had, and there was plenty of ammo. He signaled the squad leaders to be alert.

The sergeant watched the top of the hill. It was six hundred yards away. He saw movement. A pair of men crawled up to the top of the hill and looked over. An-Numan sighted in with his AK-47 and fired a single shot. Yes. He saw one of the men rear up, then fall. The other man dragged him back out of sight.

A small cheer went up down the line.

"Hold your fire," an-Numan called. "If they come, they will be charging fast. We will make every round count."

Nothing happened. For an hour, the men of the First Platoon, Second Infantry Regiment, sat in their holes, waiting. An-Numan wanted to send a scout to the crest of the hill and see who was on the other side. He didn't have a good scout left. He had one machine gun where he should have three. He had no snipers. There were only two submachine guns. The rest had AK-47s, the old ones.

Movement.

He checked with his binoculars. Another scout. Before he had a sight on the man, the Iraqi slid back out of sight.

The Syrian soldiers heard the machine before they saw it. When it came over the brow of the hill, it spat lead at them. The rig was a half-track with a .50-caliber machine gun mounted on a pedestal.

"Get down," an-Numan shouted. The heavy bullets slammed a line across their earthworks. One man shouted, but the sergeant grinned, knowing he was a clown. When the bullets walked down the line the other way, an-Numan lifted up and looked at the skyline. He shivered. Eighty, maybe a hundred men came over the top and began running forward.

"Hold your fire," the sergeant bellowed. "Wait until they get closer."

His heart thumped hard in his chest. His eyes watered. He coughed. He'd coughed when he became nervous since he was in school.

He waited.

Down the line, one man fired a shot.

"Hold your fire," He bellowed again. By that time, they were taking rifle fire from the Iraqi infantry. The .50-caliber kept working back and forth along their line of holes.

The ragged line of men was at five hundred yards. Still too far away. The farther they ran, the more tired they would be and the less accurate.

He knew: You don't have to be accurate when you're overrunning a position.

When the Iraqi were at four hundred yards, he gave the order to fire. They had been ordered before to put the AK-47s on single shot. Conserve ammunition. They were low enough.

He saw one or two of the men in the long line coming at them stagger and fall. More took their places. At three hundred yards, they slowed to a walk but kept coming. The .50-caliber had to quit firing so it didn't hit friendly forces.

Too damn many. How could he defend against a hundred men?

He kicked his AK-47 to automatic fire and began sending out bursts of three rounds. He heard other men down the line do the same thing. Now more of the Iraqis fell.

Still too many. They would be overrun.

The buzz came out of the north, then it turned into a whine and suddenly, in front of them the Iraqi soldiers fell by the dozens. A jet fighter slashed across the field and pulled up in a sweeping circle. Then another jet flashed across the field, firing some kind of machine gun or cannon. The Iraqi troops wavered. An officer barked at them and waved them forward.

Just then, a third jet slammed rounds into the line of Iraqis, and the officer went down along with twenty more men.

No more than forty soldiers were still standing. Two more times the silver jets slashed across the field and fired into the attacking soldiers.

Two Iraqis turned and ran back the way they had come.

Someone with the Iraqis shot one of the men in the back. The other one continued. Four more men from the far end of the line ran back up the slope. Then six from the middle ran.

"Fire at them," Sergeant an-Numan shouted. Six more of the attackers were put in the dirt before they made it over the ridge.

The field ahead of them was empty except for the dead and dying. The sergeant sent two of his best men up the slope, one on each end, to check over the other side. Six more men went into the field and gathered up all of the rifles and ammunition they could carry. They went back twice to collect the magazines for the AK-47s that the Iraqis carried.

Sergeant an-Numan took a drink from his canteen. He was delighted to be alive. He owed it to those U.S. fighter planes. He remembered seeing the white star on the blue field. The U.S. symbol.

A runner came into the end of the defensive line and soon found an-Numan. He opened the envelope and took out the gold bars of a second lieutenant. The handwritten note said: "Congratulations on holding your position. You are hereby promoted to second lieutenant. We have reinforcements coming. Before nightfall, you will have thirty more men to fill out your platoon. Keep up the good work. We may have stopped the onslaught of the hated Iraqis."

An-Numan smiled as he pinned on the bars. Then he called in his scouts who had looked over the hilltop.

"Must be half a regiment out there," his best soldier said. "Looks like they were mauled bad by some of the same jets that helped us. I saw some of the trucks heading back toward the border."

An-Numan smiled again, told the man he had just been promoted to sergeant and he should check the troops for any casualties.

The man stared at him a moment, then saw the bars on his shoulders and saluted. "Yes sir, Lieutenant, sir." He grinned and ran to check on the men.

An-Numan looked over the battlefield. He'd have two lookouts tonight. One on the crest of the hill in front of them and one toward the far end of the small valley. There were no friendly troops at all on their right flank. He smiled. He was starting to think like a soldier.

25

Twenty Miles from Syria
Northern Saudi Arabia

The Air Force calls it a forward logistical temporary base, or FLTB. This one was the pits, decided First Lieutenant Pete "Gotrocks" Van Dyke. He was one of the lucky pilots assigned here with his Cobra gunship helicopter. There were six of the potent birds primed and ready for action sitting outside the tent in the early-morning darkness. They had seen considerable action already, and now he waited for the sun to come up so he would be able to find his target.

The little base was as temporary as they get. It consisted of six twelve-man tents with stakes pounded deep into the subsoil and sand heaped around the roll-down sides to prevent the insides of them from becoming sand dunes.

They were situated ten miles from the Iraqi border in the middle of what he could only describe as a desolate desert. There were no settlements within a hundred and fifty miles of them. The six Cobras and two search and rescue choppers would be rotated every six days to get the sand pumped out of their vitals.

They didn't need a landing field. There was nothing but shifting sand and a few hardy shrubs and grasses for as far as anyone could see. The entire base had been flown in by

choppers, dropped, erected, and maintained by more birds.
The kitchen was the most important tent on the tiny base.
The whole place had only forty men. Half of those were
pilots, gunners, and aviation maintenance men. The rest were
cooks and missile handlers and some headquarters guys.

Lieutenant Van Dyke came to the small ready room section of the ad tent and checked the assignment sheet. Not a
formal situation. They received radio orders during the night
for the next morning. At least that's what happened the first
and only two days of their existence on this desert wonder-
land.

He grunted when he saw that he and Jimmy pulled the
supply line from Syria back into Iraq itself. Yes, lots of
trucks, but no tanks. He called his munitions handlers and
ordered a double load of 20mm rounds for the three-barrel
Gatling gun in the nose turret, and a full helping of nineteen
of the 2.75-inch rockets in the pods.

He hit the chow tent. Everyone ate together here. Rank
meant little in this outpost. He had breakfast, then picked up
Jimmy, his front-seat gunner, and they found their baby
armed, fueled, and ready to rumble.

It was almost daylight when they lifted off with two other
Cobras and flew together in a loose formation north into
Syria, then slanted a little west to find the fighting.

Iraqi forces were still moving ahead, but slower now. Two
of the gunships pulled the supply line assignment. There
were only two good routes from Iraq into this part of Syria.
Van Dyke took one and Lieutenant Platamone the other, and
they raced along a hundred feet over the desert, aiming for
the well-used roads.

Van Dyke's showed first. They were still fifteen miles inside of Syria when the chopper pilot found three trucks heading down the road toward the front. He used the Gatling gun
on them. Jimmy triggered the three barrels and blasted the
first truck in line. That stopped the other two. Drivers hit the
ditch and ran into the desert. The Cobra hovered, and Jimmy
hit the middle truck with a 2.75-inch rocket, setting off the
gas tank in a surging explosion that engulfed the other two
rigs at once.

"Let's find some more," Jimmy said.

Three miles up the road, they ran into a line of troops

marching to the front. "Saddam is getting short on trucks," Van Dyke said. He came in low and stopped, hovering a hundred yards away, to let Jimmy have hunting time with the Gatling. The troops tried to disperse, but they didn't have time. Jimmy poured a hundred rounds of 20mm into the troops, then the Cobra moved on without taking even one rifle shot in return.

Five miles on up the road, they came to the Syrian border. A lone stone building marked the spot. It was now vacant and used only as a landmark. Ahead, Van Dyke saw the sun glint off windshields. More trucks.

As they came within range of the trucks, they saw that the two lead rigs had .50-caliber machine guns mounted on the cabs. Van Dyke jerked the chopper down and away as tracers from the .50-caliber raced through the airspace where they had been. They pulled back farther to be out of effective range of the fifty and used the minigun with the 20mm to rake the first two trucks. One slewed to the side and wound up in the desert off the road. The rest of the convoy of more than thirty trucks kept moving down the road.

"We better slide in closer and get some of the rockets on him," Lieutenant Van Dyke said on the IC. Jimmy agreed, even as he tried for more hits on the first truck with the machine gun. They swung left and came up from the side. The first two 70mm rockets missed the lead truck. It had been speeding ahead, slowing, then racing ahead again. The third rocket rammed into the engine compartment and splattered it across the dirt road.

"Now we can get in closer," Van Dyke said. He gunned the chopper into a better position for Jimmy to use the Gatling gun. Jimmy washed down six trucks with the deadly 20mm rounds when he saw flashes from the first wounded truck that had slipped off the road.

"Lieutenant, that first truck ain't dead. Shooting at us. He's coming damn close, too, and . . ."

Jimmy didn't finish the sentence. Van Dyke felt the rounds hitting his chopper. Saw part of the nose of the craft in front of him break away from the effect of the .50-caliber rounds. Then the controls went mushy in his hands and he tried to swing away, to drop down near the ground and avoid any more hits.

The Cobra wouldn't respond. He had trouble holding any altitude. He could see Jimmy thrown against the side of the cockpit, his helmet blown off, a bloody mass of tissue and bone where his head should be.

The Cobra shuddered again as more of the heavy .50-caliber rounds hit it. Distance. He knew he was going down. He wanted to be as far from the trucks as he could get. He dove toward the ground and saw the tracers fly past him. He was as low as he could get, about fifteen feet off the deck, and still racing forward at 175 miles an hour. He had to get away from the men in those trucks.

The controls felt wrong. Then he realized that he had no way to move right or left. Some more of the controls had been hit by the rounds. He looked for a place to land. Almost anyplace would do. Gradually, he eased off on the power forward and the ship slowed. He hit the radio.

"Flea Bag, this is Flea One. I'm hit. Jimmy is KIA. Having hard time controlling. I'm going in. Get that S&R bird in the air now."

"Read you, Flea One. Search and rescue on its way in two. Any coordinates?"

"Just north into Iraq a few miles from the south main road. Only two roads. I'll have the transponder on. Can't talk. Going in."

He had slowed the Cobra to forty miles an hour forward. He remembered the rockets. He fired the rest of them into the desert. At least they wouldn't explode when he hit the ground.

Then the desert floor leaped up at him. Something else snapped in the controls, and he lost it all. He was twenty feet off the ground and moving ahead at no more than twenty miles an hour when he hit. The top rotor kept spinning, and it torqued the small craft around on the skids, breaking off both of them and smashing the Cobra on its side. The top rotor broke off both blades and then the noise stopped and all he could hear was dripping fluid and the desert wind.

"Fuel," he said to the wind. He hung against his straps, almost on the left side of the cockpit. He punched the cockpit release, but it didn't work. In a small panic, he loosened his seat belt and shoulder harness and kicked hard at the Plexi-

glas cover. The whole damn chopper could blast into hell
from the vaporized jet fuel at any second.

It took him six hard kicks with his boot to budge the can-
opy. Then it eased open, and he pushed it hard and dropped
six feet to the desert. He lifted up and ran.

First Lieutenant Pete Van Dyke made it thirty yards before
the Cobra's fuel ignited in a huge fireball and seared the
ground around it for twenty yards. He was slammed forward
and singed but not really burned.

Van Dyke rolled in the dirt, but his flight suit wasn't burning. The first thing he did was make sure the portable transponder he carried was turned on. Then he reached in the
leg pocket and took out the trusty .45 automatic that he
hadn't fired in six months. He pulled back the slide and
rammed a round into the chamber and pushed on the safety.
Locked and loaded. He began walking away from the road
with its trucks full of furious Iraqi soldiers. The farther he
could get from the burning hulk, the better.

"Jimmy, God, Jimmy, you're still in there." He shook his
head. It didn't matter a lot. Dead is dead. Nobody can hurt
or help you then. He was sure that Jimmy's parents would
have liked to have a body to bury, but it was far too late
now. The fifty caliber had caught him in the head. Then his
body was cremated in the fire.

He heard gunfire. Slowly he realized it was probably the
20mm ammunition going off in the fire. The rounds would
heat up and explode, with the casing going one way and the
lead slug the other, both at the same velocity. None of
it came in his direction.

Lieutenant Van Dyke walked. He couldn't see the road.
He couldn't hear the trucks. He guessed he was only a mile
or so from the road when he crashed. At least he had walked
away from the bird.

"Damn it, Jimmy, I didn't want you to die." He realized
he had shouted the words at the desert. It was true. Jimmy
was a good kid, almost twenty-one. He'd never make it now.

Water. Did he have any water? They told the flyers to
carry a pint of water in a flat flask in one of the leg pouches.
He didn't know any of the pilots or gunners who did. Yeah,
no flask where it was supposed to be. So he'd have a dry

morning. At once he was thirsty. Damn psychology. He held
the .45 in his right hand and kept walking.

Twice he heard jets screaming over, high above him. Once
a chopper sounded, but that was followed by gunfire, so that
wouldn't be the S&R. He didn't even remember if the rescue
birds were armed. He figured it was bad luck to know too
much about the rescue guys and their helo. Now he'd find
out.

Van Dyke heard a motor. He dropped into the sand and
dirt and waited. It came closer, then the sound drifted farther
away. Before he moved, the sound came toward him again.
A truck of some kind searching for him on a grid pattern?

Then he saw it. On a slight rise to his right he spotted the
top of an open jeep-type rig with a whip antenna. What was
it they learned in survival school? Stay still and there was a
good chance a searcher wouldn't see you. Move and you
were as good as dead. Van Dyke lay totally still. He didn't
even move his eyes. The rig stopped and he could see the
sun glinting off binoculars. He should have spread sand over
himself. Why didn't he when he had the chance?

Then the man on the jeep lowered the glasses and the rig
moved out of sight. How far away was it? Three hundred
yards? Maybe. At least his flight suit was made in cammie
colors to help it blend with the desert. He was damn glad of
that. Should he move or stay still?

He could hear the jeep engine again, straining when it must
have hit loose sand, then growling as it moved away.

He decided to stay put. The chopper should find him. He
wasn't more than a half hour from the field. Had it been a
half hour yet? He hadn't started his stopwatch when he got
away from the ship. Should have.

Time? His watch showed 0814.

It would be getting hot soon. Then he'd wish he had
brought along that water.

"Damnit, Jimmy, I didn't want you to die." He shouted
the words at the sky this time. Van Dyke shook his head
where he lay in the sand. He now pulled hands full of sand
over his flight suit. He had lost his flight helmet when he got
out of the ship. Good thing. It would have been a beacon to
the man with the binoculars.

Then he heard the jeep again. It came closer, then moved

away. On the next pass it was no more than a hundred yards away. He had pulled a floppy hat from another pants pocket and put it over his head when he first left the ship. Now he ducked his head under it and turned his face away from the jeep. If the man used the glasses this time, he'd almost certainly be found.

Damn, found, caught, captured, maybe shot. A .45 against an AK-47 was no contest. The Iraqis would never be in range of his pistol.

He had to know. Lieutenant Van Dyke turned his head slowly, a half inch at a time, until he could see in the direction where he had heard the engine. The jeep had stopped and now he could see two men. One a driver, the other one standing in his seat and searching with the binoculars.

They wanted his scalp bad. Yeah, but they weren't going to get it. He'd heard about prisoners the Iraqi captured. No fun. Not nice at all.

Again, the man in the jeep sat down and the rig rolled away. If their search pattern was working this way, he had to do something. Move, get away. He stood and ran away from the jeep, on farther away from the burning plane as well. They had used that as the center of the search. There might be three or four jeeps out there looking for him. What a prize he would be for their propaganda machine.

He ran harder until he began to wheeze. He wasn't in the best shape for this kind of workout. The jeep sounded again, but now it was farther away. He dropped into the sand and rocks, glad for the breather.

He lay there five minutes, couldn't hear the engine, so he stood and began walking away from the crash site.

He topped a small rise, and fifty feet away he saw the jeep with two Iraqi soldiers standing in it and aiming rifles at him.

"Well, Lieutenant. We have been looking for you. Time you had a ride out of the desert. Just keep walking this way. My English? I learned it at San Diego State on a student visa. Yes, my English is as good as yours, perhaps better. I was a straight-A student at State."

Van Dyke had no place to run. He lowered the .45 to his side but didn't move.

"Come, come, Lieutenant. You have no chance. Either you

surrender, or we kill you. Now, is that an offer you can refuse?"

A second later, he heard a roar and clack of a chopper as a search and rescue helo with USAF markings lifted up behind the jeep. A gunner in the open door of the rescue bird chopped up the two Iraqis with twenty rounds from a door-mounted machine gun. The soldiers slammed out of the jeep and sprawled on the ground.

The S&R chopper settled slowly to the ground.

First Lieutenant Pete Van Dyke ran up to the jeep and checked the two Arabs. Both were dead. He grabbed one of the AK-47s and ran for the chopper.

He jumped in the door, and the bird took wing at once.

"Just one of you?" a sergeant asked. He handed Van Dyke an ice-cold can of Coke.

"Yeah, just one. My gunner . . ."

"That's all right sir, we understand. Need to report in to base. We'll have you in a nice cold shower in thirty-five minutes."

First Lieutenant Van Dyke leaned back against the side of the chopper and closed his eyes. He said it to himself this time.

"Damnit to hell, Jimmy. I didn't want you to die."

26

US *Enterprise* CVN 65
Southern Persian Gulf

Don Stroh came back and found Murdock just as he finished his meal, and they went to his compartment. Murdock sat on his bunk and Stroh tried to pace, but there wasn't room.

"Like I said, we know where Saddam has his poison gas, we know what it is, and we know how to destroy it with as few deaths in the entire area as possible."

"Sure, meaning a dozen or so SEALs."

"You will not be in serious danger if you do the work the way the NBC boys say it should be done."

"How long do we have to train for this job?"

"Roughly twelve hours."

"I'll have all the men write suicide letters before we leave. Make it easier on you when you have to write our next of kin."

"Stop that, Murdock." Stroh said, his impatience tingeing his words. That caused Murdock to look up.

"You're serious about this mission?"

"Damn serious, and so is the President. He says it must be done, and done quickly and done right. He suggested you and your platoon."

"He didn't know how shot up we are."

233

"This isn't going to be a hundred-mile marathon. You'll have all the support we can give you, and that's a hell of a lot."

"Chopper in?"

"Absolutely, with four to six Cobra gunships for protection."

"Chopper out?"

"Yes, it's too far to walk."

Murdock eased up from the bunk. He felt the twinges again, the little hurts that bothered him sometimes from the shrapnel still in his ass from several missions back. "Just what the hell can we do with nerve gas? There's no easy way to destroy the stuff without spreading it around the whole damn globe. We going to do that?"

"Absolutely not. We have a proved way to do the job."

"Nerve gas doesn't deteriorate quickly. It won't burn. It can't be broken down chemically without a whole fucking cracking plant. So how the hell can twelve of us do the job?"

"This gas is called ectoprocy. Don't ask me what it means or how to spell it. It's a known nerve gas but hasn't been used much. It is generally considered too unstable to qualify for production or installation on weapons. Saddam didn't agree. He's done it. He has it. A whiff of a minute quantity of ectoprocy will shut down the nervous system of any animal on earth. It happens in a shorter time than I can tell you about it."

"How would Saddam deliver it?" Murdock asked.

"Missiles. He's still flush with the Scuds and can fire them from mobile units. Which means he can drive them right up to his borders and have a much greater range for them than we figured."

"So the Scuds are the key. Destroy them and you checkmate his gas."

"For a while. We know he has artillery he can use the gas with. That limits his range, but with the right wind, this stuff can be deadly."

"It's a nerve gas, so it bursts out of the shell or missile and clouds across a populated area, killing everything that breathes it?"

"Now you're getting the idea."

"How can we destroy the stuff?"

"You ever seen one of the cloud bombs we have?"

"No."

"It's a combustible liquid chemical, and when released, it vaporizes and forms a huge cloud, maybe a quarter of a mile wide. That is ignited, and the whole quarter of a mile explodes with a fury that hell would like to get the franchise for. This could be burned or exploded something like that."

"You're telling me that this nerve gas will burn? Be damned. You want us to be the trigger?"

"No. We need an accounting."

"We going to be counting warheads and missiles and canisters that hold the deadly shit?"

"That's what we're thinking right now. Unless you have a better plan. The situation is, we must make sure that we get all of the gas. It's manufactured at this plant; the shells and missile heads are assembled there. They have had accidents. Once two years ago, twenty men died when a tiny leak developed in one artillery shell. The shell was containerized and buried at once."

"Gas masks for the tender twelve?"

"Yes, two, actually. We have a new one that will filter out particles down to microns smaller than ever before. This mask has worked in every test it's been given. Using animals, of course. Then you'll have a regular-issue gas mask that is pretty damn good."

"What kind of security does the place have?"

"Doesn't need much. It's in the middle of the desert, a hundred miles from the closest village or oasis. There are twelve buildings in the complex, and on last count, about three hundred military guards. No wall, no electric fence, no guard towers. They tried not to make it look like a military location."

"How many workers at the plant?"

"The work is done. Now it's just a maintenance crew and specialists in case something goes wrong. Not more than twenty-five men."

"So all we have to do is knock down three hundred troops, then outwit twenty-five maintenance men who are undoubtedly armed with Uzis or Kalashnikovs, and then go in and count beans."

"Roughly put, yes. We plan a small surprise for the troops.

There will be a helicopter landing of a hundred Marines twenty miles from the target. They won't make a secret of the landing. They will be moving slowly toward the target. This should bring out most of the troops guarding the missile site and factory."

"So, say we can get inside and put down the locals, then count the beans and radio out our totals, how do we burn up the gas?"

"You don't."

Murdock did a double take. "What the hell you mean, we don't burn up the gas? Why else would we go in there?"

"To count the beans. We have to know that everything they have is in that one complex."

"So, we pull out, you use one of those big gas cloud bombs and hope to hell you burn up everything."

"That's what we're hoping."

"Bullshit," Murdock said. He stood and faced the CIA man. "You know that won't generate enough heat to blast open those missile heads or the 105 artillery shells, and whatever else he has loaded with your ectoprocy. You'll get some of it but not all of it. All Saddam has to do is come in, salvage, put the warheads on new missiles, and he's ready to go."

Stroh looked at him with eyes as cold as Murdock had ever seen.

"So, you know that won't work; you won't do it. Which leaves only one sure way to do the job. A way that the U.S. hasn't used in fifty-five years."

"That's enough. You don't have a need to know."

Murdock laughed. "Oh, hell, yes. You send us in there, into the fucking lion's mouth, and tell us to pull his teeth and then get out and you don't even tell us that the lion isn't even sedated. You think I'm stupid, Stroh?"

"No."

"You're talking like it. The only way to burn up all that shit in the desert and be sure it's gone is with a nuclear weapon. A small yield, maybe only five thousand kilotons. Just enough to vaporize everything in that complex and for five miles around. That keeps the three hundred Iraqi troops in the clear. Of course, the twenty or thirty maintenance men are still inside when you pull the cork."

"Thirty men dead is a small price to pay to keep an estimated ten million from being gassed to death."

"If it came to that."

"If Saddam goes down, it will come to that. Already, his advances are stalling. They have overextended their supply lines, and they're running out of gas, food, and ammunition."

"So when will his retreat start?"

"We figure in two more days, the tide will turn and the Syrians, with U.S. airpower help, will start driving Saddam back toward the border."

"And then Saddam will wipe out Damascus, Syria, for a start, and maybe Haifa for good measure."

"All of this is off the record, Murdock. You didn't hear me say a damn thing about any nuclear weapon."

"Hey, when it happens, it will be an accident in a secret site where Saddam was building nuclear weapons. An easy out. So we didn't throw in a bomb after all."

"Your men aren't to know."

"Oh, yeah, we get away in a chopper and a fucking mushroom cloud boils up behind us and I tell them, 'Damn, just a lucky accident.'"

"A warning, Murdock. Anyone, and I mean anyone, who says a word about this to anyone else, will suffer a serious and fatal accident. This isn't one we can fuck around with."

"The nuke is the only way?"

"You have a better plan?"

"Stroh, you don't need us in there. Just nuke it now and hope you get it all."

"Won't work. The President says you SEALs have another job. You have to make sure all of the personnel left in the complex are routed out and moved at least twenty miles away before the blast. We'll have four choppers there to lift out up to eighty personnel. We pull any civilians off site and dump them out near a road."

"So we're baby-sitters, too, on this one? Bean counters and baby-sitters. What a great assignment."

"You can tell your men you're going in to neutralize the poison gas facility and get the guards out before the place is bombed off the map. You can't tell them how. That's all they need to know."

Murdock slammed the flat of his palm against the bulkhead. "What you're telling me is there is no chance I can say no to this assignment."

"That's what I'm saying. When it happens, there is a special bonus for your men. Everyone is advanced one grade in rank by presidential order. You realize what that's going to mean to your men, to have a presidential order promotion in their permanent service file?"

"It ain't no medal of honor."

"But comes damn close. You can go to full commander, and the JG to full lieutenant."

Murdock shook his head. "Not for me. I move up to full commander, they yank me out of the field so fast my silver leaves would curl up and fall off. I'll stay put and take a commendation instead."

"Done. Now get your ass in gear. We've set up the security on this as tight as next Thursday. Your point of departure will be Forward Logistical Temporary Base One. It's about ten miles from the Iraqi border and about twice that far from the Syrian border. The spot is almost six hundred miles northwest of Riyadh, Saudi Arabia. I'd say just your usual weapons, maybe twice the ammo. You'll be riding both ways, so I'd think all of your men not in the hospital could make the trip."

"I'll decide that, Stroh. When do we get the COD off this floating vacation land?"

"Anytime after five o'clock, I mean 1700. That gives you almost five hours to get ready."

Ten minutes later, Murdock called his thirteen men together in their assembly room and told them quickly what the mission was. He said they'd clear the complex, then haul ass in a chopper and the Air Force or the Navy would blast the place into rubble.

"Won't that release the nerve gas?" Ching asked.

"Extensive tests have shown that this type of nerve gas will vaporize once released and then becomes flammable," Murdock said. "It will explode like one of those gas cloud bombs the Air Force uses." Murdock hoped they bought his explanation.

"You'll get briefed again in the COD. We've got some traveling to do before first light tomorrow morning."

Murdock made a sick bay call. The JG was better, but still

not out of danger. He spoke little, and Murdock left feeling lousy. Adams was in good spirits, saying he knew his arm would heal perfectly and he'd be back in SEALs in six months.

Bill Bradford, with his stomach wound, looked the best of the three. He joked about his "no guts" operation and Murdock told him they were off on another joy ride.

"You'll be on the next one, or one soon," Murdock said. Then he hurried out to pull his gear together and move the men up to the plane. He'd worked it out with Senior Chief Dobler to take over the Bravo Squad for this assignment and the rest of their current deployment. Murdock didn't know what he'd do about the JG once they returned to Coronado. He'd worry about that later. Right now, he had to go in and do a setup for an atomic bomb blast without getting any of his SEALs killed.

27

Forward Logistical Temporary Base
Northern Saudi Arabia

First Lieutenant Pete Van Dyke shook his head in amazement. He'd never seen so much activity in this corner of Saudi in his three days here. There was a line of six big CH-47 Chinook double-rotor vertical assault choppers just beyond the six resident Cobras. They had landed an hour ago, and 200 Marines billowed out of the hatches of four of the birds and stretched their cramped muscles.

Five minutes later, the Marines were doing a fast doubletime hike with weapons into the desert. They came back in fifteen minutes and ate box lunches they evidently had brought with them.

A different breed of fighting man came from the fifth Chinook. They wore cammies and a wild variety of headgear from stocking caps to bandannas or floppy hats. They all had a lean, hungry look and the dark eyes of men Van Dyke didn't want to fool with. They stayed together, ate at the chow hall, and climbed back in their helo. Somebody said they were Navy SEALs. He watched them. He'd heard of some of the amazing things they did. He wondered why they were here.

He would find out. He and the other three Cobras had been

ordered to fly cover and security for two Chinooks. They would fly into the desert and sit down. One Cobra would be in the air at all times for cover. When the SEALs were ready to return, they would cover them and give them ground support if they needed it in the return to the choppers. They were not told where they were flying or what the mission was. Tons of fuel, ammunition, and supplies had come in during the night by helicopter.

The Marines in their four helicopters had been gone two hours with two of the local Cobras for escort when the last two Chinooks lifted off. They were followed closely by four Cobras. Lieutenant Van Dyke led the gunships, putting one of his birds on each side of the big choppers and two above them.

He had no orders where to go or how long the flight would last. They slanted almost due east with a slight twist to the north. He had never flown into this space before. The big Chinook drivers seemed to know where they were going. He kept a tight rein on his Cobras, and they raced into the desert.

The Chinooks could do 150 mph with their load. The Cobras could beat that speed by 25 mph, which gave them a little maneuvering room.

Inside one of the Chinooks, Murdock talked to his men.

"We are heading into Iraq now. We have about a hundred miles to go to the nerve gas center. You saw the Marines take off. By now, they should have landed and made so much noise that most of the military unit at the nerve gas site is on its way to confront the Marines. All are probably walking, so it should take some time. The Marines were supposed to land fifteen miles from the complex. That gives us time to get there, get inside, and do what we have to do. We expect some of the military to remain behind. We'll take them out and herd the civilians into one area. Then we make a count. Hell, we don't even know what we're counting."

"Sound like they just want us to clear the facility of all people, so nobody can say we killed a bunch of military or civilians when we bomb shit out of it." That was Jaybird.

"Could be. At least we'll have secure transport on the ground and enough tools to do the job. We herd the civilians out as soon as we can and take down any military. We'll land two hundred yards from the main gate and get in that way, then we spread out in twos and take it down."

"How much time do we have?" Senior Chief Dobler asked.

"Until dusk," Murdock said. Then we have to be back in this bird. The civilians will go in the other one and any surplus in here. They can put fifty men in each Chinook."

Holt came up with the SATCOM. "I made it through to the Marines, Skip. Some captain wants to talk."

Murdock took the handset.

"SEALs here."

"Yes, SEALs. We've landed and made our presence known. Our scouts tell me there are about two hundred men coming toward us on transport and walking. Are you down yet?"

"Close, Captain. We'll keep you apprised. Let you know as soon as you can disengage. Then put your gunships on the Iraqis and get out of there."

"That's a roger, SEALs. Keep in touch."

Murdock looked out the porthole and saw the ground coming up fast. He looked ahead as much as possible and saw a dozen buildings, all painted desert brown. Nice try.

The pilot asked Murdock where he wanted to be set down, and he told him as near the front gate as possible. It was a gate, with high poles and everything. A dirt road about fifty yards long led to the first building. He saw an Iraqi flag flying on a pole in front of the first building.

A minute later, the big bird hovered a moment, then settled to the ground and a crewman pushed open the side doors. The SEALs rushed out the door and ran toward the gate, through it, and straight at the first building.

There was no gunfire.

They hit the first building. Murdock rammed open the door and slanted inside. It was an administration office. Two men looked up in an area where two dozen could work. They were surprised and then worried. One held up his hands. Then the other one did. Ken Ching ran to them, led them outside the front door, and fastened plastic riot cuffs on their hands and feet.

The SEALs cleared the rest of the room, then started out the back door, when a shot jolted into the desert quietness. A slug buried itself in the doorjamb. Murdock jumped back.

He pushed the panel open and stood to one side. Three rounds came through the opening. Murdock dropped flat to the floor and looked out at ground level. He saw the shooter, a soldier standing fifty feet away, in the open.

Murdock put a three-round burst into him and the man pawed at the air for a minute with one hand, then slumped sideways and fell to the ground, ramming his face into the sand. He didn't move.

Lam checked the other direction from just over Murdock.

"Looks clear," Lam said. He and Murdock darted through the door to a small shed behind the building. They peered around it and saw four soldiers down fifty yards.

"Do them," Murdock said.

He and Lam shot at almost the same time. The four men hesitated. Two died before they could move; the third went down and crawled behind a vehicle. The fourth one sprinted into a building across a narrow street.

"Skip, we splitting up?" Senior Chief Dobler called.

"No. Too many of them so far. Let's fan out and move down the street, clearing the buildings as we go. Civilians we take back to the front. Military we drive ahead of us."

It worked on the first building. It was a supply structure. There were three civilians there, and they surrendered with no trouble. One even spoke English.

"Yes, welcome. Want to get away from this evil place. I will take my friends to the front building and wait. You must take us with you. There is much death in this place."

Murdock waved them away.

The next building held rows of missiles and boxes of artillery shells. They all had painted red tips.

"Careful shooting in here," Murdock said. "Looks like the finished product."

They used one squad in this building and worked slowly between the missiles and the wooden boxes of shells. Ahead, somebody fired a handgun, but the round missed. Murdock sent Jaybird and three men around a stack of boxes and he went the other way. Nothing. Then two men with automatic rifles opened fire from a catwalk ten feet off the floor. Murdock felt a sting on his shoulder, dove behind some artillery round wooden boxes, and tried for some return fire.

Jaybird cut down both men from the other side. They fell off the small balcony and lay still.

"We going to count?" Jaybird called.

"Against what?" Murdock asked. "They didn't give us a total we should get to. They don't know how many units are here of shells or missiles. We might count the Scuds if we see them."

They found no one in the next building. Murdock sent Senior Chief Dobler with Bravo Squad to clear the frame building across the narrow street. He and Alpha took the one just ahead.

As soon as they stepped into the structure, Murdock knew it was different. There was a strange feel. He saw no people, only large vats and pipes and series of low worktables with tubing to each one. The whole place seemed to be a death trap.

They started through the building when a single Arab with a full beard stepped out from behind some large, wooden boxes and yelled at them in Arabic. The man held a two-foot-long canister about six inches in diameter.

He shrieked again in Arabic. They were close enough that they could see the wild look in his eyes. His movements were quick and jerky. He motioned to them with one hand and to the canister with the other.

"Franklin, get over here to the other building," Murdock talked in his lip mike. "We need your Arabic. On the double."

Murdock watched the Iraqi. He was screaming, crying, pointing at them, then at the container.

"Could be some of the nerve gas in there," Holt said where he stood near Murdock.

"Yeah, but what does he want? Why is he crying and screaming?"

"I'd say he's scared shitless about now. He wearing a uniform?"

Murdock looked closer. The man had on a military blouse with bars of some sort on the shoulders. His pants were civilian. He had no hat or weapon. Just the deadly looking canister.

Murdock laid his MP-5 submachine gun on the floor and looked at the man.

"See, I put down my weapon. We don't want to hurt you. What's in the container?"

The man frowned, wiped his eyes, then stared hard at Murdock. He jabbered again in Arabic. Calmer this time. He seemed to be getting control of himself more now. Murdock knew he had to keep talking to the man.

"We're not sure what you want. We're here to help you. To get you out of this desert of death."

The Arab slumped to the floor, but held the canister tightly. He wiped his eyes again, motioned Murdock and the others back. He put the cylinder on the floor in front of him and took out a small-caliber handgun and aimed at the silver container.

"No," Murdock bellowed. The Arab looked up. He shrugged.

Murdock heard movement behind him, and Franklin stepped in beside him.

"Talk to him, Franklin. That could be nerve gas in there."

Franklin spoke softly in Arabic. The bearded man looked up, surprised, then curious. Murdock had no idea what Franklin said. He and the Arab spoke back and forth for several minutes. Then the Arab man shook his head. He picked up the container, stood, and placed the muzzle of the pistol against it.

"Skip, the man says he's been cheated, deceived, lied to, and he's terrified. He just wants to end it all right here and right now. I don't know how to talk him out of it."

Murdock watched the man. He was serious.

"Skip, he says he'll shoot the canister open and we'll all die in seconds. If we shoot him, he'll drop the container and it will split open and we'll still all die."

Murdock watched in deadly fascination as he saw the Iraqi's finger tighten on the trigger.

28

Nerve Gas Facility
Iraqi Desert

Murdock watched the Iraqi soldier's finger tighten on the pistol's trigger. He would kill them all.

"Jaybird, do him," Murdock whispered.

The crack of the single shot from the MP-5 subgun sounded louder than normal in the closed building. The round smashed into the Arab's forehead, driving him backward.

At the moment of the shot, Lam surged forward from where he stood beside Murdock. He took three running steps, then dove toward the falling Arab, his hands extended outward like a wide receiver reaching for the football for a winning touchdown.

His hands touched the container as the dead Arab dropped it. It slid off his stretching right hand but deflected just enough to land on the Arab's chest where he fell on the concrete floor on his back. Lam twisted around, lunged forward from his knees, and grabbed the canister before it rolled off onto the hard floor.

There wasn't a sound in the building for several moments. Then held-in breaths came free and the SEALs began laughing and talking and wiping sweat off their foreheads.

Murdock moved beside Lam and took the container from him. He put it down gently on a worktable.

"Good work, guys. That could have been one hell of a long leave for all of us. Let's see what else we have in this one."

They checked the rest of the building but found nothing more.

Murdock used the Motorola. "Dobler, find anything?"

His earpiece responded at once. "Two civilians and one soldier who surrendered rather than fight. Sent them all to the administration building out front. Your excitement over?"

"All clear here. It was close. Let's move to the last two buildings in this row."

The SEALs checked outside, then ran to the next wooden structure. It had doors that looked sealed. A bar lock and lever had to be moved, then one side of the heavy door swung open. Inside, the SEALs stared in surprise. The place was filled with what they figured were Scud missiles. They were larger than they had expected.

They counted forty of them, each on a dolly that could be hooked up and rolled away to a waiting truck. Each of the missiles had red painted circles around the warhead.

Lam came up to Murdock after they counted. "Some of these could be Al-Hussein missiles. I've heard that they are about the same size as the Scuds, but I couldn't tell the differences."

"We'll give them a count and let the brass figure it out," Murdock said. There were no guards or civilians in the building. They came out, and Murdock used the radio.

"Report, Dobler."

"A batch of smaller missiles and more artillery shells, all with the red ring around the warhead or a red tip."

"Let's move on to the other row. Must be more people around here somewhere."

The platoon moved half a block to another street with six buildings on it. Just as they came around the corner of the first building, they found the people they had been looking for.

Fifty yards down the street, a machine gun opened fire. The SEALs darted back behind the building or took cover behind a low wall. Six-round bursts kept the SEALs' heads down.

Lam wormed to the edge of the frame building and looked around. "Skip, it's an MG with sandbags around it. Good protection. We'll have to flank him or use forty mikes."

Murdock waved at Dobler, who slid into the sand beside where Murdock kneeled.

"Take your squad down past two buildings and see if you can flank that machine gun. We'll throw in some forty mikes."

By the time he said it, four of the men with grenade launchers had positioned themselves out of the line of fire but so they could send the grenades at the machine gun. The first two rounds fell short but silenced the gun as the soldiers evidently dove for cover. Another forty mike hit just beyond the gun, then one at the side.

Senior Chief Dobler ran his squad down the street and around the second building, then slipped up behind cover so they could see the machine gun. A grenade burst beyond the gun, and the two men manning it dove behind the sandbags.

When they came up, four SEALs fired at them. The two machine gunners turned in surprise, then fell, slumped over the weapon they had been ready to fire. Both were dead in an instant.

"The MG is clear, Skipper. The MG is clear, and I don't see any other troops."

On the search down the street, they found another building that was a manufacturing plant for the poison gas. They searched it quickly, found no people, and hurried on. Two more structures had the large missiles, but these were crated and ready for transport to some of the sixty Scud firing sites that Saddam had spread around Iraq.

In the process, they rounded up ten more civilians and captured three more soldiers who had dropped their weapons and held their hands high.

Colt Franklin talked with each man caught. All said that the army captain and his men had gone by truck that morning down the road to meet a force of invaders. They hadn't come back. They had no contact with them by radio.

Murdock stared at the buildings. They had checked each

one. They had killed eight or ten Iraqi soldiers and captured six more and eighteen civilians.

"Jaybird, what's the count on the missiles?" Murdock asked.

Jaybird looked at his ever-present notebook. "With the last building, it comes to a hundred and sixty-eight, all with the red tips, which we believe mean they are loaded with nerve gas."

Murdock moved the men back toward the administration building near the front of the complex. Holt hurried up beside Murdock after a Motorola call.

"Get on the horn on TAC Two. Tell the choppers that we're done here and should be ready to roll in about twenty minutes. We have six Iraqi soldiers and eighteen civilians to transport."

Holt nodded and called the choppers and gave them the messages.

Murdock had the men and the prisoners at the administration building and ready to march out to the choppers when he heard the first whine.

He looked up but couldn't see the jets as they made their run. He heard the hoarse whisper of missiles as they slashed out of the sky and hit one of the Chinook choppers, shattering it into a hundred pieces. Two of the Cobras got off the ground, only to be shot down by cannon fire moments later. The second Chinook escaped the first attack and had just lifted off when another missile hit it and exploded with a huge roar that sent a shock wave across the desert.

"Stay down and out of sight," Murdock bellowed. "Nothing we can do for those men out there now. Must have been two MiGs." He looked around. "Holt, on me, now."

Ron Holt ran up with the SATCOM radio and gave Murdock the handset.

"We should be able to contact the other Chinooks on this channel."

Murdock took the handset. "Chinooks with Marines, can you read me. This is SEAL One."

He waited, looked at the burning choppers. There could be no one alive in any of the four choppers. The two surviving Cobras had lifted off and gone in opposite directions. With luck, the Iraqi MiGs wouldn't find them.

No response to the radio call. Murdock made the call again. Then a voice came on the speaker.

"SEAL One. This is Cobra with you. Any survivors on the four choppers hit?"

"Negative Cobra. Can we warn the Marines about the MiGs?"

"I tried, SEAL One. I couldn't raise them. I'll move in that direction and try again. You're without transport. Suggest you leave your captives and move to the west. We've contacted our base in Saudi about the hit here. No suggestions. We have no more Chinooks at our forward base. The Marines have four. They could stuff in thirteen SEALs."

"Roger, Cobra. We're leaving here and moving on foot to the west. Contact the Marines with your suggestion. Otherwise, it's a damn long walk for us."

"SEAL One. You sure on that survivor report?"

"Afraid so, Cobra. Sorry."

"Yeah, some good buddies. We'll stay in the area, give you cover support. Not much we can do about transporting you. Our base has been instructed not to attempt to recover bodies from the downed helos. That we don't understand. We'll stay with you."

"Thanks, Cobra. Any help now is appreciated."

Murdock turned to the SEALs. "You all heard. A scant chance we might hitchhike a ride with the Marines. Right now, we're hiking into the desert. Check this place for water. We should take some with us. Franklin, ask some of your buddies where they have water around here and how we can take some along. You have five minutes."

"Holt, let's try the Marines again. We had them before."

"SEALs calling Chinook Marines. Can you read?"

There was silence.

Murdock made the call again. Then a voice came on.

"SEALs, Chinook Marines here. We're under fire. Half mile from the choppers. Damn Iraqis are angry."

"Chinook Marines. We took a hit by Iraqi MiGs five minutes ago. Get your choppers in the air, or you're sitting ducks. Move them now. We have no transport back. Can thirteen SEALs hitch a ride with you guys? We're moving out. Mission accomplished. Heading west out of the complex."

"SEALs, we're moving ass here. Choppers warming up, ready to ramble. Thanks for the warning. Will find you. No sweat. Will call off our Marines and put the gunships on the Iraqi. Out."

"Let's move it, people," Murdock said to his SEALs.

"Skipper, what about the Iraqis we have collected?" Dobler asked.

"We'll walk them with us. Get them out of the way at least. Tell them they need to be ten miles from this place when it blows because of the nerve gas."

They walked away from the buildings and hopefully from the fatal consequences of the nerve gas.

An hour into the desert, Murdock figured they had covered four miles. The civilians were holding them up. He called a halt and made another radio call.

"Chinook Marines. Where are you? It's been an hour. SEALs here calling."

The answer came back quickly.

"SEALs. We're having some trouble here disengaging. We have three birds ready to move with troops. Last fifty men are still challenged by the Iraqi. Determined. Our Cobras are doing the final attack on them. Yes, now we're loading the last bunch. No sign of your MiGs. Hope they don't find us. Moving in ten. We'll go up this road to the buildings and turn west. We'll find you."

"Roger that, Marines. We're hung out to dry here."

Murdock told Holt to change frequencies to the satellite. He put in a call to Stroh on the *Independence*. He didn't expect to get him, but he'd leave a message. The encrypted words went out quickly:

"Stroh, the complex is sanitized. All personnel removed. We're without transport, walking five miles from the center. When we are clear by ten miles, we'll give you another call. Murdock out."

Senior Chief Dobler listened and looked at Murdock. "So where to now?"

"Go west, young man, go west. Another six miles, unless the Marines land before then."

The line of thirty-seven men had spread out as they walked. The SEALs had ten yards between them from training and practice. The civilians had straggled. Murdock was at the end of the line playing cowboy drag catching the strays.

Nobody heard or saw the MiG until the rounds hit. The cannon fire exploded in the sand around the walking men from behind them. Their spread-out formation saved the lives of a lot of them. The MiG made one pass. It was traveling at Mach 1 and coming in at an angle, so even the two-barrel cannon could make the 23mm rounds hit the ground only one every thirty feet. Murdock bellowed to the men to disperse. Franklin shouted the same thing in Arabic. By the time the MiG came back, he had a target that was spread out fifty yards wide and half again that long. He fired, but no one was hit.

The plane raced off to the east.

Murdock called for casualties. He had no reports on his radio. Franklin came on. "Two of the civilians and one Iraqi solder have been hit. One of them is dead."

"Can the wounded walk?"

"I think they both can. Not hit too bad."

They walked on to the west.

"Where the hell are the Marine choppers?" Murdock asked.

Holt gave him the handset. "We're back on TAC Two, skipper."

Murdock called the Chinooks.

"Have a small problem, SEALs. We're overloaded. Our pilots refuse to take on any more men, not even three or four per bird. I can't overrule them. We're heading for the temporary base just across the line. We'll unload and send one Chinook back for you. Hang tight for another two hours, and we'll have you."

"Let me talk to that chickenshit pilot of yours. Those Chinooks can carry over seven tons. Fifty Marines at two hundred pounds each is only five tons. That overloading is a bunch of bullshit. Tell him!"

"I've told him a dozen times. He outranks me. He's the boss of his plane. Captain of his ship. I can't change his mind."

"I'll make an appointment with him at that advanced base just as soon as we get in. Tell him to get his life insurance paid up. Out."

Murdock gave Holt the handset, his face a mask of fury. He tried to calm down. The way he felt right then, he'd change all four of those pilots' status into KIA if he had the chance.

"So, skipper?" Dobler prodded.

"We keep walking west. Get as far from that damn nerve gas as we can."

Dobler and Jaybird got the men back in line spread out ten yards apart, and Dobler led the line west.

They had walked for fifteen minutes when Lam frowned and motioned to the rear.

"Commander, we've got a vehicle coming up behind us."

"Scatter, spread out. Franklin, get the Iraqis spread out. We don't know who this fucker might be. Damn sure he isn't one of ours."

The SEALs went to the sand, covered part of themselves with it, and ducked their heads to complete the camouflage with their desert cammies.

Murdock watched to the rear. He saw it three minutes later. The rig was a half-track of some brand. It had a machine gun in front and a man scanning the landscape.

"Stay down," Murdock said on the Motorola. "This one has an MG up front with a man on it. Not sure what else he has. Hope he gets close enough before he spots us. Long guns, get ready."

"Yeah, see him," Fernandez said. "Holding."

The half-track kept coming. Murdock figured it was still back five hundred yards. The guy on the gun wouldn't be able to see the SEALs, but he might spot some of the civilians. Would he shoot at them?

"Got him dead to rights," Tony Ostercamp said.

"Hold. If he fires, we fire," Murdock said. "Weapons free at that time."

They watched the half-track grinding across the sand and rocks of the western Iraqi desert. It came to a slight rise and paused. The man on the machine gun lifted binoculars and scanned the landscape ahead of him. He passed quickly over the area where the SEALs and the Iraqis lay. Then he came back and studied it again. He went behind his weapon and fired a six round burst into the area.

One of the Iraqi civilians stood up, screaming in fear, and

held his hands high. The machine gunner splattered him with five rounds and he went down, dying in the sand. The half-track turned and charged forward at the place where the civilian died. The rig was only a hundred yards away when Murdock changed the order. No one had fired when the MG did because of the range.

Now he was in killer range. "Let's get him," Murdock said and cut loose a six-round burst from his submachine gun without the suppressor. Six more weapons fired, and the machine gunner slumped to the side, then was blown off the rig as round after round jolted into his body.

The half-track stopped. "Get the cab," Murdock said.

Ostercamp concentrated on the front tire he could see. He put ten rounds in it and watched the rig settle on that side.

More rounds shattered the windshield, then ripped into the side of the rig. Two forty mikes hit close, then two more and a WP sprayed the half-track with burning phosphorus.

The rig backed up slowly, turned, and with one wheel running on the rim, drove back the way it had come. The chasing fire tapered off, then stopped, and they let the half-track continue on out of sight.

"Let's take another hike," Murdock said into his lip mike. The SEALs waved at the Iraqis, Franklin yelled at them in Arabic, and slowly the line formed again and Dobler used his compass and led them to the west. They left the dead civilian sprawled in the sand. There was nothing else they could do for him.

"We need another two miles," Murdock told Jaybird. "Then we should be out of harm's way."

Jaybird frowned and rubbed his jaw. "That'll put us ten miles from the damn nerve gas. Thought you said it would burn up? Damn, they must be planning some bombing raid." He grinned. "Hey, bet they're gonna use one of those mile-long gas bombs."

Murdock just waved and kept hiking. If they saw the mushroom cloud, they would see it. Nothing he could do about that.

A half hour later, they were at the point Murdock figured was ten miles. He had Holt crank up the SATCOM on the satellite channel and this time caught Don Stroh near the radio on the carrier.

"We're at the ten-mile point. You have word that the four choppers of the Marines and their Cobras are out of the area?"

"We do. We plan to wait until you are into Saudi to take out the complex. Hear one of the Chinooks will be back to take all of you clear of the area."

"I've got a duel to fight as soon as I find that bastard Chinook pilot."

"Easy, easy. He had orders. We want all of those Iraqi civilians out, too, and the birds couldn't take them. No duel. Hang tough, we have talked with the Chinooks. They are now at the forward base. Should be refueled and on their way to pick you up in ten minutes. Say an hour in the air. Watch for them. You have any coordinates?"

"No, didn't bring the machine. We'll use flares when we spot them."

"Do it. Things are moving nicely. We're almost there."

"Maybe you are. We're still stuck in the middle of the fucking Iraqi desert."

Fifty-five minutes later, the big chopper roared overhead. They didn't have to use a flare. Franklin explained to the Iraqis that they were being taken to a base and later would be flown to a small village on the Iraqi border. That's what Murdock told him to say.

They loaded up and landed back at the Air Force's Forward Logistical Temporary Base. Just as they got off the chopper, Murdock heard a strange noise, then he felt the ground shake under his feet.

"They did it," he said. Dobler frowned at him.

"They did what?"

"They just blew up that nerve gas factory and all those Scuds."

Dobler laughed. "You getting psychic on me, Skipper? That place is a hundred miles away from here."

Murdock managed to work up a tired smile as they moved toward the mess tent. "A hundred miles, Senior Chief Dobler, and I hope to hell that all that nerve gas stays right there."

29

Army High Command
Damascus, Syria

General F. Jablah stared in total concentration at the expanded map of the eastern border of Syria and Iraq. The rough line of markers showed the front lines. Fighting still raged on most of the five-mile front that Saddam Hussein had attacked.

In two places, the enemy had driven ten miles into Syria. At one place directly aimed at the capital of Damascus, the Iraqi army had penetrated almost twenty miles. That thrust had been blunted, over a hundred Iraqi tanks destroyed through the aid of the United States airpower and his own MiGs and their Dassault Mirage fighters. Now that incursion had been pressed back to the ten-mile line.

His other army units were attacking the Iraqis all along the MLR. Their interdiction of the supply lines with their own fighters and the U.S. planes had made serious shortages in the already-strained umbilical of food and ammunition for the Iraqis.

Yes, they had started offensives all along the five-mile front and were pushing forward. He had urged his air force to step up the attacks on the supply lines day and night.

An aide hurried in and motioned to the telephone. General Jablah picked up the phone.

"Yes?"

"General. Major Duma from the far northern sector with the thirty-fourth Regiment. We have been attacked by at least two nerve gas artillery shells. Twenty-seven of our men died before we knew what had happened. The area has been evacuated. The gas blew into a small village, and thirty women and children there died. We have pounded the artillery unit with counterbattery, and two of our planes have bombed the unit. We're not sure of the results."

"The bastards. Order a regimental attack on that sector at once, and overrun that artillery unit and slaughter every man in the area. I want it done now. Hussein can't be allowed to use nerve gas. Get your attack formed and moving within an hour. Call in massive air support. I want that artillery unit smashed before dark."

He hung up the phone and put a large red marker on the map where the thirty-fourth Regiment battled. After checking with two more commanders, he put a push in that area. If they could get a good run, they might be able to smash forward three or four miles this side of the Iraqi border, wheel right, and cut off one of the deeper incursions of the Iraqis in the center of the front. Then he called on all the air he had to plow up the ground where that artillery battery was. If it had moved, they must find it.

It was nearly two hours after the nuclear blast in the Iraqi desert that an aide came in and turned on the TV set in the general's office.

"You should see this, General." The major tuned to CCN, which had a news special in progress.

"As near as anyone can tell, the nuclear blast took place in Iraq's western desert, a hundred miles from Saudi Arabia's border and about two hundred miles from the Syrian boundary. Iraq has not commented on the blast, but seismic recorders in Cairo and Tel Aviv report a disturbance equal to a five-point-five earthquake.

"When translated into nuclear energy terms, that would mean a nuclear blast in the five- to eight-megaton range. It has long been suspected that Iraq was working on constructing one or more nuclear weapons. No one will comment on what caused the blast. Rumors have also been circulated that the Iraqis had a nerve gas and biological warfare agent plant somewhere near the same area.

"Our correspondents are waiting now for an official statement from military headquarters in Baghdad. Yes, I understand our correspondent in Baghdad is ready."

The scene shifted to a man in shirtsleeves standing in front of a building.

"Yes, Jose Phillips in Baghdad for CNN. It has been confirmed by Iraqi military authorities that a nuclear blast did take place in its western desert. This is the official statement that the Iraqi high command gave to us on videotape."

"Iraq has been attacked by warmongering elements in the United States who dropped a nuclear weapon on a defenseless scientific laboratory and research center working on cures for cancer and AIDS in western Iraq. There has been a considerable death toll at the facility including two world-renowned scientists. A hundred and forty-eight scientists and lab workers perished, along with a security force of twenty-four.

"All roads leading into the area have been blocked off. Our own nuclear disaster team will move into the drop zone as soon as it is safe to do so. Our experts tell us that there will be a dead zone about ten miles square at this spot for up to five hundred years.

"Iraq will present a motion of condemnation tomorrow at the United Nations General Assembly and Security Council against the United States. We will ask for a worldwide embargo against the United States for this savage and unparalleled attack by a superpower on a developing nation.

"We have proof of U.S. involvement. United States Air Force helicopters were seen in the area of the bomb blast, as well as U.S. Marines that attacked the security forces at the scientific research center. Because of the intense vaporization of the downed helicopters near the complex, no physical evidence remains of the U.S. sadistic attack on a peace-loving people."

The general turned away from the set. He'd heard enough of the Iraqi lies. A new voice brought him back to the TV.

"We now have an official comment from the United States in response to the diatribe from Saddam Hussein."

The general turned to the set.

"The United States ambassador to the United Nations says he will oppose any censure motion in that body and that the U.S. has solid evidence that Iraq was producing a deadly nerve gas in the area. There is further satellite evidence that the nerve gas has been loaded into Scud missiles and artillery rounds. The same area is the home of Iraq's development laboratories and test facilities for the nation's continuing effort to produce nuclear weapons.

"Our scientists report to me that the size of the nuclear blast, estimated at five to eight megatons, is consistent with the size of a burst that could be triggered in early experiments with harnessing nuclear power. We also now have a report from the battle front in Syria, that more than fifty people, both military and civilians, have been killed by artillery shells from Iraq that contained deadly nerve gas. Iraq will be taken to task with the next meeting of the Security Council to explain this deadly development in the aggressive war it is now fighting in Syria."

General F. Jablah smiled for the first time that day. He had an offensive going, and Saddam was just caught using nerve gas in an attack. Saddam had also lost his poison gas and nuclear weapons manufacturing and development facility in the desert. The war might be over sooner than everyone thought.

USS *Enterprise* CVN 65
South Persian Gulf

Late the night before, Murdock had landed on the carrier in a COD and hustled his four previously wounded men to sick bay to have the medics look over their wounds, put on clean bandages, and generally check them out.

The medics examined Ching, Lampedusa, Franklin, and Holt. All were rebandaged and sent back to light duty. Murdock had continued into the hospital section and talked with the doctors about Lieutenant (j.g.) DeWitt. The JG was out of danger, his lung had weathered the minor puncture, and he was on his way to recovery. The doctor said it would take at least two or three weeks of hospital time, then he could get out of the hospital for extremely light duty for another two months.

Adams was chafing about his confinement.

"Hell, Skipper, at least let me clean my weapon and polish your boots or something. I'm going crazy in this damn place. It's so clean it gives me hives."

Murdock chuckled. Told him his arm was healing, but they wanted to watch it for another week, then he'd be off his leash. He growled about it and went back to his *Playboy* magazine.

Bill Bradford with the stomach wound looked the best of the three. He, too, would need another week under the white sheets before he could be released.

Don Stroh found Murdock in the sick bay and shadowed him back up to the SEALs' assembly room.

"Look, about that foul-up with the choppers."

"I've challenged that son of a bitch to a duel. Forty-fives at twenty feet. Twelve rounds. The man who lives wins. They could just as well have put us on board. They weren't overloaded. Yeah, I know, the brass didn't want any more casualties at the site than they could help. But they just sold out thirteen SEALs for the chance, the fucking *chance*, that the twenty-four Iraqis might get caught in the blast. We were ten miles out for kereist sakes."

Stroh let Murdock shoot off steam, then lifted his brows.

"Hey, I was in there punching for you. I told them you were outside the blast area. They said for twenty-four more corpses, they'd risk going back and getting you."

"That half-track could have killed off half of us. From now on out, I want guaranteed transport out of an assignment and guaranteed backup in case that first transport fucks up. If we don't get that, mister CIA master crafter, the Third Platoon *just won't go.*"

"Murdock, get some sleep. We'll talk in the morning. Looks like the war is going better than we expected. Most of the front is at a standstill or the Syrians are mounting a counteroffensive. Our airpower has just about closed off the Iraqi supply lines. So relax. I don't have any new assignment on the books for you. Relax and sleep in."

That was when Murdock realized how tired he was. Not

even a shower. He found his compartment, dove into the bed, and only managed to get his rubber boots off before he slept.

Somewhere over Syria

First Lieutenant Pete Van Dyke circled his Cobra gunship over a sector he hadn't seen before. It was to the north part of the thirty-mile front. The fighting was going for the Syrians now. He had been assigned to interdict any vehicles he saw behind the main fighting line on the Iraqi side.

His new gunner had his first day of combat yesterday and quickly proved that he could do the job. He was a natural using the Gatling. So far today he had cut up four small trucks with 20mm cannon fire and knocked out two larger transport trucks with 2.75-inch rockets.

His name was LeRoy and he came from Georgia.

As they hunted targets, Van Dyke tried not to think about the two close friends he lost in the raid on the big plant in the desert yesterday with the SEALs. He had lifted off his Cobra just prior to the attack on the Chinooks and been out of range of the explosions. Then, when he shepherded the SEALs on their hike west, he wasn't there when they needed him with the half-track.

Van Dyke was pleased that the SEALs had made it out with no casualties. He had wondered why the big Chinooks didn't stop for them. He'd seen more than seventy men crammed into the Chinooks.

"Hey Cap, we got another truck running back toward Iraq," LeRoy's slow drawl said in the IC. "Shall we give him a boost getting home?"

"That's a roger, LeRoy. Let me move in closer for you." A minute later, LeRoy's Gatling gun riddled the machine with the 20mm cannon fire from the three barrels in the nose.

Van Dyke swung up sharply when he saw men near the truck lift rifles, and he slanted away to make a harder target. They had taken a dozen rounds of ground fire on this sortie, but none had hit a vital spot.

When Van Dyke was well out of rifle range, he lifted the Cobra up higher again to check his four-mile sector. "Let's see what we can find, LeRoy. Should be some more targets out here. We have another ten minutes of hunting time before we head back."

Below, a thousand yards ahead, he saw the Syrian infantry being pushed back. He swung in for a better look. "LeRoy, check out the infantry down there. Looks like the good guys are retreating."

"Peers so, Lieutenant. Wonder why?" A moment later, the gunner spoke again. "I got him, Cap. There's a damned tank down there behind those trees just shooting to hell and gone at the Syrians."

"Yeah, a tank. First one we've seen all morning. Wish to hell we had had a TOW missile. They're made to order for tank killing. Can we do him with the rockets?"

"We can do a job on the tread if we can get in close enough, Lieutenant. We gonna try?"

"If you can knock the tread off one side, the tank will be dead in the water, and the Syrian Infantry should be able to finish him off."

"That's a go, Lieutenant. Let's get him."

Van Dyke turned around and came in to shoot at the side of the tank. He saw little ground fire and slanted in to a hundred yards. He felt a rifle round hit his machine, then another. He held the rig steady for a moment and felt three or four rockets fired. Then he surged upward and out of the way of the small arms fire from below. He turned so they could see the shots. One hit the top of the tank and did little damage. Two hit the dirt well below where the tread rolled the tank forward. The heavy machine crushed a small dirt bunker and probably tapped Syrians inside.

Van Dyke came in again, closer this time. He was no more than fifty yards away when he steadied the machine and felt LeRoy get off four rockets aimed at the tread. This time, his aim was better, and two of the small missiles hit the tread area and blasted the track into pieces. The tank swiveled around toward him as the near side tread couldn't move.

He felt two more small arms rounds jolt into the plane, then a dozen rounds ripped through the nose of the ship, and he knew the tank's .50-caliber machine gun had found him. He checked and saw that LeRoy wasn't hit. The plastic cowl over both seats had shattered. The prop wash of the rotors slashed through the cockpit, and he urged the machine higher and away from the ground fire.

"LeRoy, you okay?"

"Yes, Cap, just a little chilly."

Then they both felt more of the machine gun rounds pound into the sides of the slender fuselage that went back to the tail. Suddenly, the flight controls went mush; then, a few seconds later, the controls wouldn't respond at all. He felt the top rotor lose power and go into freewheeling.

"We're going down, kid. Fire off the rockets."

Another burst of the .50-caliber machine gun rounds ripped into the machine, and one round caught First Lieutenant Pete Van Dyke in the neck just below his flight helmet. He slammed against the far side of the cockpit as the Cobra gunship dropped straight down from three thousand feet.

It hit the desert, and the rest of its fuel exploded. That set off the rest of the 2.75-inch rockets, which detonated in place. In two minutes after impact, there wasn't enough left of the gunship to identify. The two bodies had been incinerated in the white-hot fire that raged on three hundred gallons of aircraft fuel.

Army High Command
Damascus, Syria

General F. Jablah settled back in his big chair and watched aides move markers on the wall map that showed the front lines. Today it had shrunk to a three-mile fighting zone. A mile on each end of the strip had been closed off and the enemy overwhelmed, captured, or slain. A few went screaming back toward the Iraqi border.

Yes, the war was going well. His troops had performed brilliantly once the first onslaught had been blunted and then stopped. His aircraft had helped rule the skies. The allied planes that came, especially the Americans, had also helped. The last three days there had been no reports of Iraqi planes over the fighting zone.

He was not sure why. A daring raid with fighter-bombers into the major Iraqi airfield near Baghdad had been the clincher. There were reports that Saddam had sent most of the surviving 250 fighters and 200 helicopters he had left into Iran so they wouldn't be bombed. He had done the same thing in the Gulf War ten years ago.

Now it was a case of mopping up, pushing the last of the infantry units across the border, and making them suffer as much as possible without sustaining any more Syrian casualties than absolutely necessary.

He had used his airpower here effectively. First a bombardment and strafing by helicopters and fighters, then the infantry would sweep in and mop up any of the opposition that hadn't run for the border.

Another two days and it would be over. He watched the center of the map where there had been a nearly twenty-mile thrust toward Damascus. Now the thrust had been stopped and pushed back ten miles. Elements of his tank and infantry had smashed through light resistance near the border to cut off a ten-mile corridor of Iraqi troops, guns, and trucks. They were surrounded and would all be taken prisoners or killed.

He had lost a lot of good men, especially on the sneak attack that rolled so far into his beloved land. But anyone in any country who puts on a military uniform voluntarily must come to accept the fact that he could die. War is not a tea party. War is man's greatest game. War is also a giant chessboard where the actors die as the game is played.

He heard a cheer and looked up.

"My General," an aide said. "It has just been told here that the majority of the Iraqi troops in the corridor that has been cut off have been surrendered by a brigadier general who was in command."

General Jablah sipped at the thick black coffee and stared over the top of the cup. So, soon he would have to decide. Did he pursue the enemy into his own land, capturing as much matériel as possible? Take over the tanks and trucks that would still run and the field guns and small arms and supplies of food and fuel?

Or did he stop at the border?

He knew it would be an almost impossible job to defeat Saddam on his home territory. There the Syrian troops would have the long supply lines. The Iraqis would have the emotional cause of defending their homes and protecting their women and children. It would take more than his resources to invade Iraq and dethrone Saddam Hussein.

His troops would stop at the border. Someone else would
have to take care of the devil Saddam Hussein.

USS *Enterprise* CVN 65

The SEALs had been back on board the floating island for
over a day now, and Don Stroh had not been seen or heard.
They put their gear in shape, oiled their weapons again, and,
once rested from the last challenge, they began to get bored.

They knew that operations on the big platform had slowed.
There were fewer and fewer of the F-18s screaming off the
catapults. Fewer calls for pilots to report to the ready room.
They heard reports that the war was slowing down, that Saddam was licking his wounds and making a mad dash for
home. The Syrians jolted along, hot on his heels, gathering
up as much wâr matériel as they could before it vanished
across the border.

On the second day with no action for the SEALs, Murdock
looked up Stroh. The CIA man had just finished a big meal
and sipped at an ice-cold cola.

"Murdock. Wondered where you were. Word came
through about an hour ago. I have new orders for you."

"At least this time we're rested and ready to go."

"Good. This afternoon, your three hospital cases are being
flown out of here, heading for San Diego's Balboa Naval
Hospital. The rest of you slackers will be leaving by COD
for Riyadh and the big Air Force base near there. I'm washing my hands of you. You're reassigned back to Coronado."

Murdock stared hard at the slightly plump CIA man and
scowled. "Stroh, this is not something you should joke
about."

"No joke, Red Ryder. You get on your cayuse in two hours
and you're out of here. You might want to tell your guys
and get them ready to boogie."

Murdock laughed and nodded. "Okay Little Beaver, now
I believe you. You keep yourself well, and we'll talk in about
three months. I need at least that much time to get my troops
back in top fighting shape."

"Three months? Easy. I don't know of anything that's even
cooking on the back burner. You take care, and we'll see
you when we see you." He took a drink of the cola. "When

did you say the best yellowtail tuna fishing season was there off San Diego?"

"It's mostly off Baja California, Mexico, and it could be almost anytime. But usually in the summer. Last year they caught yellows ten months out of the twelve."

"Good. We'll keep that in mind."

Murdock waved and hurried into the companionway and down to his men to get them ready for the COD transport plane on their first leg of the long trip home.

30

Naval Special Warfare Section
Coronado, California

Lieutenant Commander Blake Murdock had settled into his small office in the SEAL Team Seven, Third Platoon, building in the SEAL compound on the beach at Coronado. He'd had his platoon back in town for three days, and they were getting used to walking on land again.

Most of his time had been spent in Balboa Naval Hospital up in the park. Bradford had taken a bad turn and would be in bed another two weeks with his stomach wound. He kept joking about no guts, but that was too close to the truth. His doctor said he should be fine in two months.

Adams, whose left arm had been blown off by the mine, was progressing slowly. The attachment had taken; the blood surged through the arm almost normally. Some of the nerves weren't responding the way the doctors had hoped. He had partial use of his arm and hand.

He was still under treatment in the hospital. They wouldn't let him out until they were satisfied that they had established as much use of the arm and hand as possible.

"Yeah, Skipper, I know. I figured it out. I can't be a SEAL anymore. Turn in my trident. Sometimes I wonder, 'Why me?' Then I quit feeling sorry for myself. Hell, I should be dead by all rights. So I'm one lucky puppy. I'll do whatever I can, but I want to stay in the Navy and I want to stay with Team Seven if you can wangle me a light duty spot somewhere at BUDS/S."

Murdock said he would try.

The JG could be a problem. DeWitt had not responded to treatment the way the medics hoped. He was still having trouble with the punctured lung. Some veins were chopped up by the splattering lead, and they still hadn't found all of the fragments. He would be in the hospital for at least a month more.

That left Murdock with a problem. Did he check out the JG and ask for a replacement squad leader, or did he let senior Chief Dobler carry the load until the JG was fit for duty? He'd have to decide soon.

His other casualties were healing. Lampedusa's shoulder wound had closed and caused him little trouble. The medics at the hospital checked him and the other walking wounded and released them all.

The shrapnel in Franklin's left leg had worked its way out and was healing. The eye men checked Holt twice and decided there was no physical damage to his eyes from the exploding mine. His blindness was from shock and psychological trauma and had left no lasting damage. Ching's arm wound had almost healed, and he was ready for duty.

Master Chief Gordon MacKenzie came into the office and dropped into the chair beside Murdock's desk.

"Laddie, that after-action report. Well done. I passed it on to the commander. He's away for a month's special duty at Norfolk."

"Maybe he'll get promoted to NAVSPEC Two."

MacKenzie chuckled. "Not a chance, Laddie. We're stuck with him until he retires. You had a bunch of rough missions since you've been home."

"True, Master Chief. We got our asses shot off, is what happened. Going to take at least two months to get back in shape to go out again."

"I told the commander three months. Aye, you've got some holes to fill and some mending to tend to."

"First I better get a replacement for Adams. We've got to

figure out where to put him in the nonaction part of the team."

"First he has to get past the medical board," MacKenzie said. "I have my doubts he'll be in the Navy much longer. A medical discharge and forty percent disability is my guess."

"That could kill Adams. He's SEAL from head to gullet."

"I'll call in some favors and see what we can do for the lad. Oh, you had some fan mail this morning."

The master chief pulled out a sheet of paper from his pocket and handed it to Murdock.

"A fax," Murdock said. He read it: "Murdock. Checked by phone with Seaforth Landing. Said they had over 200 yellowtail and six dorado yesterday. I may need to come to San Diego next week. I might have a special assignment for you and Jaybird on board the *Seaforth Two*. I'll keep you up to date.

"The chief was pleased with your platoon's operation during the past month. Sorry we gave you such a large dose. Nothing on the horizon that looks interesting. Following some leads, but none are getting hot. Tell Master Chief MacKenzie to keep cracking the whip. Stroh."

"I'm afraid we've created a fishing monster here, MacKenzie."

"Do him good. He's too uptight all the time."

"And you're the picture of relaxation?"

"Aye, that's me, sir."

"I want you to arrange a leave for all of my men not in the hospital. Get them out of here. Let them get drunk and scream and yell and whore around a little. Do them good. Starting in two days. Do the paperwork."

"Aye, Commander."

"Speaking of paperwork, I better get at this. Send me four suggestions for a new man to replace Adams. Oh, are there any JGs on our roster without a platoon?"

"For a replacement or a temporary duty?"

"Right now as a temp. We'll have to wait and see how DeWitt handles the healing process. I'm hoping he'll be fit for duty within two months."

"What if Stroh yells with a problem?"

"Tell him that I've got medical reports that put six of my

men on the unfit-for-duty roster, and that the platoon won't be ready for action for at least three months. He'll have to work with another platoon if it's that big of an emergency."

"Har, har, Commander. I like that spunk. I'm moving on those leaves."

The master chief had just left the office when the phone rang. Murdock checked his watch: 1500.

"Murdock here, Third Platoon Seven."

"Just wondered if you wanted veal or T-bone steak for your entrée at dinner tonight."

"Ardith Jane." That was all he could say for a moment. Then he hurried on. "You sneaked into town?"

"I did. Your condo needed some cleaning up, but it's ready for company now. What's your choice for dinner?"

"You . . . in that thin, wispy silk thing."

"That's dessert. Welcome home, sailor. Can't wait to see you."

"Three days; you're late."

"Don Stroh promised to call me, and he forgot. He owes me. How about the veal?"

"Fine. I'll be home in ten minutes."

"I'll be waiting."

Later that evening, he couldn't remember what they had for dinner. They sat in front of the fireplace and watched the flames. She pressed close to him.

"How is Ed DeWitt?"

"Struggling. He's fighting a couple of medical problems, but his doctors think he'll come through it in good shape. It's going to take some time."

She looked up at him from clear blue eyes that showed a touch of moisture. She wiped at them. "Hey, I could get used to this. Having you here, watching the fire, not even talking. Just . . . just being together."

He held her tighter.

"I might quit my job in Washington."

He pushed her away and stared at her. "Quit? Washington? Are you joking?"

"No. I've had a good offer from here in San Diego. A big electronics/computer firm that does a lot of work for the government. They must think I can help them in D.C."

"What would you do?"

"I'd be in legal and sales and promotion. Mostly promotion with D.C., from what they said."

"So, you're considering it?"

"I don't know. As soon as Dad found out about the offer, he spread the word in the halls. The next day, I had three offers from various agencies and one from State."

"The State Department?"

"Yes."

"So?"

"I wanted to see what you thought."

"We talked about this possibility before. It has to be your decision. If I urge you to come out here and you wind up miserable in the job, we'll both be unhappy. This has to be what's best for your career first. I come in second on this race. That's the way it should be."

"I could never be miserable if I'm with you."

She stretched out on the soft rug and pulled him over her. They didn't say a word for several minutes. She kissed him long and deeply and then gave a little whimper.

"Please, darling. Right now. Right now."

Later that night, they lay in his bed and watched the shadows the small night light threw on the ceiling.

"Oh, I almost forgot. I saw your father before I left. He said to tell you he missed you by a day in Riyadh. He wanted to go up north to a temporary forward helicopter base near the Iraqi border, but some colonel told him the base came under fire frequently and no civilian was permitted up there except the President himself."

Murdock laughed. "I wondered where he was this time. Figured he'd wangle a trip over there somewhere. I spent a few hours at that forward base going and coming."

He watched her in the soft light, so blonde and sleek and beautiful.

"About those job offers," he said.

"Let's not talk about it tonight. I was hoping that you would have your paperwork caught up by now and we could drive up the coast. Maybe go to Moro Bay again."

"Yes. I'm taking off a week. We'll drive all the way up Highway One along the coast to Carmel."

She smiled, kissed him softly on the cheek, and leaned

back. A moment later, she slept. He didn't see how she could do that so quickly. At last he went to sleep.

The phone roused them in the morning. It was eight o'clock.

"Yes?" Murdock said, his voice growling.

"Wake up, you two, time to rise and shine and smell the bacon. I don't want to intrude, but it will be at least a week before I can make it out there for our fishing trip. I want one of those overnight ones so we can catch the big yellows. Something stirring here. Not too sure how bad it's going to be. We're watching it. Might not pop for a couple of months yet."

"My platoon is on medical restriction. We won't be cleared for active duty for three months."

"You're kidding."

"Talk to my phalanx of doctors."

"Fight that battle later. What do you know about Libya?"

"Libya is a nothing."

"What about Colombia in South America?"

"Nothing in Colombia except drugs."

"What about the Golden Triangle?"

"Drugs, the Far East somewhere."

"Good. I don't want to interfere with your reunion. You hang tough and get that platoon back into fighting shape. One of these days, we're going to need you again."

"Right, Stroh. Right. I love you, too. And last time, I caught the most fish." Murdock said good-bye and hung up.

"Colombia, Libya?" Ardith asked.

"Forget it, he's just probing. I have to call the master chief and tell him I won't be in for a week. He'll do the paperwork. When shall we start driving north?"

"Right now." She paused and giggled like a teenager. "Well, after we get dressed and have breakfast. No, let's drive awhile, then have breakfast up the coast somewhere, maybe at Laguna Beach."

It took Murdock two days to relax. Even then, he wondered what Stroh had meant about Libya. Qaddafi had a long history of being a thorn in the side of the U.S. Maybe the CIA had at last decided to do something about him. What? There was no excuse for the U.S. to go in there in force with the military. So, covertly with the SEALs. Murdock threw a stone in the bay and thought about it. Could happen. But not for three months.

He grabbed Ardith's hand, and they ran for the stairs leading up from the bay. They had a basket full of clam strips waiting for them in that little restaurant that overlooked Moro Bay. That's all he wanted to think about right now.

SEAL TALK

MILITARY GLOSSARY

Aalvin: Small U.S. two-man submarine.

Admin: Short for administration.

Aegis: Advanced naval air defense radar system.

AH-1W Super Cobra: Has M179 undernose turret with 20mm Gatling gun.

AK-47: 7.63-round Russian Kalashnikov automatic rifle. Most widely used assault rifle in the world.

AK-74: New, improved version of the Kalashnikov. Fires the 5.45mm round. Has 30-round magazine. Rate of fire: 600 rounds per minute. Many slight variations made for many different nations.

AN/PRC-ll7D: Radio, also called SATCOM. Works with Milstar satellite in 22,300-mile equatorial orbit for instant worldwide radio, voice, or video communications. Size: l5 inches high, 3 inches wide, 3 inches deep. Weighs l5 pounds. Microphone and voice output. Has encrypter, capable of burst transmissions of less than a second.

AN/PUS-7: Night vision goggles. Weigh 1.5 pounds.

ANVIS-6: Night vision goggles on air crewmen's helmets.

APC: Armored personnel carrier.

ASROC: Nuclear-tipped antisubmarine rocket torpedoes launched by Navy ships.

Assault Vest: Combat vest with full loadouts of ammo, gear.

ASW: Anti-Submarine Warfare.

Attack Board: Molded plastic with two hand grips with bubble compass on it. Also depth gauge and Cyalume chemical lights with twist knob to regulate amount of light. Use for underwater guidance on long swim.

Aurora: Air Force recon plane. Can circle at 90,000 feet. Can't be seen or heard from ground. Used for thermal imaging.

AWACS: Airborne Warning And Control System. Radar units in high-flying aircraft to scan for planes at any altitude out 200 miles. Controls air-to-air engagements with enemy forces. Planes have a mass of communication and electronic equipment.

Balaclavas: Headgear worn by some SEALs.

Bent Spear: Less serious nuclear violation of safety.

BKA: Bundeskriminant: German's federal investigation unit.

Black Talon: Lethal hollow-point ammunition made by Winchester. Outlawed some places.

Blivet: A collapsible fuel container. SEALs sometimes use it.

BLU-43B: Antipersonnel mine used by SEALs.

BLU-96: A fuel-air explosive bomb. It disperses fuel oil into the air, then explodes the cloud. Many times more powerful than conventional bombs because it doesn't carry its own chemical oxidizers.

BMP-1: Soviet armored fighting vehicle AFV, low, boxy, crew of 3 and 8 combat troops. Has tracks and a 73mm cannon, an AT-3 Sagger antitank missile, and coaxial machine gun.

Body Armor: Far too heavy for SEAL use in the water.

Bogey: Pilots' word for an unidentified aircraft.

Boghammer Boat: Long, narrow, low, dagger boat, high-speed patrol craft. Swedish make. Iran had 40 of them in 1993.

Boomer: A nuclear-powered missile submarine.

Bought It: A man has been killed. Also "bought the farm."

Bow Cat: The bow catapult on a carrier to launch jets.

Broken Arrow: Any accident with nuclear weapons or nuclear material lost, shot down, crashed, stolen, hijacked.

Browning 9mm High Power: A Belgian 9mm pistol, 13 rounds in magazine. First made 1935.

Buddy Line: Six foot long, ties 2 SEALs together in the water for control, help if needed.

BUDS/S: Coronado, California, nickname for SEAL training facility for six-month course.

BUPERS: BUreau of PERSonnel.

C-130 Hercules: Air Force transporter for long haul. 4 engines.

C-2A Greyhound: 2-engine turboprop cargo plane that lands on carriers. Also called COD, Carrier Onboard Delivery. Two pilots and engineer. Rear fuselage loading ramp. Cruise speed 300 mph, range 1,000 miles. Will hold 39 combat troops. Lands on CVN carriers at sea.

C-4: Plastic explosive. A claylike explosive that can be molded and shaped. It will burn. Fairly stable.

C-6 Plastique: Plastic explosive. Developed from C-4 and C-5. Is often used in bombs with radio detonator or digital timer.

C-9 Nightingale: Douglas DC-9 fitted as a medical evacuation transport plane.

C-141 Starlifter: Airlift transport for cargo, paratroops, evac for long distances. Top speed, 566 mph. Range with payload, 2,935 miles. Ceiling 41,600 feet.

Caltroops: Small four-pointed spikes used to flatten tires. Used in the Crusades to disable horses.

CamelBack: Used with drinking tube for 70 ounces of water attached to vest.

Cammies: Working camouflage wear for SEALs. Two

different patterns and colors, jungle and desert.

Cannon Fodder: Old term for soldiers in line of fire destined to die in the grand scheme of warfare.

Capped: Killed, shot, or otherwise snuffed.

CAR-15: The Colt M-4Al. Sliding stock carbine with grenade launcher under barrel. Knight sound suppresser. Can have AN/PAQ-4 laser aiming light under the carrying handle. .223-round. 20- or 30-round magazine. Rate of fire: 700 to 1,000 rds/min.

Cascade Radiation: U-235 triggers secondary radiation in other dense materials.

Cast Off: Leave a dock, port, land. Get lost. Navy: long, then short signal of horn, whistle, or light.

Castle Keep: The main tower in any castle.

Caving Ladder: Roll-up ladder that can be let down to climb.

CH-46E: Sea Knight chopper. Twin rotors, transport. Can carry 22 combat troops. Has a crew of 3.

CH-53D Sea Stallion: Big chopper. Not used much anymore.

Chaff: A small cloud of thin pieces of metal, such as tinsel, that can be picked up by enemy radar and that can attract a radar guided missile away from the plane to hit the chaff.

Charlie-Mike: Code words for continue the mission.

Chief to Chief: Bad conduct by EM handled by chiefs so no record shows or is passed up the chain of command.

Chocolate Mountains: Land training center for SEALs near these mountains in the California desert.

Christians in Action: SEAL talk for not-always-friendly CIA.

CIA: Central Intelligence Agency.

CIC: Combat Information Center. The place on a ship where communications and control areas are situated to open and control combat fire.

CINC: Commander IN Chief.

CINCLANT: Navy Commander IN Chief, AtLANTic.

CINCPAC: Commander-IN-Chief, PACific.

Class of 1978: Not a single man finished BUD/S training in this class. All-time record.

Claymore: An antipersonnel mine carried by SEALs on many of their missions.

Cluster Bombs: A canister bomb that explodes and spreads small bomblets over a great area. Used against parked aircraft, massed troops, and unarmored vehicles.

CNO: Chief of Naval Operations.

CO-2 Poisoning: During deep dives. Abort dive at once and surface.

COD: Carrier On Board Delivery plane.

Cold Pack Rations: Food carried by SEALs to use if needed.

Combat Harness: American Body Armor nylon mesh special operations vest. Six 2-magazine pouches for drum-fed belts, other pouches for other weapons, waterproof pouch for Motorola.

CONUS: The continental United States.

Corfams: Dress shoes for SEALs.

Covert Action Staff: A CIA group that handles all covert action by the SEALs.

CQB: Close Quarters Battle. A fight that's up close, hand-to-hand, whites of his eyes, blood all over you. Also called Kill House.

CRRC Bundle: Roll it off plane, sub, boat. The assault boat for 8 seals.

CRRC: Combat Rubber Raiding Craft. Also the IBS or Inflatable Boat, Small.

Cutting Charge: Lead-sheathed explosive. Triangular strip of high-velocity explosive sheathed in metal. Point of the triangle focuses a shaped charge effect. Cuts a pencil-line-wide hole to slice a steel girder in half.

CYA: Cover Your Ass; protect yourself from friendlies or officers above you and JAG people.

Damfino: Damned if I know. SEAL talk.

DDS: Dry Dock Shelter. A clamshell unit on subs to deliver SEALs and SDVs to a mission.

DEFCON: DEFense CONdition. How serious is the threat?

Delta Forces: Army special forces, much like SEALs.

Desert Cammies: Three-color desert tan and pale green with streaks of pink. For use on land.

DIA: Defense Intelligence Agency.

Dilos Class Patrol Boat: Greek, 29 feet long, 75 tons displacement.

Dirty Shirt Mess: Officers can eat there in flying suits on board a carrier.

DNS: Doppler Navigation System.

DRAEGR LAR V: Rebreather that SEALs use. No bubbles.

DREC: Digitally Reconnoiterable Electronic Component. Top-secret computer chip from NSA that lets it decipher any U.S. military electronic code.

E & E: SEAL talk for escape and evasion.

E-2C Hawkeye: Navy, carrier-based, airborne early warning craft for long-range early warning and threat assessment and fighter direction. Has a 24-foot saucer-like rotodome over the wing. Crew 5, max speed 326 knots, ceiling 30,800 feet, radius 175 nautical miles, with 4 hours on station.

E-3A Skywarrior: Old electronic intelligence craft. Replaced by the newer ES-3A.

E-4B NEACP: Called kneecap. National Emergency Airborne Command Post. A greatly modified Boeing 747 used as a communications base for the President of the United States and other high-ranking officials in an emergency and in wartime.

EA-6B Prowler: Navy plane with electronic countermeasures. Crew of 4, max speed 566 knots, ceiling 41,200 feet, range with max load 955 nautical miles.

Easy: The only easy day was yesterday. SEAL talk.

ELINT: Electronic INTelligence. Often from satellite in orbit, picture-taker, or other electronic communications.

EOD: Navy experts in nuclear material and radioactivity. Explosive Ordnance Disposal.

Equatorial Satellite Pointing Guide: To aim antenna for radio to pick up satellite signals.

ES-3A: Electronic Intelligence (ELINT) intercept craft. The platform for the battle group passive horizon extension system. Stays up for long patrol periods, has comprehensive set of sensors, lands and takes off from a carrier. Has 63 antennas.

ETA: Estimated Time of Arrival.

Executive Order 12333: By President Reagan, authorizing special warfare units such as the SEALs.

Exfil: Exfiltrate, to get out of an area.

F/A-18 Hornet: Carrier-based interceptor that can change from air-to-air to air-to-ground attack mode while in flight.

Fitrep: Fitness report.

Flashbang Grenade: Nonlethal grenade that gives off a series of piercing explosive sounds and a series of brilliant strobe-type lights to disable an enemy.

Floatation Bag: To hold equipment, ammo, gear on a wet operation.

Fort Fumble: SEAL's name for the Pentagon.

Forty mm Rifle Grenade: The M576 multipurpose round contains 20 large lead balls. SEALs use on Colt M-4A1.

Four Striper: A Navy captain.

FOX Three: In air warfare, a code phrase showing that a Navy F-14 has launched a Phoenix air-to-air missile.

FUBAR: SEAL talk: Fucked Up Beyond All Repair.

Full Helmet Masks: For high altitude jumps. Oxygen in mask.

G-3: German-made assault rifle.

Gloves: SEALs wear sage green, fire resistant Nomex flight gloves.

GMT: Greenwich Mean Time. Where it's all measured from.

GPS: Global Positioning System. A program with satellites around Earth to pinpoint precisely aircraft, ships, vehicles, and ground troops. Position information is to plus or minus ten feet. Also can give speed of a plane or ship to one-quarter of a mile per hour.

GPSL: A radio antenna with floating wire that pops to the surface. Antenna picks up positioning from the closest 4 Global Positioning Satellites and gives an exact position within 10 feet.

Green Tape: Green sticky ordnance tape that has a hundred uses for a SEAL.

GSG-9: Flashbang grenade developed by Germans: a cardboard tube filled with 5 separate charges timed to burst in rapid succession. Blinding and giving concussion to enemy, leaving targets stunned, easy to kill or capture. Usually nonlethal.

GSG9: Grenzschutzgruppe Nine. Germany's best special warfare unit . . . counterterrorist group.

Gulfstream II (VCII): Large executive jet used by services for transport of small groups quickly. Crew 3 and 18 passengers. Cruises at 581 mph. Maximum range 4,275 miles.

H & K 21A1: Machine gun 7.62 NATO round. Replaces the older, more fragile M-60 E3. Fires 900 rounds per minute. Range 1,100 meters. All types of NATO rounds: ball, incendiary, tracer.

H & K G11: Automatic rifle, new type. 4.7mm caseless ammunition. 50-round magazine. The bullet is in a sleeve of solid propellant with a special thin plastic coating around it. Fires 600 rounds per minute. Single-shot, three-round burst or fully automatic.

H & K MP-5SD: 9mm submachine gun with integral silenced barrel, single shot, three shot, or fully automatic. Rate 800 rds/min.

H & K P9S: Heckler & Koch's 9mm Parabellum double-action semiauto pistol with 9-round magazine.

H & K PSG1: 7.62 NATO round. High precision, bolt action, sniping rifle. 5- to 20-round magazine. Roller lock delayed blowback breech system. Fully adjustable stock. 6 × 42 telescopic sights. Sound suppressor.

HAHO: High Altitude jump, High Opening. From 30,000 feet, open chute for glide up to 15 miles to ground. Up to 75 minutes in glide. To enter enemy territory or enemy position unheard.

Half-Track: Military vehicle with tracked rear drive and wheels in front, usually armed and armored.

HALO: High Altitude jump, Low Opening. From 30,000 feet. Free fall in 2 minutes to 2,000 feet and open chute. Little forward movement. Get to ground quickly, silently.

Hamburgers: Often called sliders on a Navy carrier.

Handie-Talkie: Small, handheld personal radio. Short range.

Helo: SEAL talk for helicopter.

Herky Bird: C-130 Hercules transport. Most-flown military transport in the world. For cargo or passengers, paratroops, aerial refueling, search and rescue, communications, and as a gunship. Has flown from a Navy carrier deck without use of catapult. Four turboprop engines, max speed 325 knots, range at max payload 2,356 miles.

Hezbollah: Lebanese Shiite Moslem militia. Party of God.

HMMWU: The humvee, U.S. light utility truck replaced the honored jeep. Multipurpose wheeled vehicle, 4 × 4, automatic transmission, power steering. Engine: Detroit Diesel 150 hp diesel V-8 air-cooled. Top speed, 65 mph. Range, 300 miles.

Hotels: SEAL talk for hostages.

Humint: Human intelligence. Acquired on the ground, a man as vs. satellite or photo recon.

Hydra-Shock: Lethal hollow-point ammunition made by Federal Cartridge Company. Outlawed in some areas.

Hypothermia: Danger to SEALs. A drop in body temperature that can be fatal.

IBS: Inflatable Boat Small. 12 × 6 feet. Carry 8 men and 1,000 pounds of weapons and gear. Hard to sink. Quiet motor. Used for silent beach, bay, lake landings.

IR Beacon: Infrared beacon. For silent nighttime signaling.

IR Goggles: "Sees" heat instead of light.

Islamic Jihad: Arab holy war.

IV Pack: Intravenous fluid that you can drink if out of water.

JNA: Yugoslav National Army.

JP-4: Normal military jet fuel.

JSOC: Joint Special Operations Command.

JSOCCOMCENT: Joint Special Operations Command Center in the Pentagon.

KA-BAR: SEAL's combat knife.

KATN: Kick Ass and Take Names. SEAL talk, get the mission in gear.

KH-11: Spy satellite, takes pictures of ground, IR photos, etc.

KIA: Killed In Action.

KISS: Keep It Simple, Stupid. SEAL talk for streamlined operations.

Klick: A kilometer of distance. Often used as a mile. From Vietnam era, but still widely used in military.

Krytrons: Complicated, intricate timers used in making nuclear explosive detonators.

KV-57: Encoder for messages, scrambles.

LT: Short for lieutenant in SEAL talk.

Liaison: Close connection, cooperating person from one unit or service to another. Military liaison.

Laser Pistol: The SIW pinpoint of ruby light emitted for aiming. Usually silenced weapon.

Left Behind: In 30 years, SEALs have seldom left behind a dead comrade, never a wounded one. Never been taken prisoner.

Let's Get the Hell Out of Dodge: SEAL talk for leaving a place, bugging out, hauling ass.

Light Sticks: Chemical units that make light after twisting to release chemicals that phosphoresce.

Loot and Shoot: SEAL talk for getting into action on a mission.

LZ: Landing Zone.

M-16: Automatic U.S. rifle. 5.56-round. Magazine 20 or 30, rate of fire 700 to 950 rds/mn. Can attach M203 40mm grenade launcher under barrel.

M-18 Claymore: Antipersonnel mine. A slab of C-4 with 200 small ball bearings. Set off electrically or by trip wire. Can be positioned and aimed. Sprays out a cloud of balls. Kill zone, 50 meters.

M-203: A 40mm grenade launcher fitted under an M-l6 or the M-l5. Can fire a variety of grenade types up to twelve hundred feet.

M-3 Submachine Gun: World War II grease gun, .45 caliber. Cheap. Introduced in 1942.

M-60E3: Lightweight handheld machine gun. Not used now by the SEALs.

M-86: Pursuit deterrent munitions. Various types of mines, grenades, trip wire explosives, and other devices in antipersonnel use.

M1-8: Russian chopper.

M1A1 M-14: Match rifle upgraded for SEAL snipers.

M60 Machine Gun: Can use l00-round ammo box snapped onto the gun's receiver. Not used much now by SEALs.

M61(j): Machine pistol, Yugoslavian make.

M61A1: The usual 20mm cannon used on many American fighter planes.

M662: A red flare for signaling.

MagSafe: Lethal ammunition that fragments in human body and does not exit. Favored by some police units to cut down on second kill from regular ammunition exiting a body.

Make a Peek: A quick look, usually out of the water, to check your position or tactical situation.

Mark 23 Mod O: Special operations offensive handgun system. Double-action, 12-round magazine. Ambidextrous safety and mag release catches. Knight screw-on suppressor. Snap-on laser for sighting. .45 caliber. Weighs 4 pounds loaded. 9.5 inches long, with silencer 16.5 inches long.

Mark II Knife: Navy-issue combat knife.

Mark VIII SDV: Swimmer delivery vehicle. A bus, SEAL talk. Twenty-one feet long, beam and draft 4-feet, 6 knots for 6 hours.

Master-at-Arms: Military police on board a ship.

MAVRIC Lance: A nuclear alert for stolen nukes or radioactive goods.

MC-130 Combat Talon: A specially equipped Hercules for covert missions in enemy or unfriendly territory.

McMillan M88: Bolt-action sniper rifle .50 caliber. 53 inches long. Bipod, fixed five- or ten-round magazine. Bulbous muzzle brake on end of barrel. Deadly up to a mile. All types .50 caliber ammo.

MGS: Modified grooming standards. So SEALs don't all look like military to enable them to do undercover work in mufti.

MH-53J: Chopper updated CH053 from 'Nam days. 200 mph, called the PAVE Low III.

MH-60K BlackHawk: Navy chopper. Forward infrared system for low level night flight. Radar for terra follow avoidance. Crew of 3, take 12 troops. Top speed 225 mph. Ceiling, 4,000 feet. Range radius, 230 miles. Arms, two 12.7mm machine guns.

MIDEASTFOR: Middle East Force.

MiG: Russian-built fighter plane, many versions, used in many nations around the world.

Mike Boat: Liberty boat off a large ship.

Mike-Mike: Short for mm, millimeter, as 9 mike-mike.

Milstar: Communications satellite for pickup and bouncing signals from SATCOM and other radio transmitters. Used by SEALs.

Miniguns: In choppers. Can fire 2,000 rounds per minute. Gatling gun type.

Mitrajez M80: Machine gun from Yugoslavia.

Ml5: British domestic intelligence agency.

Mocha: Food energy bar SEALs carry in vest pockets.

Mossburg: Pump-action, pistol-grip, 5-round magazine, SEALs use it for close-in work.

Motorola Radio: Personal radio, short range, lip mike, earpiece, belt pack.

MRE: Meals ready to eat. Field rations used by most of U.S. armed forces and the SEALs as well. Long-lasting.

MSPF: Maritime Special Purpose Force.

Mugger (MUGR): Miniature underwater locator device. Sends up antenna for pickup on positioning satellites. Works underwater or above. Gives location within 10 feet.

Mujahideen: A soldier of Allah in Muslim nations.

NAVAIR: NAVy AIR command.

NAVSPECWAR: Naval Special Warfare Section. SEALs are in this command.

NAVSPECWARGRUP-TWO: Naval Special Warfare Section, Group Two, based at Norfolk.

NCIS: Naval Criminal Investigative Service. A civilian operation not reporting to any Navy authority to make it more responsible and responsive. Replaces the old NIS, Naval Investigation Service, which did report to the closest admiral.

NEST: Nuclear Energy Search Team. Nonmilitary unit that reports at once to any spill, problem, or broken arrow to determine the extent of the radiation problem.

Newbie: A new man, officer, or commander of an established military unit.

NKSF: North Korean Special Forces.

NLA: Iranian National Liberation Army. About 4,500 men in South Iraq, helped by Iraq for possible use against Iran.

Nomex: The type of material used for flight suits and hoods.

NPIC: National Photographic Interpretation Center in D.C.

NRO: National Reconnaissance Office to run and coordinate satellite development and operations for the intelligence community.

NSA: National Security Agency.

NSC: National Security Council. Meet in Situation Room, support facility in the Executive Office Building in D.C. Main security group in the nation.

NSVHURAWN: Iranian Marines.

NUKFLASH: An alert for any nuclear problem.

NVG One Eye: Litton single-eyepiece night vision goggles. Prevents NVG blindness in both eyes if a flare goes off. Scope shows green-tinted field at night.

NVGs: Night Vision Goggles. One-eye or two. Give good night vision in the dark with a greenish view.

OAS: Obstacle Avoidance Sonar. Used on many low-flying attack aircraft.

OIC: Officer In Charge.

Oil Tanker: One is 885 feet long, 140-foot beam, 121,000 tons, 13 cargo tanks that hold 35.8 million gallons of fuel, oil, or gas. 24 on the crew. This is a regular-sized tanker, not a supertanker.

OOD: Officer of the deck.

Orion P-3: Navy's long-range patrol and antisub aircraft. Some adapted to ELINT roles. Crew of 10. Max speed loaded, 473 mph. Ceiling, 28,300 feet. Arms: internal weapons bay and 10 external weapons stations for a mix of torpedoes, mines, rockets, and bombs.

Passive Sonar: Listening for engine noise of a ship or sub. It doesn't give away the hunter's presence as an active sonar would.

PAVE LOW III: A Navy chopper.

PC-170: Patrol coastal class 170-foot SEAL delivery vehicle. Powered by four 3,350 hp diesel engines, beam of 25 feet and draft of 7.8 feet. Top speed, 35 knots, range 2,000 nautical miles. Fixed swimmer platform on stern. Crew: 4 officers, 24 EM, and 8 SEALs.

Plank Owners: Original men in the startup of a new military unit.

Polycarbonate material: Bulletproof glass.

PRF: People's Revolutionary Front. Fictional group in *Nucflash: SEAL Team Seven.*

Prowl and Growl: SEAL talk for moving into a combat mission.

Quitting Bell: In BUD/S training. Ring it and you quit the SEAL unit. Helmets of men who quit the class are lined up below the bell in Coronado. (Recently, they have stopped ringing the bell. Dropouts simply place their helmet below the bell and go.)

RAF: Red Army Faction. A once-powerful German terrorist group, not so active now.

Remington 200: Sniper rifle. Not used by SEALs now.

Remington 700: Sniper rifle with starlight scope. Can extend night vision to 400 meters.

RIB: Rigid Inflatable Boat. 3 sizes, one 10 meters, 40 knots.

Ring Knocker: An Annapolis graduate with the ring.

RIO: Radar Intercept Officer. The officer who sits in the backseat of an F-14 Tomcat off a carrier. The job: find enemy targets in the air and on the sea.

Roger That: A yes, an affirmative, a go answer to a command or statement.

RPG: Rocket Propelled Grenade. Quick and easy, shoulder-fired. Favorite weapon of terrorists, insurgents.

S and W Mark 1 MOD: Hush puppy is SEAL name for this pistol.

SAS: British Special Air Service. Commandos. Special warfare men. Best that Britain has. Work with SEALs.

SATCOM: Satellite-based communications system for instant contact with anyone anywhere in the world. SEALs rely on it.

SAW: Squad's Automatic Weapon. Usually a machine gun or automatic rifle.

SBS: Special Boat Squadron. On-site Navy unit that transports SEALs to many of their missions. Located across the street from the SEALs' Coronado, California, headquarters.

SD3: Sound suppression system on the H & K MP5 weapon.

SDV: Swimmer Delivery Vehicle. SEALs use a variety of them.

Seahawk SH-60: Navy chopper for ASW and SAR. Top speed, 180 knots, ceiling 13,800 feet, range 503 miles, arms: 2 Mark 46 torpedoes.

SEAL Headgear: Boonie hat, wool balaclava, green scarf, watch cap, bandanna roll.

Second in Command: Also 2IC for short, in SEAL talk.

SERE: Survival, Evasion, Resistance, and Escape training.

Shipped for Six: Enlisted for six more years in the Navy.

Shit City: Coronado SEALs' name for Norfolk.

Show Colors: In combat, put U.S. flag or other identification on back for easy identification by friendly air or ground units.

Sierra Charlie: SEAL talk for everything on schedule.

Simunition: Canadian product for training that uses paint balls instead of lead for bullets.

Sixteen-Man Platoon: Basic SEAL combat force. Up from 14 men a few years ago.

Sonobouy: Small underwater device that detects sounds and transmits them by radio to plane or ship.

Space Blanket: Green foil blanket to keep troops warm. Vacuum packed and folded to a cigarette-sized package.

Sprayers and Prayers: Not the SEAL way. These men spray bullets all over the place, hoping for hits. SEALs do more aimed firing for sure kills.

SS-19: Russian ICBM missile.

STABO: Use harness and lines under chopper to get down to the ground.

STAR: Surface to air recovery operation.

Starflash Round: Shotgun round that shoots out sparkling fireballs that ricochet wildly around a room, confusing and terrifying the occupants. Nonlethal.

Stasi: Old-time East German secret police.

Stick: British terminology: Two 4-man SAS teams; 8 men.

Stokes: A kind of Navy stretcher. Open coffin shaped of wire mesh and white canvas for emergency patient transport.

STOL: Short Takeoff and Landing. Aircraft with high-lift wings and vectored-thrust engines to produced extremely short takeoffs and landings.

Subgun: Submachine gun, often the suppressed H & K M MP5.

Suits: Civilians, usually government officials wearing suits.

Sweat: The more SEALs sweat in peacetime, the less they bleed in war.

Sykes-Fairbairn: A commando fighting knife.

Syrette: Small syringe for field administration, often filled with morphine. Can be self-administered.

Tango: SEAL talk for a terrorist.

TDY: Temporary duty assigned outside of normal job designation.

Terr: Another term for terrorist. Shorthand SEAL talk.

Tetrahedral Reflectors: Show up on multimode radar like tiny suns.

Thermal Imager: Device to detect warmth, as a human body, at night or through light cover.

Thermal Tape: ID for night vision goggle user to see. Use on friendlies.

TNAZ: Trinitroaze tidine. Explosive to replace C-4. 15 percent stronger than C-4 and 20 percent lighter.

TO&E: Table showing organization and equipment of a military unit.

Top SEAL Tribute: "You sweet motherfucker, don't you never die!"

Train: For contact in smoke, no light, fog, etc. Men directly behind each other. Right hand on weapon, left hand on shoulder of man ahead. Squeeze shoulder to signal.

Trident: SEAL's emblem. An eagle with talons clutching a Revolutionary War pistol, and Neptune's trident superimposed on the Navy's traditional anchor.

TRW: A camera's digital record that is sent by SAT-COM.

TT33: Tokarev, a Russian pistol.

UAZ: A Soviet one-ton truck.

UBA Mark XV: Underwater life support with computer to regulate the rebreather's gas mixture.

UGS: Unmanned ground sensors. Can be used to explode booby traps and claymore mines.

UNODIR: Unless otherwise directed. The unit will start the operation unless they are told not to.

VBSS: Orders to "Visit, Board, Search and Seize."

Wadi: A gully or ravine, usually in a desert.

White Shirt: Man responsible for safety on carrier deck as he leads around civilians and personnel unfamiliar with the flight deck.

WIA: Wounded in action.

Zodiac: Also called an IBS, inflatable boat, small. Fifteen by six feet, 265 pounds. The "rubber duck" can carry 8 fully equipped SEALs. Can do 18 knots with a range of 65 nautical miles.

ZULU: Means Greenwich Mean Time, GMT. Used in all formal military communications.

SEAL TEAM SEVEN
Keith Douglass

__SEAL TEAM SEVEN   **0-425-14340-6/$5.99**

In a daring mission of high-seas heroism, Lt. Blake Murdock leads his seven-man unit from Team Seven's Red Squad into bulkhead-to-bulkhead battle—with high-tech buccaneers who've got nothing left to lose...

__SEAL TEAM SEVEN: SPECTER 0-425-14569-7/$5.99

Lt. Blake Murdock and his SEALs must spearhead a daring rescue mission and get the delegates out of the former Yugoslavia—where the wars still rage—in one piece—and give those responsible a taste of extreme SEAL prejudice.

__SEAL TEAM SEVEN: NUCFLASH

        0-425-14881-5/$5.99

In the New World Order there is only one fear: A renegade state will gain control of a nuclear weapon and incinerate a city of innocent people. It's up to Lt. Blake Murdock and his SEALs to bring the bad guys down.

__SEAL TEAM SEVEN: DIRECT ACTION

        0-425-15605-2/$5.99

During an attack on a terrorist group in Port Sudan, Lt. Blake Murdock and his SEAL team uncover three million dollars of counterfeit currency.

SOMETHING EXPLODED
IN THE SKY...

...something metallic, something swirling, something from hell. Four dark beasts filled the southeastern horizon like the lions of the apocalypse. The reflection of morning light off the sand splayed like blood across their wings...

Startled from the half-daze of the monotonous watch, the sentry grabbed his rifle and flung himself against the sand-filled bags at the front of the trench. It took a moment for his brain to register the fact that the planes were coming from the south and not the north—they were friends, not foes. The thick canisters of death slung beneath their wings were not meant for him.

"What the hell are those," he asked his companion as the planes roared over their positions.

The other soldier laughed. "You never saw A-10 Warthogs before?"

"They're on our side?"
"You better pray to God they are."

by James Ferro
HOGS: GOING DEEP

__0-425-16856-5/$5.99